Patricia Cavendish was born in Cape Town but left South Africa at the age of six. Her first novel, *Misunderstandings*, was published in 1990. Her hobbies are the Arts, travel and reading other people's novels.

By the same author

Misunderstandings

PATRICIA CAVENDISH

Always and Forever

Grafton
An Imprint of HarperCollins*Publishers*

Grafton
An Imprint of HarperCollins*Publishers*
77–85 Fulham Palace Road,
Hammersmith, London W6 8JB

Published by Grafton 1992
9 8 7 6 5 4 3 2 1

First published in Great Britain by
Judy Piatkus (Publishers) Ltd 1991

The verse quoted on page 316
is from *Rubáiyát of Omar Khayyam*
Translated by Edward Fitz Gerald, 1909
Published by A & C Black

ISBN 0 586 21379 1

Set in Times

Printed in Great Britain by
HarperCollinsManufacturing Glasgow

PART ONE

Germany

1

My life really began on a cold winter's day in Germany
soon after the end of World War Two. I was twenty-
three years old and still a virgin – which was not so very
unusual in those days – and less sophisticated than the
average teenager of the eighties, which *was* rather more
unusual. If anyone had told me then that my life was
about to expand so dramatically, I should have said that
it had already done so in Brussels, but that city, with all
its gaiety, fun and laughter, had only been the prelude; it
was in Germany that I was to know a love that consumed
me, to experience total joy, total misery, and to witness
the despair of countless others. And because I was so
vulnerable, all that I saw and felt and tried to understand
was to influence my deepest emotions for ever after and
to mould me into the woman I have become.

Yet, like so many of life's major events, everything
depended on chance: if I had not happened to run into
Sheena Graham earlier that year; if I had been posted
to India instead of to Brussels; if I had decided against
the move to Germany; or even if Dan and Rosalind had
not quarrelled at the top of the stairs or Emma had not
screamed at that precise moment . . . even now, after over
forty years, the memory of that night and its aftermath
never fails to make me shudder and murmur, 'Thank God
it turned out as it did.'

But on that day in Germany when Jan said: 'You've
not met Dan Cleary, have you?' I looked up only briefly
from the letter I was signing, too engrossed in its contents
to pay much attention to her. 'No, I don't think so. The
name doesn't ring a bell.' Had I worded the letter strongly

3

enough, I wondered silently, to make the American Red Cross understand how desperate was the need to trace Josef Liebovich, butcher, who had left Poland in 1912 and was believed to have settled in Chicago? That was all the information I had: no date of birth, no names or details of any family, and I was enquiring on behalf of a woman whom he had never met, for she was the niece of his second cousin and must have dredged up his name from the deepest recesses of her memory. He was her last, her only, hope because all the others of the once large family had perished, slowly and agonizingly, in the lethal fumes of the terrible Zyclon B. What must it be like, what *could* it be like to have had all hope beaten out of you for so long and then suddenly to be told that if you had a relation living abroad who would sponsor you, there would be a chance of passports, exit permits, visas, to a new life? Utterly unbelievable, I supposed, like a miracle, a glimpse of heaven . . . but over the terrifying years, minds had been forced into numbness, memories into oblivion, so that only an animal instinct for warmth, food and survival remained. How agonizing then even to start thinking and remembering again. Yet Rachel Kleinova and a few thousand other survivors were doing just that, and enquiries were pouring into every country of the free world. It was our function to make the recipients understand the need for research, no matter how scant the details or how slender the hope of success; but how *could* anyone really understand a whole people's descent into hell, where the ashes of the murdered lay ten feet deep around the camps? Of course, there were the photographs of Belsen, Dachau and Auschwitz, but for me their very obscenity made them somehow unreal: it was plain that the piled up bodies resembled those of men and women, but could speech, laughter and song ever have come from those gaping mouths? Could such shrunken breasts ever have known the lips of babies and

4

of lovers? Or living seed have issued from such withered loins?

'You've not heard a word, have you?' Jan's happy voice cut through my thoughts and I started so violently that my fountain pen skittered across the blotter, leaving a trail of inky dots. I looked up briefly. 'Sorry, Jan, but this case worries me.'

'I peeked at your report – it's very good, very warm without being sentimental, and now all you can do is wait. So, as I was saying, I think you ought to meet Dan Cleary.'

'But why?' I asked as I began to fold the letter.

'Because I really think you would hit it off together.'

I paused in the act of sealing the envelope to smile at her. 'Oh, Jan, match-making never works, you know!'

'I couldn't agree more, but I just feel that you two would be *simpatico* – at least let me fix a meeting.' Her large brown eyes were looking at me almost pleadingly.

I shrugged. 'Why not? But do tell me a bit more about him.'

'Well, he's a Group Captain on special attachment to Rhine Army HQ at Bad Oeynhausen.'

'A Group Captain!' I echoed, laughing in astonishment. 'The equivalent of a full Colonel. Oh Jan, what would I be doing with some dear old middle-aged fuddy-duddy, no doubt with dentures and a tum?'

Jan's small gamine face crinkled. 'Honey, you just don't know what you're saying! Dan Cleary is the most gorgeous male creature on two legs you're ever likely to meet, and far from middle-aged! In fact, he's only thirty, is certainly without dentures, and as he's an ex-rugger full back, I'm sure there's no tum!'

I was determined to remain unimpressed: 'And no doubt he was the RAF's most brilliant fighter ace who almost won the Battle of Britain single-handed and is now loaded down with gongs, right?'

'Wrong.' Jan looked at me over the flame of her cigarette lighter, eyes suddenly serious. 'He was in bombers and was shot down over the Ruhr. He spent almost a year as a "Kriegie" until finally escaping, and then he was sent to GHQ Cairo.'

In spite of myself I began to feel intrigued. The pilots of the RAF had been the super-heroes of the War. Besides, Ted had been the captain of a B-29 Super Fort. 'So how come you don't want him?'

'I probably would,' Jan conceded, 'he's an absolute sweetie, but you forget – I'm going home in six weeks and have my own blissful Canuck waiting for me.'

'Well,' I said, suddenly feeling very sophisticated and worldly-wise, 'I don't much care for excessively good-looking men. They're always so conceited.'

'Not this one! Although he easily could be. He's brilliant as well.'

'Good Lord, he sounds too good to be true! There must be a snag.'

Jan's smile faded a little. 'W-e-l-l, he's married – oh, yes, I know what you're going to say, but his wife is threatening to divorce him.'

'That settles it then. Thanks, but no thanks, Jan.'

The Chief put her head round the door. 'Minette, can I see you for a minute?'

'Of course.' I jumped up and hurried across the room.

'At least meet him,' Jan pleaded, 'if I ask him to bring a friend? I'm not suggesting you should start a great "thing" with him, but like all the guys out here he's lonely, and as you're still carrying a torch for that Yank, I think you and Dan would be good for each other. Come on, Minette, be a sport.'

'Oh, all right,' I said, my thoughts more on what the Chief could want. Then I forgot all about Dan Cleary so when Jan said the next day, 'Well, I've fixed it for Wednesday,' I looked at her blankly. 'Dan Cleary and his friend, Miles Henderson. We're to meet them for tea at the Twenty-One Club.'

'Tea!' I exclaimed laughingly. 'That's a new one!'

'My idea,' Jan retorted. 'As you were so reluctant, I thought a very short meeting might be best. So be here around three-thirty on Wednesday and I'll drive us over in the Beetle.'

But I very nearly missed that tea party. For I'd been detailed to meet a ten-year-old boy off the Berlin train and then put him on one for Berne.

'Book yourself into the Officers' Transit Hotel in Hanover,' the Chief said. 'It's just across the square from the Hauptbahnhof. The train is due in at four-thirty in the morning and although it'll probably be hours late, you'll need to be on the platform punctually just in case it's more or less on time. And take Morgan with you so he'll be able to find overnight accommodation. After you've seen the Eberhardt child off to Berne, I want you to go on to Hameln to interview a Lithuanian who's about to be executed for murder.

'It's a tragic case: the boy was a slave labourer who was treated very badly yet survived. Three months ago he tracked down the overseer who had made his life such hell and battered him to death. He offered no defence at his trial, and I'm afraid there's no hope of a reprieve, but his grandmother in Australia has cabled London begging for him to be seen and his last wishes obtained. I've arranged with the prison governor for the interview, and he'll lay on an interpreter for you . . . think you can handle it?'

'I should very much like to try and – I'll do my best.' I always seemed to be promising that since I'd come to Germany, and although the Chief smiled warmly, there was a slightly doubtful look in her large blue eyes. I had seen that look in the eyes of her predecessor in Brussels. As he awarded me my second 'pip' he had said: 'You've

7

done very well, Minette, and I should like you to think about moving up to Germany now.'

'Oh, yes please,' I had answered at once, avid for yet more fresh experiences. During those first weeks in Germany it seemed I never stopped looking and absorbing, my head ceaselessly turning. The devastation was on an unimaginable scale. Except in the main thoroughfares where a path had been cleared, the bricks and stones of shattered buildings lay where they had fallen in huge mounds. At first glance it appeared impossible that anyone could live within these hillocks of masonry, yet every so often there would protrude a short pipe, no thicker than a man's arm, emitting a wisp of smoke and I would realize that a human being had somehow burrowed down inside.

Then there was the silence: no birds chirped among the ruins or wheeled in the sky, no dogs barked, no children laughed or cried. Indeed, there were no children as such, only small men and women with pinched faces who, like their elders, stared at us from narrowed, hate-filled eyes. People did not pause to chat or even to greet one another, but all walked silently, the women dark-clothed, high-booted, with head scarves or large hats secured by elastic under the chin; the men in every variety of clothing, only a fortunate few wearing the favourite long leather coat and down-brimmed trilby; all shabby, waxen-faced, and over-burdened with bundles and bags. With the complete absence of vehicles, the only sound was of footsteps crunching on rubble and, now and then, the rattle of a crude handcart made from a box mounted on pram wheels. It was a scene duplicated in almost every town and city throughout the British Zone and I would have needed a heart of stone not to be stirred by it all.

Yet even as I looked on so much hardship, I saw in my mind's eye the barbarous cruelty and degradation of the camps; and horrendous stories of fire storms

8

sweeping with gale force through Dresden and Leipzig, and of phosphorous bombs shrivelling bodies to doll size in Hamburg, inevitably brought memories of all the nights when we had crouched under the stairs, listening to the whining scream of the bombs, and seeing the candle flicker in the huge explosions of the land mines. And of those other nights when guilty relief replaced fear as the bombers merely passed over us on their way to London, Coventry, Birmingham, or our sister ports of Southampton and Portsmouth.

Back in the office my mood would swing once more as the mountains of mail brought letters from the former torturers and their victims alike, all begging for help, the intensity of their suffering permeating the very paper on which they had written.

2

'You are leaving, *Fräulein Leutnant*?' asked the night porter in astonishment when I appeared in the vestibule of the transit hotel.

'Yes,' I replied in my halting German, 'I have to meet a little boy off the Berlin train.'

'*Ach so*, but there is no need to go yet, *Fräulein*. The train will be at least two hours late . . . it is the Russians at the border, you understand.'

'Nevertheless, I must wait at the station, just in case. He would be very frightened if he were to arrive and not find anyone there to meet him. If I were to miss him – '

'You care about a *German* boy?' The tone was incredulous.

'Naturally,' I replied sharply, 'as I would for any ten-year-old travelling alone.'

'But you cannot go alone across the square at this hour, *Fräulein*. I will accompany you to the station – '

'Oh, but won't you get into trouble for leaving the hotel?'

'Perhaps, but it is my duty to go with you.'

'I wouldn't want – ' But already he was putting on a battered cap and pulling down the ear flaps. 'Please, *Fräulein Leutnant*,' he said stiffly as he held open the street door. He was a tall man, thin as a rail, with a gaunt, tight-lipped face and a badly damaged leg. He wore no overcoat and the elbows of his thin jacket were patched. He carried a short club-like stick in a very purposeful way, and I was aware of his alertness as he looked sweepingly around the vast square. 'There are bad people about at such an hour,' he said matter-of-factly, and indeed I was

10

only too glad of his presence for it was an eerie, utterly silent scene, with the moon creating bright light and dense shadow on the snow-covered ruins. In the few remaining buildings, the sockets of what had once been windows were like huge black eyes, keeping sinister watch upon us. And the cold was so intense that it was like a physical blow against my face; every in-drawn breath resembled splintered ice rasping against the back of my nose and in my throat. Yet the middle-aged man beside me appeared not to feel the cold and, despite the pronounced limp, he strode along much more sure-footed than I on the frozen ground.

When a large rat suddenly ran across our path, I could not suppress a cry of revulsion and instinctively drew closer to my companion. His laugh was short and bitter. 'Only *one* rat, *Fräulein Leutnant*,' he said curtly, and I quickly glanced up at him. He was looking straight ahead, but his expression was eloquent: to be frightened of a solitary rat when the ruins were a seething mass . . . Nevertheless, there was a note of concern in his voice when we arrived at the station and found it completely deserted. 'I think it is better that you do not wait, but come back with me now,' he said after looking keenly along the platform. 'There is no one here: the train is not yet expected.'

I hesitated. The last thing in the world I wanted to do was to stay, but Karl Eberhardt had been found wandering and starving, and now all these months later, when he had left his native city, there had only been a foreign woman to see him off. If he arrived at Hanover and I was not there . . . If he wandered away again, I might never find him . . . on this, my first major assignment alone. 'No, I must remain here,' I said.

'But I must go back, and to leave you alone – '

'That's all right,' I replied, trying to sound confident, even though my heart was beginning to thud loudly in

11

my ears. 'It was most kind of you to come with me, but of course you must now return to your post.' I quickly dipped into my shoulder bag and produced a packet of twenty Senior Service. 'I hope you will accept – '

'Thank you, *Fräulein Leutnant*.' The bony hand had whisked the cigarettes out of sight almost before I had offered them. He turned abruptly, walked a few paces, then swung round to face me. 'You will not return to the hotel at least until it is daylight?'

I shook my head. 'No, I really must be here when the train comes.'

'*Also denn, wiedersehn!*' he said, washing his hands of me.

I have never forgotten the hours I waited on that platform, nor my fear. The station had been bombed many times, so it was roofless and ruined, twisted into grotesque shapes which, together with the utter silence, made it a haunted, sinister place. I did not know whether to stand in the moonlight or melt into a patch of deep shadow for I felt that many living things watched me, and all with hostile eyes. Not only was I a hated member of the Occupying Power, but everything on my person was valuable: as well as my shoulder bag and a small holdall, my outer clothing consisted of black woollen stockings, good leather shoes, gauntlet gloves and a superb greatcoat from which the insignia could easily be stripped. All of it, even the beret on my head, would command enormous prices on the black market, and immediately in my overbright imagination I saw the headlines: BRITISH WOMAN'S NAKED BODY FOUND ON GERMAN STATION. A slightly hysterical giggle rose in my throat. What a place to be found naked *and* murdered! And how astonished everyone at home would be: 'Surely not Minette Glyn, not that quiet little thing who could never say boo to a goose?' Or: 'What on earth was she *doing* in Germany anyway?' Yes, I thought, as the cold forced me to pace

12

back and forth, it had all been astonishing, not least the meeting with Sheena Graham whom I had not seen since we'd attended a secretarial course together just before the war began. Yet she had greeted me like a long-lost friend.

'What fun to meet you like this!' she had exclaimed vivaciously. 'Come and have a cuppa and tell me all about your war.'

So we had repaired to the nearby Copper Kettle where Sheena immediately launched into a sparkling account of her life and loves. When eventually she paused to sip her tepid coffee, I had asked, 'Now that the war is almost over, I suppose you'll be getting married?'

She had put down her cup sharply. 'Not likely, ducky, I'm off to India in three weeks' time!'

'India!' I exclaimed, feeling a distinct stab of envy. I had been brought up on tales of that mysterious land and had always longed to see it.

'Yes.' Sheena already had a far-away look in her eyes. 'The Red Cross is calling for volunteers to work in Service hospitals throughout India. I applied as soon as I heard, and was accepted at once.' Her eyes suddenly focused on me. 'Why don't you have a go, Minette? Oh, I know you weren't eligible for the Forces, but we Red Cross personnel are civilians and I don't think our conditions of service are so rigid. We even travel on ordinary passports.' She paused momentarily, then added with the complacency of a very pretty girl who has the world at her feet: 'But *I* shall have officer's status and be entitled to all the perks – I wouldn't dream of going otherwise!' Laughter had bubbled suddenly in her throat. 'Imagine having to kow-tow to all those ghastly ATS officers! As a VAD I've already done more than enough of that to all the battle-axes in hospital!'

But I was hardly listening. 'Surely special qualifications are required by the Red Cross?'

'No, one just has to be over twenty-one. You see, it's

13

for welfare work, not nursing. We shall be setting up recreation rooms and libraries for the patients, teaching them handicrafts and writing letters for those unable to do so themselves. Really, you know, it's almost identical to the non-nursing work started by Flo in the Crimea.'

How furiously I had pedalled home afterwards, not even bothering to prop up my bicycle before rushing to the far end of the garden where my aunt and uncle, both scarlet-faced, were trying to catch a hen in the orchard. Above the captured bird's squawks I breathlessly asked them: 'Do you think I have a chance?' Uncle Julian, who never failed to encourage me in everything, answered at once, 'You must certainly try. I suggest you write straight away and if you want any help with your letter, let me know.'

It was Aunt Alexa, always the more detached, who had doubted. Sitting on an upturned box, wearing her shapeless garden clothes and battered hat, and with the hen in her arms, she still managed to retain all the dignity of the Memsahib, the Colonel's Lady. 'You must not forget, Minette, that physically you have your limitations and, believe me, the climate throughout almost the whole of India can be most trying.'

Her words only made me more determined and within a month I was seated at the end of a huge shining expanse of mahogany facing a semi-circle of ladies, all uniformed, hatted and staff-tabbed, with rows of medal ribbons and gleaming badges of rank – a formidable sight. And later, the dreaded medical.

'Ah,' said the elderly doctor when, stripped to the waist, I stood before him, 'what have we here?'

'I'm afraid it's a double curvature,' I said, boldly taking the initiative, and then rushed on: 'But I've had a twelve-inch bone graft, so I'm quite strong.'

He was very kind. 'Yes, my dear, and it is most interesting, but India –?'

'Oh, I'm sure I wouldn't mind the heat – I was born in Kenya, actually on the Equator – '

'I was not thinking primarily of the heat, but rather of the conditions in which you might be called upon to serve, for we do not know how much longer the war in the Far East will continue. No, Miss – er – Glyn, I'm afraid India is not for you.' He must have seen my desperate disappointment for he added at once, 'But there are plenty of other locations for which I can confidently recommend you.'

Then the news that it was to be Brussels Headquarters, disappointing at first, but soon followed by excitement as I realized that I was going *somewhere*.

'Let Gieves kit you out,' advised Uncle Julian, 'I always went to them and they never let me down. You may care to mention my name.'

'Your uniform must be very carefully tailored, so be sure and explain about your shoulder. Remember, Minette, you must not be tiresome and shy about this,' said Aunt Alexa, looking at me meaningfully.

But of course I *had* been shy when the hateful fact had to be pointed out and my cheeks had instantly flared into hot colour. 'No problem at all, madam,' the fitter had said smoothly. 'There are very few of us who are quite perfectly built, and in your case the jacket needs only to be cut rather more fully on the one side with, I suggest, a small amount of padding on the other to balance the whole.'

And of course they had made an excellent job of it. Looking at myself sideways in the full-length mirror I seemed, even to my critically anxious eye, merely to be slightly round-shouldered. The nightmare had receded then – the nightmare that had started thirteen years before when my father had said without preamble: 'I'm sending you home to live with your mother's elder brother and sister.' As I remained speechless, he had glanced up quickly in his usual cold way. 'You need treatment for that spine. If you stay here, you'll end up a hunchback.'

'No, no, *of course* not, my dear!' Uncle Julian had sounded outraged when I told him of this and Aunt Alexa had followed with a withering, 'I've never heard such nonsense! All it means is you have one shoulder slightly higher than the other. But it does not show, you know, you must always remember *it does not show*.'

And of course I had believed them. Until the war, when I was about to be called up, and had inadvertently overheard my uncle telephoning the local Department of Labour: 'It is a most unfortunate fact that my niece is slightly deformed with a double curvature of the spine. She underwent major surgery on this a few years ago, but I can assure you that no medical officer would pass her for active service. As she is already doing a very useful job within her somewhat limited capabilities, I would ask you to allow her to continue. Do you wish for medical corroboration?' But because he was a well-known local dignitary and spoke with a lifetime of authority, he had been believed.

For me it was the moment of truth: I was crippled. Deformed. Ugly. And there was nothing, absolutely nothing to be done about it, except to hide the humiliation of always having to explain why I was not in the Forces – 'I'm afraid rather a weak back' – and knowing that the moment I turned away, eyes would scrutinize that back and then realize . . . But the harsh lessons of my early childhood helped. 'I'll have no wallowing in self-pity,' my father had declared, and even Aunt Alexa's later admonition: 'We never let the world see when we are beaten to our knees,' had echoed again and again in my head.

So seeing myself in that mirror I felt that a magic wand had been waved over me: I was Cinderella, clad not in a ball-gown but impeccably tailored barathea. No matter that the stiff Van Heusen collar chafed my throat, that my shoes were flat lace-ups, my grey silk stockings far too thick – I looked so *straight*, so *normal*. And so alive. Nor was that all, for on each narrow shoulder there gleamed the symbol of my officer's status, a solitary brass 'star' with a tiny enamelled red cross in its centre, and in my brand new passport was stamped an Exit Permit enabling me to leave the United Kingdom, together with a British Liberation Army – that wonderful, evocative title – Permit to travel throughout North West Europe.

They had all been waiting silently at the bottom of the stairs: Uncle Julian, the habitual sternness of his expression belied by the kindness in his deep blue eyes; Aunt Alexa, grave, dignified, reserved; and Daisy, who had come to my grandmother as a kitchen maid at the age of fourteen and had stayed on to become cook-general to us all, old now and crotchety, ruling us with a rod of iron, but as much a part of my background as the others.

'Turn around slowly,' commanded my aunt, while her eyes ranged over me from head to foot. When I had turned full circle, they were still silent and my newfound confidence had begun to waver. Then, 'Quite perfect, I think. Would you not agree, Julian?'

'Most beautifully turned out,' said that dear man, his naturally deep voice lowered to a growl-like tone, a sure sign of emotion. 'Charmingly feminine, too, in the strange way that a uniform can appear on some very young women. Yes, undoubtedly a real English rose.'

And Daisy, not to be outdone, added: 'I don't know about no rose, but you looks a lot be'er than when you come ter us – scrawny li'le thing you was, tiny frightened face under that 'orrible 'at and match-stick legs in them black wool stockin's . . . like a 'alf-starved sparrer, you was.'

'That will do, Daisy,' said Aunt Alexa firmly, but Daisy

17

gave her a malevolent glance and stood her ground, aggression in every line of her stout five-foot nothing body. Life was a running battle between the two women, with my aunt ever the loser. 'I ain't goin' till I seen Miss Minet h'orf ter the war.'

'Now, Daisy,' began Uncle Julian patiently, 'you know perfectly well that the war in Europe ended over a month ago.'

'Still,' said Daisy, thrusting out her chin, 'you nefer knows yer luck, an' Miss Minet might not come back – '

'Of course she'll be coming back,' said Uncle Julian sharply. 'Please don't say such stupid things.'

And suddenly I had not wanted to go, not because I was afraid for myself, but because they were all I had and I was leaving them. 'I shall miss you all terribly,' I said, hearing the quiver in my voice.

'Darling Minette, we shall all miss you too,' my uncle replied, and just for a second I saw tears gleam in his eyes. 'But it is time you left the nest and went out into the wide world.'

'High time indeed!' Aunt Alexa added. 'Why, at your age I had been married four years and had already travelled the length of India!'

'And I had just obtained my captaincy and sailed with my regiment for Egypt,' said Uncle Julian, letting the merest trace of pride creep into his voice.

'Yes, an' I knows wot I was doin' too,' said Daisy, not to be outdone for an instant, 'an' it was th'same as I'm doin' now!'

After that it had been excitement all the way, from the porter asking, 'Where to, *Sister*?' to the troops lining the rails of the ship shouting 'Hooray!' and stamping their feet when a booming voice announced over a tannoy that 'Three British Red Cross Officers are approaching to board.'

And Brussels – so clean, so *intact*, its streets brilliantly lit, its shops full of pretty things – had seemed a world away from the greyness, the austerity and the bombed-out buildings of Britain. Best of all, though, had been my immediate acceptance as part of the Headquarters team: 'You're coming, too, aren't you, Minette?' – to a party, the opera, to watch the Guards' Brigade march through the city; to cheer Churchill as he passed in an open car with his flat-topped bowler on the end of his upturned stick; to the Allied Officers' Club, the Habinera, the Slav Night Club, the Rendez-Vous Club and the British Officers' Club, where during the celebrations on VJ night young men had actually queued up to dance with me. So many young British officers everywhere, all anxious to wine and dine us, all hanging on our words, laughing at our jokes, all so joyous to have come through the war unscathed. How strange, therefore, that it should have been an American who was the first to stir my heart, after all those weeks of avoiding them when they and their vehicles had lined every road at home, waiting for D-Day. But Ted had been special, giving the lie to all those snide remarks about American Servicemen, and I had felt real happiness when one of the two GIs saluting him but looking at me, had said irrepressibly, 'You got somethin' good there, Capt'n.'

'I sure have, soldier!' had been the instant reply. Yet his month in Brussels had been his end-of-tour leave before returning to the States and all too soon he was gone like so many others . . .

It was all very different from the evenings spent knitting sea-boot stockings, Balaclavas and gloves for the Forces. Very different, too, from the few Home Guard dances where my partners had been high-ranking elderly gentlemen with distinguished careers and perfect manners.

3

Dawn was breaking and somewhere nearby a train was being shunted. Then there was the sound of footsteps and German voices, and two railway workers appeared, their conversation ceasing abruptly when they saw me. They did not attempt to hide their amazement as they touched their caps and muttered a '*Guten Morgen, Fräulein Leutnant*.' I croaked a reply, then stumblingly asked about the Berlin train. They shrugged. 'Who can tell? It is the Russians, you see.'

Poor child, I thought, what a terrible time it must be for him with his mother dead, his father missing in Russia since 1943, and now this interminable journey, without water, lighting or heating, and he is only ten years old . . . the same age I had been when my father took me to Nairobi station. 'I hope you're not going to start blubbing,' he had said harshly as he bent to peck me briefly on the cheek.

'But when shall I be coming back?' I had asked desperately.

'I don't know.' He had not even tried to make it easy for me. 'Can't you understand what I've told you – that the farm has failed and I'm bankrupt? I've had great difficulty in scraping up sufficient money for your passage. So good-bye now, Minette, behave yourself and do everything Mrs Mannington tells you.' Then he had turned away, leaving me to stand alone with ice seeping through every vein. Look back, just look back once and smile at me, I had begged him silently, but he had not done so, and all I could do was to stand there, obeying his last command not to 'blub'. In fact, for years afterwards I had not been *able* to cry in public.

The Berlin train was almost four hours late and when it eventually wheezed slowly into the station I gazed at it, unable to believe my eyes, for clinging to its sides like human flies were tightly packed figures, while on the roof along the whole length of the train other figures lay supine; there were even two perched precariously on the buffers of the engine.

There were no barriers or exit points on the station and as people began to pour off the train, panic gripped me. How was I ever going to find one solitary child in such a huge jostling mass? Not that there was any shortage of children – quite the reverse, and of all shapes and sizes. Some dazed with sleep or the lack of it; some obviously longing to cry – with hunger? Exhaustion? Fear? – but not daring to; most in urgent need of a lavatory because there would have been no facilities on the train or now on the battered station, all walking awkwardly, their small faces twisted in a desperate effort to hold on, all clinging to overburdened adults whose eyes in their hollow-cheeked faces had a strange glazed look. I stood on tiptoe, trying to see between the bobbing heads. At least, I thought, he is used now to our uniform so perhaps he will look for me.

'*Entschuldigen Sie, Fräulein Leutnant –* '

I looked down. A very small figure stood before me, greatcoated and with long trousers tucked into ski boots, knapsack on back, head enveloped in a thick woollen scarf tied neatly under the chin. Large blue, curiously old, eyes gazed up at me unflinchingly from a white triangle of face. He bent forward in a little bow. 'Eberhardt.'

Coldness and surprise must have numbed my brain for I asked in disbelief: '*You* are Karl Eberhardt?'

'*Jawohl, Fräulein Leutnant.*'

'But,' I said stupidly, 'I was expecting a much older boy.'

The already rigid little figure seemed to draw itself up even more. 'I am aged ten years and four months, *Fräulein.*'

I smiled, anxious to make amends. 'Yes, of course, and I am so glad to see you. Was your journey terrible?'

'Not so terrible, except that the Russians – ' the small body gave one totally convulsive shudder and then was still ' – made us all get off the train and line up. They took many people away and we did not see them again.'

'Well,' I said, trying to sound matter-of-fact, 'you'll not have anything like that to worry about on the next stage of your journey. But now, we have so little time – ' How on earth can I get him to a loo? I thought, even as the lights went on in the RTO's office across the station. Perhaps, as there was nowhere else . . .? 'We have to cross over to the far side,' I said, and immediately the small figure began to plod silently beside me. But although he was trying to walk normally, I saw that he was limping. 'Have you got a sore foot?' I asked, and immediately wished I could bite back the words, for the boots were old and obviously not his own.

'No, thank you, *Fräulein Leutnant*,' he replied politely, but the tell-tale flush instantly suffused his pale skin and I remembered that grey, damp day when the Union Castle liner had docked and I'd heard Mrs Mannington say gushingly, 'She had no warm clothes, so I've had to put her into some of Clarissa's . . . I thought I just *had* to because of that poor back, but she is so very small for her age . . .'

Despite the cold I had suddenly burned with embarrassment, horribly conscious that the strange garment called a liberty bodice, the scratchy woollen stockings, huge knickers, the dress and coat reaching almost to my ankles, were all at least three sizes too large. But the wide-brimmed felt hat was the worst of all. Clarissa had been doubled-up with laughter. 'You look just like a mushroom!' she had gasped, with all the unconscious cruelty of childhood. Yet I was lucky for my new aunt had said to Mrs Mannington, 'How very good of you . . . and how very fortunate that my niece *is* small. I find the lumpy stage that so many gals go through utterly unattractive, do you not agree?' Her tone had been so pleasant, her words so smooth, yet somehow they dripped ice and she had looked briefly but with great disdain at Clarissa, who was distinctly lumpy. Then Uncle Julian had put his arm warmly around my shoulders. 'A most dainty little girl,' he had said in his deep, rich voice, and immediately I felt as though a protective wall had closed around me: I was part of this unknown, rather intimidating couple and therefore to be protected. I put my arm around Karl Eberhardt's shoulders as I asked, 'Is it long since you last saw your aunt?'

'I have never met her, *Fräulein Leutnant*, but – but she and my uncle have promised to be waiting on the station at Berne for me.' There was the faintest note of apprehension in his voice and I tightened my arm around his shoulders, wanting to say 'I understand. I know just what it's like . . . '

How my heart had thudded in my chest when Mrs Mannington had told me they were on board and how curiously I had looked at them: the grey-haired, rather stern-faced man and the woman wearing a coat and hat of skins. That had really astonished me, for although I was used to capes of cow-hide, anklets of Colobus monkey fur, and had slept in a bed of skins stretched between four poles, I had never seen a woman in a fur coat. Then she had smiled. 'Welcome home, my dear child,' she said, and bending had kissed me on the cheek, her skin feeling papery and ice cold against mine. 'We are so pleased and delighted that you have come to live with us,' the tall man had said, sweeping off his hat as he, too, stooped to kiss me. But at that moment the terrible knickers had fallen down around my ankles and I thought I would die of shame. As Mrs Mannington fussed, commanding Clarissa to stand in front of me, my uncle had about-turned and, with hands behind his back, gazed down at the dock with rapt attention. It was my new aunt who said calmly, 'Just step out of the garment, Minette, and give it to me. In five minutes we shall be in the car and able to wrap a rug around you.'

Aloud, I said now: 'How very exciting it will be to meet your aunt and uncle for the first time. I am sure you will love living in Switzerland – everyone says how beautiful it is.'

'Yes, *Fräulein*,' Karl said in the same detached, polite voice and I thought, Fear and grief have turned him to ice inside, just as they did me. I could only hope that the unknown aunt and her husband would be as welcoming, as kind, as my mother's brother and sister had been to me.

The Corporal in the RTO's office rose with alacrity as we entered. 'Good morning, ma'am!'

'Good morning, Corporal,' I said, smiling – I hoped – winningly. 'I need your help. This little boy has just arrived from Berlin and in fifteen minutes I have to put him on the train for Berne, but he must have a wash before he leaves. Would you very kindly let him use your facilities?'

'The lad's German, isn't he, ma'am?'

'Yes.'

'Well, then, I'm afraid – '

'I know the rules,' I said pleadingly, 'but he's quite alone . . . an orphan from the Russian Sector. Wouldn't you . . . just this once – ?'

A young private had come from an inner office to lounge against the door frame. 'Wouldn't take a minute, Corp.'

'That's right,' I encouraged, beaming at them both and counting heavily on the innate kindness of the British soldier. The Corporal looked at the small silent figure beside me then threw his pencil down on the desk in capitulation. 'You'll get me shot, ma'am! See to him, Jim, but for Gawd's sake make 'im be quick!'

The young soldier straightened at once. 'You bet, Corp!' He crooked a finger at the boy. '*Kommen Sie mit*!' he shouted as though to a deaf person, and the child swung round to me, all his careful defences down and stark terror in his eyes.

'It's all right,' I said, bending to him, 'it's really all right – just for you to have a little wash and – ' Oh, God, what was the equivalent in German of 'spend a penny'? I had no idea. 'And I'll wait for you here,' I said aloud. It was obvious that he was not reassured, but he followed the soldier obediently.

'Tough on the kiddies, int'it, ma'am?' said the Corporal.

'Oh, yes, desperately.'

'About seven, is he?'

'No, over ten.'

'Reely? I've got a nipper who's just ten, but he's twice the size of this lad. I think I've got – ' out came the paybook from the breast pocket of his battle blouse, and with it a small photograph from between the covers ' – yes, 'ere's my Gary, ma'am.' A tousle-haired, round-faced boy squinted into the sun. He clutched a small dog of indeterminate breed and both seemed to be laughing. The edges of the photograph were ragged, and I wondered how many times it had been produced and admired during the years that the corporal had fought across the desert and up through Sicily, Italy and into Germany, as his medal ribbons confirmed.

'A fine, sturdy boy,' I said admiringly. 'I wonder if he'll ever know how lucky he is to be British at this time.'

'That's wot I always say to the wife. But for the grace o'Gawd – '

Karl and the private returned. 'All present an' correct!' said the latter chirpily. He looked at me meaningfully.

25

'Dun our dooty, we 'ave, an' 'ad a reel nice wash!' The woollen scarf was off, revealing baby-fine, blond-white hair, neatly combed over the small round head, and there was a pink tinge to the thin cheeks. But he still looked frightened and his eyes had searched at once for me.

'We're just brewin' up, ma'am,' said the Corporal, now completely won over. 'Would you and the lad like a cuppa?'

I looked at my watch. 'That would be wonderful,' I said gratefully, 'if you're sure?' Two steaming mugs were produced and once again Karl looked up at me. 'It is permitted?' When I nodded, his hands closed eagerly around the warmth. He bent his head for a tentative sip and I thought how thin, how terribly vulnerable the back of his neck looked. '*Es ist gut*,' he said, looking up again, this time with the ghost of a smile. When it was time to leave he carefully replaced the scarf, turned to the two soldiers and bowed. '*Vielen dank, meine Herren.*'

'Many thanks, indeed!' I echoed. 'You have both been so kind.'

'Glad to be able to help, ma'am,' said the Corporal, and as we went through the door I heard him say, 'Bloody shame, int'it?'

'This is for you,' I said, unzipping the holdall when Karl was settled in the train.

'There are two hard-boiled eggs with bread and butter, some corned beef sandwiches, and biscuits. In this medicine bottle is milk – from a tin, you understand, because we do not have fresh milk in our rations – but it is mixed with water, so it's not too thick. And here is some chocolate.' As I showed him each item, tiny sounds had come from his throat, but at the mention of chocolate he burst out incredulously: '*Schokolade*! You have real *Schokolade*?'

'Yes, here it is.'

'Is it permitted to eat it *now*?'

'Well, yes, but not too much in case it makes you feel sick. Better to eat it after some of the other food.' But he was transformed into a normal small boy wanting a sweet, eyes focused on the chocolate and tongue licking his lips. I broke off a piece of the large bar. 'Have this for now, but try to eat it slowly. I must find the guard.'

'Here is the boy,' I said, having tracked down the guard and brought him to the compartment. Karl stood up at once. '*Guten Morgen, Herr Schaffner.*'

''*Morgen,*' replied the man brusquely. He couldn't care less, I thought angrily, bloody man. Aloud I said, 'I am especially fearful because, as you see, he has food.'

He cleared his throat noisily and spat thick greenish-yellow mucus on the ground by my feet. 'We are not animals, *Fräulein Leutnant*, we do not steal food from children.'

Furious anger boiled in me then, I wanted to scream that he was a bloody old man without a heart . . . a damned German with as much feeling as the ground he stood upon. Instead I said carefully, 'I am not suggesting anyone is an animal, but these are abnormal times and hungry people, seeing an unescorted child eating a sandwich – '

'I have much work to do, *Fräulein Leutnant.*'

'Yes, but could you try to keep an eye on him when he eats?'

He shook his head. 'Not possible.'

I dug into my bag: two packets of twenty? Better make it three. It was highly illegal to give away our NAAFI ration of cigarettes in this way, but a few of us non-smokers did so when we felt the cause was good. I held the packets in my hand. 'It is a most tragic case.'

He eyed the cigarettes greedily. 'I will look after the boy,' he said and, as I hesitated, added: 'You may count on it.'

'Thank you,' I said, 'I felt sure you would be able to do so.'

But he beat me even then. 'Of course, you understand, *Fräulein Leutnant*, that I leave the train tonight, when it will be shunted into a siding, and in the morning another guard will be on duty.' He must have had a spark of feeling after all, for he added, 'I will lock the boy in the compartment for the night.'

'But will there be light and – and heating available?'

His tight-lipped, contemptuous smile plainly said, What a stupid bitch of an Englishwoman! 'There is no lighting, heating or water on German – '

'I know that, but I thought as an international train?'

'Yes, but it starts here and the fact that it goes beyond the German border makes no difference. Only trains for the use of your army have facilities, *Fräulein Leutnant*.'

I bent down to Karl and put my hand on his shoulder. 'I am afraid it will not be very nice, but try not to be frightened and think only of how lovely Switzerland will be.'

He took a step back, politely shaking off my hand. 'I am a German boy, *Fräulein Leutnant*. I shall not be afraid.'

There was nothing I could say in reply to such pathetic courage, but then I remembered the rug which Uncle Julian had sent me. 'I'll be back in a minute!' I said over my shoulder and ran, regardless of dignity, to where I hoped Morgan would be waiting with the Volkswagen. He was, and I snatched up the rug. They were closing the doors as I flew along the platform. I just had time to thrust the rug into the child's hands. 'Wrap yourself in this tonight,' I gasped, 'and good luck!' I saw him nod and his lips, now endearingly smeared with chocolate, moved, but I could not hear through the closed window.

The rug was the one Uncle Julian had wrapped around me on that morning when I had arrived in England thirteen years before.

4

By the time I got back to Headquarters I was hungry, frozen and emotionally battered, the interview with the Lithuanian murderer being the hardest task I had ever been involved in. I was astonished and desperately grieved to know that a young man, little more than a boy, should be condemned to death by a Court of the British Military Government after he had endured such misery, and to be told that his was by no means the only such case made me feel physically ill.

So when Jan said, 'Oh, you're here at last! Don't take your greatcoat off. We must leave at once,' I looked at her blankly. 'Now don't tell me you've forgotten we're having tea with Dan and Miles?'

'Oh, Jan, I can't! I've had no lunch, I'm frozen solid, and my nose has started to stream. You go without me and give them my apologies.'

'No,' Jan said doggedly, 'I'm not going without you, and we can't stand them up – not when there are so few of us out here! No, don't say anything. Just come on!'

'Oh, all right,' I said ungraciously, 'but I must do a bit of tarting up first.'

'No time, honey, we're very late as it is.' She hustled me off, and although the 21 Club was half empty, I was very conscious of looking scruffy beside Jan who was immaculate in her Canadian Red Cross khaki and gleaming dark leather belt. Then I looked up and forgot everything, for standing before me was the most magnificent man I had ever seen.

I have always said since that the fairy godmothers at Dan's birth gave him everything. He could have had those wonderful looks with only a mediocre body, yet in reality he stood just over six feet tall and exceptionally broad at the shoulder; he could have had all that but been as dull as dish-water – or humourless – or with little brain-power. Instead, he was a great raconteur with a ready wit and an extraordinarily quick brain. And even the wonderful looks could so easily have been marred: if the face had been wider, the eyes narrower, the mouth looser, then the straight, powerful nose with its flaring nostrils would have dominated, giving an entirely sensual look, perhaps even a slight coarseness, to the whole. But from the high, wide brow his face, with its slightly hollow cheeks, narrowed to a surprisingly square chin; the eyes were large and finely set; the mouth, although wide and mobile, was firm. So while remaining ruggedly handsome, it was a face that had been finely pared, a sensitive face. I was dimly aware of Jan making introductions and quite automatically held out my hand.

'What a very small, cold hand,' Dan Cleary said, looking down. Then, with his left hand, he gently rubbed the back of mine once, twice, as though we were already old friends.

'I'm so sorry we're late,' I heard myself saying quietly. 'I'm afraid it's all my fault. I've been driving around Hanover and over to Hameln all day and have only just got back.'

'I've never really understood exactly what all you girls do out here,' Dan said. So we told him, and both he and Miles Henderson listened attentively, asking very pertinent questions and expertly drawing us out. Then Jan looked up suddenly from pouring the tea and exclaimed, 'Oh, Minette, you haven't put it up!'

'What, for goodness' sake?' I asked with a start, apprehensively wondering if something vital were missing.

'Why, your third "pip" of course!' She turned to the two men. 'Minette was given it at least three days ago and here she is, still without it.'

'Well, congratulations,' they both said, and then Dan added, 'Do we call you Captain?'

'No,' I said, speaking quickly to cover my embarrassment, 'it's only an honorary rank, so we don't hold the King's Commission.'

'She's a Staff Officer, Grade II!' said Jan impishly, and Dan laughed the gently mocking laugh of a senior officer whose own rank had been hard won in a devastating war.

'This calls for a celebration,' said Miles Henderson, whom I had hardly noticed. He was a Lieutenant-Colonel with a plain, round face and a smile which could only be described as cherubic. 'Why don't we all meet for dinner tonight so that we can celebrate Minette's third – er – badge of rank?'

'Miles,' said Dan Cleary solemnly, 'that's the best idea you've had in weeks!'

But I took fright. 'Yes,' I agreed, 'it's a lovely idea, but please do excuse me this evening. I've been up since four this morning and I seem to have started a cold in the head as well.' Incredibly they both looked as disappointed as two small boys.

'Well, we must fix a date as soon as your cold is better,' Miles persisted. 'I'll ring you, Jan, in a few days and then we'll have – we'll have an orgy!'

'For God's sake, Miles, why did you have to say that? You'll frighten her off completely!' Dan said, and I turned quickly to look at him and saw by the amusement in his eyes that he had guessed the real reason for my excuse.

Miles was instantly contrite. 'Oh, Minette, *of course* I was only joking – '

'And what were you doing up at 4 A.M.?' asked Dan with mock severity, but when I told him his tone changed to utter incredulity: 'Are you seriously asking us to believe that you waited alone on Hanover Station in the early hours?'

'Y-es.'

31

The two men just looked at each other and then Dan said, 'My God, *anything* could have happened to you!'

'Well,' I said, falsely bright, 'nothing did, so that's all right, isn't it?'

'It most certainly is not,' was the curt reply. 'Even if you don't care about being raped or murdered, you might have spared a thought for the repercussions – how do you think the troops would have reacted to such news? And what about the effect it would have had upon our relations with the local Germans?'

I manufactured a small giggle to cover my by now intense embarrassment. 'I believe you're giving me a rocket!'

'Yes, I am!' was the instant retort. 'But it appears to be having no effect whatsoever! It was not a clever thing to do, you know. In fact, it was bloody stupid!' He spoke as a man very used to wielding authority and it was hard to stand up to him, but I made a great effort.

'Actually, I am aware of that,' I said, trying to sound cool, 'and I was quite terrified. But it had to be done. You see, Karl Eberhardt and his mother lived in what is now the Russian Sector of Berlin, and when the Russian Army began pouring into every building during their advance into the city, his mother locked Karl in a cupboard and told him to keep absolutely quiet, no matter what happened . . . Well, the poor child tried, but he could see through the keyhole that she was being raped again and again. At first his cries were not heard above her screams, but when she died the Russians dragged him out and clubbed him – I suppose it was a miracle they didn't kill him – and he was only found four days later, still crouched over his mother's body, starving and half mad. He fought like a little wild animal when taken away – of course the city was in total chaos, and when it was found that Karl went back again and again just to sit in that room, he was locked up.

'When our team began functioning he was brought to them, and they've worked so hard all these months, trying to get him to accept what happened. They were overjoyed when his aunt in Switzerland offered him a home. The train journey was to be the great test; for one of the team to travel with him would have been ideal, but no one could be spared and it was thought that as Karl would be with his own countrymen, he should be all right, so long as he was met at Hanover and put on the Berne train. So you see, I just had to be there.'

There was silence for a few minutes, broken only by the clatter of tea cups and the sound of quiet conversation at the far end of the Club. Then Dan said quietly, 'Christ, it's heart-breaking to realize what these children have endured. How was the poor little chap?'

'Very controlled, very – German, I suppose. Outwardly he appears to have got over it all very well and to be normal, but who knows what terrible scars are hidden beneath the surface?'

Both men murmured assent and then Dan leaned forward to look into my eyes, 'Well, Minette,' he began earnestly, 'all I can say is that you should never ever consider doing such a foolhardy thing again.'

'Listen to Daddy!' chortled Jan, but Dan's eyes flicked over to her with anger in their depths. 'No, Jan, this really is serious, and if ever you have another similar assignment, Minette, you *must* take a driver with you.'

All might have been well if I had not said stupidly, 'Oh, but I did, only as he doesn't speak any German I didn't think I'd need him, so I – I told him to come for me at nine o'clock this morning.'

'But don't you have any German drivers in your set-up?'

'Yes, we have Wolfgang, but I didn't take him because he would have had to sleep in the car and it would have been so desperately cold for him.'

33

'And what did this Wolfgang do in the war?' asked Miles quietly.

'He was Luftwaffe ground crew in Russia. He – he was very badly wounded in the lungs, so you see . . . ' My voice trailed away as I thought, Oh, Lord, I've done it again!

When Dan said, 'Someone should take her in hand,' I threw a look of appeal at Jan who responded at once: 'Yes, well, that may be so, but I'm afraid we're going to have to leave you guys now. Our Chief is having a lot of top brass to dinner and we have to be there to do our stuff – all part of her plan to put the Red Cross on the map.'

Back in the car, I said: 'Heavens, did you let me in for something!'

'Yes, and I'm sorry,' she leaned forward to switch on the ignition and half turned her head to smile at me, 'but it really was a damn silly thing to do!'

'I know,' I said, suddenly feeling exhausted, 'but I still don't think that gave Dan Cleary the right to blast off at me as he did.'

'Well, they've fought a long war, and although they were probably less than saintly towards many of the foreign women they've encountered, they are very protective of us – I think because they see us as an extension of their own womenfolk back home. Also, they must remember that for some time the war was touch and go and we could have been the ones to end up in some foreign brothel or on our knees scrubbing some fat Frau's kitchen! But what did you think of Dan?'

'Oh, he certainly is the most wonderful-looking man, and seems so nice too, despite the rocket! His wife must be mad to want a divorce.'

Jan nodded. 'Yes, that's what everyone thinks. Dan *is* nice, and brilliant too; everyone predicts a great future for him.'

'I can't imagine what made you think he'd be interested in me,' I said with absolute sincerity.

She gave me a brief smiling glance. 'Can't you? Want to bet on it?'

'No,' I replied with a small laugh, 'not worth it, and you'll need all your money if you're going to walk up the aisle trailing clouds of tulle.'

'I think I'll ring Jack Martin at the Medical Directorate and tell him I can't go to the party tonight.'

'Isn't he the guy who followed you into the Ladies' at the Club and refused to leave until you'd given him a date – yes, I thought so! What's wrong with him?'

'Nothing,' I said, flopping wearily into a chair, 'but it's been an awful day – searching through the ruins of Cologne for Otto Lange's one room and then finding it just as his coffin was being taken away! I tried to explain to his widow that we'd only received the phials of insulin from London yesterday, but my bit of German deserted me entirely. I appealed to Wolfgang to explain, but he was in such a state he couldn't understand my English! Incidentally, I think his nerves are getting worse. His fingers were drumming on the steering wheel the whole time, and his head kept jerking about in that strange way – '

'His legacy of Russia.'

'Of course, and I'm sorry for him, but with my own nerves twanging – anyway, we went on to Frau Dorf only to find her son suffering from a terrible throat infection. The German doctor says he is in urgent need of penicillin, but of course they have none and nothing more can be done for the boy – he can't even be taken into the isolation hospital because that no longer exists . . . Oh, lord, what a mess it all is! And Cologne absolutely stinks, even in this weather – I can't imagine what it's going to be like in the summer. I suppose there's nothing in from Moscow?

Stupid of me to even ask! I thought I'd better see Frau König, but it was a great mistake because I could tell that despite her agony, she thought I'd brought her news from the Russian Red Cross and her poor old face lit up! Of course, I had to say that although we'd written several times to them asking if they had any information about her son, there had never been a reply – or to any of the other hundreds of requests we'd sent, enquiring about possible POWs. I'm sure poor old Frau K. is only clinging on in the hope of hearing about her boy, but the cancer seems to be spreading over her whole body and there's no more morphine for her – '

'Yes, it's grim,' Jan said, 'but you have to remember that the Russians suffered terribly at the hands of the Germans. There must be thousands and thousands of Russian mothers yearning for news of *their* sons – and we know now that Russian POWs were treated most brutally by their captors. All we can hope is that the Chief will succeed in resuscitating the German Red Cross and then they'll be able to deal with much of this work.'

'But the Chief can't do much about the Red Cross in East Germany.'

'True, but once the West gets going, the East might also start.' Jan lit a cigarette and looked at me through its smoke. 'Meanwhile, there's no sense in your moping over all this. The best thing you can do is go to the party.' As I began a refusal, she went on: 'Do you realize that when the no-fratting ban is lifted, there'll be masses of German girls available? And I'm told they'll do *anything* for a chocolate bar or a few packets of cigs!

'Also, it's rumoured that later this year the families will be allowed to join the married men out here and that means loads of pretty daughters and perhaps even flirtatious wives. So I'm warning you, kiddo, that all the Women's Services are likely to be left out in the cold!

Better make hay while the sun shines – you can always stay at home with a good book later!'

But it was a sudden idea, rather than Jan's words, that made me to go to Jack Martin's party and he and I were hardly settled in the car before I said with elaborate casualness: 'I suppose there's plenty of penicillin available to all the medical services now?'

'Yes, the supply is pretty good, but or course it's all needed for the "Skins and Sins".' He turned briefly to give me a lopsided smile. 'VD wards, you know.'

'Yes, I do know,' I replied frostily, 'and I wonder if you can spare a very small amount to save a little boy's life?'

'You're surely not asking for a German boy?'

'Yes, but his mother's a Brit. Nat.'

'What the hell's that?'

'British National, one of the several hundred British women who married Germans between the wars. We're making contact with them all and giving them the surplus food parcels that London used to send to our POWs in German camps.'

'That so? Interesting, but I don't think – '

'Her husband was killed in France in 1940 and she's had a very tough time coping with German animosity *and* all the bombing of Cologne; the food parcels have been a God-send to her and the boy, but now he's got a terrible throat infection . . . He's all she's got. Couldn't you possibly – ?'

'All right, give me his address, and I'll see what I can do.'

'I have it here,' I said, taking the paper from my bag and holding it out. As Jack Martin's fingers closed over it, I held his hand. 'Thanks,' I said quietly, 'thanks so much.'

'Anything to please a pretty lady!'

'Well then,' I replied, taking a deep breath, 'there's an old German woman who is riddled with cancer and

37

cannot get any pain-killers. Although in terrible agony she's clinging to life in the hope of hearing whether her son is alive . . . he was only twenty-one when he was sent to Stalingrad.'

'Sorry, sweetie, no can do! The old girl would need ongoing doses, each more massive than the last, and I couldn't swing that amount. Cheer up now. Here we are!'

Even from the entrance it was obvious that the party was in full swing. There was a babel of voices, interspersed with shouts of laughter, and suddenly all my confidence seemed to ebb away, leaving only the old paralysing shyness.

'What's the matter?' Jack Martin asked as I drew back.

'It must be a huge party,' I said, my steps slowing by the minute.

'Don't tell me you're *shy*!' He made it sound like some outlandish disease, but when I did not reply, said bracingly, 'A decent-sized G.&T. will soon cure that, my girl!' Once inside, he handed me a huge glassful, introduced me to a circle of uniformed figures and then melted into the crowd. I stood silently sipping the almost neat gin and trying vainly to gather myself together. It was then that I heard the music: a Chopin étude, being played softly and with great sensitivity. I turned at once in the direction and saw across the smoke-hazed room a girl seated at a grand piano. She wore some kind of uniform – UNRRA, I think – and although I could not see her face, the light from a standard lamp shone directly on to her hair. If the music had not held my attention, that hair certainly would have, for it was magnificent. It fell in a shining sweep almost to her collar, the ends just turning upward, the strands of blonde, auburn, brown and gold intermingling, vibrant with colour, and seeming almost to sparkle under the light. I was just thinking it would need oils rather than water-colours to bring out all the shades, the gloss and the life, when Jack Martin spoke beside me.

'You wouldn't think she'd been in Auschwitz, would you? I believe she was quite bald when found, but nine months of good food and being a Brigadier's popsie have certainly paid off. Perhaps "popsie" isn't quite the right word, though. I'm told the randy old goat finally burnt himself out between Cairo and Rome, and she *had* it burnt out of her in the camp brothel where she lasted three months – not bad, when you think that meant being available twenty-four hours a day, seven days a week. When they threw her out, a God-damned Kraut doctor got her for gynaecological experiments – mainly without anaesthetics, I believe. Yet she still survived. Perhaps those Yids have become extra strong after the two thousand years of hide-and-seek they've had to play.'

The casual brutality of the words appalled me and I edged away from him. It was then that the woman turned and looked directly at me. Involuntarily, I took a step back, knocking myself against a table and slopping my drink. For the eyes that seemed to bore into mine were black pits, expressionless and dead, set in a face made mask-like by the tight stretching of the skin over every bone. It was a death's head made totally macabre by the hair flowing from it, so colourful and alive. Yet once she must have been beautiful, before unimaginable suffering had destroyed her. Now her presence made the ever-flowing drink and the shrill laughter obscene. How could people dare to be carefree when in their midst was a fellow human being whose soul had died in torture?

I turned abruptly to leave and a voice said: 'Good evening, how is your – what *is* the matter, Minette?' And there was Dan Cleary, the smile suddenly wiped off his face, his warm hand reaching out to enclose mine. 'You're shaking!'

'The woman – the woman at the piano,' I stammered, close to tears.

His eyes flicked very briefly to her and then returned

to look concernedly into my own. 'Eleni? Yes?'

'Dead,' I whispered, 'breathing, but quite dead – haven't you noticed? Except for the hair – so wonderful and so horrible.'

'I know,' he said quietly. He paused momentarily, then took my glass, sniffed it, muttered 'Almost neat,' and slammed it down on the table. 'Time to go,' he said as though speaking to a small child and, still clasping my hand, led me out. As he helped me into my greatcoat, I roused myself sufficiently to whisper, 'I believe I've only been here a few minutes.'

Dan shrugged. 'These parties are all the same – a bore from beginning to end.'

It was then that Jack Martin bustled out: 'Minette! What on earth – ?'

'We're just off,' said Dan cheerily.

'Oh, but I say, sir, Minette is with me,' Jack Martin protested.

Dan stood like a rock, his shoulders massive in the heavy blue greatcoat. He put on his cap with its single row of gold oak leaves on the peak and instantly became the senior officer. 'Correction,' he said, his tone suddenly brisk, 'Minette arrived with you, but now she is leaving with me.' Then he took a firm grip of my arm above the elbow and propelled me to the door; as he held this open for me, he half turned to the gaping Jack Martin. 'Sorry about this, chum, but you should know by now never to leave a pretty girl alone at a party. Good night!'

Outside he fell into step with me, courteously shortening his stride to mine. I looked up at him shyly. 'Perhaps I shouldn't have – '

'Nonsense! The fellow's a goon and hasn't a clue how to behave!' He led me to where a magnificent Mercedes stood, its long body gleaming in the moonlight.

'What a splendid car!' I exclaimed admiringly.

'Yes, that's what I thought when I "liberated" it,' Dan

40

said as he helped me into the front seat. After he had slipped into the driving seat, he turned to me, his gloved hand coming to rest lightly on both of mine. 'Better now?' he asked quietly.

'Yes, thank you,' I said, sounding extraordinarily prim.

'Good! But you know, Minette, you'll have to toughen up or else all that you see out here will break you. I think you're soaking it all up like a sponge and at the same time seeing everything in three-dimensional vision. You cannot – you *must* not – try to take on the tragedies of the war. We didn't seek that, but it happened, and in various ways we're all its victims. Neither can we turn back the clock for Eleni and the thousands like her. All we *can* do is to be grateful for our own survival, try our best to alleviate the suffering and vow never to let it happen again.' He swivelled in his seat and sat staring straight ahead, as though deep in thought, but when he spoke again his voice had lost its serious note: 'There now, homily over! I think a quiet dinner and some dancing is indicated, don't you?'

And suddenly, over-riding all the tragedy, was the wish to be happy and to stay with this fascinating man whose physical presence was so reassuring. I stole a glance at his profile, faintly illuminated by the dashboard light, and instantly thought: The David, that's it! Although the nose is stronger, it's a similar shape; the strong neck is the same too, so is the full eye – but of course without the David's frowning expression. The hair is quite different, the mouth and chin much longer and firmer, but then Michelangelo was sculpting a youth and Dan Cleary is very much a man . . .

He was handling the large car with casual expertise and we went racing through the deserted countryside, headlights piercing the darkness; we might have been the last people left on earth, but I did not even ask where we were going. When eventually we drew up in the shadow of a splendid Schloss, I exclaimed: 'Oh, how lovely! Are we really going inside?'

I heard, rather than saw, the smile in his voice. 'I knew this would appeal to your romantic soul, and yes, we are most definitely going in. You don't know it? Bad Lippspringe, the ancestral home of Prince Bernhard of the Netherlands? Part of it is now an Officers' Club.'

'*Guten Abend, Fräulein Hauptmann, Guten Abend, Herr Oberst* . . . for two? But of course, at once.' The head waiter's bow was deep, his voice unctuous. Minions were summoned with a flick of the fingers, a perfect table offered, chairs held out, table napkins unfurled and menus presented, all within seconds. The eyes of every woman in the huge room were turned on Dan who appeared supremely indifferent, even unaware, but instinctively I tried to hold myself straighter and was glad of my Gieves uniform, of Ted's last pair of black nylons, and of having splashed on a liberal amount of *Je Reviens*.

I saw, too, how the waiter's eyes, cold as a snake's, had flicked over the RAF wings and medal ribbons on Dan's jacket. 'They hate us, don't they?'

Dan looked up from the large menu and his level gaze held mine. 'Yes, of course,' he said calmly. 'Just as we would if the circumstances were reversed.'

'Have you noticed that all the German dance bands always end the evenings with *Lilli Marlene*? Someone told me that in the Paris night clubs the bands similarly played *J'attendrai* and all the German officers applauded, not realizing it was a Resistance song. Do you think *Lilli Marlene* means the same?'

Dan shrugged. 'I've heard the story, of course, but I've no idea if there's any truth in it. What I *do* know is that National Socialism is not completely dead and that we need to be vigilant, both now and in the future.'

'*Is* there an underground movement?'

'I believe so, but as an escape organization rather than

for resistance against us. Although some of the really big fish must have got away before the war actually ended.'

'And almost all the "ordinary" Germans deny they were ever in the Party.'

Dan laughed. 'Yes, I know! If all the denials were true, the Nazi Party would have been almost non-existent. Now, what are you going to eat?'

From then on he concentrated on entertaining me with stories of his war service, all related lightly and with so much humour that soon I hid my face, laughing helplessly, and he began to laugh too. 'You have a most delicious little giggle,' he said at last. Instantly I tried to straighten my face. 'I'm sorry, giggling is only for schoolgirls.'

'Not yours,' he replied in his decisive way, 'let's hear lots more of it. But now come and dance.'

We went on to the floor and his arm was already around me when I was suddenly and totally overwhelmed by an urge to be close . . . to melt against his large frame. It was as though I was being drawn irresistibly forward by a magnet and to fight it was so hard, so very hard. Yet I knew I must. It was with the greatest difficulty that I took a step back, trembling a little and bewildered. Never before had I experienced a feeling so intense, so all powerful.

'Do you always stand a foot away from your partners when you dance?' Dan was looking down at me, as he was always to do, with shoulders straight and only his head lowered, in a stance that was both protective and tender.

'No – yes – well, it's – it's because we shall bounce off each other's buttons otherwise!' It was the best I could do in my chaotic state and a smile of almost boyish mischief flitted briefly across his face. He started to say something, changed his mind, and instead drew me gently towards him. 'I'm sure we shall be able to manage,' he said as he swept me into the dance, but I remained as rigid as a board. The band was playing one of the latest hits, *Temptation*:

You came, I was alone,
I might have known,
You were temptation.

'Hmm,' Dan said, 'very nice. *Je Reviens*, I think.'
'Yes,' I replied, amazed at how breathless I sounded.
'It's the only perfume the NAAFI seems to have
permanently in stock.'
'I know. I have a standing order with a shop in
Brussels to keep me supplied with *Mitsouko*, Ros's
favourite.'
'Ros?'
'Yes, Rosalind, my wife.'
'Oh, yes, of course. Is she "Fair Rosalind"?'
'Of face? Yes, most definitely. But of colouring – well,
she has a remarkably fair skin, but she's a tempestuous
redhead.'
I was glad when the dance ended and I could sink
down on to a chair. Across the table Dan looked at me
thoughtfully, even slightly speculatively.
'Do you have any children?' I asked, anxious to break
the tension which suddenly seemed to have arisen between
us.
'Yes, a daughter, Emma. She's four years old.' A fine
crocodile skin wallet with the initials D.M.C. stamped in
gold across one corner was produced. 'This is Emma,' he
said, his voice now very gentle, as he handed over a
photograph of a pretty little girl clutching an elaborate
baby doll and laughing into the camera.
'Oh, sweet,' I said sincerely. 'Very sweet. She takes
after you in looks, doesn't she?'
'So people say, but I can't see it myself. To me, she
looks far more like Ros. Here – what do you think?'
Another photograph was given me and this time I was
speechless, for I was looking at a woman whose heart-
shaped face was dominated by huge eyes, its perfection

marred only slightly by the small tight mouth and discontented expression. No one would ever call Rosalind Cleary *lovely*, for that would imply softness, but certainly she was very beautiful. What a couple, I thought, admiration momentarily making me detached, what an incredibly striking couple! Aloud I said: 'How very beautiful she is.'

'Yes,' it was said with a sigh, 'Ros is certainly that.'

'And so tall,' I said, thinking of my own small stature with distaste.

'Yes,' he said again. 'She's one of those girls whose legs seem to go on forever.'

Why should I suddenly feel like a pricked balloon? Why think at that precise moment of my own crooked back? And in place of the laughter, why should I now feel tired and depressed? I must have known in my heart of hearts and just have been unready to face it. 'Will they be coming out to join you?'

'I don't know.' There was a weary note in Dan's voice too now. 'You see, my marriage is only hanging together by a thread and I just don't know from day to day what will happen.'

'Oh.' I felt totally inadequate. 'That's a terrible pity – can nothing be done?'

'Only if I agree to leave the Service.'

But he appeared so right for command, for quick thinking and unusual situations. 'You don't seem like a nine-to-five man to me!' I burst out involuntarily.

'No, nor do I intend to be! And so far as Ros is concerned, I've almost got to the point where I'd be prepared to cut my losses, but there is Emma.' He leaned across the table, utterly serious now. 'She is my daughter and I want to be with her, guide her, be responsible for her until she is grown up. But if I agree to a divorce, Ros will certainly remarry and then some other chap will take my place with Emma, and I shall remain the stranger who comes to collect her for a few hours or a few days at infrequent intervals.'

How strange that the deep hurt of my own father's neglect of me should surface then. I had never known what a father's love or even liking could be, and seeing Dan's obvious devotion to Emma brought tears to my eyes. 'Oh,' I said, in total empathy with him, 'that would be terrible – unthinkable. But – but why does your wife so dislike the RAF?'

'Actually, she doesn't. It's the constant moving about and the rather parochial life-style that she objects to.'

I gasped in astonishment. 'And that's all – that's the only reason?'

'Yes.'

'But,' I said longingly, 'there would be Kenya, Malaya, and all the Mediterranean stations, not just to see but to *experience*.'

'I know, that's what I tell her, and so far she's only lived on one bomber station in England; when I was shot down she moved back to her father's country house and remained on there after my escape, because almost at once I was posted to Cairo.'

I shook my head in bewilderment: how could any woman give up this wonderful man to whom she was *married* – actually *married* – and jeopardize her child's future, just because she did not like his chosen life-style? 'I'm afraid it's beyond me,' I said quietly. 'But I suppose when one is so beautiful and has literally everything in the world, it's very easy to become spoiled and perhaps rather self-centred – or just to have a different set of values.'

Unexpectedly he smiled, then clasped my hand as it lay on the table. 'What a very modest girl you are – modest and compassionate.'

I felt myself flushing. 'No, not at all,' I said, absurdly pleased, 'but thank you.'

46

He stood up, still holding my hand. 'We must dance to this, it's the perfect tune for you.' It was a dreamy little waltz, meant for lovers dancing as one, cheek to cheek. It would have been so easy to curl my arm around his neck, so easy . . .

Instead I strained away from him. 'Why not just relax?' he suggested very quietly, and then with laughter in his voice, 'I can assure you, our buttons won't matter.'

I made no comment, but instead with panic rising, asked: 'What is it called?'

'This tune? It's German – *Hörst Du Mein Heimliche Rufen? – Do You Hear My Secret Call?*'

'Typical German sentimentality,' I said with what I hoped was a cynical laugh, and inwardly thought: I must not come out with him again, I really must *not*. It was a resolution which I kept repeating silently as we drove back to my Mess, and when we reached the porch I held out my hand. 'Thank you for rescuing me from the party and for dinner,' I said formally, and tried to withdraw my hand, but Dan only tightened his hold. 'No, it is I who have to thank you,' he said quietly. 'It has been a wonderful evening and we must do it again.'

'That would be nice,' I answered, feeling my heart plummet, for of course I had wanted him to make another date, whatever my resolution.

'So how about the same time tomorrow?'

My heart raced in a surge of joy, but: 'Oh no, not tomorrow, I couldn't come tomorrow,' I said in instant panic.

'Why not? Something else on?'

'N-no, but – '

'So will you give me one good reason why you can't have dinner with me?'

'Ah well, you see, we were specifically told at our last briefing in London never to go out with a married man!'

His deep laugh was loud in the silence. 'That certainly

narrows the field, doesn't it? And I wonder how many of you have adhered to it? But, anyway, it hardly applies to me. As I've told you, I'm not really married any more.' He abruptly let go of my hand, stepped back and gave me a parade-ground salute. 'So I'll be here at 7.30 tomorrow. Good-night, sweet Minette, *Schlafst Du gut!*' And was gone, leaving me silent, but feeling both extraordinarily happy and very afraid.

'This evening it is your turn to talk and tell me about yourself,' Dan said once we were seated in the Bad Salzuflen Officers' Club. He had arrived punctually at 7.30 and of course I was waiting, as I had been waiting since first opening my eyes that morning, in a complete mixture of eagerness and apprehension for I knew in my heart of hearts that Dan Cleary was too fascinating, too *nice*, and too dangerous. Yet I knew equally well that it was going to be impossible to resist him. But just remember, I told myself sternly, he's only taking you out because he's very lonely.

'Oh, there's really very little to tell,' I said hastily, 'and I wouldn't know where to start.'

'You could always try the beginning,' Dan said solemnly and then sat back as though ready to wait forever, his eyes never leaving mine. So I took a deep breath and, once launched, found it surprisingly easy to talk of my parents' elopement in 1919; of the farm in Kenya which they'd been allocated under the Soldier Settler Scheme; of my mother's death seven years later and of my father sending me home when I was ten.

'To go to boarding school, I suppose?' Dan said, leaning forward now, chin on hand, in seemingly rapt attention.

I hastily took a sip of wine to cover my hesitation; if I told him the absolute truth, it would be of my back and I just could not bear to let him know about that. Yet in my family's strict code, to tell a lie was unforgivable.

'No, it was because my father was bankrupt . . . I couldn't go to school because of being too backward. Father had taught me the three Rs but little else – he really didn't like me very much, you see, and had no patience with my mistakes.'

Instantly Dan's hand covered mine. 'I find that very difficult to understand,' he said quietly.

'I think – I think he blamed me for Mummy's death. It seems she was never strong after my birth – '

'Oh, for God's sake! What the hell was the matter with him – a grown man! – to blame his own child for being alive!' The words were quietly spoken and yet with a scarcely controlled anger and I basked in the unexpected protective warmth.

'He and Mummy were very devoted, you see.'

'Really? And so, how were you educated?' He was not going to let me off the hook, and soon I was making him smile over the eccentricities of Miss Pearson with her funny feet always set at ten-to-two and her long hair secured by string. 'I suppose she wasn't really a governess because she didn't live in but came every morning on a very high, old-fashioned bicycle. But it's very unkind of me to make fun of her because she was really a dear and I was devoted to her.'

'But you must have known girls of your own age, the children of your aunt and uncle's friends?'

'Actually, no, because Uncle Julian was twenty-five and Aunt Alexa eighteen when Mummy was born.' I giggled, hoping to sound very worldly. 'I suppose she must have been the grandparents' last fling; they'd married when Granny was seventeen.'

'Hmm,' said Dan cryptically.

'And so, all the friends' children were already grown up and getting married when I first arrived – ' I broke off, suddenly remembering the first wedding they'd taken me to: a grand military affair with full dress uniforms, swords and white gloves, clinking medals and jingling spurs. I had been totally silent, lost in the glamour of the tulle-enveloped bride, the music and scent of the banked flowers. Afterwards I had pinned an old lace curtain to my head and walked down the curving stairs, solemnly tossing torn up scraps of newspaper over myself and humming the Lohengrin March. Uncle Julian, standing at the bottom, had remained grave-faced as he said: 'May I have the honour of escorting the bride?' With a regal nod I had taken his arm, and together we had proceeded slowly across the wide hall, humming in unison, until Daisy, coming to sound the gong for luncheon, had broken the spell.

'You have the most angelic smile on your face,' Dan Cleary said softly, 'so a *pfennig* for those thoughts.' But of course I could not tell him of anything so childish. The band struck up the fashionable *Hear My Song, Violetta* and I was immediately all animation – 'Could we dance? This is one of my favourites' – and the next minute just managed to restrain myself from rushing into Dan's arms. Not that he let me stand away for he held me close, yet with absolute propriety, as once again I became rigid. 'You've not been in the Red Cross for the whole of the war, have you, Minette?' His voice was gentle, even soothing.

'No,' I said hesitantly, 'I was in the Home Guard!'

That certainly startled him out of his calm. 'The Home Guard!' he repeated, laughing. 'I had no idea young girls were in that outfit. Tell me more!'

So I explained how Uncle Julian had been asked first to raise and then command the Local Defence Volunteers in Solenthaven. 'As their numbers grew and they became ever more efficient, there was a tremendous amount of paperwork and so I was a mixture of Girl Friday and general dog's body to them all.'

'But weren't you called up?'

I had such a moment of panic then that I stumbled and instantly Dan's arms tightened around me. 'Oh, heavens, something's happened to my feet – sorry! Yes, I was called up but – but was not considered strong enough for the Forces.' I saw the dreaded question hover on his lips, but good manners stopped him and instead he said, 'What bad luck.'

'Yes and no. I certainly missed all the excitement of the war, but on the other hand I had a very comfortable time and all the old gentlemen were sweet to me. They called me "The Daughter of the Regiment" and really spoiled me.'

As Dan silently guided me back to our table I felt I should speak up for them all: 'I expect everyone in the regular forces looked upon the Home Guard as dear old fuddy-duddies more likely to trip over their rifles and shoot themselves than an enemy, but they were all most distinguished and extremely efficient. For most of the time we had a retired Major-General as my uncle's second-in-command, and towards the end of the war a retired Lieutenant-General took over the battalion.'

Dan smiled into my eyes. 'How they must have enjoyed having you around!'

To my horror I felt an upsurge of tears and quickly turned away, blinking furiously, but of course he saw and said very quietly, 'And I'm glad they spoiled you because I think you deserve a lot of cosseting.'

It was stupid to feel so warm, so happy at that, and to cover it I said flippantly, 'Oh, I'm tougher than I look, you know!'

I was still sternly trying to convince myself of this as we drove back to the village, but as we approached, our headlights picked out many hurrying figures, loaded not only with the usual bundles but pushing heaped handcarts, prams and ancient bicycles. 'What's going on?' Dan queried, immediately drawing the car into deep shadow and switching off engine and lights. Few of the dark figures seemed aware of us, so determined were they, and after a few minutes of silent study, Dan laughed quietly. 'Now I understand! Look, there are a few wagons and an engine in the station, obviously broken down. I guess it's a coal train which your locals are busily robbing!'

'Oh,' I said perturbed, 'I'm sure you're right, but do you *have* to do anything about them?'

Dan turned to look at me. 'What would you suggest?'

'Nothing!' I said at once.

'Carried unanimously! Life must be endless misery for them with almost non-existent heating and so little food.' He switched on the engine and eased the big car forward. 'Let's just wish the poor devils the best of British and let them get on with it.'

Dan waited until the night-watchman opened the door for me and then with a brisk, 'Thanks for another lovely evening, Minette,' dashed away almost at a run, leaving me open-mouthed with surprise. Once in my room I rushed to the window: Dan had already roared away, headlights blazing, and from my elevated position I could see the great car hurtling along the country road, as though he could hardly wait to get away.

'You're not doing anything this evening, are you?' Jan asked at breakfast. I shook my head. I had spent an almost sleepless night trying to convince myself that it was all for the best: Dan obviously had no intention of spending any more evenings with me and I should be grateful. He was married, with a remarkably beautiful wife and a daughter he adored, and that was that. So why should I keep remembering his every word and how he had looked at me? Why should I keep hearing his quiet voice saying, 'My marriage is almost at an end.' I knew the answer but would just have to live with it, together with my turmoil of emotions and my desolation.

'Good,' Jan was saying, 'because Miles and Dan want us to join them for the celebration dinner they promised you.'

Oh, the joy, the utter joy, surging up from the depths of my being. 'How very nice of them,' I murmured, astonished at the coolness of my own voice. How clever I was at disguising my deepest feelings: it was my only talent and one which I resolved to exercise that evening: I would be pleasant, but just a little distant and cool, definitely cool, when dancing with Dan.

He took one look at me on arrival and there was no mistaking the amused glint in his eyes. 'How lovely to see you again.'

'Thanks,' I said lightly, and even managed a slight toss of the head, but then ruined the effect by not being able to resist a sideways glance at him. His fine mobile mouth lifted at the corners, but his tone was solemn as he said: 'The Ice Maiden act is very attractive – even provocative – but you'll never be able to keep it up, you know, you're far too warm and sweet. Shall we go?'

'I think heavy water is called for, don't you, Dan?' Miles asked when we were all seated at the Twenty-One Club.

What on earth is 'heavy water'? I wondered in silent alarm. 'Most definitely,' Dan replied and then, as though reading my thoughts, he turned to me: 'That is, if our guest of honour likes champagne?'

'I adore it!' I exclaimed, relief making me over-enthusiastic. When it arrived they all congratulated me and then Dan dipped a finger in his glass and carefully anointed me behind the tip of each ear. 'And here's to the best-looking Staff Officer of any grade in the whole of Rhine Army!' he said, holding my glance with his own before adding so softly that I barely heard, 'A man could drown in the depths of those gentle eyes.'

53

It was as though a hurricane swept through me, lifting me off my feet and entirely blowing away my frail resolutions . . . yet everything might still have ended differently if Dan had not said later: 'I've been watching you dance with Miles and you look so supple, so full of rhythm – how come you *feel* quite different when you dance with me?'

'Oh,' I stammered, 'well, it's because Miles is so much shorter than you . . . he's easier for me to follow, you see.'

'Strange,' he mused, straight-faced, 'I've never heard of that before.'

And because I was sure he knew the real reason, I panicked and said the first thing that came into my head: 'Dan, will you do me a great favour?'

He was instantly alert. 'Yes, of course.'

'Will you – will you teach me to drive?'

He drew in his breath sharply, surprise making him temporarily silent, but then as always he quickly recovered. 'Certainly.'

'Thank you . . . that would make life so much easier. I could be independent.' My voice stumbled and finally faded as I realized I had ensured our continuing to meet, and there was no excuse I could now make without revealing the real reason: that I was very afraid of the outcome.

'Miles,' Dan said at the end of the evening, 'will you take Jan back in your car?' She looked up sharply. 'What about Minette?'

'Minette is to have her first driving lesson.'

'Now?' I gasped, for it was after midnight.

'Why not? Couldn't be a better time!' Dan's laugh was cheerful and assured.

From the first I loved the power, freedom and excitement engendered by the big car responding to my touch and, as I gradually assumed more control over it, so the reserve built up by my father's rejection and the long years of illness began to crumble. 'Oh, isn't it lovely – isn't it thrilling?' I would ask, laughing joyously, and it was left to Dan to bring me back to reality by saying: 'Concentrate now! Keep your eyes on the road and don't press your foot down so hard!'

Yet my happiness must have been infectious for Dan, too, began to laugh more often and even to play boyish tricks on me such as silently putting on the hand brake just as we were about to move off, or diverting my attention while he switched off ignition or lights, so that I exclaimed in panic: 'What's happened? What have I done?'

On the evening before my leave, when Dan successfully fooled me for the third time, I turned to him in mock fury. 'Oh, you – you . . .!' I spluttered, quite lost for words, and began to pummel his arm with my fists.

'Hey, hey!' he protested, still laughing. 'Stop attacking me in this brutal way!' He snatched at my flying fists and held them lightly. 'You know, you're a real little spitfire beneath that demure exterior!' he said, trying hard to sound shocked.

'Oh, but I can do better than this!' I retorted, still battling ineffectually with his restraining wrists.

'Can you?' he asked softly, and instantly then everything changed: my arms were stilled by an iron grip and all his laughter was gone. Instead, he was gazing deeply into my eyes and it seemed to me that the world itself stopped in its orbit. I did not fully understand, only sensing that this was a super-charged moment, with us both at a point of no return. I felt stunned, just a little frightened, but intensely, overwhelmingly excited, wanting only that Dan should take me to that point.

Instead he abruptly dropped my hands and turned away. 'Let's get going,' he said curtly.

But I could not adjust so quickly and sat numbly while Dan lit a cigarette with hands that shook. He took a long pull on it, inhaling deeply as though desperate.

It seemed that within seconds I had ceased to exist for him, and sick at heart, I swivelled in my seat to face the wheel.

'Is there a problem?' I felt his eyes on me, but did not trust myself to look up.

'No,' I whispered almost inaudibly. I switched on the ignition, but for the first time could not put the car into gear. Trembling, and beginning to panic, I did turn then: 'I can't – '

'You've not depressed the clutch.'

'I have, but it won't – '

'Then keep your foot down hard!' His hand covered mine as it rested on the lever's knob and, like a sheet of lightning, all the tension returned and was as quickly gone, for under Dan's pressure the gear slipped smoothly into place and he whipped his hand from mine. Almost simultaneously the car leapt forward, completely out of my control, for not only was my foot seemingly glued to the accelerator but I was also incapable of steering. We were in imminent danger of crashing over the side of the Autobahn and I screamed, 'Help me, help me!' then watched, mesmerized, as a hand grabbed hold of the wheel and another unceremoniously pushed my leg aside and thus off the accelerator.

'Flap over now,' Dan said quietly and, as the car slowed, he added: 'Brake gently now, that's right, gear into neutral – handbrake on!' He did not raise his voice, but the tone of command was so absolute that somehow I brought the car to a standstill and then promptly burst into tears. Dan waited a few seconds before shaking open a handkerchief and trying to peer into my face. But I quickly turned my head away. 'Now what?' he said, sounding hurt, and of course I could not let him misunderstand. 'I look ugly when I cry,' I whispered, with a gulp.

Dan's instant laughter was loud in the silence. 'Oh, that's a very healthy sign! All right, my sweet, I won't look! So dry your eyes and have a good blow before we move off. I think perhaps the short route back to your village, don't you?'

From the depths of his handkerchief I said, 'Yes, but you'll drive, won't you?'

'I most certainly will not!'

'But I can't – I really can't, and – and I never want to drive again!'

'Well that's just too bad because you're definitely going to do so, right now!'

'Oh, please, Dan. *Please.*'

'No!'

'I – I never realized you could be so cruel.'

'Well, there are many different kinds of cruelty and most of them are obscene, but at this precise moment I'm trying to be kind. Don't you see, Minette, you *must* drive now? It's the same as crash landing a plane or falling off a horse – you have to try again straight away. So get going, unless you want to spend the rest of the night on this bit of Autobahn. And while you're making up your mind, I'll take a short snooze. You don't mind, do you?'

'Dan Cleary, don't you *dare*!'

For the first time his laughter was without a strained note. 'All right, I promise not to tease you any more, so long as you'll get us back to civilization! It's under five miles, after all.'

So I made a great effort and drove those five miles at a snail's pace, at the end of them feeling utterly exhausted. 'Thank God,' I murmured, when we finally arrived.

'Well done, that girl!' Dan exclaimed heartily. 'Very well done indeed!'

'So you're not cross any more?'

He turned quickly to me. 'Cross? Of course not! How could any man ever be cross with you? But let's get you indoors. It's late, and you'll have a hectic day tomorrow.' Then, as we walked up the path, his arm suddenly swept around my shoulders, pulling me close. 'I'm very proud of my pupil, you know, and I'll miss our evenings like hell.' As we reached the door he bent and kissed me hard and lingeringly on the temple. 'Have a lovely leave, darling, but come back to me soon, please come back to me.' And then was gone, leaving me mute and turned to stone.

'You look as though you're in a trance,' Jan said the next morning.

'Do I?' I manufactured a small laugh, instinctively trying to cover my feelings. But Jan knew me too well and paused only to take a sip of her coffee. Then, with her head on one side, she looked at me meditatively: 'You're falling for each other, hook line and sinker, aren't you?'

'Of course not!' I retorted with another laugh, but then in an uncharacteristic urge to confide, added: 'Yes, *I* am, but Dan certainly isn't. In fact, last night I seemed to make him rather angry, even though he tried to deny it.'

'Want to tell auntie all about it? Two heads, you know.'

So, to my own surprise, I found myself telling her about the previous evening. She listened without interruption until my voice finally trailed into silence. Then she put down her coffee cup very decisively and said, 'Am I right in thinking you've had a very sheltered upbringing, Minette?'

'Well, if you mean protected and looked after with great kindness – yes, I suppose I have.'

'But without friends of your own age because of not having gone to school?'

'Y-e-s, although I did begin to make quite a lot of friends when I went to secretarial college, but we'd hardly finished our course before the war started and everyone scattered.'

'And you've not had many boy friends?'

'Well, there was Ted – '

'Yes, but you only knew him for a few weeks and it never developed beyond a good-night kiss, did it?'

'Oh no! In fact, you know, romance couldn't develop all that easily in Brussels. We usually went out in a crowd because there was a lack of unit transport, and although we all lived in a house taken over for HQ staff, there was no sitting-room and boy friends waiting for us had to sit on the stairs!'

'So a mature, experienced man like Dan Cleary would be a complete mystery to you?'

'I – I don't know what you mean, Jan.'

'Well, first you have to appreciate what a difficult time this is for our men out here: for the past five years they've lived on a constant "high" of intense excitement mixed with equally intense fear. Now all that is fading, and I believe the majority are already remembering only the good times. For some, the present may even be an anti-climax. Certainly for all of them it's boring and tedious because there's so little for them to do out here and they can't even officially have German girl friends – although I'm sure many of them do!'

She paused to refill her cup and then continued slowly, as though choosing her words carefully: 'For Dan Cleary there are added difficulties. As a senior officer it would be extremely embarrassing for him if he were found to be having a clandestine affair with a German girl, yet he's young to hold such rank and is obviously very virile, so celibacy is definitely not for him. Added to this, is the uncertainty over his marriage and his future.' Jan paused again and looked at me with sombre dark eyes. 'I'll give it to you straight, Minette. I believe Dan is greatly attracted to you, but is desperately trying not to become sexually involved, for both your sakes. Last night he almost failed.'

'Jan, you – you must be having me on!'

'Minette, this is the last talk we shall have. In a few hours you'll be off on leave and by the time you return I'll have left for home, so – I ask you – at such a time would I say anything I wasn't absolutely sure of?'

'Perhaps – '

'Also, I feel very guilty because it was I who brought you together; I really should have known, but I didn't quite realize your complete inexperience. Sometimes, you know, you give the impression of being more sophisticated than you are!'

I was trying hard to put my thoughts in order and said slowly, 'Even if what you say about Dan *is* true, it's only because of there being so few of us available. In different circumstances he wouldn't even notice me.'

'Honey, I do wish you'd stop putting yourself down in this silly way! I agree that Dan Cleary, with his fantastic looks, must be used to having the pick of any local "talent", but he's also a very discerning man and would certainly notice you in a roomful of beauties, except it might take him a little longer than out here! Although you pretend not to know it, Minette, you're an extremely pretty girl, with beautiful colouring and a diffident, most appealing manner, guaranteed to bring out the protective instincts in every male. You're also that rather rare combination: a very good listener who can become quite vivacious when happy.'

Embarrassment made me cut her short. 'Thanks for the wonderful build-up.'

'I mean every word,' Jan said seriously, 'and don't kid yourself that you're shy, because you're not. It's rather a chronic lack of confidence, but I wouldn't mind betting that in time you'll become a very strong lady. It may need some soul-shattering experience to bring it out, but the potential sure is there!' She rose to her feet. 'Perhaps Dan Cleary will be the one to do just that. He won't be able to hold out indefinitely, and the decision on whether you go to bed together or not will be yours. I'm sure he would be a wonderful lover for you, but just remember, honey, that affairs with married men always end in tears.'

For the second time within hours, I was left speechless.

5

'The dear girl has brought gin, whisky *and* champagne,'
exclaimed Uncle Julian happily, 'so we must obviously
celebrate this evening!' And in honour of the occasion
he put on his best black trousers and maroon velvet
jacket which only faintly smelt of moth balls. Aunt
Alexa went even further with her floor-length woollen
skirt and the last of her pre-war crêpe-de-chine blouses
(very expertly patched under one arm). She wore her
long string of large, perfectly matched pearls and even
her engagement ring, which was normally only seen on
the most special of special occasions. 'Because it is of
quite vulgar proportions,' she had once told me. It was a
half hoop of two huge round diamonds flanking an equally
huge square sapphire. 'It will, of course, be yours one day,
Minette, and the pearls too.'

'Although it is not Saturday,' Uncle Julian said, 'it is
most definitely a special occasion, so I propose a Gin and
It before dinner.' All through the war years the highlight
of his week had been the Gin and It he prepared for us
all on Saturday evenings. Unless we were entertaining or
at an evening function, it was the only alcohol we drank
and as there was never a refill the mixture was always
strong and meant to be lingered over. Invariably we were
still flushed and warm by the time the Anthems of all the
Allies were played at nine o'clock, and when we silently
stood for *God Save The King*, Aunt Alexa was inclined
to sway very gently.

'What a splendid idea,' she said now, 'and how very
lucky we were to find some logs *and* a man willing to
deliver them. I told Daisy to light the drawing-room

fire early today and not to stint on the fuel!' Coming
from the centrally heated luxury of the Mess, my home
seemed desperately cold, and I realized how difficult life
still was in England. Also that my family was far from
affluent. Nevertheless, when we filed into dinner it was
obvious that a great effort had been made: on the table
was my grandparents' Sèvres dinner service bought on
their honeymoon in Paris and almost never used by us,
together with frail crystal glasses whose delicate engraving
of gold fleur-de-lys had so fascinated me as a child. Even
the Georgian silver was there – the silver which in the
dark days of 1940 had been buried in the garden, 'because
if the Hun does invade, nothing will be safe.' What a time
we had all had trying to get it clean after Uncle Julian had
dug it up towards the end of the war! But now it was in
pristine condition, glinting in the light of twin candelabra.

'Oh, that smells wonderful!' I exclaimed as Daisy
appeared carrying, as though a great weight, a very
small roast duckling on an exceptionally large plate.

'Yes, I was most fortunate to get it,' Aunt Alexa said,
'and clever Daisy – ' giving her an almost friendly smile
' – managed to charm the greengrocer into letting her
have an orange for the sauce.'

Daisy leaned towards me confidentially. 'I says you was
comin' from Germany where you bin starvin',' she said
with a cackle of triumph.

Uncle Julian barely waited until her departure before
he said, 'We have told her over and over again that you
are being perfectly well looked after.'

'And besides, she understands that from your letters to
her,' Aunt Alexa said. 'You know, every afternoon when
she is off duty, she sits in the kitchen with her spectacles
on the end of her nose, laboriously reading through all
your letters to her. She must know them by heart and
yet still she persists in this idea that you are starving!'

I was deeply touched and felt the sudden prick of

tears, which I hastily blinked back. 'Perhaps,' I began tentatively, 'it's because we're all she has, and she needs to feel she is the only one capable of looking after us.'

Surprisingly, it was Aunt Alexa who answered: 'Yes, of course that is right, but – ' she sighed, and just for a second her face sagged with tiredness ' – we have all been through a most difficult time and life is still *very* trying, so it's hard to be patient with Daisy.'

'Yet,' said my uncle, 'we are very lucky to have her and she *is* a splendid cook! Now, my dear, you must tell us all about Germany.'

So I talked at great length, omitting only Dan. Since our parting he had dominated every moment of my waking hours – and many of my dreams – and when Uncle Julian said with elaborate casualness, 'I suppose you've not heard from the American pilot you met in Brussels?' I wondered fleetingly who he meant. Later, in my freezing bedroom, sleep eluded me and my thoughts whirled endlessly, always returning to that magic moment when Dan's arm had swept around me. He had called me 'darling', had asked me to hurry back to him – me! Could he really have meant *me*? Could any of it really have happened, or was it just a wonderful dream? Then I remembered the pressure of his lips against my forehead and how they had lingered; there had been such hunger, such yearning in that kiss, and in the darkness of my familiar room I finally acknowledged that I, too, hungered and yearned for his kisses, for the strength of his arms about me, and – yes, oh, yes – for the warmth of his powerful body against mine. At the mere thought of this I seemed to burst into flame and then to melt, my very bones dissolving in a storm of emotion, a tenderness such as I had never known existed . . . Inevitably, then, my thoughts turned to Aunt Alexa: could she possibly have been wrong on that day when she had come so unexpectedly to 'talk about married life'? Years before she had prepared me for 'becoming a woman' but had stopped short of talking about sexual relationships until I was almost eighteen. Then, choosing a day when I was confined to bed with 'flu, she had perched – as though ready for instant flight – on the very edge of the bed, and in deep embarrassment embarked on a short biological account of the sexual act.

' . . . and so then there is a series of rhythmic thumps – '

'Thumps!' I had exclaimed, astonished. 'Thumps against what?'

'Against *whom*, my dear! Oh, oneself, of course!'

'But why?' I had asked, genuinely bewildered, 'why should the man do that?'

'Well, that is how it is: rhythmic pushes and thumps, slow at first and then becoming – er – quite frantic.'

'Oh, no!'

'Indeed, *yes*! And then in a few minutes it is all over; one's husband turns his back and seconds later is fast asleep, leaving one feeling slightly battered and just praying that a baby will not result!'

'And that's it? Just a few minutes of *thumping* and *pushing*? Nothing else?'

Aunt Alexa's mouth had twisted then. 'Believe me, my dear, that is more than enough! One is only too delighted to get it over and done with.' She had thought for a moment and then added very seriously: 'Although, of course, one must never refuse – oh no, a good wife never, never does that.'

'And what does the wife do – during the thumping?'

'Nothing, absolutely nothing. Although I-I always put my arms around Arthur's neck . . . It seemed a nice, affectionate thing to do, you know.'

'It all sounds rather nasty.'

'It is thoroughly uncomfortable at the best of times, and can be *most* unpleasant. But then, men go mad for it . . . will do anything to get it.'

'*Do* they?'

65

'Oh, yes,' she had sighed deeply, and turned away. 'In India, whenever we left our husbands to go to the hills, we knew that they took Indian mistresses. Once, during the hot season, I stayed behind, feeling it was my duty, but Arthur still went to his – woman. I was too exhausted, you see.'

Tears had come to my eyes then, for I knew already that her husband had finally fallen in love with a very young Englishwoman and Aunt Alexa had divorced him. But I thought, if he had an Indian mistress *and* a wife, why should he want another woman just for a few minutes of strange movements before going to sleep? Yet I knew that he had demanded a divorce, even though it caused a great scandal and meant a transfer from the regiment which he was about to command and a blocking of future promotion. It was all very bewildering, and for a long time after she had left me, I lay with both hands clasping the sheet which I had unknowingly pulled up over my mouth. There was a great feeling of disappointment, for hadn't all my favourite heroes and heroines in romantic fiction married and 'lived happily ever after'? And what about the others who had died for love? What about the poets who had written and sung about the 'magic' of love? Why had they made such a fuss over so little? Oh, well, I had thought finally, if it never happens to me, I don't think I'll have missed much. But now I knew that Dan, by that one kiss on my temple, had made me think quite differently.

'I've discovered a delightful thatched cottage over at Mimstead, with an orchard just coming into blossom,' Uncle Julian said at breakfast. 'I wonder if you'd care to try it, if it's not too cold for you?' He was a most skilled water-colourist and had taught me all I knew in a partnership which had begun very soon after my arrival from Kenya. Our expeditions to paint the local countryside had continued throughout the war.

'Oh, yes, do let's go. Will it be by car or bicycle?'

'Car. I've been saving my petrol coupons for weeks.'

'I'll just tell Daisy to make you the usual flask,' Aunt Alexa said, rising briskly, 'but which would you prefer in your sandwiches: sardine or corned beef?'

Soon we were seated in our usual companionable silence, with Uncle Julian working swiftly, but instead of the cottage I saw Dan's face. Charcoal, I thought, to emphasize the fine bones – very dramatic. Yet how splendid a head and shoulders would look in line and wash, or in pastels: burnished hair against tanned skin, eyes almost matching his uniform, medal ribbons as the most definite block of colour. But would I ever be able to capture the expression – that mixture of sadness and, yes, *goodness* when his face was in repose? Or should I make him very alert, very much in command as the senior officer? I very much doubted whether either would be possible, but one thing I knew quite definitely and that was my wish to return to him as soon as it was humanly possible.

It was as we were eating our sandwiches that I suddenly heard my own voice ask abruptly: 'Do you think divorce still means the end of a Service career?'

Uncle Julian swivelled round on his camp stool to look at me in great surprise. 'Well,' he said slowly, 'I can't really say. Certainly after the First World War there were enormous social changes and I would imagine much the same would happen now. Why d'you ask?'

'Oh,' I answered, elaborately casual. 'I've been thinking about Aunt Alexa's divorce. I know her husband fell in love with someone else and demanded a divorce, even though it blighted his Army career. I just wondered . . . '

Uncle Julian studied his soggy sardine sandwich with distaste. 'It wasn't quite so simple,' he said, obviously choosing his words carefully. 'The fact is that Arthur Hamilton had an affair with another man's wife and was caught by the husband in – er – a most compromising situation. The husband insisted upon a divorce, even refusing to let his wife divorce him – which was always considered the done thing, whatever the real circumstances – and although Hamilton was in no position to demand a divorce, your aunt was only too glad to be rid of him.'

'Yes, poor aunt, but – but, it doesn't sound *so* awful.'

'It certainly was terrible for your aunt – such humiliation – and suddenly being left alone with very little money. I don't know how she would have managed if I'd not been able to offer her a home. As for Hamilton, it wouldn't have been so bad if he'd been caught with an Indian woman, but instead it was the wife of his best friend and brother officer. Worst of all, they both belonged to the same regiment.'

Uncle Julian paused to wipe his fingers carefully on a paper napkin. 'You see, Minette, a regiment is like a very large family and, in a way, what affects one member, affects them all.' He turned to look briefly at me. 'And, after all, no family likes a divorce.'

Was it my imagination, or was there the faintest hint of warning in his voice? I could not tell, but said quickly: 'So what happened to the couple?'

'Hamilton managed to wangle a transfer to another regiment – which couldn't have been easy for no one wanted him – but of course he did not last long. He and his – er – wife were rather cold-shouldered, and he soon resigned his commission.'

'Oh,' I said, feeling guiltily sympathetic towards the hapless couple. 'That sounds very hard.'

'Well, yes,' Uncle Julian admitted reluctantly, 'and they came to a very low ebb, living in a flat almost on top of Paddington Station and Hamilton working as a door-to-door salesman of encyclopaedias.'

'Oh, no!'

'Oh, yes, Minette! Of course, when the war started he was offered a second lieutenancy in the Pioneer Corps, and was only too eager to accept, I believe.' It was impossible not to wince and feel for the unknown Arthur Hamilton . . . to have been second in command of an élite Indian Army Lancer regiment, and then to be brought so low that even at the start of a global war all he was given was a commission in the Pioneer Corps! 'What happened to the wife after his death?'

'I've not the faintest idea,' Uncle Julian said with most unusual callousness.

'I suppose she was – beautiful?'

'Oh, I believe very much the chorus girl type, very painted!'

I thought of Aunt Alexa so austere, so reserved, so *cool*, and I wondered . . . 'It still doesn't seem *so* ghastly,' I said, greatly daring. 'After all, it wasn't as though he'd committed some awful crime like – like murder, or even that he'd stolen the Mess silver!'

Uncle Julian tossed away the dregs of his coffee then said quietly: 'No, but it was still a crime because, d'you see, he allowed himself to be found out.'

It was my first experience of society's double standards and one I was to remember for a long time.

The station at Bad Oeynhausen was crowded when the military train from the Hook pulled in, but almost at once I saw him and saw, too, the smile instantly softening his face when he caught sight of me. He came forward at once and saluted. 'Hello, Minette.'

'Dan! What a nice surprise!' And that's the understatement of all time, I thought confusedly. 'How are you?'

'Fine, *now*.' There was no mistaking the emphasis and I was lost for words. 'Here, let me take that,' he said, bending to my holdall.

69

'But – aren't you meeting someone?'

The familiar gleam of amusement lit his eyes as he looked up at me. 'I just did.'

I was rooted to the spot. 'You mean – you've come to meet *me*?'

'Of course. Who else?'

My thoughts were entirely chaotic, yet I heard myself say primly, 'How very kind of you.'

'No, very cunning. I thought if I got to you before anyone else, you'd have to come out to dinner tonight. A-ha, I can see an excuse hovering, but don't say it, Minette. Please don't say it!'

I laughed then, feeling utterly joyous. 'I was only going to say, thank you, I'd love to.'

He was as entertaining as ever that evening, yet whenever there was a pause in the conversation his face fell into lines of such sadness that eventually I could bear it no longer and burst out: 'Dan, I'm sure there's something wrong. Please, won't you tell me?'

He answered at once, as though eager to speak. 'Yes, everything's wrong. You may remember my telling you that my father was terminally ill – well, he died two weeks ago. It was a merciful release and one could not have wished his life to be prolonged, but he was a fine man and of course I shall miss him, especially as he was the last of my Cleary relations. Obviously I went home, but returned before my leave was up. Because you see, Minette, it's all over between Ros and me.'

'Oh, she's definitely going ahead with the divorce then?'

'Well, no, she can hardly do that unless I give her grounds.' He shrugged indifferently. 'No problem there – just an hotel bill and the usual evidence of a chambermaid – but so far I've refused to co-operate. However, I realize now that it really is time to cut my losses.' He stubbed out his cigarette, moving it over the whole ashtray in harsh little movements.

70

'I-I don't know what to say,' I murmured truthfully.

'There is nothing,' he confirmed, and then looked up into my eyes, 'except that you now have a spare husband on your hands.'

I know it is not possible for the human heart to flip over, yet it certainly felt as though mine did just that, and with it went all the breath from my body. For could it be that Dan and I were to be part of each other's destiny? Could anything as utterly wonderful, as *miraculous* as that happen to me? No, of course not, not with the world so full of beautiful, fascinating women, not with Dan so handsome and able to take his pick of the most *perfect*. As though coming from another person, I heard my own voice say evenly: 'That's very nice for all of us, but tough for you. And – I'm so sorry about your father.'

He had been chain smoking all evening and now, as he opened his slim gold case yet again, my hand reached out to cover his. 'Dan – must you? It can't be good for you.'

Gently he put my hand aside. 'Yes I really must.'

'What will you do about Emma?'

Again he shrugged. 'What can I do? Custody is rarely, if ever, given to the father by a divorce judge.'

But he will marry again and there will be other children, a voice inside my head said. And so why should I then remember the consultant saying to Aunt Alexa, 'With that lower curve, I think it would be difficult for your niece to bear a child, or at least to carry it full term. But, of course, she is only ten years old and we just do not know what new techniques may have been developed in obstetrics by the time she is an adult.' Coldness enveloped me then, the coldness of despair and anger: why, *why* couldn't I have grown up like other women? Why did *my* back have to be crooked?

When I said, 'I think I'd like to leave now, Dan,' he nodded at once. But when we drew up outside the Mess he made no move to get out and instead

71

took off his cap and tossed it on to the back seat. More than any other part of his uniform, even the rings on the sleeves, that cap, with its single band of gold oak leaves around the peak – known irreverently as 'scrambled egg' – represented his senior rank. With that careless toss I felt he was throwing aside all that such rank demanded and the next second, as though in confirmation, his arms swept around me and his mouth came down hard on mine. It was as though I'd never been kissed before. I had certainly never known such magic, such tingling excitement. Yet, without conscious thought, I struggled and tore my mouth away. 'No, Dan! No, we mustn't!'

'Why not, Minette? For God's sake, why not? You must know I've been wanting to kiss you all these weeks, and have only just managed not to by dashing away.'

'No – I-I didn't know.'

'Well, you do now.' There was just a hint of laughter in his voice. 'So why don't we finish that kiss?'

'No! No, Dan!'

'Don't you *like* being kissed, Minette?'

'Why, yes – of course I do – sometimes.'

'But this is not one of those times?'

'Dan, please, you must see we can't – we mustn't – '

'No, I don't see! Just give me one good reason why.'

'Well, because . . . because you're married.'

'But haven't I just spent half the evening explaining that I'm not?'

'Yes . . . but officially – '

'So I have to wait until I can wave my decree absolute in your face before you'll let me come near you!'

'Dan, don't be like this, don't be hurt. I can't bear to hurt you.'

'But you *are* rejecting me, aren't you, Minette?'

'No, of course not! You know that's not true! Please try to understand.'

'OK,' he said tautly and leapt from the car, slamming the door. We walked silently to the Mess entrance. 'Goodnight, Minette,' he said curtly, and turned away. If the night watchman had arrived at that moment I might just have managed to get inside the building, but instead old Herr Kunzle took longer than usual and I just had time to see Dan, with shoulders uncharacteristically hunched, walk disconsolately from me. My precarious control snapped then and I rushed forward, arms outstretched. He snatched me up instantly, lifting me off my feet until our faces were almost level, and as my arms went tightly around his neck, he kissed me again. There was everything in that kiss: passion, tenderness, hunger, longing. It sealed my fate. Henceforth I was to be Dan's and never to love another man.

'Good morning, how are you?'

'Why . . . why, Dan, good morning! I'm fine thanks, and you?'

'Oh, never better. Listen, darling, a new leave centre at Altenau in the Harz Mountains has just opened and Miles and I thought we'd go down this weekend – could you come with us?'

'I should love to, but of course I'll have to ask permission. HQ staff usually work only until lunch-time on Saturdays unless there's a flap on. But should we be able to get rooms at such short notice?'

'No problem there, except you'd probably have to share with the WVS girl Miles is bringing. Just leave it to me!'

But when he collected me, he was alone. 'I'm sorry to say Miles has had to cry off because Sally's Queen Bee is expected from UK and she couldn't get away, but it's a great day and *we're* going to the mountains.' He sounded like a small boy setting off on a special treat and I glanced at him covertly, marvelling at the change. As for myself – well, I was in a dream world, full of happiness, yet apprehensive because that happiness was of such gossamer fineness. It was only a few hours since I had run into his arms, but already our relationship had changed: now when we met, Dan's habitually sad expression gave way to a smile which lit his whole face and, so long as we were alone, he came with long quick strides to put his hands on my shoulders and kiss me.

So on that brilliant afternoon in early spring we sped south through sleepy villages which showed little or no evidence of the war and whose inhabitants regarded us only with curiosity. Once in the leave centre it was not necessary to wear uniform and this, together with the magnificent scenery and crystal-clear air, so different from Westphalia, lent a dream-like quality to everything. Dan was no longer the senior officer, beset by marital problems, nor I the inhibited girl. Instead we were simply a man and a woman, clad in old slacks and sweaters, walking with arms entwined, in the pine forest where only birdsong and the soft crunch of our footsteps broke the silence. And every minute we grew closer, yet even though his arms were like steel about me, even though I seemed to melt into him and our lips to cling as though unable to withdraw, it was still not enough and I craved, I ached, for something which I neither understood nor recognized. Yet when Dan slipped into my bed that first night, I had no immediate feeling of astonishment, only of inevitability and complete conviction that even if the future brought only disgrace and heartbreak, I would not send him away.

'A pyjama girl,' he said very softly as his fingers expertly undid the tunic buttons. 'I felt sure it would be a nightie.'

'Oh no,' I said in a husky, unfamiliar voice, 'Aunt Alexa said I must always wear pyjamas . . . ' The words trailed away to nothing as Dan's hand slid over my breasts in a warm and gentle caress which sent little ripples of delight through me. Apart from examining doctors, no man had touched the bare skin of my body before; when Dan lowered his head and I felt his lips close around a nipple, sensation took over completely. I was only vaguely aware of making tiny, involuntary movements, of my arms being tightly around Dan's neck, hands cupping his head, and of the whimpering sounds coming from my own throat. But when his hand moved to the cord of my pyjama trousers, I came back to reality and clutched at him. 'Oh no!' I gasped in sudden panic.

Dan turned his head to look at me in the moonlight. 'But I must, darling, I must! Surely you know that!'

'Oh, but I-I – '

'Or is it that you don't know anything, anything at all?'

'Why, of course I do!' I said, absurdly indignant, and heard Dan's whisper-soft laugh.

'But I am the first, aren't I?'

'Yes,' I breathed, overwhelmed by shyness.

'Then let me be your teacher . . . let me show you . . . oh, my darling, I want it to be so wonderful for you, so unbelievably wonderful.' In one quick movement he had removed the trousers and again I felt his warm hand sliding over my flesh, then beginning gently to explore; felt, too, my body beginning to arch in unbearable longing. 'But loving always means sharing,' he said, taking my hand and guiding it. 'Oh no, no, I mustn't!' I exclaimed, deeply shocked now, and thought wildly: Aunt Alexa said nothing of this!

Again there was the gentle thread of laughter. 'Don't be afraid . . . don't be shy . . . there's nothing wrong about it. It just means that I want to give myself to you as completely as I know you want to give yourself to me . . . so . . . like this, darling. Yes, that's right . . . '

Dawn was already breaking when Dan stirred and said, 'I must leave you now, angel.'

Instantly I clung to him. 'Oh, no, don't go. Please don't go.'

'Sweetheart, you don't think I want to, do you? But I must, just to the next room.'

'Much, much too far away,' I protested.

'I know, I know.' It was said with a sigh, and once again his hands slid over my body caressingly. 'Such a dear little body, so sweetly passionate, so much more entrancing than I'd ever imagined, and with skin like silk.'

It was then I knew I had to tell him, even though it would shatter the magic and might make him turn away in disgust. 'Dan, I must tell you – ' The words died in my throat and what I felt then was the bitterest, most terrible hurt I had ever known, for more than anything else at that moment I wanted to be beautiful for him.

'Whatever it is, darling, I shall understand – so tell me, please tell me.'

'My back,' I began in a choked whisper, 'my back is crooked, Dan. I-I'm deformed.' I did not dare look up at him, but I heard his quick intake of breath. He's horrified, I thought wildly, he'll regret what's happened and might even find me repugnant.

'Is that all?' His voice seemed to be coming from a great distance. 'I quite thought you were about to tell me of some monstrous family secret!'

'You mean – you don't mind?!' I was incredulous, trembling on the edge of joy.

'Of course I mind – for you, and it explains so much. Now, turn over and let me see it.'

'No – no, please I couldn't – don't make me!'

'Minette, how can you bear to shut me out after all that's happened between us?'

'Oh, but it's not that at all!'

'I think it is. Darling, unpleasant things have to be faced; the longer you duck them, the harder you will make life for yourself. So – please turn over.'

76

Silently I did so, until I lay on my stomach with eyes closed and burning cheek pressed against the pillows. Please God, please – and felt his lips travelling down the length of my spine in kisses as light as a butterfly's touch. Then he gently turned me until once more I was looking up at him as he leaned over me, huge shoulders blocking the incoming light. 'It's a poor little back,' he said softly, 'and it just makes me want more and more to look after you, protect you, for now you're my love, aren't you?'

'Yes, oh yes,' I breathed tremulously, 'always – always and forever.'

6

Spring came early to Germany that year and with it came signs that people were awakening from the trauma of defeat and ready to begin life afresh. In the rural areas of Westphalia orchards and fields lost their look of neglect, while in the meadows below the Mess a few lean cows appeared from nowhere to graze, and occasionally one or two dilapidated barges crept over the Weser's broad sweep. Even in the cities there was renewal: people walked more purposefully, even smiled a little at each other or nodded a greeting, and along the main thoroughfares teams of women, aproned and kerchiefed, loaded rubble on to containers pushed along a miniature track. Here and there tiny shops opened to sell a few pieces of wrought-iron work or boxes painted in the Bavarian manner, while in private treasures of silver, glass, and exquisite porcelain would be offered in exchange for cigarettes, chocolate or coffee. The black market flourished and it was said that farmers could conjure up milk, eggs and vegetables for a kilo of coffee. Ancient cars, with loaded interiors, could be seen crawling along between farms and cities, each bearing a large wood-burning cylinder on its rear and emitting thick fumes.

For the Occupying Forces life continued to be extra-ordinary: with no hotels, cinemas, bars or night-clubs, entertainment centred around the Officers' Clubs and individual messes, with every possible excuse for a party being found to relieve the boredom and loneliness. People thought nothing of travelling up to a hundred miles for an evening of dancing and laughter, the only obstacle being lack of transport. Friendships and romances flourished overnight and although partners might be seen through an alcoholic haze rather than rose-coloured spectacles, it was still possible for enduring relationships to form.

As for me – oh, I was in a trance of happiness such as I had never even remotely imagined possible: every evening I dined out with Dan, and on the few weekends when I was free we sped away to Altenau or to the lovely villages of the Rhine, driving at speed as far as Heidelberg and, as the summer advanced, to Norderney and Travemunde in the north, always with the hood of the Mercedes down, the sun and wind on our faces.

'Come closer,' Dan would say, and I would inch along the smooth leather until I could hug his free arm and rest my head on his shoulder. Then he would invariably burst into his extensive repertoire of popular songs, singing lustily as we swept through countryside and village alike. I was still too shy to join in, but I laughed – oh, how I laughed, and how good, how novel this was! And how wonderful were those scented summer nights when we came together with hunger and passion and tenderness – always so much tenderness. I was totally unfamiliar with the simple, day-to-day demonstrations of affection and even of touch, but Dan was a wonderfully warm man, and through him I came to realize that love could extend to my finger-tips, and my hitherto despised body could give him comfort, even delight. I saw the lines of tension fade from his face and felt fiercely protective when I discovered how vulnerable he was behind the senior officer façade. Sometimes, too, I felt real apprehension because it seemed he had been given too much and in my fanciful imagination I feared that fate might make him pay a high price for it all.

Years later Dan was to ask me: 'What on earth did we find to talk about on all those trips?' But I could only remember the enchantment, the laughter and the overwhelming happiness. Except for Norderney. It was high summer when we drove up there, but although the sun was bright, the North Sea was grey and choppy with a fresh breeze blowing off it, and the sand dunes were deserted.

'Not much of a place,' Dan remarked, 'but I'm interested to see it. It was from here that Dorniers of the Second Aufklärungsgruppe used to take off in search of the Navy – it must have been every bomber squadron's dream to bag the Home Fleet.' He paused to pick up a pebble and send it skimming over the water. 'And of course *we* used to pass over here on our way to Berlin and many of the other North German targets.'

'Tell me about those times,' I urged.

Dan shrugged. 'Nothing much to tell,' he said laconically. 'We never had the glamour of the fighter boys, you know. And of course the Germans labelled us terror fliers; many of the chaps who baled out were set upon – some almost lynched by villagers or farmers.'

'But no doubt their bomber crews were heroes!'

'No doubt,' Dan agreed calmly.

'What I can't understand is why you weren't all terrified.'

Dan glanced quickly down at me. 'But we were, Minette! Of course we were! Only a mindless cretin would not have been! And terror can sweep faster than wildfire through any group, so it was up to me as skipper to appear in full control of myself. All the others took their cue from me. Intense concentration, too, can blot out fear.'

'But, night after night, flying over all those miles of enemy territory – '

'Better that than being labelled LMF – Lacking in Moral Fibre – if one couldn't take it and had to be shunted off to some desk job so as not to contaminate others.'

'Oh, but how dared they put such a label on any young man? How *dared* they?'

'Very easily, darling. We were engaged in total war which had to be won at all costs, as you well know. And our sorties could not have been worse than what our fathers endured when they went repeatedly over the top of those hellish trenches.'

'Yes, but tell me more about you: there must have been German fighters?'

'Yes, swarms!'

'And flak coming up at you from all directions?'

'Oh, yes!'

'But surely that must have been terrible?'

'Rather like flying between *walls* of tracer and shell.' He smiled down at me just a little wryly. 'Pretty lights though!'

As I slowly shook my head, Dan said: 'I'll tell you what really scared us witless – cold, fire and this sea. The cold was indescribably awful. Anything metal touched by a bare hand caused instant frostbite; the tiniest draught near eyes made them close as though glued together; fingers inside gloves would often be too numb to press the inter-com button or fire a gun. As for fire – well; that was always a problem, especially if we still had our own incendiaries on board. Yet extraordinary things could happen. Once, when the interior of our fuselage was well ablaze and I was about to order everyone to bale out, along came a lone fighter who blew out my perspex hood – with the result that the wind rushed in with such force it completely blew out the fire! The only snag then was that every cloud we flew through also billowed in and obscured the instruments in front of me! And cold forced us to fly at only ten thousand feet, which made us very vulnerable to attack.'

'Oh, Dan, Dan! And you must have been frozen almost to death.'

'Well, I was certainly stiff. I had to be lifted out of my seat in the kite when we finally made it. But that was nothing. The navigator and wireless operator were very badly burned about the hands and legs. Yes, come to think of it, that trip was a bit hairy!'

I flung my arms around his waist. 'Oh, I *wish* I were the most beautiful, most fascinating woman in the world, so that I could make you forget all the horrors!'

'But you *are* beautiful, darling!'

'No, I mean *perfectly* beautiful all over, with a lovely straight back, legs that reached up to my armpits – and a really *gorgeous* bosom!'

'But *I* think your bozooms are lovely, and what's so nice is that they're even better without your clothes on! So many of you girls wear – what are they called? – uplifts. Take those off, and it's all fall down time! And anyway, I'm off impossibly beautiful women.'

I looked incredulous. '*Can* any man be?'

'Quite easily, I assure you. Come and sit down in the shelter of this dune and I'll tell you how. Ros and I met on a 'plane returning from Canada where I'd been on a course; I was a twenty-four-year-old Flight Lieutenant, considered by the Service to be quite bright and, in my own estimation, a man of the world. Yet after one look at Ros I was – well, there's only one word for it: dazzled, utterly and completely dazzled, and by the end of the flight besotted as well. Not only was she unbelievably beautiful, but full of fun and, seemingly, very intelligent. We talked and laughed our way across the Atlantic and although it was plain that her father tolerated me with difficulty, I was determined that this was the girl I was going to marry. To my intense astonishment, Ros seemed just as keen on me, and subsequently we spent every available moment together.

'I was a bit overwhelmed by the size and grandeur of her home and the fact that her dozens of friends were all society people, apparently with unlimited money and leisure. But I was, after all, a Wykehamist so I knew the form and Dad was one of Salisbury's most respected solicitors. We lived in an old and rather lovely house in the Cathedral Close, but there'd only been the two of us since Mother's death four years before.' Dan paused to light a cigarette cupping his hands around the flame against the strengthening breeze. 'Well, Ros and I married in December '39 – a hell of a great society wedding in London – and then went to live near my station in Lincolnshire. I'm sure Sir Reginald would never have given us his blessing had the war not already started, he obviously wanted Ros to marry a title, but when he heard I was to be a bomber pilot, I honestly believe he thought I'd soon be "chopped" anyway, and he ended up making Ros a very generous allowance.

'So we seemed all set for a life of bliss, even if for me this should be very short, but the trouble started almost at once: Ros had no inclination to housekeep and although wonderful at arranging flowers she was hopeless at cooking or budgeting; she pronounced the other young wives impossibly dreary and all the WAAF girls vulgar, which was completely untrue. Many of them were far better bred than she. The marriage might have foundered there and then, had it not been for the nights: I don't know if Ros was a virgin when we married, but she was certainly no shrinking violet, and I – ' Dan turned to give me a quick, half-smiling glance ' – I'd been around, as they say. So my only disappointment was her not wanting a baby. I think most men facing imminent death want to leave a child as an extension of themselves, but Ros had told me on our wedding night not to make her pregnant as she did not want her figure ruined.

'At that early stage of the war bomber squadrons went out on daytime missions, but when our losses became too great, strategy was changed and we bombed at night. As you can imagine, those of us who got back in the very early morning were pretty exhausted and it was then that the real trouble began. I only wanted to sleep whereas Ros expected sex followed by a full day's entertainment – for herself. When I just could not comply, hours of non-stop whining petulance would follow, until I was driven almost crazy. Eventually, towards the end of my second tour, she would either not be there, or we'd arrive home together, with her still in evening dress and having travelled back from Town on the first train. I was bitterly hurt by her lack of understanding and love. Of course all the other wives waited up all night, listening for sounds of aircraft and no doubt praying hard too. When I once asked Ros why she never did the same, she just said, "I couldn't bear to." To this day, I don't know whether she meant it was too nerve-racking or just too boring!

'The real crunch came after the penultimate mission of that tour: I'd seen Jim Rowlands, my closest friend, go down in a fire-ball with all his crew – they'd not had a hope in hell of baling out – and I was pretty over-wrought, especially as we ourselves had only just made it. We'd even had to ditch all our ammo over the sea. Our fuselage was riddled from stem to stern and, as a result of all the uncontrollable wallowing, we'd all been air-sick. Then our petrol finally ran out as we approached the airfield. I got us down, but the old kite slewed violently and almost flipped over.

'I had to beg Ros to go over to Jim's wife, Christine – which she eventually did, only to return before I'd even got out of my gear. "How was she?" I asked, and remember Ros saying, "Oh, like a deaf-mute, but I told her it was no good being like that and the best thing she could do would be to come up to Town with me and I'd take her to Quag's or one of the other Clubs where one can still get decent champagne."'

Dan picked up another pebble and turned it over and over, looking at it intently as he said hesitantly: 'I must have gone a little mad then. I did something I'll always be ashamed of: I lashed out with the back of my hand and hit Ros across the mouth with such force that my signet ring tore her lip and she staggered back against the wall with nose and mouth bleeding. And I – I just sat down and bawled like a baby. By the time I'd managed to get hold of myself, Ros had walked out – literally, taking only a handbag and her car keys. I could not even try to follow her. All our petrol ration had gone into her Aston Martin and my little MG was empty.' Dan threw down the pebble as though in despair. 'That night we went to the Ruhr and were shot down.'

For the second time that afternoon I flung my arms around him, holding him close. 'Darling, darling Dan,' I whispered, 'how unbelievably awful it must have been having such a bitter, bitter personal experience and then to face all the horrors of baling out and capture! But . . . you and Ros must have become reconciled eventually?'

'Oh, yes. At first we were posted as "Missing, believed killed", but when Ros was notified that I was a POW she did write and offer to forgive and forget, which I agreed to at once, even though I knew that the heart had gone out of our relationship. Then I managed to escape, and when I returned to the UK Ros astonished me by saying that she wanted a baby; this proved to be much more difficult to achieve than we'd expected and I was already in the Middle East when she told me she was pregnant. I was thrilled of course and really thought we'd be able to settle down once the War was over.' Dan's face softened into a smile of great tenderness. 'And Emma was – is – such a darling little child.'

The smile faded and he sighed deeply. 'But disillusionment set in again as soon as I returned: Ros took very little notice of Emma and openly admitted that she'd only wanted a baby to avoid being called up. In fact, her own old nanny looked after Emma. So while every other young girl, including Princess Elizabeth, did her bit, Ros's war work was to party and dine with the Allied top brass, although I don't think this included bed.' Dan suddenly turned to me, smiling as though determined to be cheerful. 'Now, after that great spiel, you know why I'm off very beautiful women.'

'I find it quite impossible to understand her,' I said. 'Apparently she could have married anyone, yet she chose you; she hasn't ever tried to make the marriage work at all, yet keeps you on tenterhooks all the time.'

'I think she wants to have complete power over me, although perhaps she would call it love. But it's certainly not your kind, my darling. Her father, you know, is entirely self-made and only achieved his fantastic success through financial wizardry and utter ruthlessness. By the time Ros and her younger sister were born he was already in the millionaire class and indulged their every whim. Ros is very much her father's daughter and I don't think her undoubted beauty helped. Her sister, who is just pretty, is quite different and a very much nicer woman.' Dan quickly got to his feet. 'That's enough of my woes!' He held out his hands. 'Come on, let's go in, it's getting really chilly.'

I scrambled up, my hands in his. 'You're cold,' he exclaimed, looking really concerned. 'What you need is a hot shower, and as we're the only ones in the leave centre, I don't see why I shouldn't join you.'

My head jerked up. 'Oh no!'

Dan's shout of laughter was loud in the silence. 'You are the dearest, funniest little thing!' he exclaimed, wrapping his arms about me. 'We spend every available night locked together in the closest intimacy that two people can achieve, yet the suggestion of showering together turns you saucer-eyed with horror! Why so shy, sweetheart?'

'Not shyness,' I whispered, hanging my head, 'just not pretty enough to be seen.'

'Oh, darling, *really*! Is that why you always want to have the light out?' I nodded silently and Dan's arms tightened around me.

'You take an awful lot of convincing, don't you?' Then, as I remained silent, he said: 'All right, my love, I'll not tease you any more and of course you may take your shower alone.'

But that night for the first time I had sufficient confidence to take the initiative and make love to Dan, letting all the passion and love I felt for him flow through my hands as I caressed and held him. Soft laughter and tiny shivers of pleasure stirred his large frame as I locked myself around him. 'Don't stop,' he begged and so desperate was my desire to make him happy that I found a strength I never knew I had until finally we were simultaneously overwhelmed and I collapsed against him. For a few moments we lay still, then Dan turned me over and smothered my body with kisses and I knew without doubt that for a little while I had made him forget all past unhappiness and horrors.

7

It seemed that everything was going in my favour that summer: in my work, because being in love made me acutely perceptive of the tragedy all around me and I wanted to share my happiness by doing all I could for the survivors; and in my off-duty because Dan and I were accepted as a couple and invited to parties together. Even when the Women's Services were allowed out of uniform for social functions and I said I had nothing to wear, Dan produced a chit with an impressive signature and rubber stamp, giving me access to a fabric warehouse full of velvets, brocades and other beautiful materials. I could choose as many as I wished and, after all the years of clothing coupons, it was like being in a particularly exciting Aladdin's cave. Nor was that all. I discovered that in our own village there was a wonderful dressmaker, a refugee from Berlin who had been trained in Vienna and was able to faithfully copy the most exclusive models. For the first time in my life I possessed beautiful clothes, so expertly cut and fitted that my back looked almost normal.

But then the frail, rainbow-hued bubble of my happiness burst. Yet as I came down the stairs on that fateful evening I felt only excitement. I was wearing my brand new blue and silver gown whose billowing skirt rustled deliciously, and for once I felt pretty. At the foot of the stairs Dan stood looking up at me, his handsome face alight with admiration. I smiled at him, thinking that all I felt for him must show in that smile and in my eyes.

'You look – incredibly lovely,' he said, sounding almost

awed, and as I reached him, he bent close to whisper, 'And I could eat you!'

I laughed softly. 'I think I'd like that.'

Even Miles pursed his lips in a silent whistle and said, 'If I were not a staid married man, I'd give you some stiff competition with this one, Cleary, old chum!' Walking into the 21 Club, knowing that all eyes were upon me, remembering to hold my head up and stand straight, I felt strangely confident. Dan's hand was on my elbow and his tall presence close.

Later, as I stood up to dance with Miles, I was incandescent with happiness that Dan, partnering Sally, had looked at me openly with all the tenderness, longing and understanding of a lover.

Miles said, 'Quite besotted, aren't you?' and I looked up at him in mock dismay. 'Oh, Miles, is it so obvious?'

'Actually, no,' he said seriously. 'In fact, I'm always surprised when I see you at parties. You so often appear detached, even off-hand.'

'But that's only because I don't want to be a clinging vine! To tell you the truth, Miles, I begrudge every minute I'm apart from him.'

'But it won't do, you know, Minette. It simply will not do.'

'I-I don't understand.'

'Well, have you forgotten that he has a wife and child?'

'No, of course not. But there's to be a divorce.'

'Don't you believe it, sweetie, don't you believe it!'

'Oh, but she wants one and Dan has said – '

'Yes, but that's just a game she plays.'

'A – *game*?'

'Yes, to keep Dan on his toes, although I know that's not how he sees it. She knows he can have anyone he wants and I believe she feels that if she plays the devoted wife, always waiting patiently at home, he will become bored with her. So by constantly keeping him in a state of uncertainty, she holds him. It's not as difficult as you might imagine. She is of course supremely selfish and egotistical, but of course her tactic would be useless if she were not also the most beautiful, most alluring woman as well; in fact, just as devastating to men as Dan is to women. Seen together they are unbelievably magnificent, just like a couple out of a romantic novel. And then there is Emma, Ros's greatest trump card. Dan adores her and Ros knows perfectly well that he will put up with anything to keep her. That's why he's constantly badgering the top brass, visiting MPs and journalists, to get the families out here.'

Miles must have taken pity on me then. He added gently, 'Don't misunderstand, Minette. Dan really loves you and often says you would make the perfect wife, but if *he* asked for a divorce, I have no doubt Ros would refuse point blank. So, my dear, disentangle yourself while there's still time and look around you: you have the whole of the Rhine Army here, and I guarantee you could have the pick of many very eligible chaps.'

Mercifully the music stopped then. It seemed to me as though a great black abyss had opened before me and that I was about to fall into it. I was dimly aware of Dan rising to hold my chair and of his saying with concern, 'Whatever is the matter, darling? You look absolutely stricken.' And, amazingly, there was the sound of my own voice replying calmly, 'I'm fine, thanks.'

But Miles, as though determined on a complete showdown, said, 'I've been telling Minette about your efforts to expedite the arrival of families to Germany.'

'Yes,' said Sally, 'we've been alerted about them. I believe there's to be a points system according to the husband's length of service and that the first families will be arriving in September.'

'But nothing is certain yet.' Dan's voice was hoarse and constrained, and when Miles and Sally got up to dance, he turned urgently to me. 'Minette, we must talk – '

I felt drained of all feeling except a terrible weariness. 'There's really nothing to talk about – ' I began, but Dan said grimly, 'Oh yes there is, and we're leaving right now.'

He put his hand through my arm, almost forcing me to rise, then hustled me through the Club and into the car, slamming the doors and revving the engine into angry life. The big car hurtled through the garrison, and even when we were out on the narrow winding road Dan continued to drive with uncharacteristic recklessness. Rabbits and hedgehogs, frozen in our lights, were scarcely glimpsed before we were upon them, and at each corner banks of foliage rose up like walls before the car was flung round with a screech of tyres. We did not speak and Dan's face, faintly illuminated by the dashboard light, was tautened into an expression of the utmost grimness. As for myself – well, I sat huddled in a ice-cold heap, my thoughts incoherent.

When we reached the spot where we had watched the coal train being robbed, Dan pulled up and switched off the engine. Then he turned to me, sliding his arm along the back of my seat and saying without preamble, 'A month ago I wrote to Ros telling her that I, too, now wanted a divorce and urging her to consult her lawyer. I planned that you and I would go on a seventy-two-hours leave and that I'd get us air passages to the UK. We'd find somewhere nice to stay for the "evidence" – though of course you would not have been named – it would simply have gone down as my adultery with an unknown woman. I hoped that as an undefended case it would all go through quickly, and by the New Year I – we'd – be free to marry.' The staccato voice stopped abruptly as Dan took off his cap and passed his hand over his brow. When he spoke again his voice was quiet, even weary. 'To my astonishment Ros rang through to the Mess – God knows how, because civilian calls to Service establishments over

91

here are not allowed, but nevertheless she did get through. Then she completely floored me by saying that she had had second thoughts about a divorce and wanted to give our marriage another chance; she would agree to my remaining on in the Service and would come – even "wanted" – to come and live with me here. I told her it was too late, but she reminded me of all we'd gone through together. We were caught in the Café de Paris bombing, you know, and had to be dug out more dead than alive; then there was my return from the POW Camp and all that had meant.

'When I still said it was too late, Ros told me flatly that she would only ever divorce me if I agreed to forgo all my rights to Emma, whom she would then take permanently to the States.' Once again Dan paused and I heard the sob in his throat as he said, 'I-I could not bear to let that happen . . . so I agreed to try again and that is why I have been badgering everyone to get the families out here, because I still can't believe that Ros will actually come, and I can't bear much more of this being in limbo.'

Deep inside my head a voice was shouting, But what about me? Oh, what about me? As I remained silent, Dan turned to me with desperation in his voice. 'If Emma were a boy, perhaps it would be different . . . but I must see that she has a happy and secure childhood for I do not know what she will have to face later on. I've seen what war can do to a woman. Everywhere we went, from Cairo to Sicily, Italy to Germany, after the fighting we had one thought in our minds: women! "Hot & Cold Running Women" we laughingly called them and they were everywhere – from princesses and duchesses who would normally have given few of us house room, right down to those on the game, all eager to do anything for a few cigarettes, a tin of bully beef or a bar of chocolate.'

A strange sound, half a sob, half an hysterical giggle,

came from my throat as I whispered, 'And I, the one for Germany, did it for nothing!'

'No!' It was a shout and there was no gentleness in the way Dan took hold of my shoulders and twisted me so that I faced him. 'I beg you, I implore you, Minette, not to think that! Those other women . . . they knew the score, they knew that we were all lonely men seeking a little diversion, a little warmth between all the killing . . . that we would move on within days, sometimes hours, and be replaced by others equally desperate . . . and many of them wouldn't have had it any different. But you, my darling, you have given me so much, and with you I have learned what real happiness is. If it weren't for Emma, I swear I would not hesitate for a moment.' He let go of me and turned to look through the windscreen as though suddenly deep in thought. 'There's another reason which I'd better mention so that you can understand fully – Because of a low sperm count, I've been told it's highly unlikely I shall father another child, so perhaps you can understand why Emma is doubly precious to me?'

My laughter definitely was hysterical then. 'Well, that certainly makes us a pair if nothing else does!' I said with a brightness which even to my own ears sounded horrible. 'I've been told that with my back I'd never be able to carry a child full term, so what the hell?'

An Army lorry unexpectedly came towards us and in its headlights I saw the torment in Dan's eyes, and my terrible brittleness changed at once into a sob: 'Oh no . . . no,' I said, and held out my arms. 'Of course I understand . . . really I do . . . and-and I'm so sorry.'

He gathered me into his arms, holding me closely but with the utmost tenderness, and I felt his lips on my hair. 'You'll never know how much I love you,' he said.

We had just two and a half months left and they were

to be the most bitter-sweet of my life, but for Dan they were even worse; always a thinking man, he knew that responsibility for all our lives lay with him, and he fought an unending emotional tug-of-war, made infinitely worse by never knowing from day to day whether Ros really intended to join him.

As for me, I felt as though my very life's blood was being slowly drained away, yet I did nothing to further my cause, not even when an inner voice screamed at me, Don't let him go, fight for him! Not even when Dan said, 'I have been allocated a house in Bad Oeynhausen and am to choose the furnishings, but you should be doing that with me, Minette, and it should be your house, no one else's.' Not even when finally worn-down, he said, 'I want you more than anything else in the world, and I'll do whatever you ask.'

But I only whispered that it was too late, telling myself that I, of all people, could not deprive a small girl of a father's love. Yet in my innermost heart I knew this was not the main reason, but fear – fear that if I forced the issue everything might turn out disastrously. A divorce, if ever agreed to, would be messy, I instinctively knew that Ross would see to that, so might it not damage Dan's potentially brilliant career and make him bitter? I thought so often of Arthur Hamilton, brought down to doorstep selling by a passionate affair; had *he* regretted it, had *he* ever tired of his poor 'painted chorus-girl' wife? And I, might I not prove lacking as a wife, for I could never play 'games' but only be loyal and devoted. Supposing this eventually bored Dan, just as Miles had predicted? The very thought was enough to stifle any pleas I might have made and I became so silent that Dan said: 'You are like a little mouse these days, so quiet, so small – but not of course like an ordinary mouse, definitely not. Rather a pink and white marzipan, entirely delicious, entirely edible mouse – I know! I shall call you Mäuschen – it's what the Germans call little girls – and it will be a secret between us, only to be used when we're alone.'

In those last weeks we snatched at every opportunity to be alone and it seemed that as we grew spiritually closer, so physically we could never be close enough. 'Tell me how I can make it really wonderful for you,' I begged, agonized by wanting to show what I could not put into words.

'You always do,' my love assured me. 'With you, every time is like the first time . . . '

But there were other times in the closeness of the night when his control faltered and he would cry out in appeal: 'How am I ever going to manage without you, Mäuschen? Without your sweetness and warmth and love?' and even once: 'I wonder if Emma is worth all this agony I'm putting us both through. What if she still grows into a typical rich brat, spoiled and selfish? Then all this will have been in vain!' until finally: 'If only Ros would find someone else and leave Emma to us!'

And it was then that I would wrap my arms tightly about him and try to assure him that it would all be so much easier than he anticipated. Ros obviously wanted them to go on. She would surely make a great effort and to watch Emma develop would be a continuing joy. I never knew whether I convinced him, but he would always then make the most tender love to me and afterwards I would think, Remember it all: every look, every word, every gesture of love, for these moments will never return, and soon all that you treasure, long for, and love will be given to someone else. It seemed then that ice enclosed my heart and brain and when time finally ran out and only minutes were left to us, it was Dan who almost broke, while I was completely calm.

'You have given me so much, Mäuschen, and asked for so little; you have been the angel who saved my sanity and there'll never be anyone like you again in my life, yet I'm leaving you with nothing . . . try to forgive me, my darling, and then forget me.'

But through the numbness I realized that this was the very last moment in which to speak. I clutched the lapels of his tunic with both hands. 'I shall love you all the days of my life,' I said quietly. 'Yes, always – always and forever.'

Mutely he took my hands and held them for a long moment against his mouth. 'God bless you and keep you safe, my darling love,' he said at last and with a sob in his voice. Then he turned and rushed blindly away and I went on leaden feet to the nearest window where I watched the lights of the Mercedes receding farther and farther away.

8

'There's to be a cocktail party at Rhine Army on the 30th to welcome the families,' the Chief said at luncheon one day, 'but I shall be in Geneva for a conference with the International Red Cross, and I'm taking Mary with me; Fiona will be up in Hamburg and Joyce on temporary duty in Berlin, so I want you, Minette, to represent us at the party.'

'Right-ho,' I said, hoping that my expression would not give me away. I had known all along that in such a small community I was bound to meet Rosalind Cleary one day but I shrank from the thought of actually doing so.

Yet as I arrived at the party I was a mass of contradictory emotions: half of me apprehensive and trembling, the other half consumed by a curiosity of quite frightening depth. When the beloved voice said 'Darling', I spun round instinctively, but he was not speaking to me. 'I want you to meet a special friend, Minette Glyn, who is at Red Cross Headquarters; Minette, this is my wife, Rosalind.'

I had known from her photograph that she was beautiful, but I was quite unprepared for the effect of colouring upon that beauty and gazed at her speechless. She was radiant, like a being from another world – so tall that I had to look up, with creamy velvet skin and hair of a Titian richness that was drawn back in a soft chignon to reveal all the lovely contours of her face. But most striking of all were her eyes. Instead of being the usual pale blue, brown or green of most redheads, hers were a brilliant periwinkle blue, and she wore a halter-necked velvet gown of a darker shade. The depth of

97

fabric, contrasting against skin, hair and eyes, was totally dazzling. 'Minette?' she queried in a low, slightly husky voice. 'Rather unusual, rather pretty.' She half-turned to Dan. 'We should remember it, darling, and *if* we ever have another daughter, we might call her Minette. It would be a jolly way of remembering your friendship.'

Was she being deliberately cruel to him, I wondered, or had she guessed?

'But I don't think I'll have any difficulty in remembering Minette,' Dan said in a strangely flat voice.

Rosalind turned back to me with a low laugh and a slight raising of her discreetly darkened brows. 'You *are* honoured! I've never heard him say that of anyone else!' There was no hint of animosity in her tone and it was obvious that the thought of my ever being a threat had not even entered her head. It was purely for Dan's sake that I said quickly, 'Oh, it's only because Dan has been kind enough to teach me to drive, and I've given him so many hair-raising moments that he couldn't possibly forget! But it has made all the difference – being able to drive, I mean. We have to go on such long journeys and there's always a shortage of drivers – '

It seemed that, having started, I could hardly stop talking, but Rosalind broke in smoothly, 'You're in the Red Cross so you must know Marjorie Rockingham?' Coming from anyone else it might have sounded horribly patronizing, but Rosalind Cleary spoke as though it was quite natural that I should know the Duchess, who was also one of the wealthiest women in England.

'No, I don't know her personally,' I said, struggling with my chaotic thoughts, 'but she was on my selection board.'

'Oh yes, dear old Marjorie went *completely* overboard and was on *every* conceivable committee . . . I can't think how she's going to amuse herself now the war is over.' She sighed. 'But I suppose that applies to us all.' She took a sip from her drink and then turned, smiling and suddenly vivacious, to Dan. 'Except that we, of course, are going to live as second honeymooners for the rest of our lives, aren't we, darling?'

There was the slightest pause before Dan said 'Yes,' in the same flat tone. The pain I felt then was like a sledgehammer against my heart and it seemed as though my whole body opened under the blow of one great wound. I had carefully avoided looking at him, although intensely aware of his nearness as he stood between Rosalind and myself, and from the corner of my eye I saw him lift a glass from a passing waiter's tray. 'Have a drink, Minette,' he said. As I took the glass his finger touched mine. It was like a burn. My composure might have broken then if Miles had not appeared and said, 'You must allow me to take Minette away now as I want her to meet *my* wife.'

'Thank you, Miles,' I whispered shakily as we turned away.

'I'd have come before if I could, but you've coped wonderfully well. I must tell you how much I admire your remarkable composure. I know you must be going through hell, but no one would ever guess.'

Jean Henderson smiled but looked at me with wary curiosity and I realized despairingly that she saw me as a potential danger, a husband-stealer. And if she, who must have been given all the facts, thought that, what would others, who knew far less, think? It was another mortal blow to my ever fragile self-confidence, yet somehow I managed to circulate at that party, to smile and to chat until my face felt stiff and my throat rasped.

When a great bellow of laughter rang out, almost all conversation stopped and everyone turned to the dozen or so officers who stood in a semi-circle around Rosalind. They were all beaming delightedly at her and their rather fatuous expressions were of men utterly bewitched. Beside her stood Dan, glass in hand, his profile softened by a half smile. 'A couple straight out of a romantic novel,' Miles had called them. 'Quite unbelievably magnificent.' And I thought that nothing could be more apt. At that moment Rosalind moved so that her back was towards me and I saw how perfectly the halter-necked gown displayed her shoulders and delicate arms – and saw, too, that beautiful, that exquisite back; the gown was cut daringly low and revealed the slender frame as it tapered to a long narrow waist. No heavy muscles or protruding shoulder blades marred its perfection, no freckle or mole the surface of the magnolia skin. Even the spinal cleft was delicate – and straight, oh, so perfectly, so wonderfully *straight*, until it dipped into the slight hollow of the waist. For a few seconds I saw it all only as an artist who wanted to capture its beauty, but then I realized how exquisitely feminine and how totally desirable Rosalind Cleary was. All coherent thought stopped then, leaving only a desperate need to run – run as fast as my legs could carry me, away from such despair and hurt. Quickly, while all attention was still focused upon the group, I put my glass on the nearest table and slipped through the door. No good-byes, no 'Thank you for a wonderful party' to the PMC, but who would remember that Minette Glyn had ever attended the party? So – thank God for the Beetle and the ability to drive it, and thank God, too, for the early autumn darkness which hid the tears that streamed down uncontrollably.

The Mess was empty and without any lights. Herr Kunzle, having been denounced as the biggest Jew-baiter in the district, was no longer employed and none of the servants lived in. But I, who usually hated darkness, now found it friendly. I went to the window from where so often I had followed the Merc's lights: there were none on the road now, nor in the village, and only the Weser gleamed in the moonlight, the outline of its blown bridge darkly silhouetted against the flat landscape. I might have been the last person left alive, and in that utter silence I faced reality. That Dan had never really loved me seemed only too obvious; I had been an interlude such as lonely, desperate men sought everywhere when they were far from their roots. But, thinking in my simplicity that I *was* loved, I had been buoyed up and had wanted to make the end easy for him. Also, there had been the desperate hope, only ever half-acknowledged, that Rosalind Cleary would fail to join him, whereas now she was very much here and planning a life-long honeymoon; together they would go forward, a gilded, brilliant couple, enslaving all whom they met. But, dear God, how was I ever to live without Dan? How would I bear the thought that everything I had loved was to be given to *her*? Not for a few days or nights not for a few weeks – months – but *always*. All the days and nights of their lives, sharing all the highs and the lows, the joys and the sorrows.

Surprisingly, the answer came from the voices within my own head: Aunt Alexa's cool tone reminding me that Dan had never been mine and urging me to remember all the wives and sweethearts who had lost their men in death . . . and Uncle Julian, ever the more compassionate, saying, 'You must not let your obsession with physical beauty take over; there are other, more important values. And remember, always remember, that by the grace of God you were born to the winning side. Think of all the other young women who longed to live and had much to live for, but who were put to death; remember that a whole continent has been drenched in blood, with human suffering on a scale never seen before . . . it would be a crime – a sin – not to enjoy the most precious gift of life.' And when my own rebellious voice whispered, 'but what has all that to do with me?' it was my father whom I heard. 'Pull yourself together and stop all this mawkish self-pity.' And Uncle Julian again: 'Try, try always to be bigger than you are, Minette.'

So by the end of that night I had resolved to try and make the best of things. I would laugh and socialize, and if there were those who thought me a selfish husband-stealer – well, I would just have to live with it. Though the world might think my time with Dan merely a shabby, sordid affair, no different from hundreds of others, to me it had meant everything in the world. Aunt Alexa had once told me when I was in the orthopaedic hospital that if I ran from that unpleasant situation, I would run from every other throughout my life. I was not going to run now, nor let the world see that I was beaten to my knees.

'You'll enjoy Berlin,' the Chief said some weeks later.

'I'm sure I shall,' I replied, trying to sound enthusiastic and wondering if I had fooled her.

'Yes,' she continued, 'there's a great deal going on in the Western Sectors now – in complete contrast to the Eastern. Remember, you are able to move freely about all four Sectors of the city, but not into the Russian Zone.'

'But isn't the whole of Berlin deep in the Russian Zone?'

'Yes, of course, that is why we have a special military train to take us straight through. We have a number of Brit. Nats living in the Eastern Sector of the city so you'll need to drive over to see them. We're beginning to get good co-operation from the German Red Cross, so there's a great deal of work to be done, Minette, especially now that the no-fratting ban has been lifted. We must expect there to be many marriages and already we have been told that all transportation arrangements to the UK for German brides must be handled by ourselves.' The Chief took off her spectacles and sat back in her chair with a slightly weary sigh. 'But remember, it's important to avail yourself of all the leisure facilities too, otherwise a claustrophobic feeling can develop. Because of this, you'll find much more going on than here.

'Now, I'm sure you realize that the city is governed by a Kommandantur made up of the four Allied Powers but at Spandau, where Hess is imprisoned, each of the four Governors takes it in turn to administer the whole set-up for a month at a time. You might just wangle an invitation to luncheon when the British Governor is in the chair. Also, Hitler's bunker is very accessible, but there's a Russian guard at the Chancellory to get past so you'll need to tag along with a party of visiting VIPs. See it all, Minette. This is an extraordinary time in the history of our century and we are very lucky to be living in the midst of it all.'

So I went to Berlin on that military train, locked into my sleeper just as a precaution in case we had any nonsense with our Russian Allies at the border. There was no wall dividing East and West at that time, yet the contrast between the two halves of the city could not have been more apparent: in the East very little clearance had been started and the almost total absence of traffic was very reminiscent of cities in the British Zone a year before, but without any sign of their subsequent re-birth. All the battered, pock-marked buildings bore mute testimony to the ferocity of the last battles as they had raged, street by street. Even the once famous Unter den Linden was completely devastated, with only the Chancellory and shell of the Reichstag recognizable. The shell-torn Brandenberg Gate still stood, but the red flag flew from it.

The devastation was not of course confined to the East: the Tiergarten was a mass of shell and bomb craters, its trees reduced to a few blackened stumps, and only the huge towers above the air raid shelters still intact. On each side the streets were reduced to rubble as far as the eye could see, yet all forms of transport roared up and down the broad avenues and everywhere gangs of large, raw-boned women, covered in dust, worked energetically at clearing the rubble. The Ku'damm, once the most fashionable of streets, also lay in ruins, only distinguishable from all the rest by the burnt-out Church at one end. Yet all the pavements were crowded with people, still shabbily dressed but walking purposefully, and even with a 'Let's live for today' spark of gaiety. It was in the Ku'damm that a shop of sorts had been constructed from the broken stones where it was possible to acquire the most exquisite items of Meissen. Dresden and Viennese porcelain, mainly small items that people fleeing from their great town and country houses could easily carry: figurines, tiny enamelled boxes, small pieces of silver – almost all crested – a few frail liqueur glasses or almost transparent coffee cups being the most popular. All were very highly priced in marks but discreetly offered in exchange for coffee or cigarettes.

But I suppose the two most dramatic sights of that dramatic city were the bunker and the stadium. I still find it hard to believe that I once stood where one of history's greatest monsters and his lover lived out their last days as their world disintegrated in flames around them.

The stadium was silent, deserted and very eerie, but by half-closing my eyes I could still see the blood-red flags and grandiose standards held high, the massed ecstatic faces and forest of raised arms, still hear the great concerted shouts of '*Sieg Heil!*' And hear, too, a mediocre-looking man tell the ranks of bewitched youth that they would soon rule the world . . . Oh, but how he had betrayed them. In a few short years they were to die in their millions for him.

Almost every morning when we opened the office it was to find a small group of people waiting. They had come, often on foot, from all over Eastern Germany with one thought in their minds, one thought that had kept their exhausted bodies in motion: to get to the West, away from the fearful revenge of the Russians. Somehow word had reached them that the British Red Cross would help to find them money, shelter, and the all-important ration cards. Their stories were all the same: loss, violent death and rape. Sometimes there was not much we could do and to see final despair in so many eyes was unforgettable. But then, so was the sight of the city's children whose under-nourished bodies were so vulnerable to all diseases. We worked hard to get many off to Switzerland or England for holidays. Then there were the thousands of tiny orphaned babies and toddlers whose only known details were sex, colouring, approximate age and where found: 'Dug out of rubble, only survivor' – 'Found alone on bombed station' – 'In a ditch' – 'Lying injured in the middle of the road, believed to have been blown there by bomb blast' – all too young or too traumatized to give their names, all with photographs and papers rubber stamped: UNKNOWN.

Against tragedy on such a huge scale I told myself that my own loss was insignificant, but of course Dan still dominated my every thought and I found no solace in other men's admiration, even though it seemed that everyone wanted me. Except the right one. Yet I kept to my resolution and dined, danced and laughed so that no one realized how hard I was struggling through the barren desert life had become. I did not realize how great was the strain until one day I picked up the telephone and a voice said, 'Hello, Mäuschen.' The world spun, stopped, then shattered into brilliance.

'Dan – oh, Dan, is it really you?'

'Yes. How are you?' The voice was terse, almost curt.

'Why, fine – absolutely fine!' Because at that moment I was.

'Good. I'm ringing because I'm being posted to SHAEF in Paris and we're leaving next month.' There was the slightest pause and when he spoke again his voice was much lower. 'I couldn't leave without telling you.'

'Paris! Oh, how wonderful! You must be thrilled.'

'Yes. It's a plum posting and will no doubt be very interesting.' Again there was a pause. 'And – Ros is delighted; she has many friends in Paris and was just beginning to feel bored here.'

Bored! The very idea rendered me speechless.

'And how about you, Mäuschen, are you enjoying life in Berlin?'

The brilliance had faded now, leaving only an empty void as I realized the implication of his words. 'Yes . . . it's a very vital place and there's a lot going on. Dan – ?'

'Yes?'

'Are you – are you happy?'

Another pause, then a tired note in the voice, 'Oh, happiness is a pretty elusive thing, isn't it? I find concentrating on my career far easier and more rewarding. I mean to get to the top.'

'I-I'm sure you will.'

'Thank you, darling, and good-bye. Look after yourself.'

'Oh, don't go, please, don't go – ' But the line was already dead and I was left trembling, with all the wounds open and raw once more. I knew then that I could no longer continue and that night wrote to the Chief saying I wished to go home. Within two months I was on my way, escorting a party of German 'Brides for Britain'. All would become British citizens on marriage and all appeared to believe they were sailing to a land of milk and honey. As I saw the lines of waiting fiancés, all dressed in their dreary demob suits, I wondered how many of the brides would regret their marriages. We were all returning to a grey, battered country where rationing and many shortages still

106

continued. And how many of the men would have second thoughts about their *Fräuleins*? British girls, on the whole, were so much more attractive. Already within minutes of docking it had been necessary to tell two of the brides that their weddings were cancelled and that they would have to return immediately to Cuxhaven. Their lamentations could be heard all over the ship and I silently shared their feelings, for while their greatest adventure was just beginning for the majority, for me it was over. What – oh, what – was I going to do with the rest of my life?

PART TWO

England

9

They were waiting at the open front door, all so much greyer, but all smiling in welcome.

'You ain't 'alf lost a lot o'weight,' was Daisy's greeting, and even Aunt Alexa said concernedly, 'You *do* look very peaky, my dear.'

'Rest and some good air will soon put that right,' said Uncle Julian in the special growl he reserved for moments of deep emotion.

And so I returned to my roots to find that nothing had changed: the rose-patterned chintzes, the fine old mahogany furniture, the two elephant feet on the landing, Aunt Alexa's papier mâché from Kashmir in the drawing-room and Uncle Julian's paintings on the walls – all so familiar, so enduring, so English. Everything in that house brought balm to my tortured spirit, and in time I was able to pack my uniform in the tin trunk and help to take it up to the loft. It was immediately apparent that my family wanted me to stay with them indefinitely, but I had to work and there was little to offer in Solenthaven.

'I think I'll try for a secretarial job in London,' I announced one evening at dinner. 'After all, I've had the training, and if I take down the radio news in shorthand for a few weeks, I'll soon get my speed back.'

'But why not stay a little longer?' asked Uncle Julian. 'You still appear very tired and I've noticed that the essential sparkle is missing.'

Daisy, coming in with the pudding at that moment, added irrepressibly: 'Tha's rite! I nefer 'ears you giggle these days, Miss Minet.'

And Aunt Alexa, instead of reproving her, said: 'I fear those experiences in Germany have left their mark. Perfectly understandable, of course, but now you must look to the future, my dear.'

'That's why I'm anxious to start work,' I answered, glad of the opening she had unwittingly given me.

In the event it was very easy: Whelan & Whelan, structural engineers of Hamilton Place, advertised for a secretary to their Financial Director and I got the job. Somewhere to live was more difficult as the housing shortage in London, as in all big towns and cities, remained acute. A flat was out of the question, but I managed to find a bed-sitter in another girl's flat. Fiona was an air hostess, bright and stunningly pretty. Tourism was still in its infancy, but there were plenty of businessmen and VIPs flying around the world and Fiona was away for days, even weeks, at a time. She made it clear from the start that I was to be a lodger, not a sharer, except that in her absence I would have the flat to myself. She was looking for a dependable person to keep an eye on her many lovely possessions and seemed satisfied that she had found such a woman in myself. She never invited me to join the lively parties she gave and her guests seemed to hardly notice me as I scurried between the kitchen and my room. 'A little mouse,' he had called me, and I certainly was now, although minus the marzipan. My life-style resembled that of a bereaved person unable to come to terms with her grief.

I did my job conscientiously because of not wanting to lose it, but discovered very early on that all I had seen in Germany still coloured my judgement: when a drop in the firm's profits brought a near-crisis and endless meetings of the Board, I just could not take it seriously. What did the loss of a few thousand pounds matter when a whole continent of *people* had lost everyone and everything dear to them? Ironically, my attitude earned me praise and when my director said, 'Miss Glyn has remained very cool,' I could only murmur my thanks and turn quietly away.

The theatre provided the best salve for my misery, and although my emotional and physical energies were still very depleted, I could always manage the effort of getting to a theatre; in those days many of them still had galleries where admission was half-a-crown, plus one shilling for a stool which could be placed in line outside to save one queuing. Once the performance started I could usually forget my loneliness. Uncle Julian, too, helped all he could; he was regularly holding exhibitions of his paintings and whenever these were successful he would come up to Town for the night, sometimes to take me to a play, but always to have dinner at his Club, the United Service. It was on one such evening that he said, 'Do you remember Philip Conroy, the water-colourist?'

'Yes,' I said slowly, 'wasn't he the one who did for Indian women what Russell Flint did for the Spanish?'

Uncle Julian nodded. 'Correct. Before the war I knew him quite well, and of course you will remember that we have his fine "Village Women Drawing Water" at home.'

'Oh, yes,' I said at once. 'It's always been one of my favourites.'

'Well then my dear, I hope you'll soon have an opportunity to tell him so!'

Oh Lord, I thought, suddenly weary, what's he letting me in for? Aloud, I merely said: 'I can't think how.'

'Because I want you to meet him – now, Minette, *don't* look like that! Wait till I tell you: I'd not heard from Conroy for years, until last week; it appears that up to 1944 he was an official war artist, but then began to develop arthritis of the hands which is now so bad that

113

he cannot paint at all. It's a great tragedy and means that he's very badly off. He wrote to say that he was starting a small class for gifted amateurs to teach the technique of water-colour painting and, my dear, I should like you to join it.'

My first instinct was to refuse, but as I searched for words to do so without hurting my uncle, he forestalled me.

'Not exactly an enthusiastic response,' he said wryly, 'and I can see you are about to say that you cannot and that I don't understand. But I have to tell you, Minette, that I understand only too well; it has not been difficult to deduce what is causing you to be a shadow of your former self, with all the spontaneous happiness of a particularly charming young woman appearing to be gone. It cannot be illness because your final Red Cross medical would have shown that, therefore, it has to be something which has hurt you so badly that grief is draining you of all vitality, all will-power, and it hurts me deeply to see you in such a state. But, my darling girl, this *cannot* go on; you are young, you *must* try, however slowly, to pick up the threads of your life again. You used to love painting, and if you will only make the effort to go to this class, I am sure you will find interest and relaxation in it. Conroy has only a small studio, so there will be just five other students. You have real talent, Minette, so why not develop it to its fullest extent?'

I was most deeply touched and could only whisper, 'Thank you for caring so much. May I think it over?'

But Uncle Julian was not going to let me wriggle out of it. 'No, it would not be fair to keep Conroy waiting.' He finished the last of his wine, wiped his lips and continued: 'I remember a little girl coming from Africa who was so heartbroken that she was almost entirely silent, no matter what Alexa or I tried to interest her in. One day, in desperation, I appealed to her, telling her that we so much wanted her to be happy, but being two old fuddy-duddies, we did not know what else to do. "You must help us," I said. "Please tell us what we can do to make you happy." But she only looked back at me with great sad eyes. I turned away in despair, but then I felt a very small cold hand take mine and a little voice said very quietly: "Will you teach me to paint?" I picked her up and kissed her. "Of course, I will," I told her, and from that day I greatly loved the little girl because I knew she had made a colossal effort for *me* rather than for herself. And so, Minette, I am asking you once again to do something for me.'

After that, there was only one thing I could do – apart from Dan Uncle Julian was the person I loved most in the world. I promised to attend the class, even though I knew that when the time came, it would need every ounce of willpower I had to keep that promise. Once at the class, however, I immediately became fascinated by my fellow students. We were a very strange assortment: there was George, who was 'something in the City' and well into middle age; he arrived in dark pin stripes and bowler and explained with false joviality: 'The old nerves have been playing up a bit and my quack thought a spot of painting might help!' Then there was Alison, who worked at the Foreign Office, a large 'jolly hockey-sticks type', and seemingly the last person who would *want* to paint; Hilde, the smiling, ever wanting-to-please refugee who told us in her heavily accented English that she had spent the war in a factory machining men's underwear, but had always wanted to try her hand at painting, and lastly David, whose brief upward glance at me had instantly changed into a long look of shy but undisguised admiration. He had been in a reserved occupation during the war which had been spent at the Ministry of Information where he had designed posters for railway stations and hoardings. It soon emerged that of us all, he was the most talented, with perhaps myself as the next most experienced. When asked in turn what our preferred subjects were, I was the only one who said portraiture, with the work of Sorine Savely being my favourite.

'Then this is not the right class for you – ' Philip Conroy began, but I quickly cut him short: 'Oh, but I've really only done landscape and should so like to improve my technique at that.' It was not strictly true, but I suddenly found that having made such a great effort to get to the class, I now wanted to stay. And as time went on, I really began to enjoy the sessions. Philip Conroy was an excellent teacher and always had some praise for me: 'Your perspective's a bit ropey, dear, but I like the contrasts of colour and tone.' Or: 'Fine grouping, Minette, and the light is excellent but you must take more care with perspective.'

David's work was always highly and quite rightly praised: 'You know, you really should think about becoming a professional.'

Poor Hilde's work was hopeless, George's very mediocre, but Alison was surprisingly good.

At first when the class finished Philip would offer coffee, but as time went on we all tended to excuse ourselves and disperse. Then gradually I became aware that David was either leaving with me or very soon after, and in no time at all we started travelling together as far as Oxford Circus where we parted, I to go on to Lancaster Gate, David to Victoria. 'Not the most elegant of addresses,' he said with a small nervous laugh, 'but wonderfully handy for the Tate.' He paused to look intently at the ground, his brow deeply furrowed. 'Do – do you often go to the Tate?' he managed at last.

'Y-e-s,' I answered hesitantly, half anticipating what was coming, but anxious not to rebuff him. 'Although

116

I really prefer the two Nationals and I never miss the Academy Exhibitions.'

'Nor I!' He was gaining confidence rapidly and I braced myself when he added: 'Perhaps we could – would you consider coming to the Summer Exhibition with me when it opens?'

'That's awfully nice of you, David,' I said, turning to smile at him, 'But my uncle always comes up from Hampshire for that and I go with him. I-I think he would be hurt if I did not – he's the one who first taught me to paint, you see.'

'I quite understand,' David answered at once, obviously anxious to be on the same wavelength, 'but perhaps one Sunday afternoon we could . . . spend a little time at the Portrait Gallery? I'm very interested in portraiture too, you know.'

Oh, Lord, I thought miserably, what on earth has brought this on? I don't want to go! Aloud I said: 'It's a nice idea, David, but I always seem to have so much to do at weekends.'

'You must have dozens of friends all wanting to see you and take you around,' he said wistfully.

'Oh, not so many,' I replied, thinking of all the hours that I sat alone and totally without human contact. Inside my head a small voice whispered: Why not go with him? but I instantly rejected this; it will only escalate, I told myself tiredly, and before I know it, there'll be another emotional crisis on my hands. And the last thing I want to do is hurt him.

When he said, 'Well, sometime perhaps – ' I knew his confidence was evaporating. He did not issue any more invitations during the rest of the term and on our short walks to the Underground we talked about our latest subjects and of painting generally. Once on the train there was too much noise to carry on a conversation satisfactorily and we invariably sat side by side in silence.

117

At Oxford Circus I was always careful not to linger and it was a relief to say good-bye, for I could not help but be aware of his admiration for me and it made me uncomfortable.

Then came the end of term. Philip Conroy had not set a subject for our last session, but instead had said we might choose our own, 'Anything you like, chums.' He tried so hard to be patient and pleasant, even amusing, but did not suffer fools gladly and I felt we often tried his patience. His was such a brilliant talent and to be reduced to teaching a bunch of bumbling amateurs must have been difficult for him. Nevertheless at that last session, he was full of praise for my effort. I had done a head-and-shoulders of Uncle Julian, posed against the huge wall map of Europe which he kept in his study. All through the war he had charted the Allies' progress and my job had been to make and colour the tiny national flags which were pinned at all strategic points. It made a colourful background for my uncle's fine leonine head with its high, broad brow and waving iron-grey hair. 'Very nice, Minette,' Philip said, 'and an excellent likeness. The background, too, is most appropriate.'

Then Alison put up her painting. 'I've cheated a bit,' she explained in her rather deep voice, 'because it was actually painted last year when I went to stay with my sister in Bonn.' It was a view of Altenau and the totally unexpected sight caused me such agony that for a few seconds I was near to fainting. I clenched my hands and folded my arms tightly across my chest in a desperate effort to remain composed as all the memories came flooding back. And with them came all my suppressed yearning and hunger for Dan.

When David's painting was put up I saw only that it was of a young woman, her face closed in rapt concentration as she leaned forward in three-quarter view to an easel. A shaft of light fell on her fair hair, touched the curve of

118

a temple and cheekbone and outlined her straight nose. Shock sent the blood suffusing my face as I realized that it was a painting of myself.

'Most charming,' Philip was saying heartily. 'And you've captured Minette's wistful expression perfectly.'

I longed to get away from them all and like an animal, hide myself and my overwhelming emotions, but then George proposed we should all take Philip for a drink, and of course I had to go too.

'What's the matter, Minette?' Alison asked when we were all seated in The British Grenadier. 'You look very pale and about a thousand miles away.'

'It's just that I've never been to a pub before,' I said, anxious to avoid any more probing.

'Never been to a pub!' echoed Alison. 'My dear girl, where have you been hiding all these years?'

'What's such a big deal about visiting pubs?' David demanded, instantly belligerent on my behalf.

'Nothing – nothing,' Alison answered hastily, 'but it just surprised me. I mean in this day and age when women have just stopped parachuting into enemy territory, blowing up bridges and stealing the most valuable secrets . . . '

'In this world, but not of it,' boomed George unexpectedly, 'thought so the moment I set eyes on her. This confirms it!'

'Oh, really,' I protested, forcing a strange little laugh, 'you're all quite wrong, because I've actually been living very much in the world – in Germany.'

'Germany?' Alison echoed yet again. 'How interesting! My sister's married to a chap in the Control Commission. What were you doing?'

'Yes, come on, Minette,' George urged, 'just for once climb out of that shell and tell all!'

So I gave a quick resumé and then Hilde said very quietly: 'Which DP camps did you work in?'

'None,' I answered, 'but I was in very frequent contact

with them as one of my jobs was to trace relatives and friends who might sponsor a DP for an Exit Visa. There were also thousands of incoming enquiries too, and with so much devastation all church and government records were lost. It was up to us to try to find those people.'

'Excuse me,' Hilde said, jumping to her feet, 'I have to leave now – good-bye, everyone!' She was gone before we had time to assimilate her words, leaving her beer and rushing away as though in sudden panic. Naturally then everyone started talking at once, until Alison said: 'It must have been something about Germany, wouldn't you think, Minette?'

'I've not the faintest idea,' I replied hastily, but quite untruthfully. I knew that it was not impossible for a desperate person to take the identity of someone else, someone who had died . . . no, not at all impossible when there were so few Exit Visas, not when it only needed a relation, a grandmother perhaps, to have had TB for a whole family to be ineligible, with nothing but endless years ahead in a Displaced Persons Camp. I was never to know about Hilde. At the start of the new term, Philip announced that she had withdrawn.

Soon afterwards Alison was posted to the Embassy in Rome and with George's 'nervous trouble' making his attendance erratic, David and I were naturally thrown much more together. When Philip asked us if we made full use of all the wonderful art on view in the capital, David answered at once that he had asked me to visit some of the galleries with him. 'But I was not able to persuade her,' he said, looking at me smilingly, but with pleading brown eyes.

'You should go with him, Minette,' Philip urged, 'it would surely be better than going alone and this lad is surprisingly knowledgeable, you know.'

So in the end I agreed to meet David on a Sunday

afternoon, although when the time came, I had to force myself to go.

He was walking up and down, looking pinched and anxious: a tall, thin young man, very casually dressed, with brown hair perpetually tousled. He would never turn heads and after the battle-toughened men I had met in Germany, he seemed 'soft', almost what Aunt Alexa would scathingly call 'namby-pamby', but there was no doubting his essential niceness and sensitivity.

'Sorry I'm so late,' I said, and saw his face light up with something like joy.

'It's all right,' he said quickly. 'You're here now and that's all that matters. Gosh it's wonderful to see you.'

After that, we had regular 'dates' on Sunday afternoons, always ending with tea at a Corner House. I steadfastly refused to think of inviting him to my bed-sit, nor did he ever suggest I should go to his flat. He looked after me so well, always taking my elbow when we crossed roads and actually putting his arm protectively across me when we came to any crowded spot. 'I'm not breakable, you know,' I said, turning to laugh at him. 'Well, you certainly look as though you are and I'm not taking the risk!' he replied seriously. It was impossible not to realize that he was becoming fond of me and this caused me much emotional conflict: I was in turn irritated, yet desperately anxious that he should not be hurt; then angry with myself, because I knew in my inmost heart that his feelings were balm to my loneliness. How can you be so cruel? I raged silently at myself. You know you should stop seeing him now, not wait until he actually tells you he loves you.

But of course I left it too late. We were walking up Regent Street after our usual tea at the Leicester Square Corner House when I got a piece of grit in my eye. This was a frequent occurrence. With so many bombed buildings everywhere, it only needed a breeze for dust and grit to rise up everywhere; when a piece got into an

121

eye it was extremely painful and very difficult to dislodge. 'Oh damn,' I said, as my eye started to stream, 'it feels like a rock and I don't think it's going to come out with the usual holding down of my lid.'

'Let me try,' David suggested, steering me into the lighted doorway of the Galleries Lafayette. He produced a very clean-looking handkerchief, twisted a corner into a tight point and stood close to me while he gently pulled down my lower lid. 'Yes, I see it,' he said, 'it's not a rock – but, gosh, it is larger than most. I'll try not to hurt, Minette.'

'It's all right,' I answered, standing stiffly. 'It hurts so much anyway that taking it out couldn't be worse – heavens, have you got it already?'

'Yes,' he sounded quite triumphant, 'there!'

'Thanks so much, David,' I said, wanting to move away from him, but realizing that I was standing with my back to the shop's closed door. And before I could do anything he had cupped my face in his hands and kissed me very gently.

I tore my mouth from his and pushed him away. 'David!' I exclaimed, dismay making me sound angrier than intended. 'Whatever made you . . . with all these people around.'

He had taken a step back, but made no further attempt to move. 'They're all too busy with their own affairs to bother about us,' he said quietly, and of course I knew he was right: of the many people hurrying past in the early evening dusk, I doubted if more than two or three had looked twice at us.

'The fact is,' he was continuing, 'I've fallen in love with you, Minette, and I want to marry you.'

Remorse and sadness hit me hard then and I answered with difficulty. 'Please don't – don't say any more, David. I . . . cannot marry you.'

'I know you don't love me, Minette, but that doesn't

matter. I have more than enough for us both. I swear I would do everything – *everything* – to make you happy.'

Oh dear God, I thought, as memory flooded back, reminding me that I had so often felt I loved Dan enough for us both. 'David dear,' I said aloud, 'I am immensely flattered and deeply touched that you should love me, but you see I loved someone in Germany just as you love me, and I cannot – it is not possible for me to love anyone else. Please try to understand and not to be hurt – I can't bear to cause you pain.'

'It's all right,' he said, 'I've always known there must have been someone else – not that you've ever said, of course, but it wasn't necessary. Although you have such a beautiful smile, Minette, and you smile often, your face in repose always looks so – so heartbroken. But I could help you put the past behind you. We wouldn't have much money to begin with, but I know we could be happy. We have so much in common – and Minette, we needn't even stay in this country. People are wanted in Australia and South Africa; we could go and start an entirely new life, explore together – '

Yes, and he would make a wonderful husband, said a small voice within me, you would have love, companionship, emotional security, instead of this emptiness, this bitter, bitter loneliness, and he would never look at anyone else . . . but I would be *taking* all the time, battening on his devotion, and no matter how I tried, I would be able to give him so little in return.

'David, I *can't*. I just can't.'

'Ah, now, don't be so upset, Minette dear. It's my fault, I should have chosen a better place and time. But don't decide right away, just think about it and take as long as you want. Perhaps in a little while you might think differently?'

But within forty-eight hours my future was irrevocably decided for me. I had gone to dine with Uncle Julian at

123

his Club and as we rose to leave he said: 'I suppose you want to go and have a look at your hero as usual?'

'Yes, please,' I replied, forcing an enthusiasm I no longer felt. The Club owned a splendid portrait of Charles II and as a very young girl it had fascinated me. The King's lazy charm always seemed to reach out to me, his fine dark eyes to be looking directly at me, but as I gazed up at him on that evening, I thought only of how unjust it was that he should be remembered mainly as a womanizer when he had also been such an able man. I wonder if you found them worth it, I silently asked him, for with the possible exception of Nell, they were all such greedy viragos – and what a dance they led you! But I'm so glad you were always kind to your Queen. She must have seemed a little brown mouse too . . .

'I see the fascination still persists,' Uncle Julian said teasingly, and I managed to laugh and agree, while silently crying out that I was only fascinated by one man, a man with burnished hair and a face that was both ruggedly handsome and sensitive . . . Ahead of us a door opened and a figure emerged to the sound of laughter and many male voices. I stopped dead, heart and brain, seeming to spin. Dan was standing before me, resplendent in white tie and tails, with two rows of pristine miniatures pinned over his left breast. He, too, had abruptly stopped, and for a few seconds we just gazed at each other. Then he swept forward, medals tinkling and face alight with animation. 'Minette!' he exclaimed, taking both my hands. 'What an incredible, absolutely wonderful surprise! How are you?'

'I can't believe you're real!' I said, only half conscious of shaking my head. 'I thought you were still in Paris.'

'No, I'm at the Air Ministry now.'

'But you didn't get that tan here in London.'

'Too true! It's the result of a month's skiing at Chamonix before we returned here.'

We were making trivial conversation, because I believe

we were both too shocked to know exactly what to say, and all the time we never took our eyes off each other.

Beside me a throat was cleared rather noisily and I felt strong pressure on my elbow. I swung round guiltily. 'Oh, I'm so sorry, Uncle Julian – may I – may I introduce a friend from Germany, Group Captain Cleary? Dan, this is my uncle, Brigadier Maitland.' They shook hands, but Dan immediately turned back to me: 'I still don't know what you're doing here, Minette.'

'I'm living in Town now and working as a secretary in a firm of structural engineers.'

'Really? In the City?'

'No, Hamilton Place – '

'But you're so near us! Ros's father has loaned us his house in Eaton Place and I'm in Whitehall.'

'Oh – and how are Ros and Emma?'

'Emma is wonderful, but Ros is still missing her Paris friends and is rather fed up.' He paused fractionally and then added, 'I'm afraid I'll have to go back in.' He turned to my uncle. 'A Rhine Army reunion dinner.'

Uncle Julian nodded. 'Ah, yes.'

'So good-bye, Minette, it's been really wonderful to see you again.'

'Yes – you too,' I said, my voice suddenly hoarse.

Dan's bow to Uncle Julian was that of a younger man to an older, rather than to a senior officer. 'Sir.'

'Good-night to you, Group Captain, good-night!'

Dan walked quickly to the door but then, as though against his will, turned and looked at me with such intense sadness that I almost cried out. Yet the next instant he had resolutely about-turned and walked from my sight, the door closing quietly behind him.

'An exceptionally handsome man,' commented Uncle Julian, and I could only nod silently.

10

Dan was waiting for me outside my office the next evening, bowler-hatted and carrying the inevitable umbrella and briefcase, all of which he managed with great smoothness. 'Hello, Mäuschen,' he said softly, and then laughed at my amazement. 'Didn't you think I would come?'

I shook my head dazedly, 'I didn't think you even knew the name of the firm.'

'Quite true, but it only needed a few enquiries to find out. I wanted to telephone but thought you might not be allowed personal calls. Now – will you have dinner with me?'

'Oh, I-I would *love* to, but ought we? Aren't you expected home?'

His bark of laughter was suddenly harsh. 'No problem. I'm working late at the office.'

Somewhere in the dim recesses of my brain a warning bell sounded, but I was too stunned to heed it. 'I'd like to change first,' I said tentatively.

'Yes, of course.'

'But I've only got a bed-sitter.'

He smiled down at me with a faint semblance of the old mischief: 'I promise not to look. But now, a taxi.'

'Impossible at this hour.'

He did not answer, but walked casually to the kerb, unhooked the umbrella from his arm and raised it almost languidly; a taxi seemed to materialize out of nowhere. As he opened the door for me, he said: 'You should know by now that nothing is impossible.'

But I could see that he was shaken out of his calm by my bed-sitter. 'This is it?' he queried, looking around in disbelief at the narrow room with its one sash window and vista of chimney pots.

'Yes, I'm afraid so. Do sit down.' He seemed to fill all the available space and his tall figure to exude power and maleness. I got out glasses and my solitary bottle of sherry, but when I tried to pour the liquid my hands were shaking so much that all my determination was needed to keep bottle and glass in contact.

'Here's to us,' Dan said, touching his glass with mine. He took a sip, then said, 'You're very pale and thin, you know, Mäuschen, what have you been up to?'

'Why, nothing, nothing at all,' I answered, brightly inane. How could I tell him that I had been totally bereaved, totally lost without him? 'And you – are you happily settled here now?'

'Job-wise yes, it's very interesting and I do enjoy being in on all the big decisions but, my God, I'm having problems with Ros! She was great in Paris because she had lots of friends to keep her amused, but life was hellishly expensive there and I was constantly struggling to make ends meet. It's much better here because we have the loan of the house, but now Ros is bored and never lets me forget it for a moment – Christ, what a prison marriage is! I swear I'll never be caught again.'

I realized then that he was very different: the vulnerability had died in him and been replaced by a toughness, perhaps even a ruthlessness, which had certainly never been evident before. Even the boyish mischief in his smile had almost gone. He's been hurt, I thought, desperately hurt. Yet the magnetism and intense physical attractiveness had even increased. I jumped up and pointed to the radio beside my bed. 'You see, I still have the little Telefunken you gave me. If I leave you with this, the paper and the sherry, will you excuse me while I take a very quick bath?'

127

'Of course, darling,' he answered, making the endearment sound quite natural, 'but come back quickly, won't you?'

I felt such joy then that it would have outshone the brightest sun. My face in the bathroom mirror was hardly recognizable in its excitement. But as I got out of the bath I realized that in my confused state I had forgotten to bring fresh underwear with me. I can't go out in the things I've had on all day, I thought agitatedly. I hated the thought of going to fetch the clean garments wearing only a dressing-gown – it seemed so blatantly provocative, yet the gown was anything but glamorous, being well-worn and made from coupon-free curtain material. I'll just dash in and out, I thought, wrapping the gown tightly about myself.

Dan was sitting on the edge of my bed turning the knobs of the little radio. 'I can't get a sound out of this,' he said in the tone of a man totally unused to having anything that did not function instantly.

'Well, sometimes it needs a little slap,' I answered, hurrying forward to administer the blow. The mellow tones of Mantovani came through at once and I smiled into Dan's eyes . . . I've never quite known how it happened: one minute I was bent over the radio, the next I was in his arms, crushed against him, his kiss so fiercely demanding that my head snapped back.

Eventually I tore my mouth from his, gasping, 'You take my breath away – '

'Good.' His tone was both unequivocal and harsh; it wrenched at my heart and I put my arms around his neck. 'Oh, Dan – Dan, my dearest darling,' I whispered, longing to break through the bitterness, but when his hand pulled at my dressing-gown's cord, I tried to push him away. 'No – oh no, no, we mustn't!'

'Of course we must; you've known it and so have I since we set eyes on each other last night . . . I warn you, darling, not to play games with me. I've had more of those favourite feminine tactics than I can take.'

So then it was I who opened my gown and myself to this man for whom I had ached, yearned and throbbed in misery for so long.

When eventually he drew away, he looked at me and said, 'You've grown up, Mäuschen, you've become a passionate woman. I'll have to watch out or else you'll be the death of me!'

In a rare moment of confidence I was able to laugh softly and twine my arms once more around his neck. 'I only want to love you, make you happy,' I whispered.

'I know you do, Angel, and that's what you've always done – but, oh Christ, I'll have to leave you now and go back to that never-ending petulance that starts as a whine and ends like the spitting of a hell-cat. I swear one day my control will snap and I'll do her an injury.'

I wanted to say, 'Stay. Stay here for ever,' but instead as a sudden convulsive shiver shook me, I put my cheek against his shoulder. 'Don't,' I begged, 'don't ever think of such a thing.'

He had quickly recovered his poise. 'No, of course not,' he said, jumping up and beginning to dress. 'It's just that Ros cannot or will not accept that she is married to a man who has no private income.' He paused as he knotted his tie. 'I expect it's really my fault – I should never have married a rich man's daughter. And especially not a woman who's also a spoiled beauty.' He shrugged into his coat and came over to me. 'Good night, sweet Mäuschen. I'm sorry not to have given you dinner after all, but next time I promise a really slap-up meal – something to put a bit of flesh on those little bones!'

'When?' I asked hesitantly. 'When shall I see you again?'

'I don't know,' the tone was instantly decisive, 'but soon, definitely very soon.'

129

And so I joined the large number of women who exist in the twilight zone of married men's lives, who wait for the telephone or a knock on the door, shunning friends and unwilling to make any definite appointments in case they should clash with 'his' visits. It was certainly not a role which I had ever envisaged for myself, or would have chosen, and after the first stunned amazement, guilt set in. While a war-time affair might be excusable, one with a married man while he was still living with his wife, was definitely not. Like any woman in love, I longed to share everything with Dan, to be seen with him and to introduce him to my family, but his circumstances made our times together clandestine and entirely physical. In Germany I had thought he wanted to marry me, but now he made it perfectly plain that he would not marry again, even if he were free.

'It's nothing but a life sentence,' he said bitterly, and never knew that the last of my self-esteem crumbled at that moment for no matter how much I despised myself, I knew I could not do without him – his touch, his kiss, his possession of me. It seemed that I was forever waiting and longing, like a starveling, for the crumbs from a rich man's table. Yet when at last Dan was with me I would often be beyond joy, beyond ecstasy.

It was some time before I even thought of David, or of the class, and when I eventually rang to cancel my attendance, Philip said, 'David has been asking most anxiously for your address. May I give it?'

'No, please don't,' I said hastily. 'I know his and I'll write to him.' But to my everlasting shame, I never did so.

Then one evening as Dan and I were leaving a secluded little wine bar, I heard my name called urgently. I turned and there was David, smiling delightedly. 'Minette! Where have you been? I've – God, but you look radiant!'

'I couldn't agree more,' Dan said stiffly, by way of establishing his role.

Remorse at my cavalier treatment of David made my face flame and instead of introducing the two men, I could only mumble: 'I've been too busy to attend the class.'

But David, with his artist's eye for detail, had seen how tightly Dan's arm was through mine, with hands clasped and fingers laced. All the animation died from his face. 'Yes,' he said slowly, 'I understand and – and I won't keep you. All the very best, Minette. Good-bye!'

'Who is that fellow!' Dan demanded as David rushed away.

'Just one of the others at Philip Conroy's class.'

'Really? Well, he's in love with you, isn't he?'

'He – he seems to think he is.'

'I would say there's no doubt about it,' Dan said quietly. 'And you, Mäuschen?'

Astonishment stopped me in my tracks on the crowded pavement and I broke away from him so that I could face him. 'Dan! How can you even *think* I might love David when you know perfectly well there is only one man in my life?'

'Yes, I do know it.' It was said with a sigh and later after we'd made love, he said: 'I'm keeping other men – eligible men – away from you, aren't I, Mäuschen?'

'No, no of course not!' I replied in instant panic.

As though he had not heard, he burst out: 'What an utterly selfish brute I've been to come back into your life, take everything and always waltz off leaving you with nothing!'

I flung myself into his arms. 'Don't, Dan! Please don't. You know how much I care – not only about you personally, but about your career too. I-I don't mind staying in the background so long as you need me.'

'Ah, but I'll always do that, Mäuschen. You are the only person who brings sweetness, love and understanding into my life. I just wish I could do something constructive about

131

the whole situation but Ros, after all those months of threatening divorce, won't let me go and Emma needs me so much – she gets very little from Ros. No matter what happens, I'm determined to stick it out until she's grown up, then I'll know that I've done my very best for her.' He paused to light and pull deeply on a cigarette. 'The tragic thing is,' he said slowly, 'that I'm safeguarding Emma's future at the expense of yours.' He moved restlessly to stub out the cigarette. 'Why don't you throw me out, Mäuschen – for God's sake, why don't you?'

'Because I know what life is like without you,' I burst out passionately. 'I lived it in Berlin: it was like walking across an endless desert, without food or water.'

'Yes, but in time – '

'But don't you know how difficult it would be for any other man to follow you? Don't you know that I don't *want* anyone else?'

'Nor do I!' Dan said with a break in his voice. 'Oh God, nor do I!'

'Then love me,' I begged, wrapping myself around him, 'love me again. I can never get enough of you.' So we made love again with all the desperation of despair, even though we did not know that it was to be for the last time.

Two days later I received a parcel from Philip Conroy, together with a brief note: 'David wanted you to have the enclosed and to know that he is leaving England at the end of this month.' Inside was his painting of me. This, together with my shabby treatment of him, the guilt and hopelessness of the situation with Dan, and all my emotional insecurity, took a heavy toll.

The crisis began the weekend that I travelled down to Solenthaven where great shock was expressed at my appearance.

'Minette, you're obviously on the brink of illness and I have a proposition to put to you,' Uncle Julian said over our Saturday evening drink. 'Now that travel is becoming a little easier, I think I could pull a few strings and get us passages to Mombasa. Why don't you and I go on an expedition to Kenya? The farm is, of course, still yours, and although the house must be quite derelict by now, we might go and see it. Or we could spend all our time painting. When I visited your parents before you were born, I was enthralled by all the vastness and colour, and I'm sure we'd find a very great deal to paint. And to relax, to get away from everything here for a month or two, would do you the world of good. So what do you say, my dear?'

I was reduced to instant panic: to leave London even for one month when Dan might be there, to miss him, was quite impossible. A small voice inside my head murmured that he could be away for anything up to six weeks on an extended trip on Ministry business at NATO headquarters or for 'talks' in Washington, but I paid no heed. 'It's a lovely thought,' I said aloud, 'but of course I couldn't go.'

'My dear, why not?'

'Well, for one thing, I'd have to leave my job.'

'Yes, of course, but now that you've had London experience, surely it would not be difficult to find another post?'

'No-yes – oh no, no, please no!' I felt the pressure behind his quiet words, and when the gong sounded I uttered a small shriek and dropped my glass.

There was complete silence for a few seconds, then Uncle Julian rose and went to the door. 'Daisy, we shall not be in to dinner for a while. Please keep everything hot.' When he turned back to me, his face was tense. 'Minette, I am appalled.'

I had never heard his voice so stern. 'I-I don't understand,' I faltered in dread.

'Ah, but I think you do! It is only too painfully obvious that you are in the throes of an intense and unhappy love

133

affair which is bringing you close to complete nervous exhaustion.'

A strangled sound came from my closed throat. Aunt Alexa said coldly, 'I hope you will not insult us by attempting to deny it.'

'Oh, you know how much I love you both,' I burst out passionately, 'and I can't bear to hurt you! I *wish* with all my heart that the circumstances were different – were natural – but I cannot give up Dan.'

Again it was Aunt Alexa who spoke. 'Where is your pride, your self-esteem, girl?'

I turned to her, pleading for understanding. 'I have no pride, no self-esteem, where Dan is concerned. It's true that he has a wife, but they're unhappy and only stay together for the sake of their daughter. I-I did not cause the unhappiness and Ros does not know about me.'

'But a wife *always* knows!'

'No, Aunt. Ros is a most beautiful, most confident woman, and now that she and Dan are officially together, I don't believe it would occur to her that he could prefer anyone to herself.' I spread my hands. 'I only want to make him happy.'

'And have you any proof that you do so?' asked Uncle Julian in a cold, interrogatory tone.

'I – yes, I believe so.' They just looked at me silently and I rushed on, 'He – always comes back and – '

Uncle Julian laughed harshly. 'You poor, *foolish* girl! A man does not necessarily keep such a liaison going because it makes him *happy*!' Uncharacteristically he tossed off his drink in one gulp. 'Besides, it is perfectly possible for a man to love two women simultaneously – but, believe me, he cannot be loyal to both.'

My composure was rapidly disintegrating. I jumped up and began to walk about the room, with hands over my ears. 'No – no, I won't listen, I *won't*!'

But my aunt's implacable voice still reached me: 'Are you proposing to remain a whore for the rest of your life, or only until this man tires of you?'

I swung round, suddenly furious, but Uncle Julian forestalled me. 'We had such hopes for you, Minette; we both looked forward to the day when you would meet some suitable young man and I – I would have the privilege of giving you away in marriage.'

The tears fell then, cascading down my face and dripping on to my clenched hands. And with them all my defensive anger evaporated. 'I am sorry,' I whispered humbly, 'so desperately, desperately sorry, and if it were humanly possible to give Dan up, I swear I would try to do so. But, you see, he is my life, my whole life. I only feel alive when he's with me and – and yes, Aunt, I would rather be his whore than any other man's wife.'

They were reduced not only to silence but to the rigid immobility of shock, and before they could recover I walked quietly from the room. Outside I was dimly conscious of Daisy's stricken face, but I did not pause. Once in my room I packed my weekend case and put on my coat. At the door I turned to look for the last time at the room which had held such wonders for the small frightened child who had first seen it: the tiny ruby vase which always held a few flowers, no matter what the season; the hissing gas fire in winter; the thick soft carpet and puff-ball of eiderdown; the chintz curtains and glowing water-colours on the walls – all entirely novel and fascinating then, all touched and marvelled at. The room had welcomed me as a child and had continued to do so through all the years, but now I wondered if I would ever return to it.

When I opened the drawing-room door my aunt and uncle looked up, white-faced and suddenly not just elderly but very, very old. 'I'm going now,' I said quietly, not quite able to keep the tremor from my voice.

Uncle Julian immediately struggled out of his chair. 'Oh, now, Minette. There's no need – '

'Please,' I said humbly, 'I want to be by myself.'

'But, my dear child, you're ill – you need rest.'

I just shook my head, unable to speak, and as I closed the door I heard him say, 'Oh, my God, what *are* we to do?'

11

This was a thought that echoed and re-echoed in my mind through the endless train journey and sleepless night. The answer stared me in the face the following day when I saw the placards: MYSTERY DEATH OF AIR ACE'S WIFE. The words might not have registered had there not been a blown-up, full-page photograph of Rosalind Cleary on the front pages of the midday editions.

'Wich yer wan', Miss, *Standar'* h'or *Evenin' noos* – y'aw rite, Miss?' The crumpled face of the old newsvendor swam before my eyes, but I must have paid for the paper because it was thrust into my hands. Slowly, I read:

Mystery surrounds the death in the early hours of this morning of Mrs Rosalind Cleary, the beautiful twenty-nine-year-old wife of Group Captain D.M. Cleary, DSO, DFC and Two Bars, AFC, one of the RAF's most famous war-time bomber pilots.

It is understood that Mrs Cleary had a fall on the stairs of her home in Eaton Place, and although Group Captain Cleary called an ambulance at once, his wife was found to be dead on arrival at St George's Hospital. Earlier the couple had spent the evening dining and dancing with friends at the Savoy Hotel. Mrs Cleary was the elder daughter of Sir Reginald Chandler, the well-known financier, of Friary Court, Godalming, Surrey. Her marriage at St Mark's, North Audley Street, in December, 1939 to the then Flt Lt Cleary was the wedding of the year and followed a whirlwind romance, the couple having met on a plane returning to England from Canada. Flt Lt Cleary had been on a training course in that country and Miss Chandler was returning with her father after his successful missions to Washington and Ottawa.

There is one child of the marriage, a daughter, Emma Jane, born in 1943. Group Captain Cleary, who was shot down over the Ruhr in 1942, spent ten months as a POW in Stalag Luft III before finally escaping, after several unsuccessful attempts.

After his return to England the Group Captain held a staff appointment at the Air Ministry before being posted to Cairo. He has since held important appointments at Rhine Army Headquarters at Bad Oeynhausen, Germany, and SHAEF, Paris. It is understood that he had only returned from Washington a few hours before his wife's death.

His current posting is at the Air Ministry, where he is regarded as one of the most brilliant of post-war RAF officers. Group Captain Cleary was unavailable for comment today.

I have little recollection of the remainder of that day; I know I did not return to the office and believe I walked for hours, because there is some memory of dashing up the stairs to my room in time for the six o'clock news, and then being almost unable to hear for the pounding in my head that: 'Following information received, the police are to investigate Mrs Cleary's death.' There is some memory, too, of sitting without light, heat or food – did I sit in that room all night? Did I think? Could I think? Looking back now, I believe I anticipated what was to happen and certainly events were to proceed with all the inevitability of a Greek tragedy: the following day Dan was shown in the newspapers accompanying police to Knightsbridge police station to make a statement. The photograph was of him sitting in the back of the car, staring ahead, his face a mask; later 'A man was helping police with their enquiries,' and finally the charge: 'Group Captain Cleary was being remanded in custody for the murder of his wife.'

Within minutes of the announcement Uncle Julian was on the line: 'Minette, you have heard the news?'

'I – yes.'

'What? I can't hear you.'

It needed a superhuman effort to raise my voice above a whisper, but I must have succeeded because my uncle continued, 'Well, then, listen carefully: you must not try to see or communicate with – the prisoner.'

'Oh, but I *must* let him know that I believe completely in him.'

'NO, MINETTE. NO! You will do him the greatest disservice and only succeed in getting yourself involved. Don't you see, if there's any doubt over a motive, the suggestion of there being "another woman" could provide one? So I implore you, for everyone's sake, to remain absolutely silent. And I also strongly advise you to keep away from the Court hearings.'

'Yes, yes, but Dan must be going through such hell! There must be *some* way of letting him know that he still has friends.'

'*I* will write and remind him of our meeting at the Club and express, on behalf of my family, our faith in him and good wishes.'

'Oh, Uncle Julian, thank you, thank you – oh, bless you! Will you write tonight? Will you be *sure* and let him know?'

'I give you my word – and, Minette?'

'Yes?'

'I want you to remember that your home is where it has always been and always will be – at Solenthaven. We want you to come and rest there.'

'Darling Uncle Julian, thank you. I-I don't know what will happen when Dan is freed, but I must stay here for now, I must be near him.' After that conversation

I felt a little less distraught, for Uncle Julian was the type of Englishman whose word was known throughout the world to be his bond: I never doubted for a second that he would write to Dan and, in the most discreet words, manage to convey my feelings. At that stage, too, I was sure that Dan would soon be freed; the police had made a terrible mistake, and my main concern was for his humiliation and grief – and, it must be admitted, for the effect the whole situation would have upon our relationship.

But then Dan was committed for trial at the Old Bailey and it was announced that he had resigned his Commission to 'save bringing further disrepute upon the Service'. And I finally faced the reality: he was to be put on trial for his life; if found guilty he would be hanged. I think I became a little mad then. Certainly I was a haunted wraith, tortured by nightmares and seeing a noose in a scarf, a shoelace, or a strap-handle. Trains and buses moved to the rhythm of 'Hanged by the neck until you are dead . . . dead . . . dead.' It was in the rustle of trees, the swish of tyres in rain and the moan of wind through war-torn buildings. It echoed in my head when I tried to swallow, and closed my throat. And all the while my mood swung wildly from despair to an hysterical belief that God would never allow the execution of a totally innocent man. I had only to pray hard enough and Dan would come walking towards me, smiling and free. When a voice whispered that prayer had not saved the people of the camps, I tried to block it out. No wonder that when I set off for the Old Bailey I felt light-headed and barely able to concentrate for more than a few moments at a time.

Although I arrived a good half-hour before the door to the public gallery was to be opened, a queue, formed mostly of fashionably dressed women, was already waiting. This was something I should have anticipated for the glamour, beauty and wealth of the drama's principals had been just what the newspapers needed to boost sales when the excitement of victory was fading. All the national dailies had done their sensational best, giving the case front page coverage. I railed at myself for not arriving sooner, and the fear that I might not get into No. 1 Court made me push forward ruthlessly as soon as the street door was opened.

There were several flights up to the various Courts, but although they were short, by the time I reached the top I was struggling for breath and my legs felt like jelly. Will-power alone propelled me forward and into one of the last remaining seats in the small public gallery. The Court was smaller than expected and very light with cream-washed walls and pale woods, the only real colour being in the scarlet and gold scabbard of the City's sword which hung over the huge centre chair, always reserved for the Lord Mayor. Although the gowned and be-wigged figures were moving about in a leisurely and relaxed manner they, and everything about the Court conveyed the whole weight, the absolute inexorability of the Law. I thought of all the men and women who had stood in the dock and heard that their lives were to be terminated. And how many, like Dan, had really been innocent? I wondered, with a shudder.

When a stentorian voice commanded 'All stand!' I stood with difficulty to see the Judge enter, robed in scarlet, sashed with black, and carrying – to my surprise – white gloves. But when the usher began the traditional greeting, his voice seemed to ebb and flow, while heat washed over me. But I mustn't faint, I thought desperately. I'll be taken out and might not be allowed back.

'Bring up Daniel Michael Cleary!' boomed another voice, and the heat suddenly gave way to an icy coldness that left me shivering. Then my darling appeared, and as he walked towards the bar of the dock to face the Judge, my first thought was of how thin he looked, but he was utterly calm and automatically stood with shoulders back and head held high.

141

'Daniel Michael Cleary,' intoned the Clerk of the Court, 'you stand indicted on a charge of murder, in that you, on the 20th January last, did murder your wife, Rosalind Anne Cleary. How do you plead: Guilty, or not Guilty?'

'Not guilty,' Dan answered in a clear even tone.

Oh, Dan, my dearest darling, I am here, as near as I can be, sharing all this agony, this nightmare with you. And I am praying, Dan, every second I am praying . . .

He sat so still, only slightly turning his head to watch the swearing in of the Jury, and not moving again until the Prosecuting Counsel ended his opening speech to them with the terrifying words: 'You have heard the indictment put to the defendant on arraignment and you have heard his plea of Not Guilty. The issues are these: the Prosecution will submit that on the evidence the defendant is guilty of murder, or at least of manslaughter. If the Prosecution fails to prove either murder or manslaughter, then the facts into which you will be enquiring amount only to accident, in which case your verdict will be Not Guilty. These issues are for you and you alone to decide, according to the evidence.'

The nightmare lasted four days and my memory of them is strangely vague, no doubt because I was unable to either eat or sleep, and felt perpetually light-headed. Fortunately, I kept some of the newspaper reports and so have been able to record a certain amount of the evidence verbatim. And I also remember the excited buzz – hastily repressed by the Judge – when the Home Office pathologist stated that death had not been due to strangulation.

'What then is the significance of the marks on Mrs Cleary's throat?' persisted the Counsel for the Prosecution.

'There is a confusion of markings indicating the possible use of two hands,' conceded Dr Franklin, 'but the cricoid bone was not broken and both the internal and external bruising is extremely light.'

142

'Is there any possible connection between attempted strangulation and heart failure?'

'Yes, of course, as in any violent attack, especially on the frail or elderly. But Mrs Cleary was a perfectly healthy young woman.'

'Where there is an attempted strangulation, but the assailant's hands are released before death occurs, does the victim, if standing, tend to fall?'

'Yes.'

'Were there any injuries to Mrs Cleary's face consistent with a fall?'

'There was extensive bruising to the face, head and body, consistent with a head-long fall down a staircase.'

'Is there any evidence as to what caused Mrs Cleary to fall downstairs, such as marks of a blow or punch on any part of her body?'

'There are none that I could categorically attribute to such a blow.'

'Thank you, Dr Franklin, no further questions.'

Mr Gervase McMahon, KC, leader of the team for the Defence, then rose. 'Dr Franklin, in your experience, do victims of manual strangulation invariably struggle violently against their attacker?'

'Yes.'

'Were there any signs upon the body or dress of the victim to indicate that she had fought for her life?'

'None at all, except for some blood-speckled shavings of skin beneath the finger-nails of both hands.'

'Ah, yes.' Mr McMahon referred to his notes. 'The police surgeon has recorded inch-long scratches on the cheeks of the accused; is the debris under Mrs Cleary's finger-nails consistent with her having raked her husband's cheeks with her nails?'

'Indeed, this has been proved to be so.'

'Are you able to state whether the victim was conscious or unconscious when she fell to her death?'

'All the evidence points to her being conscious.'

'Can you elaborate, doctor?'

'Yes. Not only is the bruising very light, but there is no scratching of the skin, no haemorrhaging of the whites of the eyes, no protrusion of the tongue.'

'You have reported that there was a large amount of alcohol in the victim's blood-stream: was she drunk at the time of her death?'

'That would depend upon how used she was to alcohol; there was certainly sufficient in the blood-stream to create drunkenness in a person unused to alcohol.'

'Even if the victim were used to say, cocktails before dinner, wine with the meal, liqueurs or brandy afterwards, was there sufficient alcohol in the blood-stream to relax her body muscles to such a degree as to show minimum physical damage, as we have already heard?'

'I would say so, yes.'

'In your opinion, if Mrs Cleary had not been in a drunken state when she fell downstairs, would her injuries have been more serious, and the damage to her body more severe, due to tensing of muscle reaction throughout her body?'

'I would agree with that, and consider there would have been every probability of a break in the skin at some point and possibly a fracture of one or more bones.'

'Thank you, Dr Franklin. No further questions.'

A scientist from the Forensic Laboratory was then called and Mr Eustice Romilly, KC rose again for the prosecution. He picked up a plastic bag from the central table and crossed to the witness box. 'Does this contain the evening gown the victim was wearing at the time of her death?'

'Yes.'

'When you examined it, did you find any damage to it?'

'A few small bloodstains and one hole.'

'Will you find the hole, please.' The beautiful taffeta

144

gown in the blue of Rosalind Cleary's eyes was shaken out, its huge skirt rustling.

'Here,' said the witness, and Mr Romilly took the gown and moved to the Jury where he held it up to display a small round hole near the hem at the rear. He picked up another plastic bag and returned to the witness. 'Are these the shoes Mrs Cleary was wearing at the time of her death?' he asked, holding up a pair of satin shoes, one of whose long stiletto heels was almost completely broken off from the sole, and dangling. When the scientist confirmed that they were the shoes, he was asked if both gown and shoes had been examined in the laboratory and if it had been established how the hole and broken heel were caused.

'With regard to the hole, yes. We found that this was caused by the wearer stepping back and catching the heel in the gown. The heel, being extremely long and slender, could then have snapped, or it could have done so during Mrs Cleary's fall down the stairs.'

'In either event, would her balance have been affected?'

'Yes. The heel catching in the gown could have caused her to fall back or forward and, if the heel broke simultaneously, it could have precipitated her fall – in any direction – but I am unable to state categorically that the heel did break at that moment.'

'Were the shoes still on the victim's feet when she was found?'

'Yes. They were extremely expensive hand-made shoes and the fit was so perfect that they were not dislodged even by the violent jolting of the victim's body as she fell the length of the staircase.'

Mr McMahon then called Dan to the stand. He was extremely pale, but still calm, and his hand, as he took the oath, appeared to be quite steady.

'Group Captain Cleary – '

'One moment, Mr McMahon,' interrupted the Judge,

'I understand the accused has resigned his Commission in the Royal Air Force?'

'That is so, my lord, but at this moment in time I submit that he is still entitled to be addressed by his rank.'

'Quite so, Mr McMahon. Please proceed.'

'Thank you, my lord. Group Captain Cleary, did you on the evening of 20th January last return from an official trip to Washington?'

'Yes.'

'What was the exact nature of the trip?'

'For talks on defence and to visit certain locations. I regret I cannot be more specific as it was all top secret.'

'Quite so. The trip lasted eight days, I believe. How would you describe them?'

'Extremely arduous.'

'At what time did you return to Eaton Place?'

'Six P.M.'

'You have heard your host at the Savoy Hotel state that upon arrival your wife said to him, "Dan's in one of his bloody-minded moods."'

'Yes.'

'What exactly did your wife mean by the phrase "bloody minded"?'

'It was an expression she invariably used when she could not get her own way.'

'And what had occasioned her to call you "bloody-minded" on the evening in question?'

'There were two reasons: for the previous three weeks my wife had been pestering – '

The Judge looked at Dan over his gold half-moon spectacles. 'What do you mean, "pestering"?'

'Anything from snide remarks, barbed witticisms at my expense to screaming fury,' Dan paused, and when told to continue, added: 'My wife had been asked by friends to join them in a two-month tour of South Africa and I told her repeatedly that it was out of the question because I could not afford it. We had quarrelled many times about this, although before I left for Washington I thought she had finally accepted the situation, but as soon as I returned she started again – '

Mr McMahon forestalled the Judge by seconds. 'What precisely do you mean by "started again"?'

'She began by saying she hoped I'd had second thoughts about South Africa; then progressed to why did I expect her to remain in cold, wet, dreary London while I was swanning around the States.'

'*Swanning*?'

'I beg your pardon, my lord, I meant travelling around the States. I tried to tell my wife that it was not a pleasure trip, but she just laughed in my face. Then, when she told me we were to dine out that evening, I refused to go, saying that I was too tired and had to finish a report on my trip. My wife then began a long tirade on my shortcomings as a husband, always leaving her to socialize alone, but I remained adamant that I was not going to the party – until she accused me of cowardice: I was refusing to go because I could not face telling our friends that I was too much of a scrooge to let her accompany them to South Africa. I then capitulated and went to the Savoy.'

'You have heard evidence concerning the large amount of alcohol found in your wife's blood-stream, and your host has also testified that you each had four vodka martinis before dinner, champagne with the meal and liqueurs or brandy afterwards.'

'Yes.'

'Were you and your wife used to consuming that amount of alcohol in an evening?'

'We were used to cocktails and wine, but rarely drank champagne at home, although occasionally we would each have a brandy after dinner. When dining out we did, of course, drink considerably more.'

'At what time did you and your wife return from the Savoy on 20th January last?'

'At two A.M.'

'Did you both go immediately upstairs?'

'No, into the drawing-room, because my wife then told me that she had been asked to join a house-party at Gstaad the following week for a month's skiing, and if she could not go to South Africa, she would go to Switzerland. I told her it was out of the question.'

'What was her reply?'

'That she was going anyway. I asked her what she proposed to do about Emma – our daughter. She said Nanny would be here as usual.'

'Was that not acceptable to you?'

'No, because for two of the weeks I also would have been away, attending a NATO exercise in Germany.'

'Was that the only reason?'

'No. I did not want my daughter forever left solely in the company of a Nanny, no matter how good or caring. I felt very strongly that, as parents, my wife and I should spend all our available time with her, and I told Rosalind this.'

'Did she accept it?'

'No, she said she would not have Emma molly-coddled and was not prepared to give up her whole life to the child.'

'Was this a heated exchange?'

'I felt coldly furious, but my wife was shouting and visibly shaking with anger.'

'Were you both drunk at the time?'

'I suppose we must both have been very nearly, if not actually drunk, but we were affected in different ways.'

'How different?'

'I felt utterly exhausted, wanting only peace and quiet, whereas my wife appeared to draw on fresh energy for her aggressiveness.'

'So – did you continue to argue in the drawing-room?'

'No, I walked out, saying that if she went to Gstaad she need not bother to return.'

'What was your wife's reaction to this?'

'She followed me closely as I began to walk up the stairs, all the time ranting at me that if she left she would take Emma with her to America. I replied that I'd have the child made a Ward of Court, but my wife only laughed and said she and Emma would be out of the country before I could take any action.'

'Now, Group Captain Cleary, will you tell His Lordship and the Jury exactly what happened next.'

'By then I had reached the top of the stairs and I-I suddenly could not take any more. I turned round, saying something like, "If you don't shut up, I'll throttle you." My wife was immediately behind me and as I put my hands around her throat, she put up her hands and raked my cheeks with her nails . . . but then I heard Emma scream behind me. I dropped my hands and whipped round to her . . . I was conscious that in doing so the point of my shoulder had hit some part of my wife's body and I heard her cry out . . . but my total concern was for Emma, on whom I thought the scene would have the most traumatic effect. I ran to pick her up – the landing was dim and it was only then that I saw she was looking with terror beyond me. I turned back in the direction of the stairs, with Emma still in my arms, and saw my wife's body hurtling down them. Emma started to scream for her mother and mercifully Nanny appeared at that moment. I handed the child over and rushed to the bottom of the stairs. It . . . it was immediately apparent to me that my wife was dead.'

'And what did you do then?'

'There was a telephone extension in the hall. I dialled 999 and . . . when the ambulance came, I accompanied

149

my wife's body to St George's Hospital where the Casualty Officer confirmed that she was dead.'

There was utter silence and I do not think one person in all that crowded Court moved for a few seconds. Then Mr McMahon said very quietly: 'Group Captain Cleary, did you intend to murder your wife?'

'No, sir.'

'Did you intend to knock or push her down the stairs?'

'No, I was thinking only of Emma.'

'Thank you. No further questions.'

In order to try and stop the ceaseless darting of my thoughts, I had recorded the above in shorthand and when Dan's evidence was concluded my hopes soared. I looked at the Jury, convinced they would now show some sign of emotion: perhaps a lightening of expression to indicate their belief in his innocence, or sympathy for his ordeal. Instead, their faces remained impassive, with one man even stifling his yawns. The Judge, too, appeared entirely engrossed in shuffling his papers and I wanted to scream at them all to think, to understand that they were trying a man for his life.

I could record no more. Not only was I on the brink of collapse, but my overbright imagination had taken off and I kept seeing the noose being put around Dan's neck – such a powerful neck, such a young, strong body – and the only way to shut out the spectre was to pray. I had always prayed in times of great stress, but my aunt and uncle were not churchgoers, so I had been brought up with only the usual lukewarm faith of the Protestant majority. Now my petitions ranged from: 'You cannot let him die, You know he is not capable of murdering anyone in cold blood, and You must have loved him to give him so many talents, such splendid looks. You *cannot* let all that be lost to the world . . . not when so many millions have died', to: 'Dear God, if You will only spare Dan, I *promise* I'll never ask for anything else so long as I live', or: 'If You want me to, I'll go away, I'll not see him again, but please let him live, please God, please.'

The Judge's summing up was long, but I only really heard the end when he advised the Jury that if they were quite convinced that murder had been committed, they must bring in a verdict of guilty, but that if they had any doubts, the alternatives were involuntary manslaughter or acquittal.

The Jury were out for two hours. When they returned I again searched their faces for some sign but, apart from extreme tiredness, they remained without expression.

'Members of the Jury, are you agreed upon your verdict?'

A small roly-poly man stood up, his ugly Utility suit badly creased, his face solemn and flushed. 'We are.'

'Do you find Daniel Michael Cleary Guilty or Not Guilty?'

Please God, please, please . . .

'Not Guilty of murder, but guilty of manslaughter.'

'It's all right, just take it easy,' said the white-coated figure above me. 'You're in Bart's Out Patients, brought in from the Bailey because you kept on fainting, but you're OK.'

'The sentence,' I croaked, 'have you heard?'

'Yes, he got four years.' My face must have given me away. The young doctor continued, 'He'll be out in just over two and a half with remission. You know him, do you?'

Even then Uncle Julian's words came back to me and I shook my head. But I understood what St Peter must have felt when he denied the Lord. The room spun, 'Oh!'

'Yes, look, I want you to come in for forty-eight hours so that we can do some tests on your heart – it's a bit

151

tired. Nothing to worry about if you have rest. Been overdoing it rather badly, haven't you?'

I attempted a nod, but he misunderstood my expression. 'It's all right, you know. It's all free under the new National Health – treatment, nursing, medicines, food, the lot. Why not stay for a couple of days and let us set you on the right road?'

12

To everyone's surprise, Dan did not appeal and was sent
to the Scrubs to begin his sentence. On the first day that
he was allowed a visitor, I was there, waiting with all the
other women. We were a very mixed bunch, ranging from
young to middle-aged, from the haunted and vulnerable
to the hard-eyed and thin-lipped. I wondered if any felt
as excited, as tremulous, as I. All my clothes hung on
me and I'd had to resort to safety pins, but my hair
was newly shampooed and set, my nails varnished, and
for the first time in my life, my cheeks were carefully
tinged with rouge. The overall effect looked attractive,
I thought, and I just hoped Dan would be too pleased
to see me to notice how ill-fitting my suit was. And
at least I smelled delicious. He had given me for my
birthday a large bottle of *Je Reviens* and I had splashed
this liberally about my person. In one hand I clutched
a box covered in pretty striped paper and filled with a
selection of English fruit, and in the other two paperbacks
wrapped in the same paper. Thinking of what to take him
had exercised my mind for days beforehand, especially
the books. How could I take crime stories to someone
who had been on trial for murder? Or travel books to
someone incarcerated within four walls? Even a fast
moving adventure story seemed inappropriate, so in the
end I chose biographies.

Dan saw me as soon as he appeared in the doorway
and I smiled with all the love, all the joy I felt in my
heart, but his eyes seemed to look through me; he spoke
briefly to the Warder beside him, then turned and walked
back the way he had come. Oh, he's forgotten something,

I thought. *Oh, Dan, my darling, don't be long – there's not very much time.*

I was still smiling when the Warder came up to me and said, 'I'm sorry, Miss, he doesn't want to see you.'

I was speechless, gazing at the man with the smile frozen on my face. 'I'm sorry,' he said again, and I thought wildly, Surely I can't have changed so much that Dan doesn't recognize me? 'He also said, "Tell Miss Glyn not to come back again,"' said the Warder.

'I-I don't understand,' I said in a strange, husky voice.

'They're often a bit odd when they first come in, Miss – feel ashamed, or want only to be alone. I expect he'll write when he comes round and wants to see you.'

'Yes,' I said, nodding with great emphasis and then wondering why. 'But at least give him these.'

'I told him you had something for him, but he said he didn't want it, whatever it was.'

Oh, but Dan, I took so long sticking the paper and matching the stripes and the fruit is lovely – surely you'd enjoy that? And the books, I chose them so carefully.

'If you take them and give them to him later – ' I began.

'I'm sorry, Miss,' the man said yet again, 'but he was definite that he didn't want them.'

Why, Dan? Why? I don't understand, why are you shutting me out?

'Perhaps one of the others, someone who doesn't have visitors?'

'If you're sure, Miss?'

'Yes, quite sure, thank you. And – and when you see – Group Captain Cleary, could you – would you give him my love?'

He was a tough-looking man, that Warder, but I thought I saw compassion in his eyes. 'I surely will. And, Miss – don't take it to heart; I wouldn't mind betting that he comes round soon.'

'Thank you. Thank you very much . . . goodbye.' All the others had their men with them, many were smiling, most were holding hands and leaning towards each other, talking softly.

Never let the world see . . . but I didn't have to try very hard. No one even looked up as I passed.

It was a bad time, and coming so soon after all the horrors and then all the excitement, it was hard to bear. But soon I was putting all my hopes into writing the two letters a week which prisoners were allowed. I was sure that Dan's attitude was due to a misunderstanding and, telling myself that I'd always been better with the written rather than the spoken word, I settled down to tell him all that I felt. I knew he must be nearly out of his mind about Emma, who I assumed was being looked after by the Chandler family, and I offered to see her or do anything Dan could think of to help them both. Every evening I rushed back from the office with racing heart to look for a reply, and each week I wrote my two letters. At first I tried to write at length, but eventually the letters became little notes, telling him how much I loved him and begging for a reply.

One evening some eight weeks later when I came into the entrance hall I saw a foolscap manilla envelope with the unmistakable writing. I clutched it, so overcome by a mixture of emotions that all the breath seemed to leave my body and my legs to be suddenly so weak that I had to haul myself up the stairs, like an old woman. Even finding the key to the flat door and inserting it in the lock was a major operation because of my trembling hands. Eventually I got myself into my room and frantically untangled my fingers from the string bag of groceries, the umbrella and handbag. It was such a bulky envelope, and I thought, He's written telling me everything and now it will be all right . . . I tore it open and drew out the bundle which was held together by a rubber band. It consisted of all the letters I had written. Not one had been opened.

'You must let him be,' Uncle Julian said decisively. 'Good heavens, Minette, the man has lost everything! His wife – and no matter what he thought of her, she *was* his wife – his child, his career, his good name, and his liberty! It is perfectly understandable that he does not wish to see you or anyone else at present. I imagine he is licking his wounds. So let him make the next move.'

The words made sense, and now that Dan's life was no longer in peril, I began to realize just what he must have been suffering over the past weeks. My heart bled for him and I wished – oh, how I wished – that he would let me share it all with him. I still waited every day for a letter, but there was never any word, and over the months hope gradually faded. So often I came near to writing again and that first Christmas I did send a card, just with a message: 'Always and forever – Mäuschen.' Cunningly I had typed the envelope, hoping that curiosity would make him open it; there was no response, but at least it was not returned.

'If you're determined to wait for this man, as I suppose you are,' Uncle Julian said on one of his visits, 'then I suggest you occupy yourself. Sitting alone in that dingy room night after night will not help Cleary and will definitely be detrimental to *your* mental and physical state. I suggest, for a start, you return to Conroy's class.'

As usual he was right and Philip greeted me warmly, but with concerned eyes. 'What on earth have you done to yourself, Minette? You never did look robust, but now you're a wraith!'

I managed to fob him off without any lengthy explanation and then asked about David. 'No, I've not heard since he left for Australia,' Philip said, 'nor do I expect to.' He turned to lay out his brushes. 'David took a real shine to you, didn't he?'

'Yes,' I said sadly, 'but I honestly did not encourage him or lead him on – '

'It's all right, dearie, don't look so upset! Haven't you ever heard that all artists and writers need heartbreak to make them produce their magnum opus? You've probably done young David a very great favour!'

Only George remained of the original class, seemingly with his 'nerves' under complete control. He, too, was welcoming but when he sidled up to me some weeks later to say quietly: 'Fancy a spot of dinner some time, do you, Minette?' I did not hesitate.

'Thank you, George,' I said, trying hard to sound cold, 'but I am entirely committed, both emotionally and physically.'

'Oh, right, dear girl, right! Best of luck to you!' he answered, backing off. He never approached me again.

In the New Year another great sorrow overwhelmed me. Uncle Julian died in his sleep, a lovely death for a dear and gentle man. It was a terrible shock to us all and hit me particularly hard for he had taken the place of my parents and for so many years had been my 'guide, philosopher and friend'.

'Of course the house and furniture will have to go,' Aunt Alexa said after the funeral. She had borne the brunt of the whole tragedy, but characteristically had also retained all her habitual calm and reserve.

'Could we keep the house if I got a job here and came home to live?' I asked tentatively.

'Certainly not, Minette!' The reply was instantaneous and I looked at her sadly.

'You'll never forgive me will you, Aunt?'

'Forgive is too strong a word, but I will certainly never condone your behaviour.'

Of course it would be impossible for her to understand, I thought, she'd obviously had a very insensitive husband and just didn't have the faintest idea what all-consuming

157

love was. 'So what will you do?' I asked aloud. I had been shocked at the very small amount of money Uncle Julian had left. Apart from a bequest of one hundred pounds to Daisy, everything had been willed to my aunt.

'You must realize, Minette, that when Julian made that will he was convinced that by the time he died you would be safely married – that is why he did not leave you a half-share of everything. But of course you must take the Sèvres, the silver and all the linen, together with as many of his paintings as you wish. I should be obliged if you would pack these before you return to London and arrange for their removal as the house must be put up for sale immediately. I shall find a small hotel in Eastbourne and settle there.'

'But wouldn't a small flat be better?' I asked, knowing how much she valued her possessions.

'You simply do not understand,' she said, and I knew by her curt tone that she was concealing deep feeling. 'Since the Japanese conquest of Malaya, I've had no income at all – the few shares I owned were in rubber. With Arthur's death in 1944, my maintenance stopped and since then I have been entirely dependent upon Julian; that is another reason why he left everything to me, and I require all the capital I can obtain in order to live at all.'

'I had no idea,' I murmured, horrified. 'And – what about Daisy?'

'Daisy will go to her great-niece,' my aunt said firmly.

'Oh, not that awful Gladys!' I exclaimed. 'Daisy has never been able to stand her!'

'Nevertheless, she is fortunate to have a relation willing to take her. The alternative would be an institution.'

'Oh, no!'

'Oh, yes,' said Aunt Alexa implacably, 'for some time Daisy has been failing; she has arthritis of the hands and feet, so other employment is really out of the question.'

'But – she's spent her whole life with us – we have been her family!'

'Well, what can I do?' my aunt exclaimed, for the first time showing signs of strain. 'I cannot take her with me! If I live too long, I shall also end up in an institution.'

I ran to put my arms about her shoulders. '*Of course* you won't! As if I should let that happen!'

She very gently threw off my arms, but there was a faint smile on her face as she said: 'Thank you, Minette, but I think you will need all your resources to look after yourself.'

There was no difficulty in selling the house and its contents for Solenthaven had been heavily bombed and people were desperate for accommodation, but it was a great sadness to see all the lovely old furniture being carried out and to walk through the empty rooms knowing that I would never set foot in them again. Worst of all, though, was saying good-bye to Daisy. The awful Gladys did come for her, but her smile seemed entirely false to me, and Daisy, suddenly shrunken and with all her old fighting spirit quite gone, was a pathetic little figure. My aunt, ice calm and ramrod straight, held out her hand. 'Well, Daisy, I shall write to you and I hope you will write to me, but for now, goodbye and good luck to you.'

'Goo'bye, ma'am,' Daisy quavered, 'I 'ope you'll be 'appy in H'Eastbourne. Thank you for everythin' an' – an' I'm sorry for all the times I h'argued wit'you.'

'Thank you, Daisy.' Aunt Alexa inclined her head graciously, but I swept Daisy up in a great embrace. 'Oh no,' I cried, 'you've given your whole life to us, Daisy, and it is we who should be grateful to you for looking after us so well . . . I'm so sorry we have to part, but we will keep in touch and I do so hope you will be happy.'

'An' you, too, Miss Minet, an' mind you h'eats proper food now – '

'Aw, come on now, Auntie, do!' said Gladys impatiently, even as she smiled ingratiatingly at us. 'Cheers, ladies!'

So Daisy picked up the two brown paper carrier bags – is that all, I thought wildly, just two paper bags after a life-time? Not even *one* case? – and, sobbing noisily, she turned away. Gladys did not even offer to take one of the bags.

'What did she mean, saying "cheers"? We'd not offered her a drink,' demanded Aunt Alexa indignantly.

But my thoughts were too chaotic to answer and instead I burst out angrily, 'I don't trust that woman!'

'No, of course not,' agreed my aunt calmly, 'she is only after the money Julian left Daisy. Let us hope she at least makes life bearable for the poor old woman.'

But there was no need. Within a week Daisy, too, was dead; 'heart failure' was the official verdict, but I thought 'heart break' more likely.

'You'd better take these,' my aunt said later, and with a start of surprise I saw that she was holding out my mother's wedding ring and the only photograph taken of my parents on their wedding day; these were so precious that I had always left them in Uncle Julian's safe, but with so much happening I had entirely forgotten them. Later, I slipped the ring on my finger; it fitted perfectly, but I quickly took it off, feeling strangely that I had no right to it, for on the inner rim were the letters 'H. to L. 19.6.19'. I studied the photograph and marvelled that although they had eloped, my mother had still managed to wear a picture hat, with a full-blown rose dipping its brim, and a softly draped dress. She was seated, one foot in its strapped shoe with a Louis heel placed forward, as though she were ready to leap from the chair, but her face was dreaming and tender. My lovely mother, whose romantic attachment to the Stuarts had caused her to name me after a Princess of that House, Henriette Anne, who was always known

160

within her family as Minette. Strange, I thought wryly, that she, too, should have had one shoulder higher than the other . . . In the photograph my father was standing and still wearing the uniform and badges of a Captain in the Hampshire Regiment; he looked young, confident and happy, so different from the broken man I remembered. When I took the photograph out of its frame, I saw written on the back in faded writing 'Lorna Glyn', and underneath 'Mrs Hugh Glyn', and I remembered the day in Germany when I had written 'Minette Cleary', looking at it longingly before guiltily tearing it into fragments.

Perhaps it was all that, and the solicitor's letter coming so quickly after, which first gave me the idea – the idea that was so daring, so exciting, that it was to occupy almost all my thoughts over the remaining two years. In the letter, the solicitor in Nairobi stated that he had received an offer for the land I still owned and did I wish to sell? I wrote back at once, saying that in no circumstances would I do so.

They were frugal, those two years. I was struggling to save every penny, so there were no more theatres or concerts, and the only holiday was a very occasional weekend at Eastbourne. Yet, because of the idea engendered by that letter, I was galvanized into action, joining first a dressmaking class and, soon after, a cookery class. 'Not to learn the Cordon Bleu type,' I explained, 'but bread-making and the ability to conjure up nourishing meals from only the basics.' Fortunately, after years of food rationing, such cookery was widely known and still taught.

But my dressmaking teacher was puzzled: 'Why do you always bring cotton materials and only to make shirts and very simple frocks, Minette! Don't you ever go to parties?' 'No, never,' I replied, hoping that my enigmatic smile would be sufficient to discourage her. A second-hand

161

sewing machine purchased, after much deliberation, for five pounds was my only extravagance. But it will really be a necessity, I told myself firmly, and will save hours of hand sewing, which I'll not have time for. Apart from reading voraciously, my other great occupation was visiting my favourite museums and galleries, for if my plan came to fruition I doubted whether I'd see these treasures again. Yet with my leisure time now very limited, my life was also very solitary. I had very little in common with most of my fellow art students and at the office only the middle-aged remained. It was also a time of readjustment for people everywhere, with money, fuel, transport and even food still scarce, and at the end of the day everyone tended to hurry away, knowing there would be long queues for transport with, at the end, a cold or at best only a moderately warm home.

So when a London pigeon suddenly swooped down to rest on the open top half of my sash window, I was absurdly pleased. I never knew why it should have chosen my window out of the many thousands, but every morning at first light it would fly off, returning every evening just to fold its wings and sleep. Its presence and the tiny sounds it made were strangely comforting.

Then, as the day for Dan's release drew near, I was in a fever of excitement and apprehension. Over and over in my mind I rehearsed my first words to him – yet when the moment came, I could not speak and was only just able to walk towards him, trying to smile. He was extremely thin and very pale, but he walked through the small door quickly, head down, looking neither left nor right. When he realized there was someone in his path and looked up, I saw shock in his eyes, but his expression did not change. Nor did he stop, but said as he passed me, 'What are *you* doing here?'

'Dan, darling, I've come to take you home – '

His bark of laughter was harsh. 'Home? That's the joke of the year! Anyway, I'm not coming, so you can just clear off!'

'Dan – wait! We have to talk!'

'Oh no, we don't, not on your life!' I could not tell whether his choice of words was intentional or just unfortunate and my main concern was to keep up with him. Always before he had walked in step with me, but now he strode out briskly, and because I was turned towards him, I was having to take strange sideways skips and hops.

'Dan, I love you, I want – '

'Then that's just too bad!'

'Dan, if you'll only – '

He stopped so abruptly I almost lost my balance and instinctively put my hand on his arm; he shook it off instantly and turned to face me, eyes narrowed. 'Can't you get it into your head that I don't want you? Or does nothing register? Listen now, and for God's sake try to take this in: I don't love you, I don't want you, I don't even like you. So, once and for all, will you leave me alone?'

There are no words that can even begin to express what I felt at that moment; all the accumulated pain and grief of the past years could not remotely compare with it, and the fury in his eyes alone was like a stake through my heart.

I was still standing there, motionless, long after he had walked from view. I have no recollection of making my way back to the flat. But somehow I did get there and took to my bed, burrowing down in it with the clothes over my head, in an animal wish to hide in darkness. I remained there for the next forty-eight hours, getting up only to go to the bathroom, and even that became almost too much of an effort in the end. The truth was that I had come to a full stop, and had neither motivation nor wish to do anything other than remain in bed without food, sleep or even movement. Deep clinical depression was already setting in when the telephone rang, and continued to ring at intervals during the day, but I was incapable of answering it. When hammering on the flat door started, I ignored that too, even though it became more and more urgent. It was only when blows started to thud against it and the wood to creak, that I dragged myself out of bed and went, barefoot and clad only in a nightdress, to open it. Then I fell back with a cry. I had instantly recognized the figure that stood hunched, ready to hurl itself with clenched fists against the door. I thought only that he had come back to torment me, and closed my eyes tightly so that I could not see the hatred in his.

'Oh, my God,' cried a furious voice, 'what have you done to yourself?'

I was swept off my feet and carried back into my bedroom. 'You stupid little thing! Don't you know that no man, least of all I, is worth letting yourself go for, like this?'

I did not answer, nor open my eyes, and was dumped none too gently on to my bed and the clothes thrown over me.

'This room's like an ice house,' the voice went on, sounding more exasperated than furious now. I heard the gas hiss loudly and the scraping of a match, then the fire ignited with a tiny explosion and there was the pad-pad of feet moving towards the window. The cords were pulled vigorously, then there was a startled exclamation. 'Christ! There's a bloody bird here!' And my pigeon, equally startled, took off with a squawk. The window was closed with a bang, and I sensed that Dan was looking at me. 'Why have you got your eyes shut?' he demanded harshly, but I only slightly shook my head and pulled the sheet over my mouth. 'Oh, don't be so stupid – open your eyes!' The sheet was whipped away from my face. 'Well, tell me why not then?'

A tear fell from the corner of my eye as I whispered: 'Because I can't bear to see you look at me with such hatred . . . '

For a few seconds there was complete silence and I thought wildly, this will be the *coup de grâce*, but instead he said brokenly, 'Oh, Mäuschen,' and, unbelievably, I felt gentle hands on my shoulders. Hardly daring to breathe, I opened my eyes: Dan was down on his knees beside my bed, his bright head abjectly lowered so that I could not see his face. When I heard the first harsh sobs, I drew him against me so that his head was nestled into my shoulder. And I just held him, making tiny, soft sounds, like a mother soothing a distraught child. The tears of an infant are always heart-rending, those of a pretty woman appealing and dramatic, but neither is as moving as the sobs of a strong man . . . yet as I held my love I felt the tension slowly leave his body, and when at last he turned his ravaged face to me, I could see that he was exhausted but calm.

'Forgive me, Mäuschen, if you can,' he whispered humbly. 'I knew you would be terribly hurt . . . but I had resolved . . . ever since the trial that I would not drag you down with me. That's why I refused to see you or open your letters . . . I knew it would take a lot for your love to die, and when I saw you waiting for me, I thought I must finish it once and for all by being as brutal as I could make myself . . . but afterwards I remembered Eleni, and your saying that she was dead, although still breathing, and I was afraid I had killed you in the same way . . . I couldn't go through with it, Mäuschen, I had to know. I kept ringing and ringing this number, and then waited all day outside your office. When all the other secretaries came out but not you, I asked one of them and was told you had not been in and they knew nothing about you. I was so afraid, so desperately afraid. I was ready to break down the door . . . '

Shyly I took his face in my hands and looked into his eyes. 'Nothing you could ever do would kill my love for you . . . but if you hadn't come, I might never have got up from this bed.' He kissed me then and it was wonderful . . . wonderful. All the sadness, the terror, were as nothing. We were together and as close as it is humanly possible for a man and a woman to be; my only regret was that I did not have more than one pair of arms and legs to wrap around the body of my love.

Afterwards, a *very* long time afterwards, I realized I was ravenously hungry. 'Stay there,' Dan said, 'while I make scrambled eggs for us both – I tell you, Angel, that until you taste my scrambled eggs, you've not tasted scrambled eggs at all.'

Although he was joking, I found his words to be true and I just could not have enough. 'How long is it since you've eaten?' Dan asked, after making me a third helping.

'Years,' I mumbled, rudely speaking with my mouth full.

'Oh, darling!' he chided smilingly, but in a sense it was right: I had eaten to remain alive, but it was certainly years since I had enjoyed a meal, or even actually *tasted* food.

'Your nose is bright red,' Dan commented, his eyes tender.

'I don't care,' I answered as I scraped my plate, then settled back with a happy sigh.

But great as my euphoria was, it soon became apparent that Dan was greatly changed; formerly he had always been amusingly extrovert, but now when we were silent for even a few minutes, he would sit hunched forward, staring into the fire, the lines deeply etched on his haggard face. Poor darling, I thought with great sadness, my poor,

poor darling. Eventually I knelt down beside him to lay one hand against his cheek and he turned first to kiss my palm, then to rest wearily against it. 'Was it absolutely terrible?' I asked softly, and as he hesitated, I pleaded, 'Please tell me.'

The words seemed to burst out then: 'I could have stood it all, had it not been for the other inmates; they seemed to think because I spoke the King's English and had held rank, that I'd literally got away with murder and goaded me constantly. Then one day I realized . . . I acknowledged . . . that they were right: I *was* guilty!' At my involuntary gasp, he turned quickly to me: 'No, I didn't murder Ros, but I did cause her death, because I should have had more control. After all I'd faced during the war, I should have been able to cope with one furious woman.' The mere ghost of a smile touched his lips as he said: 'After all, it was not an uncommon occurrence.'

'Perhaps it was *because* of all you'd endured during the war that your control finally snapped,' I suggested. 'But I, too, am guilty, darling. Our association must have added to all the tension. I shouldn't have let it develop.'

'That's not as I see it, Mäuschen.'

'Nevertheless, I believe these feelings will haunt us for the rest of our lives and it would be stupid to suggest we could forget them, but there's also the future to think of too.'

'No, that's where you're wrong: there is no future,' Dan said. 'I'm finished, Mäuschen, *kaput*, washed up, as they say. All I can do is fly, but pilots are two a penny now and, anyway, who would employ a man just out of prison?'

My heart began to thud loudly: this was the moment I had planned for and rehearsed so many times in my mind . . . now, NOW. 'But *I* know what you are going to do,' I said evenly. 'You're coming to Kenya with me to farm.'

Always in the past I had admired the quickness of his reactions, and this was the first time I had ever seen him lost for words. 'I'm quite serious, you know,' I said, determined to keep my advantage. 'The land is mine, all three thousand acres of it, but I shall ask my father's solicitor in Nairobi to draw up papers making you joint owner with me. Of course, we shall have to start from scratch; it will need clearing, and the house has long since vanished, but I'm sure we shall manage.'

Dan found his voice at last. 'I'm utterly flabbergasted,' he said, looking and sounding as though he were. 'It's a wonderful thought, and your generosity makes me feel very humble, but of course it's quite out of the question.'

'Why?' I asked, preparing for battle.

'Well, for one thing, I know nothing about farming.'

'Nor did ninety-nine per cent of the settlers who went out after the First War.'

'Yes, and didn't you tell me that many failed? Including your own father?'

'That's true, farming is always hazardous and particularly so in Africa, but many families did prosper and are still there. As for my father, well, he just gave up altogether after Mummy's death . . . and then, of course, there were the locusts: they came for three years in succession, turning day into night just by their huge numbers – stripping everything – breaking branches off trees by their weight – ugh! They were everywhere, and when one walked over them they emitted an awful odour *and* a revolting oily liquid – the birds ate so many that they could not rise from the ground!' I paused, unable to repress a slight shudder, and then said: 'Of course, they're not nearly such a menace now because there are agricultural pilots who spray all the breeding grounds. Dan, I know we could make it, I just know it!'

'Just give me one good reason why we should even contemplate such madness?'

'Because it's a wonderful country and it has everything: gorgeous scenery, climate, vast numbers of fascinating animals, friendly people – and it would be a fresh start for us both, so what have we to lose?'

'Apart from our lives from starvation!'

'No! We could always grow enough food to keep ourselves.'

'And what happens when the nice friendly people discover my past and become distinctly unfriendly?'

'Well, that would be just too bad, but I wonder if they would find out? After all, it will soon be three years since the trial, and an awful lot has happened on the world scene since. Also, a farm is very different from living in even a small village, and I remember Moonrise as being quite remote.'

'What happened to the farm after your father's death?'

'Uncle Julian, as my guardian, appointed a manager, but he was no good; I believe he drank rather, and let the house go to rack and ruin. When the war started, he went off as most of the young men did, and it was not possible to find another manager. Then something called, I think, the District Agricultural Committee decreed that no land was to be left uncultivated, even if this meant that neighbouring farmers had to help. Well, we only had the Mannington family nearby and by then Mr Mannington had joined the Army and been posted to Burma, where he was later killed . . . so his wife had to cope with her own huge farm and do something about ours, with only African labour and Italian POWs. After the war she sold up, and the people who bought her farm have been leasing some of my – our – land.'

We talked until far into the night, with me strenuously countering all of Dan's arguments, and at the same time trying to tell him all that I remembered of the farm. Eventually I wore him down and, to my intense joy, he said slowly: 'All right, we'll give it a try.' I ran to hug him.

169

'There's just one thing that worries me,' I said later when I felt it was slightly safer to raise the matter.

'Just one?' he said, smiling a little for the first time.

'Yes. Will Emma – accept me?'

Instantly the smile faded. 'Oh, Emma won't be coming with us . . . Ros's sister took her from the first; it was fortunate that she was married to an attaché at the American Embassy in London. Before they went back to the States, they adopted Emma. She thinks I'm dead.'

'Oh, no! Dan, why?'

'Better that than knowing her father was tried for the murder of her own mother.'

'But she saw – '

'I know. That's what nearly drove me out of my mind. I can only hope that she'll remember it as a nightmare rather than reality . . . she was told soon afterwards that Ros and I had gone to heaven together.' A mirthless laugh bubbled briefly in his throat. 'Some heaven!'

'I-I don't know what to say,' I murmured, completely defeated now.

'There *is* nothing. So – we'd better get married before we set off on this great venture.'

Coming at that precise moment, when I felt so upset about Emma, I almost failed in my resolve. Almost, but not quite. 'No, Dan darling, I'll not marry you, although of course I want to live with you for always.'

He had taken out a cigarette and, as I spoke, he paused, lighter in hand. Just for an instant I saw the hurt in his eyes, then it was gone and he looked at me steadily over the lighter's tiny flame. 'You're more sensible than I thought,' he said quietly. 'No woman in her right mind would want to marry me now that I have nothing to offer.'

So often in the past shyness had kept me silent, even when I felt most strongly, but I knew I dared not let that happen now. I grasped the lapels of his jacket and forced myself to speak: 'You have everything in the word I could

170

possibly want – yourself – but you've said so many times in the past that you would never marry again.'

'Oh, Mäuschen, you must know by now that there are times when I talk nonsense!'

'I know nothing of the kind – and I'll not let you feel that you have to marry me.'

'Well, apart from anything else, darling, what do you think people's reactions will be when they know that Miss Glyn and Mr Cleary are living together on an isolated farm?'

'That won't happen,' I said, smiling smugly. 'I intend to change my name to Cleary by deed poll and wear my mother's wedding ring – then everyone will naturally assume that we are married.'

He looked at me with the utmost astonishment: 'You're not really serious!'

'Never more so, I assure you!'

'But – but, Mäuschen, why make everything so complicated, so dangerous, when the solution is so simple?'

'Because, my love, you've just become free from one prison, and I'll not be the means of putting you into another.'

It was another long drawn-out argument, but in the end Dan gave in and we started to plan, although I do not think he believed any of it would really happen. Until the day when our passages came through: we were to sail from Tilbury in four days on an ancient cargo ship bound for Mombasa. By then I had my new name and new passport. I was still shown in that as 'Miss', of course, but I reckoned that once in Kenya this would not matter.

We were due to see Aunt Alexa the day before we sailed. 'It's better if she thinks we really are married,' I said, as I slipped on my mother's ring.

'She's not the only one,' Dan answered with such a lugubrious expression on his face that I was reduced to instant laughter.

171

'And I'll explain that she was not invited to the wedding because I wished to save her any embarrassment.'

Dan looked at me very seriously. 'I think it would save embarrassment all round if you went alone tomorrow.'

'Oh, darling, no!'

He looked down at his tightly clasped hands. 'Besides, I don't think I could face her.'

'Darling, she's had her own traumas and her motto has always been to face them head on . . . she'll probably never like you, but I can guarantee that she'll respect your courage in seeing her.' As Dan remained silent, I added softly, 'Long ago, after that first night at Altenau, you too told me that unpleasant things have to be faced and that to duck them only makes life harder. Dan, don't make me go alone.'

'No,' he said at last. 'No, of course not.'

As so often happens in life, the meeting was much easier than expected, even though I was almost as tense as Dan and he was *very* tense.

Aunt Alexa had declined our invitation to lunch but said she would 'receive' us – the use of so grand a word being particularly pathetic as the receiving was done in a room with shabby furnishing, a threadbare carpet, and only a one-bar electric fire to combat the Arctic chill. I was shocked too, by her appearance. She had lost much weight and looked slightly neglected, with a run in one stocking and her tweed skirt baggy at knees and rear, neither of which would she have tolerated even in the darkest, most difficult days of the war. She was distant at first, especially to Dan, but no female was proof against him for long, even when he was not trying, and as we left she actually smiled at him. Then she completely amazed us both by saying to him: 'May I ask a favour of you?'

'Why, yes, Mrs Hamilton, anything within my power,' Dan answered courteously.

'I have always understood that society in East Africa is very "fast" and you are an extremely handsome man. I have no doubt that many women will throw themselves at you, and I would ask you, please, not to let my niece be hurt.'

'Oh, I can assure you, there will be no one – '

'Thank you, Mr Cleary, but I have absolutely no faith in such assurances. All I ask is that you conduct any affair with as much discretion as possible, and that you do your utmost to keep Minette in ignorance of it. Even if it means lying to her.'

'Aunt, really!' I protested with a nervous laugh, but she ignored me.

'And I would ask you to remember that she has endured a great deal of suffering already.'

'I am very much aware of that,' Dan said quietly, 'and now I want only to make her happy.'

I hustled him away as quickly as I could after that, but it was impossible not to be touched and sad, for I doubted very much whether I would see my aunt again, and I knew that, in her own unique way, she loved me.

The next day, as we waited for the taxi, I suddenly had the most awful jitters. What have I done, I thought wildly, to have committed us both to a savage, distant land and a life-style we know almost nothing about? Supposing we become ill, supposing we do starve?

'Darling, you look so serious, so pale . . . I think I'm too much for you,' Dan said, but instantly I reached up on tiptoe to put my arms around his neck. 'You're not, of course you're not! Don't you dare go all cold and distant now!'

His arms enveloped me, warm and strong. 'I'm not likely to do that, am I?' he said, smiling down at me.

There was a distant hoot from the street below. 'That's our taxi.' Dan released me and moved to pick up the one case that had not already gone on board. He turned and held out his hand. 'Ready, darling?'

'Oh, yes, quite ready,' I said, feeling confidence surge back within me.

'Then let's go,' Dan said, and just for a minute all his old decisiveness was back. 'Let's go right now!'

And, hand-in-hand, we ran down the stairs together.

PART THREE

Kenya

13

My parents, like most of their generation of settlers, had travelled to their new farm by various means, starting with the long sea voyage to Mombasa, then by train, via Nairobi, to the railhead at Naivasha. From there they continued the long and often perilous journey by ox cart until a few angle irons in the ground, plus a number on a crude map, indicated that they had finally reached 'home'.

Dan and I were luckier. After much discussion and heart-searching, we had bought a second-hand Ford van, full of strange rattles and almost devoid of springs yet capable of quite good speeds, and part of our journey lay along the well-surfaced road constructed by Italian prisoners of war. It was only when we turned off this on to a narrow track and began to climb steeply that the real discomfort started, for the red-ochre *murram* was both dry and deeply rutted. Even though reduced to a walking pace, the van still stirred up great clouds of dust, but it was no use closing the windows for then the air became so dry that within minutes our throats were parched and our eyes watering. And all the while I, at least, was being bounced around – against the door, against Dan and, once or twice, even against the roof.

Dan, being so much heavier, fared better, but he was gripping the wheel so tightly that his knuckles shone white. 'God, I hope we don't break an axle,' he muttered. 'We should have bought a Land Rover or Fifteen Hundredweight. And what the hell do we do if we meet another vehicle coming the other way?'

'I don't know,' I croaked miserably, but it was obvious that we could do nothing: the earth, having once been beaten into a track, had then been eroded by rain until it was almost a foot below the level of the surrounding savannah and it would be quite impossible for our vehicle to surmount this.

'Not that there seems to be much fear of meeting anyone else,' he added. 'Do you realize that so far we've not seen a single soul since we left the main road? Nor is there any wild life.'

This was true. Apart from a few distant giraffe and a solitary buffalo, we had seen nothing. Yet in my childhood there had been great herds of almost all species around my home. And the landscape, too, was subtly different. I remembered the huge trees of camphor, podocarpus and cedar had reached down in great density to meet the lesser giants of the steep ridges. But now, although we were above the candelabra-shaped euphorbias, the thorns and eucalyptus, there were large areas of open ground where once the mighty forest had stood.

'We're climbing very high,' Dan said. 'I suppose we're on the right track. Do you remember any of this?'

'No,' I replied, 'but this must be all right because there hasn't been any turning off it.'

'Always providing we took the right turning from the valley floor. They don't seem too good on road signs in this country, but as far as I could tell from the map, this *was* right.'

Tears of tiredness and apprehension came to my eyes. It was already late afternoon, and within an hour or two the African night would descend. Then I remembered that this was just what had happened to my parents: they had still been labouring up the track when darkness had suddenly enveloped them and there had been no option but to continue, so my father had walked ahead with a hurricane lamp in one hand and a gun in the other, while one of their 'boys' had led the weary oxen. They had come to their site as the moon was rising and my mother, ever the romantic, had instantly decided that the farm should be called 'Moonrise'.

Dan's suddenly animated voice broke in on my thoughts: 'Look! the track is bearing left just ahead. Perhaps we're OK after all – perhaps we're almost there!'

And of course we were, for having curved to the left, we came upon a huge open escarpment which stretched on one side to where the Aberdares rose in a mighty wall. But it was the view from the other side which I instantly recognized; I had last seen it through a blur of tears when, as a ten-year-old child, I had left my home I thought forever, yet it had been stamped indelibly on my memory, as it must be for all who see it.

As the old van ground to a halt, I leapt out, calling urgently: 'Quickly, quickly, do come! I want to show you one of Africa's wonders!' And when Dan strode to my side, half-smiling, I grabbed his hand and pulled him forward into a run. 'There!' I said triumphantly when we reached the edge. '*There*!'

Below us the ground fell almost vertically some four thousand feet to the valley floor, where the road showed as a narrow ribbon and Lake Nakuru was a placid blue mirror, hazed with the pink of its two million flamingoes, and surrounded by the dazzling white of its soda ash. On the far side of the huge valley shadows were already darkening the steep forested slopes of the Mau, but farther to the north-west the mountain ranges were a shimmering lavender blue. It was a view breath-taking in its immensity, and as a small girl I had come every day to gaze upon it. Its beauty had never failed to uplift my spirit but now, as an adult, it made me feel extraordinarily humble. For this was Africa, a land already ancient when the first living creatures began to move over its surface, and this unique valley, which had been carved out by the most primordial of forces, had remained almost unchanged ever since. There was something quite mind-shattering, even terrifying, in the knowledge that long after all life, both human and animal, had become extinct, the setting sun would still rim the Mau with purple every evening; shadows of the great billowing clouds of white, lavender and indigo still race along the valley floor, and steam from the ancient volcanoes still rise lazily upwards, all in unbroken continuity from the beginning of the world until its very end.

'This must be one of the most magnificent sights in all Africa,' Dan said very quietly, 'and it's difficult to believe that we're almost on the Equator here – the air is so fresh and alpine.'

'Oh, yes,' I said happily, 'it's always like this, and when the sun goes down it will become really cold.'

Dan turned abruptly from the view. 'Then we haven't much time. Can you remember where your land actually begins?'

'I think so,' I said, retracing my steps, 'there was a fence with a five-barred gate about there and the drive ran in a straight line to the house which faced the valley squarely.' But of course there was nothing left, not even a few stones to indicate where the house had stood.

It was Dan who first noticed the ruts in the earth where the grasses and weeds were slightly shorter than elsewhere. 'Could this be the drive?' he asked. 'These ruts are quite deep as though motor vehicles have passed frequently, but perhaps not too recently, over the ground.'

'Yes, this must be it,' I answered. I walked forward slowly, looking desperately around, ignoring the slashing grasses and flocks of startled birds rising suddenly from them, and even forgetting to watch out for the many snakes whose habitat such ground was. At first I could see nothing familiar – then I noticed the cedar. It had been a solitary sapling when the house was built, but now it was an immensely tall, splendid tree, and suddenly I saw it all as it had been: the long, single-storey building with the five stone steps leading up to its encircling verandah, and the young cedar just behind one corner. There had been a lawn in front with flower beds all around, and at one end of the verandah, my Morning Glory. 'Minette shall plant the seeds,' my mother had said that last year, and I remembered how I had squatted down, the sun warm on my back, and with infinite care had taken each seed in my chubby fingers and put it in the narrow channel of earth. Every morning after I would laboriously clamber down the steep steps, armed with an old teapot, to water the plants. How proud I had been when they grew into a curtain of magnificent purple-blue flowers, and how happy I was when my mother sat increasingly in their shade, because of course I did not know that those were to be the last days of her life; instead, the moment she sank wearily on to the wicker-work chaise longue, I would clamber up to nestle against her softness – oh, how I had loved that softness and the coolness of her skin, no matter how hot the day. 'Tell me a story, Mummy,' I would say, and she always did.

Until that morning when she was no longer there, and instead the Mannington governess had arrived to take me 'to play with Clarissa and Charlie, you'll enjoy that'. But of course I had not, and when brought home that evening had instantly rushed to find my mother. The Mannington governess, bored and eager to be out of a difficult situation, had insisted on putting me to bed, saying only that my father would explain everything in the morning: 'So long as you are a good girl and go to sleep at once.'

Terror must have given me an infantile cunning for I obediently closed my eyes, but as soon as the sound of her car faded, I got out of bed and rushed along the verandah, screaming. It was then that a door at the far end had opened, and against the light my father's figure had loomed, large and formidable. 'Stop that bawling at once!' he had commanded in his usual brusque way which normally brought instant obedience. But not that night. I had flung myself against his knees, tugging at his trouser legs. 'Mummy! I want my Mummy!' I had shrieked again and again, until he had pulled me away from him and shaken me: 'Be quiet and listen to me! Your mother's dead, so you'd better start getting used to it at once!'

'But when is she coming back?' I had demanded, too terrified to understand.

'Never! I've just told you that, you stupid little thing! Now, go back to bed and don't let me hear another sound from you!' And I had gone, obediently trying to muffle my sobs, to clamber into bed and curl into a small ball of total misery. That night had marked the end of my happy childhood. I was just six years old. Remembering it all brought fresh grief, for now that I, too, had loved and almost lost, I understood my father as never before: he who had led men in many of the major battles of World War One, and been decorated for bravery, finally could not bring himself to accept that by allowing his young wife to become pregnant, he had ensured her early death. Instead, his grief had turned inward, and he had blamed me. Perhaps if there had been friends to help, or a less isolated farm, his attitude might have been more normal, but alone and deeply introverted, his anguish intensified until he, too, was dead. Oh, father, I cried to him silently now, as tears poured from my eyes, if only you had picked me up and cuddled me that first night, perhaps we could have comforted each other, perhaps we could have become close, for we needed each other so desperately.

'A bad moment, darling?' Dan's voice was very quiet, his arm warm and strong around my shoulders. I nodded silently, unable to speak, and crept close to him, hiding my face in his chest. He held me tightly until the worst of my sobs subsided, then produced a large handkerchief and said gently: 'A nice cup of tea is what you need, my love – oh, but what do we do about water?'

It was the faint note of near-panic in his voice that roused me. I stepped away from him, dashed away the tears, and said: 'It's all right, there should be a stream nearby.'

Once again it took a bit of finding because the undergrowth had long since obscured the path, but at last we found it, a large stream of crystal-clear water, bordered by luxuriant tree ferns and Arum lilies, running swiftly down from the mountains. A weaver bird fluttered agitatedly from its nest in the reeds and beneath the ferns there was a sudden darting movement. 'Fish!' Dan exclaimed. 'Just like trout!'

'It *is* trout,' I said, laughing now at his surprise. I bent down and swished my hands around in the ice cold water. Instantly it began to foam. 'Look,' I said, 'the oil from my skin is enough to make it lather.'

'Fascinating,' Dan answered, 'like everything else out here – it's certainly going to be a whole new way of life. Tomorrow we must explore and begin planning, but now let's get a brew going.'

Happily then I went with him to build a fire, help pitch our tent and put up our camp beds. Later there was much laughter as we tried to take baths: I fitted easily into the canvas bath, but Dan had to sit with his long legs over the sides, and with only one pail of hot water each, it was more refreshing than cleansing. Later still, when we tried to make love, we discovered that this was extremely difficult on a camp bed and were reduced to helpless laughter at the absurdity of our situation.

'The very first thing we're going to buy is a decent bed,' Dan promised, 'just as soon as we've got somewhere to put it!'

That night I felt not only great weariness, but great relief too. We had surmounted the first two hurdles: our voyage out and entry into Kenya. The latter had been very easy, but not so the former.

Dan's tension had mounted all the way to Tilbury and when we reached the dockside, I could actually see the effort he had to make just to put one foot before the other. To me, remembering the confident man he had been, always striding forward briskly, it was heart-breaking. But that was only the beginning. To enter the dining saloon was almost an impossibility until I whispered that our loitering outside would be noticeable, and then he stepped hesitantly inside, head down.

As our vessel carried mainly cargo, there were only twelve passengers, including ourselves, all seated at the one long table. As soon as I had got my own nerves under control, I surveyed them anxiously: there were four nuns and a priest bound for Uganda; two trainee managers for the Ceylon tea estates; an Indian doctor returning to Mombasa; and two wives of tea planters, also en route for Ceylon. Of course, we *had* to be seated opposite these two, the very ones most likely to have been interested in the trial. Certainly their eyes had widened slightly at the sight of Dan, but that had always happened and simply meant surprise at his splendid looks. In an effort to draw their attention away from him, I engaged them in almost non-stop conversation, which I was to keep up throughout the voyage, my voice eventually becoming quite hoarse with such an unaccustomed effort. Dan, meanwhile, continued to be monosyllabic, always eating very little and obviously impatient to leave. At all other times he shunned everyone and one night he disappeared. I searched frantically, with mounting terror, only to find him at last standing in the deep shadow of a life boat, hunched over the rail and staring at the black sea.

'Oh, there you are, darling,' I said, making a supreme effort to sound calm, but of course I could not control my fluttering breath or my body's shaking and he noticed at once. 'You're cold and frightened,' he said, putting his arm around me closely. 'What's the matter?'

'Oh, Dan,' I gasped in amazement, 'don't you realize how terrified I've been?'

'But why?' he asked, sounding genuinely puzzled.

'I couldn't find you, I didn't know what had happened – '

'You thought I might have taken a dive over the side?'

'I-I couldn't . . . Dan, you won't leave me, will you?'

'And let you face the consequences alone? No, that would be the most ignoble of all my ignoble actions.'

'Then please tell me why you are here; please let me share your thoughts.'

'I was thinking of many things: of Ros, being alive and full of fury one minute . . . and the next like a beautiful broken doll. Of Emma, who normally slept through all our parties, waking and actually coming on to the landing just at that moment – unbelievable even now!' As I remained silent, he added, 'I was also thinking of all the fellows in the Service who must have been so jealous when I outstripped them in rank; and of all those I had to reprimand, or order to pull their weight instead of just coasting along – often so much older than I – how they must be gloating now that Cleary, the blue-eyed boy, has come to such an ignominious end! God, it must be the talk of every Mess around the world!'

'But it was three years ago!' I protested vigorously. 'And probably already forgotten.' Yet I understood the bitter humiliation, the wish to hide, and the dread that someone some time would recognize him as the notorious Group Captain Cleary, and I thought sombrely, it will take years . . .

But as I lay cocooned in the warmth of my sleeping bag, listening to the sounds of the African night, I felt much more confident. Not only had we arrived safely at our destination, but already there had been laughter, and Dan had expressed enthusiasm for our surroundings. Already, too, for the first time since we had left England, he looked relaxed, with the lines of tension around his eyes and mouth less apparent. With so many new experiences to occupy him, I thought, surely the dark memories will recede. I must try to remember as much as possible about farm routine and crops, so that we don't make any unnecessary mistakes. Already the incessant rasping of cicadas sounded familiar, so did the night wind sighing through the great trees, the howling of a distant hyena, and the much nearer screeching of hyraxes. Furry little creatures, I thought sleepily, with huge soft eyes. I must remember to leave them the skins of fruit when we have some.

14

But the next morning I was made to realize just how fragile Dan's confidence still was. It had all started so well: the sky was cloudless, the sun like a benediction on our bodies, and I had managed to cook bacon and eggs on the fire – somewhat precariously, with everything tasting slightly of wood smoke, but the champagne air had made us very hungry and we ate it all with great relish.

Finally, Dan said, 'It's wonderful sitting here, but we really ought to get on. How about coming for a walk to see exactly what we have here? Then we can make a plan and decide on priorities.'

'Perhaps – ' I began, then broke off, catching my breath. We looked at each other in astonishment. 'Can it really be?' I asked, not fully able to believe my ears.

'Oh, yes,' Dan said decisively, 'and coming here too.'

The next moment it came into view, a Land Rover, slowly swaying up the drive, where it stopped, and a tall, very slim man leapt lightly out. He wore a shirt and trousers which looked as though they might once have been Army khaki and a battered double terai hat. We gazed at him as though he were someone from outer space, then Dan got to his feet, muttering, 'We'd better go and see what he wants,' and walked forward. I hastily fell into step beside him, half of me suddenly apprehensive, the other half thinking wildly, it's a bit like Stanley and Livingstone.

'Good morning to you both,' the stranger called out, with the merest hint of an Irish brogue in his fine baritone. 'I'm Patrick Keneally, your nearest neighbour.' As he came closer and lifted his hat, I saw that his face was hideously disfigured. Burns, I thought instantly, and then in panic: Oh, God, supposing he was RAF?

'Good morning,' Dan was saying, rather curtly, 'I'm Dan Cleary and this is – Minette.'

Patrick Keneally smiled, which made his face even more grotesque, and held out his hand. 'Welcome to our tiny portion of God's own country,' he said. I noticed that the first two fingers of his right hand were missing, yet his grip was surprisingly firm, the skin dry and curiously scaly. After greeting Dan he turned back to me: 'I do hope my appearance is not too much of a shock for you, Mrs Cleary? I do try whenever possible to warn people in advance – '

'Of course I'm not shocked,' I said, warming to him and suddenly wanting to take his hand again and say, 'I know just what it's like, I understand only too well!'

'The war, I suppose?' Dan was asking matter-of-factly.

Patrick Keneally nodded. 'Yes, I was caught in a blazing armoured car in the Ethiopian campaign and taken prisoner by the Italians; their medics did what they could for me, but really hadn't a clue, and by the time I was repatriated it was almost too late for even Archie McIndoe and his team to do anything.'

'What damned bad luck,' Dan said in the casual tone that fighting men always seem to use when commenting upon even the most horrendous of injuries.

'Well, I was lucky to get out alive, but it *was* tough on my wife who had said goodbye to a fairly civilized-looking cove, only to welcome back a monster!'

'But,' I said quickly, 'I'm sure she was so overjoyed to have you back that she didn't care one bit!'

Again he smiled. 'Almost her exact words! Sure, she's a great girl is my Terry-May and I can tell you're going to get on famously. She's looking forward so much to meeting you.'

Beside me, I felt Dan stiffen, but Patrick Keneally

continued: 'One of the reasons for this call is to ask you both to dinner this evening.'

'That's awfully nice of you,' Dan broke in at once, 'but I'm afraid we're not yet up to partying.'

'Ah, but this is not a party – just Terry-May and myself, plus a South African couple from Eldoret who are staying overnight with us.' As we were both silent, he added: 'Come now, you cannot plead a prior engagement, and at least it will save you opening another tin, so do say yes!'

To my own surprise, I took the initiative. 'Then, thank you, I think we'd love too, wouldn't we, darling?' I said, wrapping both arms around Dan's right and peering up into his face; to the stranger he must have looked quite normal but I, who knew him so well, could see the panic at the back of his eyes. 'Yes – yes, that's right,' he said hesitantly.

'Great! Come while it's still light so that you can negotiate the track's little idiosyncrasies. Our lands adjoin, but the house is about five miles from here – nothing in this country – and you just follow the fence until you come to our drive-in. It's the old Mannington place, of course, and still called Sweetwater Farm.'

'What I cannot understand,' Dan said, 'is how you knew we were here.'

Patrick Keneally laughed. 'I wondered if you'd ask that! Well, the old witch-doctor who lives on my *shamba* told me yesterday afternoon that you'd arrived.'

'But how could he possibly have known?'

Patrick shrugged. 'I have no idea, but these old boys often come up with some astonishing things; you just have to accept them as part of Africa's many mysteries.'

'Perhaps he could help us find the well,' I suggested.

'I can show you that,' Patrick answered at once. 'Also, like ourselves, you have a stream which is absolutely pure and gives a constant supply of wonderful water, something that the valley farmers would have given their eye teeth for in the days before proper irrigation was started. And the trout's great too!' He turned to Dan. 'Have you been farming at home?'

'No,' he said, his tone discouraging, 'I'm afraid we're quite new to this game.'

'Ah, well . . . you're not the first. And if I can help in any way, you have only to ask.'

'Most kind,' Dan replied, looking and sounding as though asking would be the last thing he'd ever do, but I rushed in with: 'If you could give us a few clues about what to grow?'

'Yes, of course. Wheat and maize do very well up here, even though we're near their maximum altitude; also pyrethrum, which is pretty trouble-free and in great demand, and vegetables for which there is always a ready market down in Nakuru. You have a very large acreage here, but I would suggest that you start by using the land I was leasing until the end of last year.'

I started. 'Oh, I should have realized! It was you who wanted to buy the farm, wasn't it?'

'Yes, but now I'm glad that you've come instead. We're still pretty isolated up here and it'll be good to have neighbours close by.' He turned back to Dan. 'Most of the acreage I did not lease has long since reverted to bush and will need to be cleared of all the tree roots, giant heathers and anthills which are not only very tall, but like concrete. To get rid of all that lot, you'd need a fair number of workers to dig down to the roots and oxen with chains to haul them out, but if you use the land I've been cultivating, you'll only need to plough and get the soil down to a decent tilth again before you start sowing. I would suggest a variety of crops and you should have some seeds, fertilizer and ground all ready for planting as soon as rain comes.'

He's so nice, I thought, and I should offer him coffee,

but I know Dan is longing for him to go. I cleared my throat. 'Our coffee seems to take ages,' I began tentatively, 'but if you can spare the time, I'll get some going.' He smiled down at me and I marvelled that despite the hideous scars great warmth, even sweetness, showed through. 'Thanks, but I must get back. You'll soon find that there are never enough hours in the day. See you both this evening, though.'

As soon as Patrick was out of earshot, Dan turned to me. 'Why, Mäuschen? Why did you ruin everything before we'd even started?'

I flung my arms around his waist, unable to bear the pain in his eyes. 'Darling – darling, it'll be all right, I know it will.'

'How can it be? Keneally's bound to ask me what I did in the war, and of course I'll have to say; then my name will ring a bell and in no time at all the whole sordid business will be known.'

'Dan, you're assuming too much – '

'Then there's the South African chap,' Dan said, as though he'd not heard a word. 'I met so many from their forces in the Middle East – he might even be one!'

'Well, so what?' I asked, trying another tactic in desperation. 'You've paid whatever debt you may have owed society, so what can happen even if they all recognize you and remember the case?'

'They can spread the story around, and if it should reach the ears of the Administration out here, things might become very sticky for us.'

I shrugged. 'Then if and when that happens, we'll just have to cope with it as best we can.'

'So you won't mind being ostracized?'

'I'll put up with it, and – and besides, we came here partly because we knew we'd be isolated.'

'Quite! Yet within hours of getting here, you jump at the first invitation!'

'Dan, don't you see? They're our nearest neighbours – no, our only neighbours. We'd have to meet them some time, and to keep on making excuses would inevitably start them wondering and thinking. Surely it's much better to go this once and then try to fob them off *if* they invite us again? At least then we could always say that we had too much to do here, or were unable to return hospitality or something.'

'Perhaps. Anyway, I'm going for a walk now.'

'Oh, right, I'll just change my sandals – '

'I want to go on my own, Mäuschen.'

The ever-present fear of rejection rose up like a monster before me then, and Dan never knew the effort I made to sound normal: 'Of course, darling, just as you wish.' Don't make a great thing of it, I told myself sternly, it's only a tiff and he'll come round after he's thought it through. Concentrate on what you're going to wear this evening! But the lump in my throat remained and I was suddenly irritated that I could not turn on a tap, or heat an iron to press the silk frock from my tin trunk. All I could do was to hang Dan's suit and the frock on branches of a tree.

He came back within an hour and put his arm warmly around my shoulders. 'Sorry, darling,' he said humbly, 'I'm so sorry.'

I turned at once within his embrace and hugged him. 'Me, too,' I whispered, 'but I understand.'

'You always do, don't you?' he said, his lips against my hair.

'And you know I always will.'

'Yes, that's something I *do* know.'

Instantly all was well with me again, but when we were almost ready to leave another crisis occurred. Dan was sitting on his bed, dressed except for putting on a sock, when he suddenly seemed to sag, with head bent and hands between his knees, the sock dangling from two fingers.

192

'What is it?' I asked fearfully.

Slowly he raised his head and the sight of his haggard face was like a blow over my heart. 'I can't go through with it, Mäuschen,' he whispered brokenly. 'I'm sorry, I just cannot face them.'

I went down on my knees before him and took his face in my hands, 'My dearest *dearest* darling,' I said, knowing instinctively that I had to be strong, and struggling for composure, 'you *must* face them, ·for if you do not you'll forever be a fugitive from meeting people. And probably without any need! This is the nearest we can get to living on a desert island, but even here we must have some contact with other human beings. And there have been scandals out here too, you know, it's not a puritanical society – don't you remember Aunt Alexa called it "fast"? And, I've just remembered, there was the Erroll case . . . You must have heard of that!'

Dan shook his head slowly. 'I don't recall.'

'Well, it was during the war: the Earl of Erroll was murdered out here and Sir Delves Broughton, the husband of Erroll's mistress, was arrested and tried for it; although he was acquitted, he later committed suicide. Now, you must admit, that's far more lurid a case than yours!'

'It seems so, but it happened during the war and is ancient history now, whereas I was tried for murder just over three years ago!'

'*And* were found not guilty!'

'Yes, but there'll always be a question mark over that: was I really innocent or just very lucky to get off with manslaughter?'

'Dan, did you murder Ros?'

Amazement replaced the beaten look in his eyes. 'Of course I didn't! You know that!'

'Yes, I do,' I said firmly, 'and it's the truth, so let's

193

always hold on hard to it. Surely the truth must still count for something!'

'You never fail to surprise me,' Dan said, the ghost of a smile touching his lips.

'That's nice,' I said, pretending lightness as I took the sock and began to ease it on to his foot, 'but I can't get this over your heel!' It worked; he bent forward, pulling on first the sock and then his shoe. I got to my feet, feeling suddenly weak. 'Do let's go,' I urged, and added silently: Before *I* start collapsing. When Dan stood up, I took his arm and hugged it against my side, 'I love you,' I said softly.

'I know you do,' he replied with great sadness in his voice.

I breathed a sigh of relief when we were finally on the track, but when we came to a belt of trees and there was a sudden tumult of noise, followed by a flash of black and white objects seemingly in flight high above us, we both started violently and Dan instinctively stamped on the brake. 'What the hell's that?' he demanded.

I peered up through the windscreen and then laughed. 'Oh, it's all right – just a family of Colobus monkeys going home for the night! If you look out of your window you might just see them high up in the trees.'

'Yes – yes, I can! They're taking enormous leaps from tree to tree – with something streaming out behind them.'

'That's a sort of cloak which they wrap around themselves and their babies in the rain.'

'I see they have young with them – good Lord, one of them appears to be climbing up its mother's tail! But is it the mother? The youngster has quite different colouring, even marking!'

'Yes, it's certainly the mother; all the babies start off white with purple faces, then change as they mature.'

'Now they've all disappeared, but what a din! How long does that go on for?'

'Quite some time.' I paused, then added gently, 'Perhaps they think the same of our vehicle.'

'Yes,' Dan answered as he put the car into gear, 'how right you are, Mäuschen!'

We knew at once that we were approaching the Keneally farm for the boundary was neatly fenced all along as far as the eye could see, and behind this the fields and pastures were in prime condition. All were empty now, but the sound of cow bells came faintly on the still evening air.

When we turned into the drive, memories came surging back to me, yet I had forgotten how attractive the house was: stone-built, with two pointed gables and a roof of golden thatch, it nestled against a back-drop of cedar, while in front lay a sweep of well-tended lawn, bordered by beds of brilliant shrubs and flowers. The scents of these, mixed with wood-smoke, filled the air. Reluctantly I looked to the far left where the paddling pool had been, and although that had been replaced by large rose beds, I saw it as it had been on that day when Mrs Mannington had suddenly told me to bend forward. I was wearing – of course – one of Clarissa's bathing suits and had felt Mrs Mannington's finger tracing a line down my bare spine. 'Look at this,' I heard her say to the governess, 'definitely curved, and already pushing out the shoulder blade on that side. Her father must be told at once.' And I remembered first my bewilderment, then my humiliation, as Clarissa had asked: 'Will she be a hunchback?' 'Be quiet!' Mrs Mannington had said sharply, but nothing could stop Charlie who, with drops of water flying off his fat little body, rushed around chanting: 'Minette has a crooked back . . . a crooked back.'

'It all looks very grand,' Dan's voice brought me back to the present. 'I wonder if we should have dressed? Keneally didn't say, did he?'

'N-no,' I answered frowning, as a memory stirred, elusive as a name on the tip of the tongue.

'Well,' Dan said, 'at least we're respectably turned out.' He ran his eye quickly over me. 'And you look *very* pretty, Mäuschen.'

He, of course, looked superb, being deeply tanned from our sea voyage, and with sun-streaked hair. He wore a light-weight suit with a silk shirt and tie left over from the days when Ros used to order both by the dozen from the Duke of Edinburgh's shirt-maker. As always, I felt eclipsed by him, but my frock of turquoise silk had been expertly made by Frau Wendel, and around my shoulders I wore a lacy mohair stole; my sheerest stockings and only pair of high-heeled sandals completed the outfit.

As we walked forward, I slid my hand into Dan's and he squeezed it, turning to look down at me with the familiar half-smile. 'More than pretty,' he said very softly, 'quite lovely, in fact.' His voice was calm, and no one would have guessed that only half an hour before he had been a nervous wreck. Somehow he had dredged up sufficient confidence to appear relaxed, and only I would know the colossal effort this had entailed.

But *my* heart began to thud as the door was opened by a very tall thin African dressed in a floor-length white *khanzu*, who murmured a greeting as he bowed. He wore a broad green sash across his shoulder and chest as a symbol of his status, and I just had time to whisper: 'The head houseboy, I think,' before two small long-haired Dachshunds and a magnificent Irish Wolfhound all erupted into the hall; the little dogs, with ears flung back and tails held high like banners, were yapping excitedly, but their huge companion merely approached to inspect us with incredibly wise eyes. Then another door was opened and the servant was obviously announcing us. We stepped forward, then froze, speechless, as the four figures around the fire rose. All were wearing dressing-gowns and pyjamas.

'Hello there!' Patrick said, coming forward with hand held out.

Dan was the first to recover. 'We've obviously come at the wrong time,' he said evenly. 'I do apologize.'

'No, no, of course you've not – Patrick, you should have told them!' A slender, dark-haired woman swept forward, the Irish lilt quite pronounced as her voice rose and fell. 'I'm Teresa-Mary, known universally as Terry-May, and I'm delighted to meet you both. Don't take any notice of our get-up, it's only a silly old pioneer custom!'

As memory clicked into place, hot colour suffused my face. 'I should have remembered,' I said contritely, 'but – it's such a long time ago and so much has happened since.'

'Oh, but it's great for us to have two such elegant guests,' Terry-May answered. 'Up here in our splendid isolation we quite forget how people dress these days. Sure now, Patrick, isn't it quite a treat?'

'Yes, and I'm thinking it is we who should apologize, but now come and meet Aletta and Janni Verhoeff.'

They were trying so hard to put us at our ease, but after all the tensions of the day I suddenly felt tired and defeated.

Aletta Verhoeff was a small, unsmiling woman with large angry-looking black eyes; she seemed barely willing to take my hand. In complete contrast, her husband was huge, with tiny cunning eyes perpetually smiling, and a grip that made me wince visibly. 'Cleary?' he said at once. 'That sounds familiar!'

For a second heart, brain, speech and movement seemed to freeze within me, and then I heard my own voice saying brightly: 'Oh, no doubt you're thinking of Jon Cleary, the Australian novelist who has had such tremendous success with *The Sundowners*. Isn't it a good story? I read it on the boat coming out and *loved* it.' It was one of those moments in life when words seem to be uttered of their own volition and without conscious thought, but now I could not stop, even though an inner voice was screaming: You're speaking too fast and too loud – shut up! 'I do hope they make it into a film,' I said aloud, 'don't you?'

'Yes,' Janni Verhoeff began uncertainly, although it was obvious from his expression that he had never heard of Jon Cleary.

Across the room Terry-May was saying to Dan: 'With a name like Cleary, you must have some Irish blood, surely?'

Oh God, I thought desperately, I'll have to stop this, but he answered smoothly enough: 'Yes, but our roots have been in England since the reign of Elizabeth Tudor.'

'So you don't practise the Old Faith?'

'No . . . we preferred conversion to the danger of being hanged, drawn and quartered.'

Terry-May shuddered slightly. 'Yes, I understand.'

All the time I was conscious of Janni Verhoeff's gaze and tried to turn away from him, but the little dogs were throwing themselves against my legs with frantic, attention-seeking barks, while like a self-appointed guard, the Wolfhound stood waist-high beside me, her tail thudding against the back of my thighs. And suddenly it was all too much: the noise, the feeling of being trapped, even the brightness and warmth of the room, all seemed to close in on me. I'm going to scream, I thought in panic, and looked wildly across to Dan, but it was Patrick who intercepted my glance.

'Minette, I'm so sorry! The dogs are behaving appallingly even though they only mean to be friendly.' His hand was on my elbow, as with the toe of his slipper he pushed the Dachshunds away, 'That's enough now, you two – be off with you! And you, madam – ' to the Wolfhound ' – must go on to your rug. I mean it, Liffey, this instant, if you please!' As she only continued

198

to wag her tail even more vigorously and gaze up at him adoringly, Patrick slapped her very gently on the rump and she moved reluctantly, walking silently and with grace to a rug in the corner where she flung herself down, sighing hugely, with head on paws and great eyes sweeping the room, full of misery. 'The complete Tragedy Queen,' Patrick said, 'but don't say a word, or even smile at her. She never misses an opportunity and will bound back here in a second. Now come and sit by the fire and relax.' He drew up a deep-cushioned chair and I sank into it gratefully. 'May I make you a Martini, Minette?' The Dachshunds had immediately turned their attention to Dan, and as one flung its paws against his legs, he bent to it.

'Damnit, stop that at once!' Terry-May said sharply, and Dan froze. 'I beg your pardon?'

'Oh, Dan, not you!' Impulsively she put her hand on his arm and looked up at him laughingly. 'That's his name! They're called Damnit and Jones! I know it's unbelievable, and when we took over the pair we tried to give them different names, but they just refused to answer to any!'

'Original at least,' Dan said, and again I marvelled at his composure. It must be due to the Keneallys' warmth, I thought, and perhaps the memory of all the official dinners and receptions he used to attend when it was necessary to appear relaxed and confident, even if he were exhausted or had just come from a blazing row . . .

'Now here's Jones, the little girl, who's looking up at you so meltingly! She wants you to pick her up, but don't because in seconds you'll have Damnit demanding the same!'

I swallowed hard on the sudden giggle in my throat as I thought: Little girls and big girls, human and canine, they all look up at him meltingly. But all the time Janni Verhoeff was continuing to look at *me*, so I pretended to

199

concentrate on Patrick who was squeezing a lemon over a lighted match. 'I've not seen that done before,' I remarked hastily, to forestall any conversation with Janni.

Patrick did not look up and I realized how difficult it must be for him with only two fingers and a thumb on one hand. 'No?' he queried. 'It's just another old pioneer custom: instead of slicing the lemon, we squeeze it and the flame ensures that the aroma will remain in the glass.' Under the strong light his disfigurement was appalling: minus lashes and brows, and with eyelids, nose and mouth obviously reconstructed, it was impossible to guess at what his original appearance had been. Only his very fair hair and the blue of his eyes under their thick lids gave an indication of his colouring, for the skin of his face was blotchy, while that at the back of his head red and shrivelled. The hair grew only patchily there, but at the sides it was still thick enough to partially cover the holes that were all that remained of his ears. Yet, strangely, none of this was revolting. After the initial shock one was much more conscious of his gentle personality. I could not even faintly imagine what his suffering had been, nor the courage needed to endure, to overcome so much. And he had such an attractive wife! Terry-May, although so slender, had beautiful feminine curves in all the right places and she exuded health; it showed in the vivid colour staining her cheeks beneath their deep tan, in the sparkle of her soft dark eyes, the whiteness of her strong teeth, and the gloss of her Irish black hair. I do hope she loves him, I thought, and that she can give him tenderness and passion. He must need so much loving kindness.

'So you've taken over the Glyn place?' Janni's harsh South African accent broke in on my thoughts and I took a long sip of my Martini before saying: 'Inherited, rather. I'm Hugh Glyn's daughter.'

'Ach so, Hugh Glyn, eh?'

'Then of course you must remember this house, Minette,' said Terry-May who, in a few quick strides, had crossed to my side.

'Yes,' I said, for the first time looking around, 'but it was nothing like this. It's such a lovely house now, and this room is so pretty.'

'Thank you. I've tried to create a real home – a haven, if you like – partly because we're so isolated up here, but mostly for Patrick. He still suffers a great deal of pain at times and he also works terribly hard, so everything is geared for comfort and relaxation: the colours are muted because after days in the brilliant sun, soft shades are restful, and – as you see – we're both dotty about books and music.'

'Oh, yes, we are too,' I said, glancing appreciatively at the overflowing bookcases and piles of records.

'Then you must borrow whatever books you want, and come often to hear our music – it's a great revitalizer, I think – but you're not likely to find it always so tidy here. The combination of dogs and children – '

'You have children!' I exclaimed in surprise.

'Why, yes, four-year-old twins. I think – yes, in fact they're here now.' Laughing she turned briefly to me. 'What impeccable timing! Come in, Wanjiri, and you, my darlings, come and say good-night to everyone.' A smiling African woman in a skimpy cotton frock that was tight over her ample body, and with a bright bandana tied around her head, advanced shyly into the room, holding by the hand two of the most beautiful children I had ever seen. They were dressed identically in pale blue dressing-gowns, pyjamas and fluffy slippers, and this sameness emphasized their great similarity in looks: each had blond-white hair in thistledown curls, exquisite rose-tinged skin and large blue eyes fringed by incredibly long dark lashes. A sprinkling of freckles lay over the bridge of each small nose. The two little figures,

201

smelling of baby soap and talc, biscuits and warm milk, went politely around the room, their small bodies pressed trustingly against the side of each adult in turn, but when the little girl came to Dan she halted and gazed up at him solemnly. He bent forward, holding out his hand and, after a slight pause, her fingers curled around his thumb.

'Hello,' Dan said softly, 'what's your name?' My heart went out to him then, for I knew he was thinking of Emma.

'I'm Bridie,' she answered in a clear, piping tone, and Dan smiled at her with great gentleness. Like many very large, powerful men, he was extremely protective and tender with any tiny, fragile creature. 'Well, Bridie,' he said, 'may I kiss you good-night?'

'Yes, please,' she answered at once and a ripple of soft laughter went around the room. So, spanning her waist, Dan lifted her up to his level and kissed her lightly on the cheek. 'Thank you,' he said gravely as he set her down again. She continued to look at him with great solemnity, then said, 'I like you, but I love my Daddy most of all.' And in a sudden swift movement she twisted away and rushed to Patrick. As he swept her up, she put her arms tightly around his neck, and covered his cheek with tiny butterfly kisses.

'Will you look at that?' Terry-May said to me. 'One hundred per cent female at four years old! What'll she be like at fourteen, I ask myself?'

'Will you take me out on Benji tomorrow, Daddy?' Bridie was asking, her face only inches from Patrick's.

'Ah no, Puss, I think it'll have to be Matu who gives you your lesson.'

'No, Daddy, you! You! Sean can go with Matu, I want you!'

'All right, then, darlint, just you and me and Benji.'

'Oh, Patrick!' Terry-May protested. And to me: 'He's like the softest putty in her hands.'

Yes, I thought, and perhaps it's partly because Bridie is the only female who sees him as completely normal; she throws her arms about his neck and rains kisses on him without any knowledge of his scars, and he adores her for it.

'Patrick, do bless them now. It's late and dinner will be announced any moment,' Terry-May urged. 'Sean, go to Daddy now.'

Patrick set his daughter on her feet and the two children stood before him, eyes tightly closed and hands together in prayer as he signed each with a cross on the forehead. 'May the holy angels fold their wings around you both and keep you safe this night and ever more,' he said very quietly, and Terry-May whispered, 'Amen.'

'Good-night, my son, God bless you,' Patrick said, kissing the little boy, and to Bridie: 'Good-night, my heart, God bless you.'

'I've never seen more beautiful children,' I said to Terry-May as the African nurse led them from the room. 'Such wonderful colouring!'

'Thank you,' Terry-May's smile was brilliant, 'and what about you? Will you be starting a family soon?'

I was completely taken by surprise and could only stammer, 'Oh, I-I don't think so, we've got more than enough to cope with for now!'

'Well, you and Dan obviously love children, so who knows. Have you been married long?'

Oh, God, I thought in panic and felt my face flame. 'Just-just before we came out,' I said.

Terry-May laughed and put her hand warmly over mine. 'Why, you're a bride, and still shy about it! But we can't let this pass! Patrick, we have a bridal couple here – I've only just discovered it. We must celebrate!'

I caught Dan's astonished look and could only gaze back helplessly.

'Ah now, isn't this just great?' Patrick said delightedly. 'A special bottle is called for, indeed it is!'

At that moment dinner was announced, and as we walked through to the far end of the enormous room I glanced round appreciatively: the walls were of softest dove grey matching the fitted linen, piped with green, which covered all the chairs. Colour was restricted to the many cushions, flowers, books, and curtains at the three long windows. The fabric of the hangings was also linen, but printed with the hounds and pink-coated riders of a hunt whose black horses perpetually jumped hedges and galloped across green fields. The Podo wood floor was bare except for a few neutral hand-woven rugs, and all the furniture was of mahogany, more sturdy than elegant, but with surfaces polished to glass-like perfection. The sashed houseboy, now wearing a matching green bolero, stood with another younger African before the large sideboard. Both wore white cotton gloves.

The starter of egg mousse, subtly flavoured with curry, was delicious but I was too tense to enjoy it. By the time the champagne came and everyone toasted us, my mind was blank with panic and when Dan, looking completely composed, said quietly: 'You are all most kind and we do appreciate it, don't we, darling?' I could only manage an 'Oh, yes,' in a croaky voice.

When Patrick lifted his glass again, saying: 'And we all wish you the very greatest success with the farm,' I almost sagged in my seat with relief. Surely this is a safe topic, I thought, but then Janni Verhoeff said: 'Your farm in Britain – was it successful?'

And Dan, in the same quiet voice, answered: 'There was none. This is our first venture.'

Janni's little eyes opened to their very limited extent. 'You have never farmed before? And you come *here* to begin? To *Africa*?'

Dan nodded briefly. 'Correct.'

As Janni looked around the table in speechless disbelief, Patrick said, 'There have been others, you know, especially after the Boer War.'

Aletta Verhoeff, who had been entirely silent, suddenly spoke. 'Yes, when they had finished persecuting us, the *Rooineks* came up here and started their madness all over again.'

There was silence for a few seconds, then Dan took up the challenge: 'Madness? In what way?'

'By insisting on bringing the Kaffir baboons down from the trees where they belonged, and educating them!' Aletta answered, black eyes diamond hard.

Dan unhurriedly spooned up the last of his mango fool before saying: 'Forgive me, but did you not come from South África yourselves?'

'Yes,' Janni answered for his wife, 'my grandparents trekked up here in '09, but when they settled on the high veld there was nothing except animals, and the blacks they did meet *they* left alone. But your lot insisted on bringing them religion, on interfering with all their stupid customs and jabbing all the babies – '

'Oh, come now, Janni,' Terry-May said, 'we couldn't stand by and let so many babies and young children die just for want of immunization.'

'And what do we have as a result? Hundreds of the bastards who would otherwise have died, alive now, with nothing for them to do!'

The two servants were clearing the pudding glasses and setting out delicious-looking cheeses and home-made biscuits. I wondered what they thought, but it was impossible to tell. Their faces were blank, eyes opaque.

'Thank you, that is all,' Terry-May said quietly, and waited until the door had closed behind them before turning back to Janni: 'Yes, the population explosion *is* a problem, I grant you that, yet it cannot be insoluble, and as for our interference in their customs – well, this has only been an effort to stop female circumcision and the deliberate killing of breech-birth babies and first-born twins.' At my half stifled exclamation of horror, she addressed me: 'You see, they believe that such babies are really devils who have inhabited the bodies, and therefore they have to be killed at birth before they put a *thaku* – a curse – on everyone else. It is necessary to understand, Minette, that they love their children very much, but to kill a new-born baby is not a crime since they believe a child is not really born until its second birthday.'

'And you really believe this practice has now been stopped?' Janni asked, smiling cynically.

Terry-May shrugged. 'Officially yes, but I fear it's still done when the women who act as midwives think they can get away with it.'

'And female circumcision?' Janni persisted.

'An extremely painful, potentially dangerous operation,' Terry-May answered at once. 'It can often lead to kidney and bladder infections, and almost always to difficult child-birth. We *had* to do something for all the poor girls.'

'Have you forgotten the old woman, the missionary?'

'Hilda Stumpf? No, definitely not, I always say a prayer for her,' Terry-May said. Once again she turned to me: 'Hilda Stumpf was an elderly American missionary who had worked at Kijabe for twenty years. She had campaigned vigorously against female circumcision and one night some Africans broke into her room as she slept and forcibly circumcised her. They also put a pillow over her head to deaden her screams and of course killed her . . . a terrible death but, God love her, I believe not in vain. It certainly drew public attention to the problem as nothing else would have done.'

Again there was silence until Patrick said: 'Faith, we are being gloomy tonight, but don't let us put you two

206

off. Kenya is a wonderful country and I've no doubt you'll love it here.'

But as we returned to the fire, Janni said to Dan: 'You have guns?'

For a second he looked nonplussed but, as always, quickly recovered. 'I have my Service 45 and a .256 Manlicher-Schonneur rifle.'

Janni shook his head dolefully. 'Not enough.' He swung round to me. 'No doubt you, Mevrou, are an excellent shot?'

'I've never handled a gun in my life,' I said, childishly pleased to prove him wrong.

He appeared to be genuinely shocked. 'Never handled a gun!' he echoed. 'What was your father thinking of not to teach you?'

'Well, having been right through the First World War in the trenches, he was utterly against shooting man or beast, and I certainly have no wish to do so.'

'But you *must* know how to defend yourself! There is much unrest in this country which the authorities are too soft to put down and I tell you, Mevrou, the time may come when every man, woman, and even child will have to carry a gun.'

'Is there really unrest?' Dan asked Patrick.

'There has always been a certain amount ever since native troops returned from the First War and were stirred up by Harry Thuku, who had formed the Young Kikuyu Association, and pointed out, quite rightly, that all they had got for fighting the war was a reduction in farm wages and a doubling of Poll and Hut Tax. When Thuku was sent into exile most of the unrest petered out, like his Association.'

'Ah, but now that his henchman, the Commie Kaffir Kenyatta is back – '

'Now, Janni, what evidence do we have that he is a Communist?'

'What evidence?' Janni bellowed. 'Why, the bastard has lived in Russia!'

'But he's also lived a long time in England,' Patrick protested.

'Yes, and has become far too clever for his own good,' Janni retorted. 'We would know what to do with him and all his kind down in the Union.' In the silence that followed, he calmly lit a cheroot. 'Don't forget,' he said as he watched a perfect smoke ring drift lightly upwards, 'that there are forty thousand of us out here against some three million blacks. If they ever decide to rise up, we shall all have to act bloody quickly and bloody hard!'

I looked towards the window and a tiny *frisson* of fear touched my spine, for the curtains had not been drawn, and although light from the room streamed out brilliantly, beyond its limit lay total darkness.

Patrick went to put another log on the fire; instantly it sent up a shower of sparks and filled the room with a delicious aroma. 'Well, Janni, my friend, you'd better modify your opinions because Independence is bound to come, with Kenyatta and the like taking leading roles.'

'You really think Independence is the best solution?' Dan asked, deeply interested.

Patrick nodded. 'I believe it is the only solution.'

Janni looked as though about to explode. 'Give this wonderful country – which *we* have made – to a bunch of lazy, thieving, lying black baboons?' he shouted, waving his arms dramatically. 'You have to be raving, man!'

Patrick laughed good-humouredly. 'No, I don't think so. Just consider for a moment what an incredible advance they have made within half a century: from a completely pastoral people who had never seen a plough, let alone a gun, or even travelled beyond the nearest mountain pass, they have learned to use modern firearms, cross the seas – think what that must have been like for a young Kuke to *see* a ship and so much water – to fight in two

208

horrendous wars *and* to absorb some education and a certain amount of religion. But now they have come to a dangerous crossroads: de-tribalized, and therefore no longer under the considerable influence of the elders, and with little to do, they could so easily drift into apathy, or violence, or lawlessness. In my view, only Independence can give them the opportunity, ambition and will to succeed further. But of course they will need a strong, Westernized leader, sophisticated and, one hopes, with some integrity. I believe Kenyatta could be such a man. And, don't forget, he *is* a Kikuyu and they, as a tribe, will be the deciding factor.'

'And you would be prepared to accept the arrogance, along with all the greed and corruption that would inevitably follow?' Janni asked.

Patrick nodded. 'I think you are taking an unnecessarily gloomy view, but yes, we should certainly remain.'

'And you,' Dan asked Janni, 'what would you do?'

The Afrikaner glared at him. 'I don't know, but I can promise you one thing for sure: no Kaffir bastard is ever going to tell *me* what to do!'

'Then,' Terry-May said lightly, 'you'd better have another cup of coffee before you rush home to start packing!'

'Don't worry,' Janni retorted, 'it will never happen. Thank God there aren't many woolly-minded liberals like this madman here, and the rest of us will fight Independence to the death!'

'I suppose you were in the Forces during the war, Dan?' Terry-May suddenly asked, and I jerked into immediate alertness.

He nodded. 'Of course.'

'Army?'

'No . . . RAF.'

'I'm sure you made Wing Co,' Terry-May said admiringly.

Put a good face on it, darling, I begged Dan silently as he hesitated. *Don't give up now that the evening's almost over*. 'Yes,' he said, in a tone that did not invite further comment, 'but you know that accelerated promotion did not mean much then.'

'And I was a Staff Officer Grade II,' I said brightly, ever the young ingénue, and everyone smiled at me.

'That sounds very interesting,' Terry-May said. 'Do tell us more.'

So I launched into a long account of Germany, the DPs and the camps.

'Fascinating,' Terry-May said at last, 'and it makes my own service as a QA Sister up at MacKinnon Road very dull! You know, there's a German doctor down in Nakuru who was in Auschwitz – Dr Engel – who treats mainly Africans and a few Asians.' There was no reason why I should remember the name, which was one of the most usual of German–Jewish, and of course I had no idea how important Dr Engel was to be to me, yet the name did remain in my memory: Dr Engel of Nakuru.

'Well,' Dan said, 'we've all got to be up early tomorrow, so I think Minette and I should be on our way now.'

As we all rose, I said: 'I'm afraid our tent is going to seem very cold and cheerless after all this lovely comfort and warmth.'

'It would be a good thing to get a more substantial shelter before the rains come,' Patrick said. 'It need only be a mud hut to start with; they're surprisingly warm in winter and cool in summer. Of course, various other creatures will make their homes up in the thatch, but you'll get used to them!'

'But how do we set about building the hut?'

'You get a few casual workers, mainly women, to do that. So long as you keep a close eye on them, they'll build the hut in a few hours.'

'But we haven't seen any Africans at all,' Dan said.

'No? But don't be fooled – there are plenty living up in the Aberdares. Oh, remember that cedar is excellent for building *anything*, so long as it is the red – only that is safe from termites. And whatever land you cultivate, fence it very securely or else you'll lose all your crops. The African night is full of predators! And that goes for hens, too. Two hundred laying hens should produce about one hundred and fifty eggs per day, or four thousand five hundred per month. At twenty cents per egg, you should make nine hundred Kenyan shillings, so they're worth thinking about, but it's only too easy to lose the lot in one night, if they're not properly housed and fenced.'

'Remember,' Janni said solemnly as we were leaving, 'Africa will do everything in her power to break you. You must fight her every inch of the way for it is only on those who succeed in taming her that she lavishes her bounty.'

'Meanwhile, we'll steal a march on the old girl by getting you some labour,' Patrick said, as he held out his hand. 'I'll send a message up to my head man straight away.'

'It wasn't too bad, was it?'

'No, and I was very proud of you, Mäuschen,' Dan said as we rattled out on to the track. He felt for my hand and kissed the back of it. 'You warded off all the awkward questions so well.'

'Yet at one stage I felt the Verhoeff man was playing cat and mouse with me. I didn't much care for him or his wife, did you?'

'No,' Dan replied, 'I thought them both quite awful! She's stuck in a time warp and he's a gross, uncouth creature. Strange, because so many of the South Africans I met in the Middle East were great chaps. But I certainly liked the Keneallys.'

'Terry-May asked me if I'd like to go with her to Nakuru market one day.'

'What did you say, darling?'

'That I-I felt we might be too busy for me to spend any time away.'

Dan's arm swept around me, drawing me close. 'Poor little Mäuschen, you'd love to go and I think you should – it would be totally selfish of me to deny you the friendship of our only female neighbour. But now, I think you're very tired, aren't you?'

'A bit,' I admitted reluctantly. In fact, I felt totally exhausted, and within seconds of putting my head on Dan's shoulder fell into a light doze, only to be started into wakefulness by his quick intake of breath. 'What?' I asked dazedly.

'Straight ahead,' he said, 'lions – a male and two females, quite magnificent.' They were at the very limit of our headlights, walking with their beautiful lithe movement across the track. They turned to look at us without much interest, eyes glowing bright green.

'Let's hope we don't break down here, with those three around,' Dan said lightly, but I shuddered and then started as an owl flew across our bonnet with a screech, the long feathers around its feet rising like tiny skirts. Everywhere the myriad lights of fire-flies danced around us, and far below in the valley other lights were pin-points of brightness in the night. Once again I felt our isolation, and once again the fear, which I had never known as a child. 'That awful Verhoeff man was right about one thing,' I said, 'we do need firearms.'

'Yes, but we need so much,' Dan answered with a sigh. 'A house, tractor, seed, saws, nails, a hen-house and birds, fences – oh God, the list is endless.' Yet as soon as we were in our tent with the Coleman lamp blazing, Dan went to his tin trunk and drew out his revolver, still in its holster and attached to a webbing belt. Quickly he withdrew it, broke it, and began to fit in the six bullets. Then he did the same with the rifle. 'No sense in having these if they're not ready for instant use,' he remarked, 'and – yes, darling, I will teach you how to use them. It makes good sense that you should be able to defend yourself.'

Moments later, with the lamp out, the blackness was once more intense: somewhere nearby a lion roared and I was suddenly conscious that only a thin canvas flap separated us from the prowling creatures of the night and the slithering snakes. Yet I had been born here and, as a child, had seen many lion, buffalo, even the shy cheetah and black-coated leopard, but never had I known such fear then . . . so, was I afraid of something else now? Something more sinister than the great cats, the lumbering buffalo, the mighty forest elephant – ? A scream, high pitched and of the utmost agony rent the air and was almost instantly cut off. It had to be an animal, but could have been a human being, and I knew at once then that I was not afraid of the animals . . . 'Dan,' I began hoarsely.

'Yes?' the reply was instant and fully alert.

'I feel a little frightened tonight – you will stay close, won't you?'

'Well, I'm not likely to be going anywhere, sweetheart, and I would certainly be a lot closer if it weren't for these bloody beds. But don't worry, the revolver is on the box beside me with the flashlight, and the rifle is propped against the side, so we'll be all right. Try to get some sleep now, darling.'

I slept fitfully until dawn when I fell into a deep sleep, only to awake with a thudding head and a great disinclination to move. Dan was already fully dressed and, as I sleepily watched him move to look outside, I saw him stiffen. 'Oh, what is it?' I asked, struggling up.

He turned to smile reassuringly at me. 'Come and see,' he suggested, 'you're never going to believe this!'

A large crowd was assembled some fifty odd yards from our tent: there were old men with grizzled heads and stick-like legs leaning on long staves; young men and totos squatting down on their haunches in the seemingly effortless position of the African; women with babies on their backs, sitting with legs straight out before them, all totally silent, all with eyes fixed upon us.

'Patrick's head man certainly didn't waste much time,' Dan said wonderingly, 'and I'd love to know how he managed to alert so many when he was only told late last night that we wanted labour, but instead I'd better go out and try to talk to them. You get some clothes on, darling, then come and say where you want your hut built.'

We had to send the majority away, but within minutes there was a long line of women all hacking away at the weeds and undergrowth with their pangas and digging sticks, all laughing and chattering in high-pitched voices, the babies on their backs silent and seemingly oblivious of the flies clustering at their eyes and mouths. Some two hundred yards away another group was clearing the ground of the original drive. I decided our new home should be built on the site of my parents' house, so as soon as the ground was cleared, I took a large stick and drew two enormous circles connected by a passage-way, with a smaller one beside the 'bedroom'. This last was to be our 'bathroom'. Fortunately, I just remembered in time that native huts do not have windows or any kind of chimney. 'The smoke from their cooking fires is allowed to waft up and through the roof,' I explained to Dan, 'and everything becomes blackened. But no doubt I'll have a wood-burning cooker – when we get one – so what can we do?'

'A flue, high enough to keep smoke and sparks well away from the thatch, is probably the answer,' he said. 'Perhaps I'd better get down to Nakuru and see what I can buy before they start putting on the roof. Will you be all right with this lot?'

I nodded, and of course I was, although they were subtly different from the workers of my childhood who had been a carefree people, shy at first but instantly responsive to a smile, and who had looked at us with a child-like curiosity. But now, although some still smiled, many tended to keep their eyes lowered or else to shift their gaze from mine, their expressions either sullen or strangely worried. I wanted so much to talk and try to draw them out, but found that all faces immediately became blank, all eyes opaque. So it was with relief that I greeted Dan when the old van trundled up the drive. 'Darling!' I exclaimed. 'Have you bought up the whole of Nakuru?'

'No,' he replied with a mischievous smile, 'but I did get the bed! And a few less important items, including the stove.'

The stove appeared to fascinate our workers. 'Ee-i!' the women shrilled, while all walking around it, chattering non-stop.

'Surely, they've seen one of these before,' Dan said, surveying the crowd with hands on hips. 'I'll have to try and find out what's causing the flap.' A few minutes later he returned, smiling. 'Would you believe it? It's the flue that's intriguing them! I've tried to explain its use, but I'd better watch carefully now they're about to put the roof on.' To our Western eyes the fabric of bamboo poles and freshly cut cedar held together by clay-like earth, looked flimsy indeed. Yet the wood had been deeply sunk into the ground and the earth between quickly dried to the consistency of cement. Reeds and grasses for the roof had been arriving all day on the backs of women bent almost double, their shaven heads and bare limbs glistening with sweat. But many of them were still able to climb nimbly up and begin densely weaving the reeds on to the circle of branches which was already in place and secured by lianas twisted into rope. The holes cut for windows were rather small and of course without glass, but Dan managed to make the workers understand that he wanted screens to fit inside the apertures. These, like the only door, were made of bamboo poles lashed together; there were no fastenings, and the window screens would have to be held in place by stones, but for the door there was a crude kind of hinge and a roughly hewn plank could be placed across to rest on two protruding branches set into the wall on either side. The floors were of beaten earth and full of miniature hills and valleys. 'But,' said Dan, 'perhaps in time we'll be able to cement it over and give the walls a coat of whitewash, inside and out.' When all was finished and the workers were all lining up, all the women again burst into a spontaneous high-pitched trilling.

'Now, what's up with the chorus line?' Dan asked, bending almost double to get through the doorway.

'I haven't a clue,' I replied, 'but perhaps they're glad to ɔve finished, or to be being paid, or just to be going home. But whatever the reason, they seem happier than they've been all day.' They all held out their cupped hands for their wages and most murmured something, and then it seemed that they just melted away: one minute we had a group of men, women and tots, and the next Dan and I were alone.

'Where are they?' he asked, swivelling quickly to look all around.

'I don't know,' I replied, and suddenly shivered as the strange *frisson* of fear touched my spine again. Then I forgot about it. Dan had swept me up into his arms and was endeavouring to carry me over the threshold, but because the doorway was so narrow, we got stuck and were immediately reduced to giggles. Once inside, his arms tightened around me and he looked deeply into my eyes. I wound my arms around his neck and said softly, 'Which would you prefer me to try first: the new stove or the new bed?' He uttered a whoop of joy, twirled me around and then ran the few steps into our second hut, which contained only the bed, our tin trunks, and a wooden box masquerading as a bedside table.

That night Dan and I slept in each other's arms. I think we both realized as never before that we only had each other, and each needed the closeness of the other for love and reassurance. 'Are you happy?' I whispered as we clung together, closely entwined.

'Oh, yes,' he said softly, 'at this moment I'm completely happy.'

15

The purchase of a tractor with plough attachment and two hundred laying hens made us really feel like farmers, and our only initial difficulty was to decide on who should do what. Dan was convinced that the tractor would be too heavy for me to manage – 'It's not like the Merc, you know – ' but after a short, rather sharp argument I won, pointing out that I could not supervise the fencing or planting of the pyrethrum. 'Remember, darling, Patrick said this had to be done by hand, with the seedlings two feet apart, and twenty thousand to an acre. How could I ever cope with that?'

'OK,' Dan said, 'you win.'

So from dawn until the light finally faded, I sat in the jolting, noisy vehicle, surrounded by great swirling clouds of dust, as I drove first up and down, then twice across the vast acreage formerly cultivated by Patrick. Behind me worked a crowd of women and totos reducing the clods to a fine tilth with their *jembes*, while on all sides came sounds of men sawing and hammering.

Every evening Dan sat adding and subtracting figures on scraps of paper, and at first I made no comment, having insisted that he alone should handle our finances, but as he began to look more and more worried, I had to know: 'Is it all right? Are we going to get by? How much have we got left?'

At first Dan tried to reassure me. 'Just keep your fingers crossed, darling – we're keeping our heads above water.' Or: 'It's going to be touch and go.' Until finally: 'It's a dilemma, Mäuschen. I'm told that a planter with a drill for seed and fertilizer costs two hundred pounds, but that

218

it can do in a day what a hundred women can only do in a month. So, do we dig more deeply into our savings to buy it in the hope that the harvest will succeed sufficiently to let us recoup the cost? It's the same with the pyrethrum seedlings. Patrick said twenty acres of the flowers could make as much as one thousand pounds next year, but do we risk more of our money to buy them?'

'Yes,' I said, 'let's get a loan from the bank and buy what we need.'

But Dan shook his head. 'The bank must be our very last resort, and there *must* be something else we can do!'

I could think of nothing, since we were already living a hand-to-mouth existence, but the next day when Dan returned from Nakuru he was jubilant. 'Guess what, darling? I managed to flog my cigarette case and lighter to an Indian who has a *duka* – '

'Oh, no!'

'Oh, yes, and don't look so upset – they meant nothing to me and he did give me enough to buy the seedlings, so we only need to take the two hundred from our savings.'

'But, Dan, they were *gold*.'

'I know, but the lighter had my initials on it, and inside the case Ros had had a message inscribed. I'm sure the wily old cove will manage to have it all erased, but of course I wasn't able to bargain very effectively.'

I must have continued to look upset because Dan came to put his arms around me and say bracingly: 'Don't waste time regretting the sale, darling, it had to be done. It rained during the night which means we must work flat out to get the planting done.'

So once again I drove the tractor from dawn to dusk, with the planter attachment spewing out seed and fertilizer, while Dan had the almost impossible task of over-seeing the young boys in the pyrethrum fields. Ten boys were supposed to plant an acre a day, but without

219

constant supervision they slowed down, went into a day dream or just wandered off. And with the sowing came a new threat: birds! There had always been plenty of green parrots, doves, pigeons and many smaller birds about the land, and the air was constantly filled with their various sounds, but when the ground was sown great flocks appeared from the forest and converged on our fields. They had to be shot and I was the one to do it. But first I had to be taught. Desperation must have given me extra skill for I learned very quickly, even though I hated to kill the beautiful, fragile creatures. It was a case of us or them, and I told myself that a bullet was far kinder than the African method of smearing the natural latex from mwerere fruit on to branches so that birds perching on these were stuck fast. As a small girl I had frequently been distressed to see the pathetic fluttering of their wings and, if the branch were low enough, I would always go and put my hands very gently around the small trapped creature, marvelling at its fragility and tiny bursting heart, until suddenly this would stop, the delicate neck droop and the large black eyes close. As an adult I realized of course that I must have added a thousand fold to the birds' terror, although I had only wanted to comfort, to enfold, no doubt because I, too, needed to be comforted and held.

And all the time we were too ignorant to recognize the greatest threat: the lack of rain, for apart from that one downpour, there had been no more. So I continued to pursue the birds across our fields, knowing that although each shot sent great numbers of them into the air, within minutes they would all return; and Dan continued to walk miles and chivvy the boys, knowing that as soon as his back was turned, they would slow down. At first we were acutely conscious of our physical discomfort: of sweat pouring into our eyes, off the end of our noses and chins, and cascading down our bodies; of dust coating our skin and perpetually parching our throats, but as time went on we became automatons, oblivious of everything except the need to continue. Speech and even food were reduced to the barest essentials, and the one longed-for moment of the day was when we could strip off our sodden clothes and get into the bath. But every drop of water had to be fetched, every twig gathered for the stove. Never had I ever thought I would wear unironed clothes, but every evening these were put into pails to soak, rinsed through in the morning and left on the ground to dry, only to be worn in the evening, rough and creased, but blessedly fresh. Although Nairobi was just over one hundred miles away, we were living like nineteenth-century pioneers and I think we realized very early on that we were beaten, but were just too stubborn to acknowledge it. We would probably have continued until we literally dropped in our tracks had we not returned one afternoon to find all the hens dead; they were quite untouched, and had seemed all right that morning. Dan and I just gazed at them silently, avoiding each other's eyes, but knowing that this was really the end.

I stumbled away, with head bent, then saw two hooves before me. I looked up dazedly and there was Patrick, mounted on a fine horse and with Bridie perched up before him, his arm strongly around her. 'I'm out riding with my daddy,' she announced, smiling at me woman-to-woman. I tried to smile back, but the combination of dust and sweat had caked like a mask on my face.

'Holy God, Minette!' Patrick exclaimed in shocked tones. 'What's happened to you?'

'All over,' I croaked, 'tried so hard . . . but hopeless, quite hopeless . . . '

Patrick dismounted effortlessly and then lifted Bridie down. She was wearing a minute pair of blue dungarees with a matching shirt and white sun hat. She stood very close to her father, her small hand clinging to his two fingers and her eyes, looking up at me with a child's candour, were of the deepest, clearest blue.

'Your voice sounds funny,' she said in the exact tone Terry-May might have used, 'and your face is very dirty!'

'Hush now, Bridie,' Patrick admonished, 'don't be saying such rude things.' And to me: 'Tell me exactly what has happened.'

So in a trembling, barely audible voice I told him of the hens that had seemed well that morning but were now dead; of the fields full of weeds but without any sign of crops; and of the pyrethrum seedlings that were dying because they were not being planted quickly enough. As I finished Dan appeared, a four gallon *debe* of water in each hand. He looked as though he might have just come from under a waterfall, so sodden were his clothes. 'Good afternoon, Patrick,' he said easily, as though the situation were quite normal and we did not look like scarecrows that had been exposed to the elements for too long. 'What a fine horse you have there!'

Patrick was not to be fobbed off and came straight to the point. 'Dan, I'm appalled to hear that you are having such a struggle and I hope you will let me see what I can do to help.'

Dan was a very strong man and in his prime, yet the past weeks had taken their toll of him too: the once slightly hollow cheeks were now so thin that it was as though the underlying tissue had been scooped out, and there were new deep lines around his eyes and mouth. But I could also see a refusal hovering on his lips and I sagged back against the wall of the hut, unable to take any more. The movement caught his eye and he looked at me as though seeing me for the first time. I saw horror and fear in his expression and knew that my own face was showing all the exhaustion I had seen in his. 'Thank you, Patrick,' he said in a suddenly hoarse voice, 'I'm afraid

Minette and I are beaten to our knees, but if you think there is anything – '

'Ah, praise be to God!' Patrick said fervently. 'I was afraid you were going to play the proud, stiff-necked Englishman, but now let's see what needs to be done!'

It did not take him long to solve our difficulties. 'I suspect that many of your seeds will have escaped the birds,' he said, 'and be germinating, but they are being choked by the weeds. You need some women and totos to clear these; they're good at weeding, they've been doing it for centuries, and you need only give them a ration of tea, sugar and posho – maize flour – in payment. Let me send Joseph, my head man, and a few of my other fellows to sort out the pyrethrum fields. I think there's still time to save most of the seedlings if we hurry. As for the hens – well, my friends, you made a very simple mistake: you did not give them sufficient runs, and they died of infection. They need four runs and four doors to the hen-houses, so that these can be used in rotation. We can disinfect the houses but we'll have to re-locate them and I can let you have some pullets, but each week you'll need to powder their rears and beneath their feathers to keep them clean.'

'We'll never be able to thank you – ' Dan began, but Patrick held up his hand. 'No need,' he said simply, 'one of the best things about farming out here is that we are not in competition, so when there is a crisis we help each other. Besides, to a large extent, we're all at the mercy of nature and I must warn you that unless we get good rains within the next few days, we'll all be in trouble.'

'But we had that deluge – '

'Yes, but we need days – weeks – of rain and then you'll see everything rocket up!'

But the rain did not come, although every day we watched the build-up of clouds over the mountains; they were darker, heavier now, but still there was sufficient

223

wind to blow them away from us. Down in the valley heat shimmered over the parched brown land, and even at our height the normally alpine air became humid. It seemed that, like us, all nature was working flat out, for every bush and plant that had burst into a final flowering, was invaded by bees and the long curved beaks of sunbirds, whose quivering wings of wine-red or blue vied with the fragile beauty of our many butterflies. Other birds fought each other for a twig or blade of grass with the victors flying wildly away, their trophies trailing; on the ground minute beetles toiled at speed in the grasses, their bodies metallic in the sun, and little turquoise lizards with brilliant orange heads, scuttled amidst the stones.

On the morning that huge cumulus clouds shrouded the Mau summit, we were jubilant, for the wind was blowing them forward at speed and within minutes the valley was lost to view. But then the wind suddenly dropped and the clouds remained to saturate the Rift's floor and lower slopes before thinning and drifting lazily away. Once more hope began to die within us and, as always, we sought comfort from each other, making love with a desperation which never seemed to be assuaged.

Finally Dan said, 'We'd better make contingency plans in case the rains don't come, because you do realize, don't you, Mäuschen, that we should not be able to carry on?'

'Well, we'd just have to use the money we've kept in case we had to go home,' I said, shying away even then from reality.

'But, don't you see, darling, we could use all that money and still be bankrupt if a real drought occurred?'

'Then we'd have to mortgage the farm.'

'But supposing the bank later foreclosed? We'd be without a roof over our heads then and have to apply for assisted passages back to the UK.'

'Oh, but would we want to go back there?'

224

'No,' Dan said after a long pause, 'not unless it was absolutely necessary. I don't think there'd be anything for us in England.'

'All that awful rain – ' I began, then laughed shakily. 'Oh, Lord, just what we're longing for here!'

'I wish to God I'd been trained for something other than flying,' he said, 'but I thought of nothing else and went straight into the RAF from school. I wonder if there'd be any chance of a job with a small local set-up somewhere in Africa? I was a damned good pilot after all.' He paused again, and when he spoke there was hopelessness in his voice. 'But of course I wouldn't know how to fly the jets.'

The idea of him flying some ramshackle plane filled me with despair. 'Oh, it's so unfair!' I burst out. 'We've tried so hard, asked for so little – why, why, can't we be allowed to stay here with just sufficient money to make life a bit easier?'

'Yes, damnit! You wouldn't think that could be so difficult, considering that we're living like the poorest of the first settlers here.'

'Never mind, darling,' I said, attempting lightness, 'we're in very aristocratic company. Lord Delamere and the Duke of Montrose, plus quite a few others, lived in mud huts when they first came out.'

'Maybe, but I can't believe they were ever short of a decent drink, or had to think twice about whether they could afford new batteries for their radios. I'd give a – what the hell's that?'

It was an explosion of sound which shook the entire hut, and its reverberations crashed through the forest; when this was followed by a brilliant flash of blue-white light, we both rushed outside. It was a storm dramatic by even African standards, with lightning which not only lit up the dark sky, but then ran in a crackling rivulet along the ground, only to be followed seconds later by earth-shaking thunder and roaring wind. I saw Dan look up anxiously at our roof. He was able to stand with legs apart, braced against the wind, but I was thrown back against the wall, and he came to wrap his arms tightly around me. 'Go inside!' he shouted in my ear, but I shook my head, preferring the great curtains of dust which rose all around to the fear that the hut might collapse on top of us. It seemed impossible that such a simple structure could withstand so great an onslaught or even that the solitary cedar standing over it could survive, for it was creaking and some of the thinner branches were being snapped off as though by a giant hand. Near the top a lone Colobus monkey was clinging to the trunk, her long fur wrapped around her like a cloak, from which peeped the tiny purple face and anxious black eyes of her baby. 'Go back to the forest,' I shouted up idiotically to her, 'where you'll be safe!' But even there the great trees were being lashed by the wind and the curtains of lichen which hung from them were billowing out like tattered, ghostly banners.

Then, with unbelievable suddenness, it was over: one minute there was a raging tempest, the next utter silence, as though the heavens themselves were overcome with exhaustion, and in the silence we heard the first plops – slow to begin with, each one sending up a tiny spurt of dust, and then deluging down, obliterating the entire landscape.

'It's rain, real rain!' we shouted deliriously to each other and, still clinging together, did a little dance, not caring that already we were soaked, for the rain was cool and in seconds had washed away the dust from our bodies. Of course it was not possible for the thatch to withstand such a downpour and soon the floor was awash. We just managed to cover our bed with tarpaulin in time, and then rushed to put every bucket and the canvas bath to catch the rain. It seemed criminal to throw all this away, but there was nothing else to be done, and already streams were cascading down the mountains. 'Somehow, before next season, we must build a dam,' Dan shouted, his voice strong and decisive as though the rain had washed away all his despair.

Thus began the rains, but between the deluges the sky cleared and then the light had a piercing brilliance in which everything glittered or shone. All over our fields tender green shoots appeared overnight to grow by the inch. Although the sun was hot, the air had a wonderful crispness and fresh new scents arose from the earth itself, while those of cedar and thyme were accentuated. Within an incredibly short time the wheat and maize were a foot high, the vegetables were becoming distinguishable, and the pyrethrum forming into tiny bushes.

Then back came all the birds from their refuge in the forest: doves, parrots, crested hoopoes, bee-eaters, weavers, starlings and a host of others, their jewel-like plumage iridescent in the sun, while far above buzzards and kites returned to circle endlessly, as though on patrol. It was Eden, and the sense of well-being it brought was extraordinary; I just wanted to take in great breaths of the wonderful air and to let the sun flood through me. Of course, as in every Eden, there were serpents and these had been particularly active before and during the rains. Mambas and puff adders were probably the worst, although I dreaded the spitting cobras most, since they were able to rear up quite high and if their venom touched the eyes it caused blindness. And they always aimed for the eyes. Fear of what such creatures could do emphasized our isolation as nothing else had done, for in the treatment of snake bite speed is of the essence. But Dan was a fine shot and, thanks to the maurading birds, I, too, was now expert with revolver and shotgun. So it became second nature for us to wear revolvers at all times and to be constantly alert.

With the ending of the rains, our thoughts were entirely concentrated upon our crops. And what a beautiful sight these were: a vast sea of wheat over four feet tall, golden, sweet-smelling, and rustling in every breeze; beside it the maize, even taller, and very strong, standing in columns of delicate green rising above a mulch of brown and yellow banana fronds; beyond a snow-drift of flowering pyrethrum and acres of market garden, all surrounded by great swathes of blue mutakwa flowers, yellow cassia and golden rain honeysuckle, the grasses beneath them starred with wild gladioli.

Dan no longer poured over scribbled figures but talked of how good it would be when we could afford batteries for our radio and a stock of beer cooling in a kerosene-run refrigerator. 'But we haven't got a refrigerator,' I protested.

'I know, darling, but you may have one before long, *and* a paraffin water heater. You'd like both, wouldn't you?'

I went to stand before him, hands on hips. 'Dan Cleary,' I said, trying to sound severe, 'you've got that look on your face that means there's something you've not told me – now what is it?'

He opened his eyes wide in a boyish pretence of innocence. 'Darling, I don't know what you're talking about!' he exclaimed, and pulled me down on to his knee to nuzzle my neck.

'You're not going to tell me, are you?' I said, trying hard to resist him.

He shrugged. 'There's nothing to tell.' But two weeks later, when he returned from collecting the mail, he waved a letter at me. '*This* is what you wanted to know!' he said, looking jubilant. 'I sent my medals to Spink and my dress studs to Asprey where they'd come from, and asked if they'd buy them back. Here's the cheque!'

I was appalled. 'Oh, Dan, not your DSO and DFCs.'

'Yes, the whole caboodle.'

'But, my darling, you were *awarded* them for gallantry.'

'To hell with that! Anyway, half the chaps who should have got them were missed out; I just wish I'd had the VC – it would have fetched so much more.'

'And your studs were black pearls . . . '

'Yes, I know, and just the thing to wear in a mud hut.' He spoke lightly, but I remained distressed. 'I wish I had something to sell,' I said sharply, 'but the Sèvres dinner service and the silver were auctioned before we left home.'

'Darling, please don't get into a state over this! Just be thankful we've got some ready money.' He paused, then said more seriously: 'Perhaps we'd better not spend it until after the harvest – that is, if you don't mind waiting a bit longer for the refrigerator?'

The Keneallys had continued to keep in close touch, although I was never able to go out with Terry-May, and we had refused all other invitations, telling them frankly that this was because we could not return their hospitality. But this did not stop them from making us gifts: I would hear a knock and find a smiling young boy holding out a covered basket, with a note saying, 'We've been given a lamb from Molo and cannot possibly eat it all. Can you help out?' And there would be half a leg. Or: 'I know you are never able to get to market, so I wonder if you've had a chance to try Nile perch or black bass?' Or: 'Kimani made this fruit cake yesterday especially for Patrick, who now tells me he's right off it; it's too fattening for me and the children will only eat sponge, so may I ask you to accept it?'

And then Patrick offered the greatest help of all: 'As my crops were planted a little in advance of yours,' he said tentatively, 'I shall finish harvesting before you, so how would it be if I brought my combine over here and helped you gather in your wheat? We could send off our crops together then.'

I held my breath, willing Dan to accept, and this time he did not hesitate. 'That would mean the end of our problems,' he admitted.

Patrick laughed. 'I doubt it! There's no end to the problems of farming in Africa, but I must say everything is looking great here and I can promise you it'll be a high spot in both your lives when you see your crops being harvested; all the toil, anxiety and bone-weariness will be forgotten, and instead there'll be a tremendous feeling of achievement.'

I hugged myself, suddenly joyous. 'I can't wait!' I exclaimed, and although Dan smiled at me indulgently, I knew he was feeling the same, for although wheat and maize were our main crops, the pyrethrum was flourishing and our vegetables were the sweetest, most succulent I had ever tasted. Already we were selling all we could produce and even the new hens were starting to lay well.

So it was with growing excitement that we awaited Patrick's next visit. Late one afternoon he drove up hurriedly, saying, 'We've just finished our harvesting and can start on yours tomorrow, if it's ready.' We held our breath and watched as he broke off some wheat to cup it in his hands. 'Perfect,' he said, as he blew off the chaff, 'very dry and completely free from rust.' He clapped Dan on the back. 'Good show, Bwana, and you too, little Mem!'

'A drink, Patrick?'

'I think not, thanks. My lot will be having a *ngoma* – a party – tonight and I always give them some beef. If I don't hurry back now, they'll take my prize animal – with some very plausible excuse, of course! Also, Verhoeff is coming to spend the night – says he has some important information about a secret society . . . something called Mau-Mau, whatever that means. So, *kwaheri* for now, chums, see you at first light with the harvester and a lorry-load of very hung-over Kukes!'

After Patrick had gone, Dan went to stand looking over our fields. He was silent but I could see from the set of his shoulders that he was relaxed and a feeling of great contentment swept over me. Perhaps, I thought naively, we have come safely through the worst of our worries. I put my arms around Dan's waist and rested my cheek against his back, but immediately he unlaced my fingers so that he could turn to face me. 'To what do I owe this unexpected pleasure?' he asked with mock solemnity.

'I'm just so happy,' I said, smiling up at him.

'Darling Mäuschen, always asking for so little.'

'I love you,' I said, 'did I ever tell you?'

He nodded, still solemn. 'I believe you have mentioned it once or twice.' In fact, I was always telling him, but although he was my ardent, tender lover, always wanting to please me, he never said that he loved me. It was a constant sadness, a hurt, and I turned away quickly so that he could not see the sudden rush of tears to my eyes. Don't be stupid, I told myself sternly, and just be thankful for what you've got – you have him all to yourself, entirely without competition, so remember the line from that Bette Davis film about not asking for the moon when one has the stars.

'Well, I mustn't loiter here,' I said aloud, pretending briskness, and behind me Dan laughed softly. 'Such a busy lady,' he said, gently mocking.

When I got back to our hut I found a tall young Kikuyu standing there. 'I have honey, M'sabu,' he said. 'You buy?'

'Oh, let me see, please,' I said eagerly, and he parted the leaves of a woven basket to reveal a honeycomb, crawling with grubs. 'Oh, no thank you,' I said, stepping back quickly in revulsion.

'Very good honey, M'sabu,' he persisted. 'Very cheap.'

231

'Memsahib has already said no.' Dan spoke with quiet authority from behind me. 'And I say no, too!' The youth muttered something and turned away, his face a sullen mask.

'I wonder if Verhoeff was right about the unrest,' Dan said. 'That one looked as though he could be a very awkward customer.' I shivered suddenly. 'Cold?' Dan asked in surprise.

'No,' I said, 'just someone walking over my grave.'

'Heaven forbid, darling,' Dan answered lightly, 'but there is a breeze springing up, so come inside now.'

That night we went to bed earlier than usual, but as Dan drew me close, he said, 'Only a little cuddle now, because I know if I let you have your way with me, I'll not be fit for harvesting at dawn or any other time tomorrow.'

This was so absurd that I was reduced to helpless giggles. 'I don't know how you have the nerve – ' I began.

'It's true,' his voice was already sleepy, 'catch you on one of your good nights and a man can wake up next morning in a state of shock, barely able to totter about.'

He was asleep, his head against my shoulder, one arm loosely about my waist. To move would have disturbed him, so I lay still, listening as the breeze freshened into a wind that sighed eerily through the great trees and caused the thorns on the lower slopes to make a whistling noise, while much more faintly came the sound of drums and the strange rhythm of native singing. I must have dozed then, only to awaken with a suddenly thudding heart, for there was a new sound which I could not identify: a roaring, crackling sound. 'Dan,' I whispered urgently, 'are you awake?'

'Well, I am now.'

'Listen, something strange is happening outside – '

He lifted his head briefly, then leapt off the bed. 'Christ, it's fire! The thatch must be on fire!' But it was our wheat, not the thatch: a blazing sea with flames and smoke rising hundreds of feet into the air. 'Come on!' Dan shouted desperately. 'Come on, we've got to stop it – beat it out!'

Of course it was quite hopeless. The fire was racing through our fields far faster than we could ever hope to contain it. Yet Dan would not give up and was frenziedly beating it with a canvas sheet and stamping the ground, seemingly oblivious of the heat penetrating the soles of his boots. It was like a nightmare, for with every change in the wind, flames and smoke came rushing towards us, scorching our skin, blinding us and filling our lungs. Sparks flew everywhere as though in a mad dance and already one of the great forest cedars had burst into a brilliant bouquet at its top. Then the bamboo paling caught and began exploding like dozens of rifles being fired simultaneously.

I ran to put my arms around Dan's waist. 'Stop it! Stop it! You'll be burned alive!' I screamed as I tried to tug him back, but he thrust an elbow into my ribs so hard that I fell backwards.

'Get away from me!' he shouted as though demented. 'Get away!'

I struggled to my feet. Many living creatures were leaving their homes and burrows in the wheat. I saw a bird rise very briefly, with body blazing and wings fluttering feebly, before it dived once more into the flames. Like us, I thought hysterically, and for an instant even wanted to throw myself into them too . . . then I saw the lights of three or four vehicles racing up our drive where they stopped. Dark figures leapt out to shouted commands and began racing towards the fire. And I ran forward to clutch at Patrick's lapels.

'Make him stop! Oh, Patrick, please make him stop before he's killed! Please, please!'

I felt Patrick's arms go gently around me. 'Yes, yes, Minette! It's all right, it's really all right!'

But then I was conscious of Janni Verhoeff beside Patrick saying, 'Just leave him to me!' and as he ran towards Dan, I tore myself away from Patrick and followed at a stumbling trot, for I was frightened of Janni Verhoeff and what he would do. But I was not in time to stop him from swinging Dan around and giving him such a blow to the jaw that he was felled and lay without movement.

'Oh, what have you done?' I shrieked. 'What have you *done?*' I flung myself down to cradle Dan's head: 'Dan, Dan, my dearest love, my darling, don't die! Don't leave me! Oh, Dan, do speak to me!'

Janni pushed me roughly aside, then stooped and picked up Dan whom he flung over his shoulder like a sack of potatoes. Dan was just over six feet and weighed some fifteen stone, but it was only later that I marvelled at Janni's strength; at that first moment, seeing Dan with head and arms hanging limply, I was convinced he was dead, and I stumbled after them, silent now but bent double, with arms folded across my stomach against the agony of grief that welled up from the very centre of my being. It was then that the tiny part of my brain which had remained calm enough to hear, see and record, finally gave up.

I have no recollection of anything else until I awoke to find bright sunlight shining through pretty curtains patterned with faded yellow and apricot roses. I looked around with a strange detached curiosity: it was a high raftered room, simply furnished with sturdy white-painted furniture and rag rugs on the wood floor. A bowl of creamy-white roses, delicately edged with carmine, stood on the dressing-table, their blooms enormous and their scent filling the room. I lay on a bed with unbelievably soft pillows and fine linen; the sheet covering me had a border of hand-embroidered Richelieu work all in white, and I thought how expert the stitching was. I wonder where I am and what I'm doing here, I thought without too much concern, but then: Where's Dan? I turned at once and found him looking at me.

'Hello, Mäuschen,' he said, his voice quiet and very flat.

I bent over him. 'Oh, Dan, your face!'

He nodded. 'Yes, and yours too, although you still have your eyebrows, but Terry-May says it'll soon fade.'

I held my head in my hands. 'I can't seem to focus my thoughts,' I said miserably, 'I feel so woolly-headed.'

'That's because Terry-May gave you a knock-out drop.'

'Only me? Not you too?'

Dan smiled wryly and ran his fingers over his chin. 'I hardly needed one! Verhoeff saw to that!'

I remembered then. 'Yes – yes! Oh, God, I thought you were dead!'

He moved restlessly. 'No, still alive, although at this moment I rather wish I were dead.'

'Oh Dan, darling – darling – what a thing to say!'

'Well, perhaps you don't realize that everything's gone and it's all my fault?'

'I . . . don't understand. How could it be?'

'Because I should have made a fire-break.'

'But you couldn't have known!'

'Of course I should have! Any fool knows that crops are vulnerable, and one of the few ways of protecting them is to have adequate fire and wind-breaks!'

A soft knock on the door saved me from answering. Two houseboys appeared, smiling tentatively and murmuring a greeting. The younger carried two neatly folded piles which I realized were our clothes, all washed and ironed, and the elder bore a tray of tea and wafer-thin home-made biscuits which he put on the bed between Dan and me. 'My Memsahib says breakfast on the verandah when you are ready,' he said in carefully accented English.

The pretty china was set on a cloth of green linen whose borders were bright with large pansies worked in the same expert Richelieu embroidery. I must not get a drop on it, I thought, but when I picked up the teapot my hand shook so much that I had to put it down again.

'Here, let me,' Dan said, 'it's shock, my darling.'

'Did you say everything had gone?' I asked hesitantly as realization suddenly hit me.

'It must have.'

'But – but – what are we going to do?'

Dan's bark of laughter was both bitter and humourless. 'God only knows! Don't ask me!'

It was his bleak look as much as his tone that broke me. As the tears just fell out of my eyes, I whispered, 'I don't think I can take any more.'

He leapt off the bed and padded round to me. 'Forgive me, Mäuschen,' he said gently as he enfolded me. 'I'm being a brute, but it's really because I'm so furious with myself. Don't cry now, please don't. I promise I'll think of something.'

'Whatever happens – we'll still be together, won't we?' I asked, looking up at him fearfully.

'Oh, of course, sweetheart! Of course!'

As always, with the worst of my fears assuaged, I began to feel more optimistic, but later when Patrick said: 'We managed to save most of the vegetables, the hens and your rondavels,' my heart went out to Dan.

'I just cannot thank you enough, Patrick,' he replied with unusual humility, 'and I am only sorry that you had to bring out your labour and do all the hard work.'

'Ah now, think nothing of it,' Patrick said quickly, 'my boys were all up anyway and full of *pombe* – sorry, native beer – so it did them good to work.'

'Well, I shall never forgive myself,' Dan said, 'to have caused so much disruption and disaster just through lack of a fire-break!' The words were quietly spoken, but I

236

sensed his deep humiliation: in the past he had been involved in the defence of a whole continent and been cognizant of the West's most sophisticated weapons, yet the lack of a simple fire-break had defeated him.

Patrick, in the act of pouring coffee, turned quickly. 'But you're being too hard on yourself!' he exclaimed. 'A fire-break without labour wouldn't have saved your crops. As it was, even without one, my boys were able to control it *and* prevent the whole forest from going up.'

'But how did it start, that's what I'd like to know?'

Patrick shrugged. 'With the forest floor covered with dead leaves and cedar, which is a juniper, and catches fire very easily, it only requires the tiniest spark – ask any Forestry Officer and he'll tell you it's the bane of his life. The locals don't help either. At this time of year they will go around collecting honey from hollow cedar trees where the bees build their hives. The technique is to smoke them out by lighting a fire inside the bole of the tree, then shinning up to collect the honeycombs while the bees are dispersed. But of course no African will ever think to put out the fire afterwards, even though such fires can rage for weeks and thousands of trees are lost through them every year.'

'Why, that's the answer!' I exclaimed. 'We did have an African suddenly appear yesterday evening, wanting us to buy honey!'

'There you are then, Dan,' Patrick said, sounding relieved, 'that ought to convince you that it was not all your fault, but just one of Kenya's many hazards – Jésu, the history of this country is made up of hazards and disasters! Anything and everything from fire, flood, drought, plagues of locusts, Antesia bugs, army worm, rinderpest and cattle fluke – to name just a few! One year you can be positively affluent, the next almost wiped out financially!' As Dan only nodded sombrely, Patrick said

237

with a smile: 'Don't tell me I've got a bloody Englishman here who's given up already!'

To my great relief, Dan then returned the smile and replied, 'Not if there's enough bloody Irish blarney to keep me going!'

But once back on our own farm it was difficult not to feel beaten at the sight of black stubble stretching as far as the eye could see. Every step we took stirred up grey ash, inches deep, and the air was still heavy with the acrid smell of burnt cedar. We just stood there silently, remembering all the toil, the sweat, the exhaustion – and the hopes we had put into our golden fields. Then Dan said: 'What do you want to do, Mäuschen?'

I knew at once what he meant, but deliberately pretended not to, 'Well,' I said, 'we still have a roof over our heads, so I vote we go to the bank for a loan.'

'All right,' Dan answered slowly after a long pause, 'let's do that straight away.'

16

Dan and I had both lived long enough by then to know that not everyone is given a second chance, so when ours came in the form of a large bank loan, we seized it eagerly. How best to use it caused much heart-searching and endless discussions, but eventually we agreed that water to keep crops irrigated must have priority, so a Sikh *fundi* was hired to build a dam; then we took on more labour to clear some of our uncultivated acreage and erect sheds for our growing number of implements. I was once more driving the tractor from dawn to dusk, and Dan back to supervising the field workers, for although we now had fifty families living on our land, we still had not acquired a head man.

When Terry-May said they were going to the Coast for Christmas and asked if we could join them, Dan vetoed it. 'I must get hold of a harvester somehow,' he explained 'and then a Land Rover, because the van won't last much longer. So, Mäuschen darling, I'm afraid we'll have to stick it out here without anything to make Christmas special this year.'

'Never mind,' I said at once, 'think how much we'll appreciate the good times when they come.' But in the event that Christmas was very special. It started when the Keneallys sent over a turkey, two bottles of wine and a pudding, making sure we could not refuse any of it by instructing their head man, Joseph, to bring it over only after they had left for Kilifi.

When the turkey took far longer than anticipated to cook, Dan suggested we should try the red wine while we were waiting. He then launched into a sparkling account of wartime Christmases which soon had me laughing helplessly. Somehow, I've never fully understood how we managed it, we ended up by drinking the whole bottle before the turkey was ready, and when at last it was, Dan said: 'It's so good that I think we ought to try the other bottle, to help our digestion, if nothing else.' And we ended up drinking all of that too. It was only when I got up and my head swam that I realized. 'Why, I'm quite squiffy!' I exclaimed in astonishment, and Dan's laugh was loud in the little room.

'Squiffy?' he echoed, smiling up at me. 'My darling girl, you're as high as a kite! And I'm not much better myself!'

'Oh, well,' I said as I rather dreamily started to gather up the plates, 'it's a very happy state.'

And then Dan burst into song, making the walls of the room reverberate to the sound of *Adeste Fideles* which I followed up with *Silent Night*. After that we were in competition as to who could think up the next carol. We were still singing lustily as we went with arms around each other into the bedroom where, given the huge meal and all the wine consumed, we might have been expected to fall instantly asleep. Instead we were wide-awake and that night we did not just make love, we *were* love; a rare experience in which we gave to each other all that we had, all that we were, emotionally and spiritually, using the physical as the best, the ultimate way of expressing all that we felt. Truly, a night of heart-stopping wonder, happiness and utter delight.

Yet eight weeks later it was the cause of the first real quarrel we'd ever had. I had been on a rare journey to Nakuru and, as I returned, Dan was just bringing in the *debes* of water. 'Hello, darling,' he called out cheerily, 'did you get what you wanted?'

I leapt out of the van, and danced rather than walked across to him. 'Come indoors,' I commanded. 'I've got

240

something so amazing to tell you that you'll need to sit down!'

'Then let me guess,' he said, entering into my obviously joyous mood, 'there was a letter waiting for you at the Post Office informing you that an unknown relation had left you a fortune?'

'No, no, nothing like that!'

'Then you've found out that we have gold under our land – '

'No!'

'Diamonds then?'

'No, no.'

'Well then, what else – copper, perhaps?'

'Dan – oh, Dan – it's something far more wonderful.'

'OK, I give up.'

'I – we – we're going to have a baby!' I had expected the utmost astonishment, even speechlessness, but not the sudden rigidity, the draining of all expression from his face and eyes. When at last he spoke it was in a hoarse, unfamiliar voice: 'You're joking, of course?'

'No, *of course* not! Darling, isn't it the most wonder – '

'Hold on,' he said, 'if you're a bit late, it doesn't necessarily mean – '

I shook my head slowly, beaming at him as the joy, which had been momentarily checked by his reaction, rose up again like a tidal wave within me. 'I've seen a doctor, I've had the test, and there's absolutely no doubt: I'm well and truly preggers!'

Again there was a pause, then he said quietly, 'Oh, good Christ, I wouldn't have put you through this for the world, but of course it's impossible – I'll have to go down and talk to Wilson.'

I frowned in bewilderment. 'Wilson?'

'Dr Wilson.'

'Oh, but – but I went to Dr Engel, the one Terry-May told us about.'

'Surely not that fellow who has a rundown surgery near the market? Good God, Mäuschen, are you completely out of your mind?'

The tidalwave of joy had ebbed once more, leaving only a sensation of choking. 'I went to him because he was in Auschwitz and only survived because he was allowed to practise as a doctor. He knows more than most about difficult births.'

'And what did he say about you?'

'Only – only that I-I might have to rest completely during the last couple of months – '

'You gave him all your medical history?'

'Of course.'

Dan started to pace about the little room, hands in pockets and head bent. 'I wonder if he'd consider a termination, in the circumstances?'

'A – a termination?' I asked, not daring to acknowledge even to myself that I knew what he meant.

'Yes, in view of what doctors have told you in the past.'

Something snapped in me then and I jumped up, overturning my chair, and rushed blindly about the room, screaming. When Dan made to grab my arm, I shrank back from him. 'Get away!' I screamed ever more wildly. 'You murderer – murderer of your own child! Don't ever come near me again!' Of course, within seconds he had caught me and then he slapped me across the face but with such force that my head snapped to one side and I staggered back against the wall. That stopped the screaming, but when he said, 'Oh, Mäuschen darling, I'm so sorry, please forgive me,' and would have taken me in his arms, I tried to melt into the wall, my own arms clutched across my stomach, 'No!' I whispered. 'No!'

'Darling, come and sit down and let's talk this over quietly – '

'No, I-I don't want to – '

He was silent for a few seconds, just looking at me with distraught eyes. 'All right then,' he said at last, 'I'll heat the water so that you can have a warm bath and then if you'd like to get into bed, I'll bring you something to eat.'

'I don't *want* anything to eat,' I said, spitting out the words and knowing that for the first time ever I was being deliberately cruel to him.

He let out his breath in a long sigh. 'Well, I'll heat the water anyway,' he said and turned away, his wide shoulders sagging. It was this uncharacteristic sight that roused me from my anger and fear; he looked so tired, so *beaten*, that within seconds I had padded after him.

'Dan,' I said in a small voice, 'I'm sorry.'

He whirled at once, arms enfolding me. 'Ah, darling Mäuschen, so am I,' he said, ready as always to meet me half way, 'and of course it's all my fault, but I swear to you that if I'd thought there was the slightest chance of this happening, I would have taken precautions.'

'I thought you'd be so pleased,' I said woefully.

'Darling, I would – I would, if only conditions were different. Why, good God, I'd be dancing for joy – but how *can* we have a baby here?'

'Well,' I said, suddenly falsely bright, 'he won't be the first baby to be brought up in a mud hut.'

'But d'you realize we haven't even got a drawer to lay it in?'

'Yes, I've thought of that, and the answer is to get one of the women to weave a Moses-type basket and then if you could perhaps make a table or just two trestles to raise the basket off the floor – '

'Let's sit down,' Dan suggested, obviously preparing for a long session. He pulled me on to his knee. 'What happens if the baby wriggles so much that the basket overturns? And what happens when we get to the toddler stage?'

'Well, perhaps you could make him one of those old-fashioned cots with high sides, so that he could stand upright within it?'

'Perhaps I could, but there's another important factor: how are we going to feed the child?'

'Oh, *that's* no problem!' I answered, sitting up straight and puffing out my chest. 'You forget, I already have built-in nourishment for him.'

But Dan only laughed mirthlessly. 'My darling girl, you look as though you need to be put on a full cream diet yourself – you're totally unfit to feed a baby!'

'I doubt that, but if you *are* right, we could always get cow's milk from Patrick's animals.'

'And another thing,' Dan said, as though continuing his own line of thought, 'where and how is Engel planning for you to give birth?'

'Well, he has a tiny building in the grounds of his surgery where patients anticipating difficulties are admitted.'

'Some sort of hut, I suppose?'

'No, it's a proper building. Perhaps a – a bit stark, but very clean and smelling strongly of antiseptic.'

'And you would be willing to go there?'

'I'd go anywhere to have our baby – '

'And didn't Engel even *hint* that there might be complications in your case?'

'W-e-ll, he did say that he wouldn't let me be in labour too long before doing a Caesarean – '

Dan set me down gently on my feet, then got up to pace restlessly about the floor. 'A Caesarean? Oh, God! And, besides, there are all sorts of hazards before we ever get to that stage: what happens if you suddenly go into premature labour? The best I could do would be to take you five miles over a pot-holed track to the Keneallys' in the hope that Terry-May could look after you.'

'Dan, I've already thought of all the hazards and – and I know it may all end in tragedy, but couldn't we at least

244

try? Our baby was conceived on Christmas Night, like a gift from God.'

I thought Dan was going to explode at that. 'I've never heard such stupid, romantic twaddle! It's high time you came down to earth, Mäuschen, and faced facts. Do you know how many – ' He saw my stricken face and made a superhuman effort to regain control. 'Please, darling, think this through very carefully, not only for our sakes but for the child's as well.'

'I *have* thought, Dan, and for anything else that concerns us, I will always bow to your judgement – I promise you that – but no one, not even you, is going to take our baby away from me.'

'I see. So you would prefer all the pain and grief that a miscarriage would mean?'

'I shall do everything humanly possible not to lose the baby, but if I do, I shall know that it was not meant to be.'

Across the room his angry eyes locked with mine, but his voice remained quiet. 'Then there's nothing more to be said, is there?'

'No,' I whispered, feeling totally deflated, 'there's not.'

That night, apart from a quick kiss on my cheek and a brusque 'Good night, Mäuschen,' Dan turned away from me, something that had never happened before in all our time together. I doubt if he slept – he lay too still – and I did not sleep either until the night was far advanced. When I awoke it was to find him already dressed and lacing his chukka boots. I scrambled up with a muffled exclamation as he said: 'I've made the tea. I'll bring you a cup in a minute.'

'But I must get up,' I said, pushing back the sheet and thin blanket.

'No point in hurrying,' he replied as he stood up, 'you'll not be able to do anything outside.'

'Not do anything!' I echoed in astonishment. 'Of course I'm going to carry on as usual. Dr Engel said I could do

245

everything except drive the tractor as the jolting might not be too good for me.'

Dan shrugged. 'Oh, right-ho then,' he said curtly as he turned and left the room.

Tears rushed to my eyes, but I blinked them back. I must give him time to adjust to all this, I thought, and I must try not to be ill – oh God, don't let me have morning sickness! The inexorable voice inside my head immediately reminded me of my promise never to ask for anything again, but this time I ignored it, and to the surprise of Dr Engel did not suffer from the dreaded morning sickness.

'I do feel very sick every morning,' I confided to Terry-May, 'but so long as I go immediately into the open air and don't eat anything, it passes.'

'Well, thanks be to God for that,' she replied fervently, 'for sure it's a great blessing. Why, I remember that every morning, the moment I raised my head from the pillow, I was horribly sick. It went on for almost three months. Patrick, the darlin' man, became expert at holding my head and emptying basins.' She must have sensed my sadness for she said, 'I'm sure Dan is thrilled to bits, isn't he?'

I broke down then and told her the truth.

'Sure now, aren't these men of ours the limit? They wed us and bed us and then show amazement at the most natural outcome – a baby!'

I nodded, but of course I could not betray Dan by telling her that he had never expected to become a father again.

'And don't you be worrying about cradles and clothes,' Terry-May was saying, 'I can lend you everything.'

But even this news failed to alter Dan's mood. 'I'm just so sick and tired of having to be forever grateful to the Keneallys!' he burst out as he paced restlessly about our tiny kitchen, clenched hands deep in trouser pockets. Irritation and hurt battled within me as I looked at him, yet deep down I did understand, for Dan was a proud man who had always been entirely self-reliant, and memories of those years when he had command of money in millions had still not completely faded. So I kept my voice quiet as I said: 'I know it goes against the grain, darling, but let's just be thankful we have such kind friends – and – and look forward to the day when we can repay them in some way.'

'But how?' he demanded. 'Just tell me how are we going to do that?'

'I don't know,' I admitted reluctantly, 'but we're going to be here for the rest of our lives, so surely there will be something, some time. And, darling, they are so pleased for us – ' I took a deep breath ' – as you will be when your son is placed in your arms.'

He came to stand in front of me, frowning and taut-faced. 'You keep on referring to this son – what makes you so sure it will be a boy?'

'Because – because we may never again be parents and I just know in my heart of hearts that I'm carrying a boy.'

'Then all I can say is, you're going to be a very disappointed woman when you wake up and find you've given birth to a mere girl!'

'Oh, no – no, of course not! I should dearly love a little girl – I want a son for you!'

'But I don't want – ' He realized too late what he was admitting and I finished the sentence: 'You don't want either, do you?' As he slowly and sombrely shook his head, I just sank down into a despairing bundle, mindlessly sobbing.

'Ah, Mäuschen, don't, please don't.' He came at once to kneel beside me and draw me close. 'I'm sorry, I didn't mean it. Please stop crying before you make yourself ill. Please stop now – oh God, I don't know what to do!'

Somehow the mixture of alarm and irritation in his voice got through to me. I swallowed hard on my own emotion, blew my nose and stood up. 'It's all right,' I said quietly, 'I'm not ill and I – I won't cry any more.'

Dan stood up too. 'Darling – '

'No, there's no need to say anything more. I understand, really I do.'

'I didn't mean it. I didn't know what I was saying. Of course I'll be delighted to have a son or a daughter.' He was trying hard to make amends, but I knew it was only for my sake and that he *had* meant those harsh words. But I pretended, nodding, and even smiling a little through my tears. 'That's – wonderful then.'

'Then you'll forgive and forget this conversation?'

'Yes, of course, Dan darling.' He came and put his arms gently around me and I rested my head against his chest as I had done so many times before, but now there was something missing; something very precious had gone out of our relationship and I wondered with great but surprising calmness whether it would ever be regained. So engrossed was I in our own troubles that I quite forgot to pass on the news I'd heard on Terry-May's radio: that Princess Elizabeth, on her first official visit to Kenya with her handsome husband, had gone to spend the night in a little Wendy house high up in a forest tree top, and when she descended the rope ladder that morning she had already become Queen of England.

In the weeks that followed I grew closer to Terry-May, no doubt partly because she was a fellow female who had given birth, but mainly because she never failed to give me confidence. Hers was truly a blithe spirit, and although I never again talked of Dan's attitude – and she never asked – she always sensed when I was particularly unhappy and would say, 'It will pass and all will be well,' words not offered as facile consolation, but said with a sunny smile and deep conviction; it was a philosophy which governed her own life in both minor and major events and one which I realized must have carried her and Patrick through all the agony and trauma of his terrible wounds.

My other great source of comfort was Dr Engel and he, too, tended to say that all would pass, but whereas Terry-May's belief stemmed from an unshakeable Faith, his conviction came from having survived the ultimate in terror, agony and horror; he did not believe all would be well, but whether good or bad, that it would pass. On that first visit to him, he had asked me why I had consulted him rather than Dr Wilson, who was the local European community's General Practitioner, and I had told him that I knew he had been in Auschwitz and must therefore have had great experience of difficult births; as I was afraid my baby's would be another, I felt he was the right doctor for me. He had asked then about my own work in Germany and, as I rather haltingly explained, he sat absolutely still, his large almond-shaped eyes never leaving my face. Ever since, although maintaining professional detachment, I felt he took a keen personal interest in my case and was as determined as I that my pregnancy should be successful.

My conviction that the baby would be a boy was also reinforced in a strange way: I had driven over one morning to see Terry-May and when told that she was up in the labour lines, I set off to meet her. I walked slowly, admiring all the sights around me of a large, very well run and prosperous farm. What a long way we have to go before we achieve anything like this, I thought as I finally left the immediate environs and walked towards the rondavels of the Kikuyu workers, where thin spirals of blue smoke were rising through their roofs. They consisted of family units, with a separate hut for each of a man's wives, and the communal grain store – a bulbous structure of interwoven thorn boughs mounted on stilts – standing in the centre, the whole enclosed in a strong *boma* of the same wood. Within these, tiny naked totos wandered uncertainly about while hens pecked at the dirt and mongrel dogs scratched, yawned or bit at their fleas. All around the ground was heavily cultivated with maize, sweet potatoes and beans. Elderly women were tending these, while others were bringing in great loads of firewood, banana fronds and gourds of water, mainly balanced on their heads, and walking effortlessly upright. It was a typical pastoral scene, set against the backdrop of the forest, pungent with all the smells of an African village, and with the sound of goat bells clonking in the distance.

I stopped to admire it, thinking how much I should like to paint it all, and then noticed the ancient man who was hunkered down in the shade of a sacred fig tree, his staff and a number of gourds beside him. He wore a shapeless cotton garment, knotted clumsily at the one shoulder it covered, and he appeared almost devoid of body fat for his bones protruded painfully at all the joints; his head was completely shaven and the hugely extended lobes of his ears had round wooden discs inserted into them. His eyes, under thick, heavily wrinkled and strangely reptilian lids, were milky-white with cataracts, yet he unhesitatingly raised a bony arm and said: '*Jambo*, Memsahib.' Clever of him, I thought, as I returned the greeting, for he must be completely blind. I suppose my footsteps sound quite different from those of a barefoot African.

'Hello there!' Terry-May's happy voice rang out as she came swinging towards me, a large medical case in one hand. 'Sorry you had to come all this way, but the clinic took much longer than expected, for didn't Mwange's youngest fall on the fire early this morning? The poor little fellow has quite extensive burns, although they're superficial, luckily.'

'Oh, how awful! Will he have to go into hospital?'

'I'd really like him to be seen at least, but it's such a flurry they all get into if hospital is even mentioned, so I said I'd try to treat him. But if there's any sign of infection, I shall insist on taking him. Totos are forever falling on the fire in these huts – not at all surprising when you think of the fug they get up in the evenings with all the family plus the goats in there, the cooking pot boiling, and not a breath of fresh air in the place. 'Tis no wonder, either, that ophthalmia is still so rife. *Jambo*, M'zee! This is our resident witch doctor who – '

We stopped in our tracks as the old man raised a fleshless arm loaded with wire bangles and pointed at me, his sightless eyes seemingly focused upon me. He spoke quietly, yet with absolute authority, but although the Swahili I had understood in my childhood had largely returned to me, I had never mastered the many intricacies of Kikuyu, so I looked with some apprehension at Terry-May, who smiled broadly and said: 'He is telling you that you carry a fine son.'

'Oh, I knew it! I just *knew* it!' I exclaimed joyfully and did a little quick-step of happiness. But the old man was speaking again and once more I looked to Terry-May; she turned quickly away, yet not before I had seen the smile wiped off her face.

'What? What?' I demanded, but she shrugged.

'I couldn't get it all – you know how these old boys waffle on.'

'But you must have understood *something*!'

It was her turn to look at me. 'Well, don't be getting in a state now, but he was saying something about "Beware the day of the lion!"'

'The day of the lion,' I repeated slowly, 'but what does that mean?'

251

'Why, nothing, nothing at all.'

'But it sounds so like a warning – '

'Ah, but isn't the whole Kikuyu culture full of warnings, superstitions and spells, good and bad? And he's a real doom and gloom merchant! Sure now, didn't he tell me we'd only leave the farm twice more: once to go to the green city, and then to be buried. And that all our bones would lie together.'

A shadow seemed to pass over the sun, but I've never known whether it was real or imaginary; I certainly shuddered, but Terry-May said brightly, 'Faith, but I'm longing for my coffee! Let's be getting back to the house now, because I want to show you my new rose and you must take some buds home with you.'

But I was still trying to puzzle out the witch-doctor's words and suddenly burst out: 'Oh, I know! In astrology August is the month of the lion, so perhaps that's what he meant. Not the day, but the month. As I shall be in my eighth month by then I really shall have to take extra care . . . although I can't see the connection between Western astrology and an African witch-doctor, can you?'

Once again Terry-May shrugged. 'No, except that it's all mumbo-jumbo, but I'm advising you to forget it. After all, you're taking every care and are not likely to start playing with lions, are you? Now here's my rose. It's called "Peace" and only appeared three years ago. Isn't it the most beautiful you've ever seen?'

It would be wrong to say that I forgot the witch-doctor's words, but I certainly put them to the back of my mind for in the weeks that followed I continued to be very well, and certainly did not even catch a glimpse of a lion anywhere. Dan's attitude seemed to soften a little after he had seen Dr Engel. He did not tell me of the visit until he returned, adding: 'Engel thinks there is every possibility of your having this baby successfully, but we've agreed that you must go into the War Memorial Hospital in Nakuru for the birth and that you may have to be admitted as much as two weeks in advance.'

'Two weeks! But – but we can't possibly afford for me to be in hospital all that time!'

'Darling,' Dan said patiently, 'whatever it costs it will be cheaper than having to rush you in as an emergency, so don't start worrying about it. And, anyway, Engel explained that much depends on the weight of the foetus; he wants this kept as light as possible to ease the strain on your spine and back muscles – no doubt he's told you this already – and also that you should spend as much time as you can resting with your legs up, so I've bought you a cane chaise-longue – '

I ran to hug him and, as his arms closed about me, he said, 'You must promise me faithfully that as soon as your back begins to ache, you'll sit down.'

'I promise,' I said, so happy at that moment that I would have promised anything.

He kissed me briefly on the temple before turning away. 'I've also bought new shock absorbers and springs for the van which I want to fit straight away, so that you'll have a decent journey next time you go out.'

It wasn't much of a change, but enough to make me feel as light as air with joy.

17

It was at this time that Dainty came into our lives and my story would not be complete without her. I have said that our bed took up most of the so-called bedroom, but even so it had been necessary to push it against the wall, and therefore under the window, and of course it made sense that I should sleep on that side, thus leaving Dan free to leap up in any emergency. The window was still just an aperture and in good weather we did not block this with the crude bamboo shutter, both of us having been brought up to believe that a bedroom window *had* to be left open, no matter what the temperature.

Patrick had been right on that first evening when he had said that other creatures would make their home in our roof and we had soon become accustomed to strange rustlings and even a faint squeak now and then. Once I had even thought I could see a tiny eye looking down at me, but at that instant Dan had blown out the lamp and I had told myself with great firmness that it was just a trick of the light. There were always at least two tiny geckos – house lizards – on the walls and if, in the darkness, I felt feather-like movement over my face, I always lay absolutely still until it had passed.

But one night I awoke with my heart thumping loudly in my ears, for *something* was blowing on me from the window and I knew it was the warm breath of some large creature. For a few seconds I was petrified, but then I realized that Dan was sleeping with his face towards me and with very little movement I could put my mouth close to his ear.

'Dan,' I whispered urgently, 'wake up, please wake up!' And never had I been so glad of his capacity for instant alertness. As soon as he stirred, I mouthed into his ear: 'There's something at the window,' and was just able to hear his command: 'Keep absolutely still!'

There was a slight rustle as he turned to feel for the torch and revolver on the box and then in one lightning movement he sat up with both pointing at the window. 'Good God,' he exclaimed, 'it's a bloody cow!' It was indeed a bovine face that gazed back at us with huge eyes blinking in the light and head so small that it fitted neatly into the opening.

'Why, how pretty and tiny she is!' I exclaimed.

'Yes, well,' Dan said, flicking off the torch, 'now that we know it's a harmless creature, we needn't worry and no doubt it'll go away in a minute.'

'But where to?'

'Well, wherever it came from.'

'Dan, don't you realize that it's most extraordinary for a solitary cow to appear anywhere in the middle of the night?'

'Maybe it is, but there's nothing we can do about it.'

'But supposing a lion gets her?'

'Darling, it's two o'clock in the morning – '

'Couldn't we – couldn't we just give her shelter until morning?'

'My dear girl, we've only enough shelter for ourselves. Where would you suggest we put a cow?'

'Well, perhaps – perhaps in the passage-way?'

'Indoors? Here? Impossible! There's no knowing what she'd get up to! Besides, how would I ever get her into such a small space?'

'There's that bit of rope in the kitchen; if you made a noose and then led her – '

'Mäuschen, it's just not on, you must know that! Now, turn over on to this side and I'll pull the blanket up around your head so you don't feel her breath, and I guarantee that in no time at all, she'll have gone!'

I turned over obediently, but instantly a mental picture arose of a lion leaping on to the cow's back, great teeth sinking into her throat, while another huge beast ripped at her underside . . . when a pathetic little moo came from the window, I shot up with a muffled exclamation: 'Dan, I'm sorry, but I'll have to get up!'

'What for?' he demanded suspiciously.

'I can't *bear* to leave her out there, exposed to all the dangers. I really can't!'

'All right, you win,' he said, sighing exaggeratedly as he tossed back the bed clothes and lit the lamp. I don't suppose any man likes getting up in the middle of the night on some non-urgent matter and Dan was no exception, yet I looked at him with great tenderness for there he was, a powerfully built grown man, somehow transformed into a truculent small boy with hair standing on end and lower lip thrust out belligerently. 'You wait here,' he commanded as he left, taking the lamp, and a few minutes later I heard him say, 'Now come along, girl, get your head out of that window and into this noose.' There followed the unmistakable sounds of man and beast engaged in a tussle of wills: 'No, not in here! Just turn around – *this* way, you stupid animal! Now go forward – oh, for heaven's sake, move! Yes, that's right. Now, whoa! whoa, I say. WHOA!'

I got to the doorway just in time to see them both come to a full stop in the narrow passage-way. 'Well,' Dan said unnecessarily, 'I've brought her in as you insisted, but God only knows how I'm ever going to get her out!' She was a little native cow, hump-backed and creamy-beige, with the biggest, most gentle eyes imaginable.

'We'll manage,' I said confidently, 'she's only little.' I moved forward with hand outstretched to pat her, but Dan instantly stepped between us and seized my wrist.

'Have a care, Mäuschen! She could easily lash out at you!'

'I'm sure she wouldn't.' But I did take a step back to please him. 'I wonder if she'd like a drink?'

'Oh, why not offer her tea and toast?'

'Really, darling, don't be so absurd!' I answered tartly, and Dan's guffaw was loud in the silence. '*I'm* absurd? Well, if that isn't the limit!' Yet he went at once to fetch the pail of water we always kept in the kitchen. When he put it down in front of her, the little cow drank thirstily until she had finished all the water, then a large purple tongue came out to lick the last drops from her muzzle.

'I think she's exhausted,' I said and, as though on cue, her forelegs buckled and she sank down.

'You do realize, don't you, that this animal is not house trained?' Dan said.

'It's all right,' I answered, for she was looking up at me as though imploring me to protect her, 'I'll clear it all up in the morning.' But in the event she behaved impeccably and our only difficulty was getting her out of the confined space. I was not allowed to help and could only watch, fighting hard to stop the giggles, as Dan strove to make her understand. Once outside, they both stood panting, and the little cow looked smaller than ever.

'I think we'll call her Dainty – '

Dan swung round, red-faced beneath his tan, and looking quite shocked. 'You're surely not planning to keep her?'

'Well, why not, if she'd like to stay?'

'Mäuschen, are you out of your mind? Any minute now an African will appear to claim this animal and I'll have a hard job convincing him that I didn't entice her away from his herd.'

'But supposing no one does come?'

'Well, she'll no doubt wander off – '

'Oh no, no, we can't let her! She'd be killed – it's a wonder she reached here safely. We've not seen any native herds anywhere near here; she must have come a long way.'

'So if she managed to get here safely, why can't she return just as safely?'

'Because, for one thing, the herd has probably moved on by now and she might not be able to find it.'

Dan looked at his watch. 'I *must* get on. Let's just wait and see what happens, shall we? We've no fodder for her, so no doubt that will be the deciding factor.' But once again, as though on cue, Dainty moved quietly across to the overgrown side of our huts and lowered her head; when, within seconds, there was the sound of tearing and chomping, I smiled triumphantly at Dan who merely shook his head and turned away. Dainty was still munching when I returned from weeding the vegetables at midday, and when I finally finished in the late afternoon she was standing beneath the cedar, ears twitching at the cloud of flies surrounding her and looking as though she had been there forever. I'll have to raise the question of shelter for tonight, I thought as I started to prepare the evening meal, but as soon as Dan came in he began pouring over figures and forms. Better wait, I told myself, and then gasped as Dainty appeared in the doorway. Dan and I were both transfixed until I said faintly, 'I-I think she wants to go to bed!'

He leapt up. 'Oh no you don't! Not again!'

'What are you going to do with her?' I asked, preparing for battle.

'Put her in the shed with the tractor.'

'But there's no door!'

'I'll drive the tractor across the opening which should deter all but the most determined predator.'

But of course I knew that was not true and spent a sleepless night waiting for a dying shriek. It did not come, but next morning I noticed that Dan hurried up to the shed, and a few minutes later when he reappeared leading

Dainty, I saw him pat her on the neck and gently pull one of her ears. I believe he really does like her, I thought gleefully, but that evening was not so sure, for by then it was obvious that Dainty needed to be milked. 'I've never done it,' Dan said, sounding quite confident, 'but there can't be much to it. I'll tie her up to the cedar, take the camp stool, and how about this for the milk?'

'Come along, Dainty,' I heard him call. 'That's a good girl. Now, all you've got to do is to stand still. It won't hurt, and I'll be as quick as I can –' But a few seconds later the silence was broken by a deep and frantic protest from Dainty, followed by Dan's soothing voice: 'I'm sorry, old girl, I'm really sorry, but just calm down now and we'll try again – now, Dainty, DO stand still! How am I supposed – this is not a dance, Dainty, and I wish you'd stop flicking your tail in my face! Now . . . oh, God!'

I put my hand over my mouth to stifle the laughter as a loud clonk clearly indicated that a hoof had struck the pail, followed by a crash as this landed on hard ground. After a few seconds of silence, Dan's language was the most colourful I had ever heard, and his voice was grim as he spoke again: 'Dainty, you are going to be milked whether you like it or not, so tantrums will not stop me. Now come along, let's try again . . . '

'How did you get on, darling?' I asked solemnly when he eventually reappeared, scarlet-faced.

'Well, now I know why bloody-minded females are always called cows,' he said, 'but still I did get some milk. Be sure and boil it, won't you?'

When I took the pail it needed every ounce of will-power not to burst into fresh laughter. The milk barely covered the bottom. 'Yes, of course, darling,' I said, swallowing hard.

When Patrick next drove over I noticed that Dan and I vied with each other in our eagerness to tell him about Dainty. 'Sure, it *is* strange,' Patrick said, 'but my guess is she belonged to a squatter family who were either returning to the Reserve or moving to some other destination. Perhaps they came upon a herd of elephants and had to abandon her. As their animals are of paramount importance to all the tribes, no doubt they would have returned later to look for her, but by that time she had taken her own evasive action and they were unable to find her again. The main reason for your not keeping her is that she will be full of all endemic cattle diseases and, although immune herself, will badly infect your land. This will mean big trouble if you eventually decide to have a herd of your own.'

'Well, I don't think we could get rid of her now,' Dan said quickly, 'Minette regards her as a sort of pet.'

'That's right,' I piped up loyally and thought: Ho, ho, ho, typically male, putting it all on to me because he can't bear to admit he's a big softie.

'I'd be interested to see her,' Patrick was saying, and we certainly needed no persuasion.

'Ah, yes, small even for a native cow, and quite a pretty face,' he said when we had led him to her. He inspected her carefully. 'And not just a pretty face either! I think she's in calf.'

'*Is* she?' Dan and I exclaimed in unison.

Patrick bent to run his hand along Dainty's flank and she turned to look at him with mild curiosity. 'All right, girl, all right – yes, I think without doubt.'

'I suppose it's very easy for them?' Dan asked with just the slightest hint of apprehension in his voice.

'Usually, so long as the head is in the right position: it must be on the forelegs, or else she'll have a terrible time, probably breaking her pelvis and with the calf eventually being born dead.'

'Oh no!' I exclaimed, experiencing a strong fellow feeling for Dainty.

'Just tell me what I have to do if things go wrong,' Dan said grimly.

'Well, in an animal as small as this one, I think it would be impossible to turn the calf around completely – '

It was Dan's turn to bend and put his hand on Dainty's underside. 'But how will I know where to feel?'

'Not outside, chum, inside.'

'In – ? Oh, good Christ!'

'It's not as bad as it sounds: you just have to bring the head forward, which means putting a noose of thin but very strong rope over the muzzle – if you can get it over the whole head, so much the better – and then pulling gently but very firmly until she drops it. The ideal thing is to have two people working in unison: one pulling while the other manoeuvres the head from inside, but you'll manage.'

As Dan and I just stared at him, utterly mute, Patrick looked quickly from one to the other and then burst into laughter. 'Oh, my friends, I wish you could see your faces! You both look so terribly shocked!'

'Aren't there any vets in this country?' Dan demanded hoarsely.

Patrick nodded. 'Of course, down in Nakuru, but by the time one of them had got here, it would almost certainly be too late. And don't forget, all the while your animal would be getting more and more distressed, so I guarantee you'd not be able to stand by without helping her.' We must have continued to look horrified because he continued, 'It's all part of farming, you know. Like so many other things, once you've done it, you'll find there's nothing to it. And of course it may not happen with this animal – but, look, if it does I'll come over and show you. That is, if I'm not helping one of my own!'

'Thanks very much,' Dan said abruptly. I don't think he'll want to keep her now, I thought, but he surprised me by spending the rest of the day making a *boma* for Dainty.

261

'It's very crude,' he said when at last it was finished, 'but at least it's strong and we'll know that she will be safe. Now, let's see how she likes it.'

But Dainty was nowhere to be found. 'She must be *somewhere*,' Dan said, then clambered up on the roof of the *boma* where he stood shading his eyes against the late afternoon sun and gazing over our fields. 'Where the devil can she be – oh, God, I wonder if she's taken herself off on to the track? I'd better look for her in the van because she may be heading for Patrick's land and I promised to keep her well away.' He dashed off while I walked right up to where the forest began to encroach on our boundary, only turning back when the light finally faded.

Dan was just drawing up as I approached our home. 'Any luck?' he called out, and when I sadly shook my head, came to put an arm around my shoulders. 'I'm afraid we have to resign ourselves, darling,' he said gently, 'she's gone. I went right up to Patrick's entrance and then on the way back drove half way down the track, but there was no sign of her anywhere. There's nothing more we can do.'

'But why?' I whispered in distress. 'She seemed so happy here, and without our protection she won't last a day: it only needs a hunting lion or a pack of those horrible hyenas to get her scent and they'll be upon her, tearing her limbs off while she's still alive – and ripping out her calf.'

'Now, Mäuschen, stop this at once before you make yourself ill!' Dan's tone was suddenly severe. 'I grant you it's monstrously cruel, but it's the law of the wild and must happen all the time.'

I knew he was right, but I was silent as we went indoors, thinking of Dainty who, like me, was waiting to give birth.

Dan had built up the fire and just put on the water for our baths when he suddenly stiffened, then whirled round: 'What was that?' But I, still deep in thought, had heard nothing. 'There's something in the passage,' he said quietly as he took out his revolver. He walked forward, holding the Coleman lamp high, while I peered under his arm – and there was Dainty, prone on the floor, sleepy eyes blinking up at us. For the second time that day Dan and I were rendered speechless, but now I was the one first to recover. Ducking under Dan's arm, I went to kneel awkwardly beside her, stroking her behind the ears as I exclaimed happily, 'Dainty dear, I'm *so* glad to see you! We've been looking everywhere for you and were so afraid you'd left us forever! But you'll be quite safe now, and when your time comes, we'll look after you, won't we, Dan?'

If I had expected any enthusiasm from him, I was to be disappointed for, man-like, his relief had instantly given way to exasperation. 'Wretched little animal!' he exclaimed. 'And what stupid, sentimental idiots she's made of us! I can tell you one thing for sure, Mäuschen, we'll never succeed as farmers out here unless we stop these nauseating, mawkish ways!'

But I made no reply and just winked conspiratorially at Dainty.

After that we never had to look for her because she followed us everywhere. I was her favourite, mainly because she loved to be tickled behind the ears and knew I was soft enough always to stop and oblige her; she would come and rub her muzzle gently against my side and, just like a spoiled child, would persist until gratified. At other times I would feel a little nudge in the small of my back and know that I was standing on her next meal. We swelled together, she and I, and increasingly were to be found resting – I, on my chaise longue, and Dainty prone beneath the cedar.

Dan's attitude to her remained ambivalent: on the good days she was 'Dear old Dainty', but on the bad 'That damned cow of yours'. Nevertheless, on the night when

263

we heard the cries of pain and terror, Dan was the first to leap out of bed while, roused from deep sleep, I was still uncomprehending: 'Whatever is it?'

'Dainty,' he replied tersely as he lit the lamp. 'Something's got in there – God only knows how – but she's obviously in terrible pain.' I could recognize the sounds myself by then and scrambled awkwardly out of bed to throw a tent-like garment and coat over my nightdress.

Dan was already dressed and lacing his boots before he realized what I was doing. 'Where d'you think you're going, Mäuschen?'

'With you, of course.'

'Oh no, you're not!' Dan said, already beginning to stride from the room.

'Oh yes, I am!' I retorted defiantly, and struggled to hop after him on one leg while latching my sandal on the other.

Dan stopped abruptly to face me. 'Mäuschen, I just cannot cope with whatever is in there and look after you at the same time.'

'But you can't cope *without* me! Supposing it's a lion? Are you going to say to it, "Just have a seat, please, while I put down the lamp and line you up in my sights?" Why, the creature would be upon you within seconds and you wouldn't have a chance! At least I can take the lamp and the revolver, which will leave you free to handle the rifle.'

'Well,' Dan said reluctantly, 'I suppose I can't stop you, but for God's sake keep close to me.' He snatched up the rifle and tucked the torch into his belt, while I pumped up the lamp to its fullest extent and grabbed the revolver.

It was a bitterly cold night and the sounds coming from the *boma* seemed to become more frantic by the second. Without me Dan could have run, but even to keep up with his full striding walk, I had to trot, while holding the lamp high above me, and within seconds I was panting.

'This is going to do you a lot of good,' Dan said sarcastically over his shoulder.

'It's not far – I can make it,' I gasped, but my heart was thudding painfully in my ears when we reached the *boma*.

Dan flashed the torch all around. 'I don't understand, it's all secure and there's nothing here.'

'Perhaps a snake?'

'Of course! It has to be!' Quickly he removed the wooden bar from across the door and as it swung open, said authoritatively: 'Keep well back now, Mäuschen.'

But again there was nothing, even though he searched the darkest corners and played the light over every inch of the roof. All the time I had been looking at Dainty. 'Dan, we're wrong!' I burst out. 'There's nothing here, but Dainty's screaming because – because she's trying to give birth!'

Dan swung round and I heard his sharp intake of breath. 'By God, I believe you're right! But do they always make this fuss?'

'No,' I replied, searching my memory, 'I believe they just walk round in circles until they drop the calf, but Dainty is obviously terrified and in agony.'

As another spasm convulsed her, Dan said very calmly, 'You go and leave me to it, Mäuschen.'

'No, I'm staying!'

He shrugged. 'I've not time to argue with you, but brace yourself – this is going to be very nasty.'

'Should we get Patrick?' I asked tentatively, and Dan's instant answer was a very decisive, 'No.'

He fetched two pails of water, poured Jeyes' Fluid into one and tore off his sweater and shirt before washing his arms to the shoulder. 'I've had the rope for weeks,' he said calmly as he took it from a paper bag; it smelt strongly of disinfectant.

'A slip knot, I think,' he murmured as he went to stand behind Dainty; he lifted her tail in one hand and, as he bent, I saw his taut face whiten; then the hand holding the rope was inserted deeply and the whiteness changed swiftly to a greenish-yellow and sweat formed along his hairline and lip. I felt my own stomach churn and clamped my teeth together, hand over my mouth, but when Dan whispered, 'Oh God,' I had to know. 'The space,' he gasped, 'so small, and she's pushing so hard against me – aa-aa!'

'Oh, what, what?' I asked fearfully.

'It blinked and I felt its lashes against my hand!'

'Then it's alive – it has a chance!'

'But I don't know if I'll ever be able to get it out – it seems wedged – and it's impossible to get the rope over the head.' He was sweating profusely now, with moisture dropping into his eyes and off the end of his nose, so I picked up his shirt and wiped his face. 'Thanks,' he gasped, 'but now, stand right back, because I've got the rope over the muzzle and I don't know how she'll react.' He straightened and wound the rope around his left hand, 'Oh, God, don't let it come off the muzzle,' he whispered as he began to tug. The tortured sounds coming from Dainty changed to a lower key and I knew she was nearing total exhaustion. I stood wringing my hands in despair, wondering how long Dan could continue for he was standing with legs braced, and every muscle on his arms, chest and throat looked ready to burst through the skin.

It seemed an eternity that he pulled on that rope, but suddenly I realized he was winding more and more of it around his wrist, and then it was all over: the calf slipped out, even as Dainty collapsed on to her side, neck thrown back and head right down on the floor. As Dan reeled back against the wall, breathing in great heaving gasps, I knelt clumsily and rolled the bloody rope off the little calf's muzzle. It lay utterly still and I thought: Dear God, don't let it be dead; don't let all that effort be in vain. I wiped the slimy membrane away from the face and head before gently forcing the tiny jaws apart and then watched in wonder as the nostrils widened and the calf breathed in jerkily. An instant later an ear twitched and the huge eyes opened slowly. 'It's alive! It's alive!' I exclaimed, even as tears of tiredness and relief spilled over.

'I'll be back in a minute,' Dan gasped as he rushed out; I wanted to follow him, but felt instinctively that he must be allowed to recover in privacy. So I remained on my knees, talking to the little calf as I wiped its body down with straw. I wanted to carry it across to Dainty, but it was too heavy for me, so I gathered it warmly against myself and wondered if I would have to hand rear it. Dainty had shown no interest at all and still lay as though in complete exhaustion, breathing heavily and with eyes glassed over and almost closed.

When Dan reappeared, freshly clothed and smelling strongly of soap and Jeyes, I was still hugging the calf and he looked quickly from us to Dainty. 'I'm afraid she's in a very bad way,' I said, and Dan nodded.

'You don't look too good yourself,' he said, 'and you certainly can't remain here. What d'you think we should do about the calf?'

I did not know, but instinct told me that if I were dying I would want to have my child close to me, and its need of me would be the one thing that might help me to live. 'I think we should put it close to Dainty,' I said, and Dan bent to take the little animal. He carried it across to Dainty and set it down against her side and, for the second time that night, we witnessed a miracle: for Dainty raised her weary head and began sniffing at the calf, then she heaved herself on to her stomach and slowly started to lick it all over, while strange deep sounds came from within her.

'But why the noise?' Dan queried worriedly, and with my new insight I said, 'I believe she's crooning to her baby.'

'Is that what it is? Well, all I can say is that she'll never rival Sinatra, but it does seem to be having a beneficial effect upon the calf – just look at him, trying to sit up already!' Dan glanced around. 'I must get this place cleaned up and then I'll stay for the rest of the night. I understand there's a danger of haemorrhage; God only knows what I do if that does happen, but I wouldn't like to leave the old girl now. And you, my darling, must get some rest yourself.'

'Tea first,' I said, and hurried away to wash, change and make a flask. When I returned with this and two mugs, Dan was sitting in the camp chair he'd brought from the kitchen and the two animals appeared to be sleeping peacefully.

'Mother and child doing well,' Dan said, a wide grin creasing his exhausted face.

'Oh, wonderful, and I've thought of a name for the baby!' I said happily.

'I bet you have, darling, but don't tell me it's Tiny Tim, please!'

'Tiny – ? *Of course* not, it's much prettier than that!'

Dan looked at me sceptically over the rim of his mug. 'Well?'

'It's – Tiffany.'

Dan, in the act of taking a mouthful of hot tea, gulped and swallowed painfully. 'Tiffany?' he gasped. '*Tiffany*? Whoever in their wildest dreams would call a calf TIFFANY?'

'It seems perfectly logical to me,' I said with a toss of the head. 'Tiffany's in New York are noted for their pretty gifts, and this little calf *is* a pretty gift, so why not name her after them?'

'Her?' Dan queried. 'Are you sure?'

That floored me, of course: 'Why, no – I just thought that so small and pretty a little creature must be a female.'

Dan laughed. 'I'll make sure in the morning and if you're right, she can be Tiffany, just to make you happy, although I still think it's a damned silly name.' He took my hand and kissed the back of it. 'But thanks, darling, for seeing everything through with me.'

I bent at once to put my arm around his neck and lay my cheek against his. 'Where else would I ever want to be?' I asked softly. 'And you did so wonderfully well.'

Tell me that you love me now, I begged him silently, after this shattering experience that we have shared . . .

He smiled up at me. 'Thanks again, but now, darling, please go back to bed.'

From that time Dainty and Tiffany became real pets. Not only did they follow us around, but Dainty would make her crooning noise when we were near, while Tiffany's stump of a tail would wag just like a dog's. I talked to them both frequently and although Dan laughed at me, he treated them both with great gentleness and was always looking around for them. He called them 'the girls' and I suspected that he also talked to them when I was not there.

I believe Dan put down his first real roots at that time, for bringing Tiffany into the world had done more to restore his self-confidence than anything previously. Until then we had survived, even succeeded, in a very modest way, but only with the Keneallys' generous help. Then Dan had been called upon to perform a totally unexpected and unknown task at which many would have baulked. He had succeeded, and the fact that he had saved one if not two animals' lives, was an added distinction.

Then an even more shattering, but utterly wonderful, experience occurred to us: I had spent most of the day picking tomatoes, peas and beans and packing them into *kikapus*, the all-purpose woven baskets that African women make so well, ready for Dan to take to market the following morning, and had finally sunk on to my chaise longue with legs trembling and back screaming for a rest. It was then that my child moved within me, kicking strongly. For an instant I was terrified, thinking it was the start of a miscarriage, until glancing down, I saw tiny, fluttering movements lifting the thin cotton of my frock over my stomach. I put my hands very lightly over them and the mixture of joy, amazement and wonder that I felt is quite indescribable. Until then I had never dared to hope or to look forward to the day when my child would be born, but feeling the movements made me realize that the tiny baby I carried was very much alive and very strong. I had no doubt then that I would be able to give him birth. 'And how I shall love you, my darling, my precious, my angel,' I whispered ecstatically. Catching sight of Dan, I beckoned him. Naturally I wanted more than anything else to share such a supreme moment with him.

'What's up?' he asked, smiling down at me. 'You look positively radiant.' I did not speak, but as he crouched down beside me, I took his hand to put it on my stomach with my own two lightly over it. His head swivelled round to look at me, eyes widening, and I smiled into them. It was a moment of the most perfect communion, silent except for all the sounds of nature around us, and wrapped in the golden glow of late afternoon.

Surprisingly, it was I who spoke first. 'I love you,' I whispered, and thought, Now, surely now . . .

Dan leaned forward to kiss me very gently on the mouth. 'I know you do, angel,' he said, then got quickly to his feet. 'I'd love to stay with you, but there's so much to do.'

As he strode away, I realized that he would never say he loved me because he did not, although we had already been through too much for bonds of fondness not to have been forged. For so long I had wanted more

270

than anything to be loved by him and to be necessary for his happiness but now, at the moment of truth, I did not feel completely bereft, for soon I would have his child and there was no doubt that I already thought of the baby as a miniature Dan – and *he* would need me, *he* would love me. But, I thought sagely, a child needs the love of both parents, so I must not monopolize him. Dan could easily feel left out. Unless I have a Caesarean, he must be present at the birth and then must take his full share of nappy changing, cuddling and bottle feeding, if that's necessary. Surely, then, he would grow to love his little boy with the same devotion I knew he still had for Emma.

Soon after that afternoon I had to give up work on the market garden, and even the weekly powdering of the hens became a great effort because to bend made me so breathless. So during those last few months of my pregnancy I spent many hours resting, with arms circling my stomach, and my mind concentrated on talking silently to my baby. I told him all about the wonderful country he would be born into: its colours and great variety of scenery; its fascinating wild life and brilliant flora. No doubt all new mothers feel that their child is unique. Indeed, there were times when I felt *myself* to be so – the first and only woman ever to have a baby – while at other moments I felt a great kinship with women of all races and colours who were also pregnant. But perhaps the most important wish of all was that our child should inherit the best of our two personalities, for he would go forward into the future, just a minute speck in the world, yet part of it, and through him Dan and I would achieve a kind of immortality . . . a thought to catch at the breath and make the heart beat faster, so wonderful, so amazing was it.

And suddenly the waiting was almost over, the months were reduced to weeks and I was going for my penultimate visit to Dr Engel.

'I think I should come with you today,' Dan said when, after quite a lot of effort, I was behind the wheel of the van.

'Oh no, darling, I can manage perfectly well,' I replied, trying hard not to gasp.

'But the wheel is pressing against your stomach,' Dan said, looking worried. 'Won't it hurt him?' He had made so few references to the baby that this sudden concern made me instantly confident, almost euphoric. 'It only looks as though it is,' I said, beaming down at him, 'there's no real pressure – truly there isn't.'

'Well if you're sure – ' But his tone was still doubtful.

'Absolutely. And, darling, don't worry if I'm a bit later than usual because I want to go to the market for another length of cotton. I'll need another nightdress for hospital.'

'All right,' he reached up to kiss me, 'but come back as soon as you can, and – and look after yourselves, darling.'

This is my lovely day, I thought happily, and I was humming the song as I drove down to Nakuru where Dr Engel was sufficiently jolted out of his professional reserve to admit that, 'Everything is going splendidly.'

It was while I was there that the storm broke – thunder and lightning, followed by deluges of rain – but nothing could spoil my happiness and I beamed at all the pregnant African women in the surgery. I've almost done it, was my unspoken message, and after a few seconds of uncertainty, there was an answering smile. The storm had ended by the time I got to the market, where I bought a length of the cheapest calico and a piece of fillet steak for Dan's supper. I wanted to give him a celebration meal with home-grown spinach, tomatoes and tiny button mushrooms, but the steak was very expensive, so I would say that it was too heavy for me to digest and just have the vegetables.

I drove quickly out of Nakuru. The storm had not cleared the air, but left it hot and very humid. Steam was rising from the track as the ground dried and on

272

each side the pink-tipped oat grass was recovering from the rain's battering. I was about half way up the track when I came upon it: a deep gully where the ground had sunk and was full of muddy water. I pulled up, wondering how best to drive through – at a snail's pace, or with my foot down hard? Finally, I put the car into first gear and went forward steadily, only to come to a full stop in the middle, with the wheels whirling helplessly and water flying everywhere. Oh, Lord, I thought, whatever am I going to do now? I tried slow revs and fast revs, but although the old van shook, the wheels remained fast, and I guessed they were already becoming embedded in the heavy red clay ruts beneath the water.

'Dan,' I whispered in near panic, 'Dan, we need you.' But after a few minutes common sense told me that even if Dan were with us, there was little he could do alone. It would take a dozen strong men pushing in unison to free the van even after the water had subsided. And meanwhile the afternoon was far advanced. 'I think we'll have to walk,' I told my baby, 'but you'll be all right, my precious, it won't do us any harm, if I go carefully.'

The distance across country was not great, but the grasses were waist-high and I thought of all the snakes there would be in the depths, almost impossible to see until one was upon them . . . it'll have to be the track, I thought, and I must concentrate on not twisting an ankle in any of the ruts.

I stuffed the length of calico into the open top of my handbag and then slung this over my head and shoulder like a school satchel, so that I only had to carry the string bag containing the meat. I put my old straw hat firmly on my head and stepped gingerly into the water; it came half way up my bare legs, with the clay at the bottom very slippery. Clinging to the side of the van, I waded through it, breathing a sigh of relief when at last I stepped on to dryness. But even then the going was very rough and I was

273

soon gasping for breath. When I came to a dead acacia tree I stopped, thinking that if I could break off one of the lower branches to use as a staff, it would help pull me along. Wiping my streaming face, I looked up and it was then that out of the corner of my eye, I caught the movement: on the other side of the track stood a thorn tree, its branches swaying beneath the weight of a dozen or more birds. There was no mistaking their bald heads and red beaks; they were vultures, and could only mean one thing: somewhere nearby a creature was dying. I stood absolutely still while panic once more bubbled in my throat and my eyes searched the grasses. Even then I might have missed him had he not started to pant: a huge, black-maned lion, staring at me with merciless golden eyes. I had, of course, heard many stories of people walking quietly past lions without harm, but I knew I would not have the nerve to do so, and I was unarmed, no longer being able to get a revolver belt around my waist.

Beware the day of the lion . . . I heard the words with terrifying clarity as the great beast got to his feet and I saw the wound in his shoulder, seething with flies. Then his long tufted tail slowly began to move, and a voice screamed inside my head: Throw the string bag! His speed and agility were much impaired, but as he launched himself into a leap, I threw the bag, which dropped immediately in front of him. The smell of the meat was sufficient to deflect him from his purpose. With an almighty roar he pounced upon it, great teeth tearing through string and paper to gobble the tiny piece of meat, while simultaneously I began to climb the tree. It must have been very old for it had many low branches, all bare and with peeling bark, but even so in ordinary circumstances I would never have imagined I could get beyond the lowest of these. Yet in those few seconds of mindless panic, I somehow hauled myself up until I was wedged in a fork, where I clung precariously, gasping for breath and uttering gurgling sounds in my throat. But then the lion came to fling himself against the trunk and shake it in impotent fury at his inability to climb after me. As the tree began to creak and sway, I had to lower one leg to steady myself. Instantly a great paw reached up and, with wide-spread claws, raked it from knee to ankle, the skin peeling back in neat strips and the blood flowing. I screamed in pain and terror while realizing dimly that I must get even higher, for the lion continued to roar, mouth wide open with the skin drawn back in a snarl to expose huge yellow fangs, and eyes glaring up at me with unbelievable ferocity.

The branches zig-zagged in a horizontal jumble as they had been blown by the wind, the thinner ones looking ready to snap off at the slightest pressure, but there was one at the top of the tree which remained straight and fairly strong. I knew that if I and my baby were to have any degree of safety, I must get us up to that. Gingerly, I pulled myself upright, arms outstretched above my head and clinging to a cross branch, but just as I got my balance, the leather soles of my sandals, worn to smoothness, slipped on the crumbling bark and I was left hanging by my arms, my great stomach protruding like a full sail. That reduced me to gibbering, incoherent sounds of terror, yet somehow I managed to retain enough sense to struggle and get my feet back on the branch until, clinging with one hand above me, I lifted first one foot then the other to unlatch my sandals and kick them off. The bark was jagged and piercing to my bare feet, but I hardly noticed the pain as I began to climb, slowly and tremblingly. When I reached the top, I was sobbing for breath and fighting dizziness.

Although my feet were now resting on a jutting branch and my arms around the trunk in a tight embrace, I knew that if I fainted I would drop straight down in front of the

275

lion. Then I remembered the calico; but to haul the bag from my back meant withdrawing one arm from around the tree, and might be enough to send me falling to the ground. Oh God, do help me, please, please, do help me, I begged, and with every ounce of remaining strength I pressed myself against the trunk while slowly pulling the bag round and clawing at the calico. My hands were trembling so much that I almost let the material fall from my grasp. Almost, but not quite. With the utmost difficulty I wound it into some semblance of a rope, then got it under both arms and around the trunk to tie it in clumsy knots across my chest. If I fainted completely, I doubted whether it would hold me, but it did give quite a lot of support, and I had drawn it so tightly around myself that one arm was clamped around the trunk.

It was then that the pains started, and as I was torn apart, I shrieked: 'Oh, no – no, don't do this to me . . . please don't . . . not my baby . . . You can't. Oh, God, can't You *hear*? Can't You *understand*? It's my baby . . . MY BABY!' Perhaps I had expected the heavens to open and a whole company of the angelic host to come to my aid, but I remained alone in the vastness of the African bush, and when only clouds continued to scud across the darkening sky, I knew the full meaning of those words: 'My God, my God, why hast Thou forsaken me?' For not only was there a lion waiting a few feet below me and a tree full of vultures waiting for us both, but my baby was clamouring to be born.

There were lights and voices, first in high-pitched, excited Swahili, then in calmer English: 'Dan – the boys have found a straw hat and sandals here, near the dead lion.'

'Oh, my God, *my God*!'

'No, it's all right, there's – there's nothing else here, but they think she's up in the tree.'

'But how *could* she be? She's eight months pregnant and not strong enough to climb trees at the best of times.'

'Nevertheless, Dan – '

'Mäuschen, Mäuschen, are you there, darling? She can't be, she'd answer if she were.'

'Not necessarily. If she were completely dehydrated she would not be able to speak – '

'Dan – Patrick – the boys are convinced there's something right at the top, but our lights aren't strong enough to let them see.'

'I'm going up!'

'No, Dan, wait! The tree is dead and the branches will be very brittle . . . we could easily shake her down. I'm much lighter than you or Patrick, I'll go.'

'But Terry-May – '

'Dan, we don't know what state she's in . . . it may be better for me, a woman, to reach her first. Give me your torch, Patrick.'

'Be careful, darlint, and don't trust any of the branches!'

'No, of course not! Patrick, give me a push up, will you? Thanks, that's fine. It's not too bad, there's a lot to hold on to – oops, sorry, I hope that one didn't land on your heads! Oh, dear God, there's definitely something up here . . . Minette, Minette, me lovely girl, it's you, I know it's you. Wait now, till I get the torch on . . . Oh, a leg . . . injured . . . Oh! Oh, Mother of God! Oh, sweet Mother of God, no . . . '

'Is she there, Terry-May? *Is* she? For God's sake, tell us!'

'Yes, Dan, she's here and she's conscious, but she's . . . she's had the baby. I don't think he's alive . . . '

It was then that I heard above Terry-May's sobs, a great cry of anguish and knew that Dan had wanted his son after all.

18

I was floating, weightless, free from pain, and full of a wonderful sense of well-being, yet at the same time I could see myself prone on the bed, white-faced, with eyes closed and a drip in each arm. I could hear, too, the doctor saying very quietly: 'Sinking fast now. I doubt if he'll get here in time,' and the nurse answering, as softly: 'It's so sad. He's been here non-stop for forty-eight hours and Mr Keneally only persuaded him to leave for a bath and a change of clothing.'

I knew then that they were speaking of Dan and that I was about to leave him forever. There was great sadness but I did not want to go back, the feeling of being drawn farther and farther away, of lightness and joy, were all too great, too wonderful . . . Then I saw the door open and Dan stride in, saw the doctor straighten and heard his quiet: 'I'm sorry . . . ' and Dan's terse, 'Leave us, please.'

He stood for a few seconds looking down at the figure on the bed, then I heard his harsh sob as he sank to his knees and gathered the head and shoulders of that me into his arms. I could feel his arms tenderly cradling me even as I looked down on the scene, and when he spoke his voice sounded so close to my ear: 'Don't leave me, Mäuschen. Please don't leave me . . . I love you, need you too much for you to go from me . . . if you do, I'll be lonely for you for the rest of my life – and we're still so young. So, please, darling, fight to stay with me . . . we've overcome so much and you've always had such a brave spirit, don't make me go on without you now. If you can hear me, try to open your eyes . . . try to fight for my sake, Mäuschen. I love you so much . . . I always have, more than anything else in the world, and I should be so lost without you.'

I knew then that I would have to go back. I had waited too long to hear those words not to heed them now . . . but it was so difficult getting back into my body, I had to fight to do so, and then it was as though great weights were over my eyes. Lifting the lids just the smallest amount was a supreme effort, but when I did so, one look at Dan's grief-stricken face convinced me that I must stay.

It was a long, very hard fight, yet from the moment that I first looked into Dan's tear-filled eyes, I somehow knew I would win.

I was never to tell anyone of my strange experience, instinctively knowing that they would assume it was an hallucination, but I knew that I had been taken to the very threshold of another life. This meant that I was never again to fear death itself, although violence that caused death was to terrify me in the near future.

But full consciousness brought memory surging back and I relived endlessly those hours in the dead tree, always with uncontrollable weeping and bitter self-accusation. I was convinced that the tragedy would not have occurred if only I had stayed in the van. 'Why?' I kept repeating. 'Why, oh why, did I leave it?'

'Because it seemed the right thing, the only thing, to do,' Dan would say, inexhaustibly patient.

'If I had stayed, Patrick would have found me, just as he found the empty van.'

'But, darling, you weren't to know that, and it was only by chance that he used that track rather than the one nearer Sweetwater. And, think, you would have had to keep the windows open – supposing that lion had managed to jump in.'

'Oh, but he couldn't have. He was too badly hurt.'

'Well, to get the door open then.'

'But I would have locked it.'

'Yes, and he would only have had to give it a good shake for the lock to break, it's so flimsy and old! My God, Mäuschen, it doesn't bear thinking about!'

But I refused to be comforted and, with the self-centredness of the very ill, demanded over and over again to be given details of the baby. What had he looked like? What was his colouring? Was he pretty and perfect in every way? And even, did he have any hair?

'Darling,' Dan would say very gently, 'he was just a very tiny baby who looked as though he were asleep.'

I do not know how many more times I would have made Dan give me the details of how they had got me down, and of Terry-May baptizing the baby with a few drops of water from a bottle and giving him Dan's second name, Michael – all of which I already knew by heart – if Dr Engel had not come in one day and asked abruptly: 'Do you love your husband, Mrs Cleary?'

'Of course,' I mumbled.

'Then why do you keep torturing him?' As I just gazed up at him, he continued: 'That man is going through hell, and unless you stop your demands for him constantly to relive that one day, he will crack!'

I was sufficiently shocked to stop crying and whisper: 'I don't understand.'

'No, because you're so wrapped up in your own misery that you've not spared a thought for his! Don't you realize that his sense of guilt is as great as yours – because he did not insist on accompanying you that day? You should be trying to console each other, but look at yourself: you have swollen, red-rimmed eyes and a face full of ugly blotches! I must tell you frankly that this excessive grief is retarding your recovery and may soon impair your sight.' Dr Engel paused briefly, then said more gently: 'Forgive yourself, Mrs Cleary.'

I shook my head woefully, teardrops scattering. 'Never!'

'Then learn to live with your guilt as we all have to do!' the doctor snapped, and walked briskly from the room.

I did not stop grieving or blaming myself from that day, but I did make an effort to be composed and not mention the tragedy whenever Dan came, and my one desire was to leave the hospital. But it was only when the Keneallys insisted on my convalescing with them that Dr Engel eventually agreed, for I was still a semi-invalid and very weak.

So then it was back to the room with the faded rose-patterned curtains and Richelieu work embroideries, to fine Irish linen sheets and unbelievably soft pillows – 'Filled with down from our own birds' Terry-May said gaily – and mornings waking to the smell of coffee and freshly baked rolls as a smiling Karangi brought in my breakfast tray.

'As you know,' Terry-May said on my first day, 'African cooks can conjure up magnificent meals, even in the most primitive conditions, and not only is our Kimani one of the best, he also has a fine kitchen and is anxious to do his best for you.' So then there were delicious meals of lamb from Molo, surely the sweetest in the world, wonderful home-cured hams and buffalo tongue which tasted far better than beef, black bass and perch, tiny grilled trout *en gelée verte*, sandgrouse, cold francolin, guinea fowl and partridge, all accompanied by home-grown vegetables and followed by light-as-air puddings. I ate all the offerings, always going to congratulate Kimani on his efforts; I took short strolls in the beautiful garden and flipped through the fine selection of books, but none of it really meant anything: my mouth should have watered at all the wonderful smells, I should have been full of enthusiasm for the flowers and, most of all, I should have devoured the books, just as I had always done in the past. But all I wanted to do was sit in a comfortable chair and be totally idle, both mentally and physically.

Dan came almost every evening for supper, but even seeing him age suddenly from his actual thirty-seven years to look more like forty-seven, failed to rouse me from my lethargy. Until one evening when he said: 'I'll probably not come over for the rest of the week because with all these supper outings, I've neglected the paperwork dreadfully and I simply must catch up. So you won't worry or mind, will you, darling?' Then, without waiting for my reply, he took me in his arms, kissed me tenderly, and walked away rather hurriedly. I watched idly as Patrick joined him and they stood talking for a few minutes before shaking hands, Patrick briefly clapping Dan on the back as he turned to climb into the van. How funny that they should shake hands, I thought, as though saying good-bye. I've never seen them do that before. . . . A little later I realized that Dan's words had also seemed strange for during the last weeks of my pregnancy I had taken over the paperwork and knew that while on a farm the size of Sweetwater this was very considerable, on ours it was negligible. Dan must have used that as an excuse for not accepting any more hospitality, I thought, until in the middle of the night I suddenly awoke and the answer was crystal-clear: it *was* an excuse, and the two men had been saying good-bye because . . . because Dan had left me and wanted to be far away before Terry-May told me. 'But he said he loved me,' I whispered in the darkness, and at once the voice inside my head said: 'You were dying, and he knew that if anything could make you live, those words could . . . and he'd felt so guilty about everything. If the baby had lived, it might have kept him, but not forever; surely you didn't hope to keep him forever in such hand-to-mouth poverty with only you, deformed and plain, for company? Surely even you could not have been so naive, so stupid? So he's decided on a clean break and by not telling you himself he's done you a last kindness. He knew you'd find it impossible to take from him, but from Terry-May your usual reserve would help you not to make too great a fuss.

In the blackness of the night it all made such sense, and of course I had been through it all before, but now I could not even cry. Although there was excruciating pain behind my eyes, no tears welled up.

At first light I got up to look in the mirror. Since my illness I had only given cursory glances at myself, but now I really looked – and saw a woman with tightly-drawn, dehydrated skin and short, straw-like hair, with downcurving mouth and haunted eyes. 'Plain, almost ugly, that's what you are,' I whispered to the face in the mirror, 'no wonder he's left you.' Somewhere, from far away, I seemed to hear Uncle Julian saying, 'You are obsessed with physical beauty, Minette, but it's not everything . . .'

'That might be true,' I whispered back, 'if Dan were just ordinary and rather plain too, but as he's so handsome, so charismatic . . . You could not hope to hold him,' I told my own reflection, 'so let him go and find happiness elsewhere. Don't forget, he too has suffered very much . . . But, oh, Dan, I did so want to spend my whole life with you – ' the face crumpled then, but only briefly – 'I did so love you.'

Surprisingly, my inner voice said strongly: That was the mistake you made; you loved too much and made him your whole life. Just be thankful for the months you've had with him. Everyone has a ration of happiness in life and they were yours. Be thankful, too, that you're not really married. There will be no complications, no difficulties. But make it easy for Terry-May. She's been such a good friend, and she'll hate having to tell you, but say at once that you've known, that you've been waiting for her to tell you. And until then, just carry on as though everything's normal – you *must* carry on.

Amazingly, I did so, except that I was unable to eat for at the sight of food my throat seemed to close up completely. 'Just a bit of a sore throat,' I said, even managing a smile of sorts, but when Terry-May said, 'I'll take a look,' I shied away.

'Oh no, that's not necessary. I'm sure it'll be better in a day or two.'

But I had never seen her in the role of Nursing Sister before, and within seconds I was pressed into a chair and my mouth opened. 'It all appears to be perfectly normal,' she said at last, eyeing me concernedly, and I wanted to scream: 'Let's get this charade over! For God's sake, let's end it. I can't take much more!'

Instead, I smiled and said, 'I told you it was only a bit sore!'

Oh, how those days dragged! I think I counted every hour of every day. I knew Terry-May would wait until the weekend; Sunday, rather than Saturday, I thought, when they return from Mass, after she'll have prayed for strength and guidance. That will have given Dan time to leave the country. But for where? I wondered, worn down to near-detachment. Certainly not England. Some obscure part of Africa where he can find employment with a small airline, perhaps?

On the Saturday morning I was sitting as usual on the verandah with the children, who were busy with crayons and colouring books, when Terry-May appeared in the front garden, complete with basket and secateurs. Oh Lord, I thought, if she sees me just sitting, she'll persuade me to help her choose the weekend flowers but I can't. I just can't walk around the garden and chat. I looked around and saw on the table a large sheet of brown paper which I pulled towards me, with a white crayon. At first, I meant only to doodle, but then realized that Terry-May might come and look, so almost out of desperation, I began outlining the heads and shoulders of the two children. It was so easy, they were busy concentrating themselves, and the effect of the white on the brown was ethereal and most attractive. The only other colours I used were a blue for their wonderful eyes and a few strokes of light brown mixed with white for their lashes. I was surprised, even delighted, when a faithful likeness of the two angelic little faces appeared under my hand and was just putting a last touch to their thistledown curls when the telephone rang in the hall behind me. I was conscious of Terry-May rushing past, as though anxious that no one else should answer, and when she began speaking very loudly, I knew it was a long distance call and that it was from Dan. I rose abruptly and padded silently into the hall to stand behind her.

'What's your news?' she was shouting. 'You *have*? Oh, isn't that just great? Well done! Oh, not quite so good, I'm afraid – what? No, not a word – it's going to take a bit of time – but *of course* we will – yes, *that's* all right. Joseph has been assigned to it and already he's swaggering around, full of self-importance – oh, you will? When? Tonight? Fine, fine – oh, yes, 'bye . . .' She was half smiling as she turned, but then started visibly. 'Why, Minette, I didn't know you were there.'

'It was Dan, wasn't it?'

'Dan? But you haven't got a phone!'

'No, but it was long distance, wasn't it?'

'Now whatever makes you think – ?'

'He's left me, hasn't he? *Hasn't he?*'

'Oh, wait now – '

But that was something I could no longer do. All my battened-down emotions suddenly erupted like a steam-jet. Rushing forward, I seized Terry-May by the shoulders and began shaking her. 'Why do you keep lying?' I screamed. 'Why can't you tell me – tell me –? I can't take any more! Don't you understand *I can't take any more!*'

She kept absolutely still until shortness of breath made me stop and I was suddenly aware of the silence: I looked around wildly and saw Wanjiri and Karangi standing like statues, mouths agape. Worse still were the two little figures outlined by sunlight as they stood in the doorway, crayons still in their hands, their expressions a mixture of fear and curiosity. Even the dogs were there, not understanding but aware that something was wrong and ready for instant action.

'I'm sorry,' I whispered, ashamed and exhausted now, 'so sorry.'

Terry-May assumed complete control. 'Wanjiri, will you take the children and get them ready for lunch? And, Karangi, what do you think you're doing, just standing there? Get on with your work now!' Then, with an arm about my shoulders, she said very gently, 'Come and sit down, darlin' girl, and I'll explain.' When we went back on the verandah, she sat facing me, hands lightly clasped in her lap. 'I wanted to tell you at once,' she began, 'but Dan thought you would get too upset, and as he obviously knows you better than anyone, I had to bow to his judgement. You were right in some of the things you said just now: it *was* a long-distance call from Dan and he has been out of the country – ah, now, Minette, don't look as though you're about to fade away completely! It's not what you think. Believe me, Dan has not left you in the way you meant, but he's spent the last week up in the Sudan.'

'The Sudan?' I whispered, amazement beginning to replace fear. 'Whatever for?'

'Because, dear, he applied to become an Ag Pilot and all the training is done – indeed, the whole outfit operates – from the Sudan. All the new pilots begin training in August and Dan had to undergo some tests to see whether he was acceptable; his call just now was to confirm this. He starts training next month but, because you've been so ill, he's been given a few days' special

286

leave to tell you, and will be on the train from Nairobi this evening! So, isn't it all just great?'

But I was still trying to puzzle it all out. 'Why? Why is he doing it? And what about the farm?'

'Oh, Patrick's arranged for Joseph to act as head man and he's doing well. As for Dan's reasons – well, the pay is very good and – and he has had some big expenses recently.'

'Meaning my hospital bills.'

'Those, and of course there's the loan repayments, but he reckons that after his six-month stint as a pilot, he'll clear the hospital bills *and* be able to repay more of the loan.'

'Six months!' I echoed in disbelief. 'Is that how long he'll be away?' When Terry-May nodded, I added: 'It's dangerous, too, isn't it?'

'Well,' she said hesitantly, as though trying to choose her words carefully, 'I suppose there's always an element of danger in flying.'

'Yes, but aren't the planes very light, and don't they have to fly very low when they spray the crops and – and often are forced to fly between narrow mountain passes?'

'I honestly don't know, Minette, but as they cover a lot of territory, no doubt there are hazards, that's what their training is for. But, look, you'll be able to ask Dan tonight. Patrick and I will disappear very soon after dinner, so that you two – '

'Oh, but I must go home!' I said, instantly galvanized into action, with all tiredness forgotten. 'I must get everything clean and ready for him!' I dashed indoors to my bedroom where I hurriedly began to pack.

Terry-May followed me, protesting all the way: 'You don't have to go – Dan can stay here with you! Minette, stop and think a minute! If you stay, you won't have to worry about cooking or cleaning, and I guarantee that we will leave you both completely alone.'

I did stop then, but only to say: 'Dan is coming *home*, Terry-May, and I must be there for him, with everything as nice as I can make it. Oh, I know it's all very primitive, but it's the only home we've ever had together, and – and if he's going away for six months, I think he'll want to spend these few days there.' She gave up trying to dissuade me then and instead concentrated on helping me.

When we eventually drove over, she put a covered basket in the car: 'Just a few provisions to tide you over this evening and tomorrow morning, so that you won't have to fuss with lots of preparation,' she said and, as always, waved away my thanks.

After she had gone it was very quiet and as I stood looking around our tiny home, grief threatened to engulf me once again. For it was impossible not to remember that the last time I had stood there I had been joyfully awaiting the birth of my baby, certain at last that nothing could go wrong . . . Pull yourself together, my inner voice told me. Close your mind to what might have been and be thankful that you still have Dan.

Driving down to Nakuru was another test. I resolved not to even glance at the tree as I passed, not knowing that weeks before Dan had sent our labour to cut it to the ground and take away every branch. And sadness gave way to excitement as the Nairobi train pulled in. I was remembering that day at Bad Oeynhausen station when Dan had met me, so long ago . . . He leapt lightly from the train, carrying a small holdall, and I noticed how jaunty was his step, how totally alert his whole bearing. Until he saw me, and then astonishment stopped him in his tracks. But as always his reaction was swift: 'Mäuschen darling, what a wonderful surprise!' he exclaimed as he swept me up in a tight embrace. 'How are you?'

'Very well,' I answered firmly, 'and we are going home – to put the past behind us and just be happy.'

That evening Dan spent a long time speaking with great

288

enthusiasm of the Sudan and I realized that the whole experience was doing more than anything else to assuage his grief and remorse. I did not have the heart to voice my own feelings on the project then, and by the next morning dreaded having to do so. I tried several times to begin but without being able to find the words, so that by the time Dan came in from his first look round, I had worked myself up into unusual belligerency. Whirling from the stove, frying pan in hand, I burst out: 'I'm not having it, you know! I simply will not have it!'

Naturally he looked at me blankly for a few seconds, then his face relaxed. 'No? Well, you could have fooled me, darling,' he said lightly. 'I was under the impression you'd been doing just that half the night!'

'Last night has nothing to do with it!' I retorted, waving the pan in exasperation.

Dan crossed his wrists over his face and looked at me through his fingers. 'All right, but don't hit me!' he pleaded in a high falsetto. 'I'm very fragile this morning!'

'Oh, don't be so absurd,' I said tartly. 'I'm serious.'

He lowered his hands and composed his face into an exaggeratedly solemn expression. 'I can see that, I just don't know what you're talking about.'

'This – this idea of being an Ag Pilot,' I said, courage beginning to ebb rapidly. 'I-I won't let you do it, I won't! It's too – too dangerous!'

'Is that what all this is about?' Dan asked, sounding incredulous.

'Well, *of course* it is – I thought you would have realized that at once.'

He sat down and held out his arms. 'Come here, sweetheart.' I never had been able to resist sitting on his knee, but this time I walked slowly and then just perched upright instead of snuggling close to him as usual. 'Darling, it simply isn't true to say that Ag Piloting is dangerous.'

'Oh no? With lots of lovely mountains to fly into, or teeny-weeny passes in between that you have to find through thick cloud?'

'Who the hell has told you all this?'

'No one. It just stands to reason: you have to fly very low to spray the crops and when there are mountains at the end, you must have to climb very steeply or find a way through them.'

'But this is partly what our training is for.'

'Oh, how nice! You're given the opportunity to smash yourselves up before you even start work!'

'Mäuschen, this is very silly. You're talking about something of which you have no knowledge whatsoever!'

'Maybe,' I retorted, 'but apart from all that, what about me? What about the farm?'

'Well, naturally, you were my first concern, but the Keneallys would be delighted to have you remain with them – '

'For six months! How could I possibly impose on them for so long?'

'I suggested that you might care to be here during the day and merely go over to their place at night. And as for the farm, Patrick said he would continue to second Joseph to me as overseer, although obviously I would still pay his wages and those of the labour he has already hired.'

'And you discussed all this with Patrick before even mentioning it to me?'

'Darling, what else was I to do? I had to settle all the most important plans before even applying for the job. You had been desperately ill and were still very weak, so how could I possibly burden you with my plans before I knew whether they would be implemented?'

'You really want to go, don't you, Dan?'

'No, I can honestly say I do not, but I've no doubt I'll make the best of it and perhaps even enjoy it once I start. After all, I love flying, for whatever reason.' He glanced at his watch. 'God, just look at the time!' He set me quickly on my feet. 'I'll have to skip breakfast and go into town straight away, if that's all right by you, darling?'

I nodded silently. He's going, I thought miserably, and there's nothing I can do to stop him. But when he returned from Nakuru there was a glimmer of hope, for he was smiling and waving two open letters. 'Good news, darling!' he called out as he strode towards me. 'I picked up these two from the Post Office and, you'll never guess, we've been given the contract to supply both the hospital and the Stag's Head Hotel with eggs and vegetables!' He bent to kiss me lightly on the cheek. 'Something else I didn't tell you about.'

'Oh, but that's wonderful, wonderful! Now you won't have to go away!'

The animation faded from his face. 'It doesn't make that much difference – '

'But how could you go away for six months when you would be needed here more than ever?'

'Well, we'll certainly need to put more land under vegetables and buy more laying hens, but I think Joseph could organize the labour to do all that, even if he needed to hire more – Patrick has great confidence in his abilities.' Dan paused, then as I remained silent, added: 'You see, darling, I can earn more in a month as an Ag Pilot than we'll make in six from these contracts. And I'm afraid we're up to our necks in debt. If the bank should foreclose . . . '

'They wouldn't dare!' I burst out. 'Not if we threatened to tell every newspaper in East Africa that we were being evicted because of my hospital bills! After all, it's not every day that a woman gives birth perched up a dead tree with – with a lion sitting at the bottom! The papers would love such a bizarre story, and it wouldn't do anything for the bank's image to foreclose as a result!' Always in the past I had tried so hard never to make a fuss, never to

291

persuade him to do anything against his will, but as the memory of that terrible afternoon came flooding back, plus all my fears that he had left me, my control snapped. 'Don't go,' I begged, while the tears I had been unable to shed for weeks suddenly poured down. 'There have been so many partings in the past, so much tragedy, I-I don't think I can go on if you're not here.'

Dan could not bear to see a woman cry. So now he strode to my side and enveloped me in his arms. 'Of course I won't go,' he said soothingly. 'I'll write and say I've changed my mind . . . and we'll get by somehow, just as we've done up till now. So don't cry any more, Mäuschen darling, you make me feel such a heel.'

He wrote the letter, although I knew it was a struggle for him to do so, and two days later we had another stroke of luck when Terry-May drove up with a flourish and rushed towards me. 'Minette darlin', you'll never guess but I've shown that beautiful drawing of the kids to all my friends and they all want you to do something for them!'

But my instant reaction was to refuse. 'That's awfully nice of them, but I'm afraid I haven't the time.'

'Nonsense!' Terry-May answered forcefully. 'This will do you more good than all the planting and weeding you can ever manage! Now, I've made it plain that you must name your fees yourself, but said I *thought* they would be in the region of three guineas for a single subject, six for two or one large – say a house and garden.'

'But I couldn't possibly charge anything at all!' I exclaimed, flabbergasted. 'I'm only an amateur.'

'What does that matter? You've got great talent, indeed you have! The drawing of our two is already framed and hanging, and everyone exclaims over it!'

'Yes, but your children are exceptionally lovely.'

'Minette, will you stop putting yourself down in this silly way and think about the commissions waiting for

292

you? I've got people in Nakuru, Gilgil, Njoro and even Nanuki and Nyeri.'

I felt completely overwhelmed and could only say, 'I'll have to talk it over with Dan.'

'Why?' asked Terry-May bluntly. 'Why should you have to do that if, as I believe, you really want to accept these commissions?'

'Well, of course I must! I always do – '

'Sure, I know that, and I know how much you love Dan, but that doesn't mean you have to live in his shadow. The world is changing, Minette, and women are changing with it. Why, didn't I just receive a letter from Bernadette in New York telling me that young women there are carving out careers for themselves – even top executive ones – and *demanding* equality with men; and Bernie herself, God love her, even though she's crazy about that lovely man Shamus, plans to be completely independent after they're married.'

'Oh, but, Terry-May,' I interrupted with a laugh, 'I'm not the career girl type and I think it would be difficult for me to be independent in our circumstances, even if I wanted to be – which I don't!'

'But, lovely girl that you are,' Terry-May persisted, 'you should have much more self-confidence and more self-esteem, indeed you should! And instead of instantly thinking yourself not talented enough to accept these commissions, you should welcome them!'

'Well,' I said slowly, 'you may be right, but I was brought up to be modest. Any sort of showing-off was considered by Aunt Alexa to be extremely vulgar!'

Terry-May ran a hand through her hair as though in exasperation. 'Why, it's nothing to do with showing-off!' she exclaimed. 'But rather appreciation of your own worth – apart from your artistic talent, don't you *know*, Minette, how strong you are? How wonderfully you've coped with all the difficulties and the heartbreak?'

'Oh, come on now, Terry-May!' I said with a nervous laugh. 'You know perfectly well that I've only done what any other woman would do in the same circumstances.'

'Faith, but you're a stubborn one!' she answered, shaking her head in mock anger. 'And I'm telling you that not every woman *could* take this life. Haven't I known quite a few who've given up and gone down to South Africa and back to Europe?'

'But why?' I asked, mystified. 'Did they have husband trouble or poor health?'

Terry-May shook her head. 'Neither. It was simply the isolation: no cinemas for miles, no libraries, no newspaper or postal deliveries, no shops to browse in except at Nairobi, and those not up to much, and almost no social life except perhaps a Saturday evening dance at a Club umpteen miles away. Worst of all, no other women to talk to, just miles of African bush.'

'OK, OK, I get the message,' I said, laughing, 'and my head is swelling by the minute! But can I at least talk to Dan before I dash off into the blue to paint?'

'Oh, yes, of course – *talk*, but not *ask*! And, Minette – '

'Yes?'

'Do remember that although Dan is just great and will always have women swooning in the aisles, most of what he has achieved out here has been through you – *you*, a person in your own right and a very strong, brave lady.'

To my surprise he was all for my taking the painting commissions. 'Just what you need,' he said, 'to get out, meet other women and socialize.'

'But don't you realize that we may get drawn into other circles as a result?'

When he shrugged and said: 'Well, we'll just have to go and hope for the best,' I was thrilled, for it meant that yet more of his confidence had been restored.

Thus began the most fulfilling weeks of my life in Kenya, for although I approached my first assignment

294

with great uncertainty, I found drawing the little girl and her Jack Russell quite easy. As time went on I progressed from drawing to painting, digging down in my tin trunk for brushes and water-colours. The brushes were still supple but some tubes had hardened, and it was an indication of my growing confidence that I wrote off immediately for replacements. The paintings of homesteads and beautiful gardens, even of horses and dogs, were invariably commissioned by their elderly female owners whose strong-featured faces and brusque manner might have been intimidating had they not re-minded me of Aunt Alexa – they were all cast in the same indomitable mould. Like her, most were alone, through divorce or death, and all ran huge farms with hundreds of workers at whom they shouted, while in the same breath speaking gently to the many dogs that surrounded them. When I overheard one such lady refer to me as 'That nice little thing', I knew I had made the grade.

Inevitably invitations came from younger families which I tried to refuse on the grounds of not being able to return their hospitality, but the first party we did attend proved to be a milestone for us both: for Dan because he was at ease, mixing effortlessly; and for me because when a fellow guest asked if I had children, I heard myself say quietly, 'No, I'm afraid not. I was pregnant earlier this year, but then I lost the baby.'

'Oh, I say, how rotten for you,' the other woman said, smiling sympathetically. 'I know what it's like, but here's to better luck next time.'

And, with seeming composure, I was able to smile too and thank her. While Terry-May had told me solely of the women who could not endure Africa, I was now meeting those who had not only endured, but triumphed over tragedy: the death of a child or husband – or both – being common, even in circumstances more horrific than my own. And so, through them, I came to terms with my own baby's death. Although I would never cease to mourn him, or blame myself for leaving the van, I was able to admit calmly that, although a mistake, it had seemed the right decision at the time, and God knew, I had only wanted to keep my unborn child safe. I even began to think perhaps there might, just might, be another chance . . . no doubt because it was a time of growing optimism for Dan and me; more of our ground had been cleared and planted, with all crops flourishing. A fairly small but steady income was now coming along from them and we actually hoped to make a good profit when the pyrethrum flowers were gathered. We now had another dozen families added to the fifty already living on their own *shambas* and James, Joseph's brother, came to us as head man.

'You'll find him as efficient as Joseph,' Patrick said in his kindly way, 'and it'll be good for him to have more responsibility. Here, he's been under Joseph's thumb and very much the younger brother. Of course, they're both Mission boys as their names indicate, but sometimes I feel that Christianity rests very lightly upon them and even that they're likely to revert at some time to the old ways of the Kikuyu god, Ngai. But,' he added with a grin, 'they're not unique in that. I suspect quite a lot offer up a few prayers to Ngai as well as to the Lord! And you'll also find James a much more friendly type than Joseph who, I know, can be a bit taciturn at times.'

And that's the understatement of the year, I thought. To me Joseph had always appeared positively sullen. Being Mission-educated, his English was fluent, and on his various secondments to us I had tried to talk to him, mainly about crops, but his answers had always been extremely brief, spoken as though with great reluctance, usually as he turned away or continued with what he was doing. My last attempt to draw him out had been when he appeared on a brand new bicycle. 'Why, Joseph,' I had

296

said with genuine admiration, 'what a fine new machine. Is it your own?'

'Yes,' he had mumbled as he continued to wipe off the dust of the track from it.

'Congratulations!' I said, knowing that to possess a bicycle was a great African ambition, and usually only achievable if an employer loaned the purchase price. Joseph did not look at me, but for the first time in all our encounters, he smiled fleetingly.

'Did Bwana Keneally help you buy it?' I asked and was astonished to see the smile instantly replaced by a scowl. 'No,' he said sharply, leaping on to the saddle and riding away, regardless of me.

It was at once apparent that James was going to be quite different: a very tall gangling youth with feet constantly shuffling and huge hands gesticulating, he talked readily in rapid-fire English, often laughing and always smiling. This was such a welcome change from his brother that at first I did not realize how ingratiating his manner was, or even that he smiled *too* much. Until the day when I was picking pyrethrum flowers and happened to turn quickly, only to find him standing very close behind me. It was impossible not to start violently with shock and take a step back. 'Oh, James, you startled me!' I exclaimed, and just had time to note how different his face seemed without its usual smile. Then, in an instant, the ear-to-ear grin was back in place. 'I am sorry, Mem, but I thought you heard me cough. I have come to carry the gunnies; I think they are too heavy for you.' Such a comment was unusual and I was pretty sure he had not coughed. 'Thank you, James,' I said rather curtly, 'but the flowers are very light and I can manage.'

But already he had picked up the large gunnies and swung them on to his shoulders. 'I will take them, Memsabu.' It was a statement, spoken quietly, even deferentially, yet somehow conveying complete authority.

For the first time I realized that instead of the youth I had been seeing, here was a tall and powerful man.

'Very well, James,' I said, turning away in dismissal, 'take them and then get back to your work.'

When I told Dan that evening, his reaction was to laugh and say: 'It's that overbright imagination of yours, Mäuschen, working overtime,' and by then I, too, was ready to laugh at my earlier unease. Yet a few days later when I suddenly felt I was being watched, I turned and there he was again, towering silently over me. This time I managed to suppress a start and to say coolly: 'Yes, James, what do you want?'

'Would you like a toto to help you with the peas, Mem?'

'Well, if and when I do, I'll tell you.'

'Yes, Mem. Thank you, Mem.'

Bloody man, I thought as he strode away. I don't know what his game is, but if this happens again I'll give him a piece of my mind. Sure enough, the next week it did and I exploded with a furious: 'How dare you come and stand so near me and without speaking!'

'But, Mem, I sneezed – '

'You did nothing of the kind!' I retorted. 'Get back to work at once!'

'But, Mem – '

'At once, James!'

He assumed a hang-dog expression and turned away as though totally dejected. A born actor, I thought, and was about to start my own work again when I saw, some twenty yards away, a woman bent almost double and walking with slow, faltering steps across the field. On her back she carried the usual cone-shaped basket held in place by a wide leather strap across her forehead. Both arms were raised, hands over her shoulders, clutching at the basket. I could not see what this contained, but it was obviously too heavy for her. To my astonishment James

298

roared at her in Kikuyu, and she came to a stumbling halt, looking up at him in terror. He's going to take the load from her, I thought, but then gasped as, with another roar and much waving of arms, he sent her scurrying forward, even aiming a kick at her behind as she passed.

I never knew how I covered the intervening ground, but suddenly I found myself beside the woman, my hand on her arm, my voice telling her in halting Kikuyu to stop and not be afraid. I do remember James's amazed expression quickly turning into the familiar grin and my own furious tone as I ordered him to 'Wipe that smile off your face and tell me what you mean by treating this woman as a beast of burden, and daring – yes, *daring*, James! – to kick her!'

He tried to bluster: 'She is a lazy sow who does nothing.'

'And you are a cruel, inhuman bully!' I retorted, almost choking in my fury. 'Anyone with only half an eye could see that she is not strong enough for such a load – what's in the basket anyway? Let me see – my God, potatoes! Pounds and pounds of potatoes! No wonder her legs are almost buckling and she's gasping for breath! Take the basket off her before she collapses!' I recalled dimly that for a Kikuyu male to help a woman of his tribe was almost unheard of. James did not move. 'Don't you dare defy me,' I said grimly, 'not if you value your job here!'

He did move then, muttering furiously under his breath, but instead of lifting the leather strap clear, he scraped it brutally across her shaven head, making her grunt with pain. Then he threw the basket down and the potatoes spilled out all around. The woman had been looking from one to the other of us. Now she moved to pick up the scattered potatoes. 'Not you, old one,' I said quietly, 'you go and sit under that tree until I call you.' She hesitated, and I realized for the first time what a complete hold James must have over her, for not to obey a memsahib was unknown. 'And now,

James,' I said as she eventually crept away, 'you will pick up all those potatoes and take the basket to the van.'

'It is not work for a man,' he muttered sullenly, the likeness to his brother startlingly apparent.

'Well, it is certainly not work for an old woman,' I retorted, 'nor do I care whether it is man's work or not – I have given you an order and you will obey at once or else I shall not wait for the bwana but dismiss you myself, here and now!' Reluctantly he started to gather up the potatoes, but only with infuriating slowness. When the basket was once more full he slung it easily on to his shoulder and would have slunk away, but my fury was not yet spent.

'One moment!' I said, speaking as harshly as I knew how. 'I must warn you, James, that if I ever again see you kicking a woman or a toto, or over-burdening either, it will mean instant dismissal without any reference. Is that clear?'

'It is clear,' he said, speaking insolently over his shoulder. I very nearly ordered him to face me and repeat the words, but instead I walked over to the woman, who at once struggled to her feet. 'Are you Wanja?' I asked gently.

'Yes, Mem.'

'Then tell me, Wanja,' I said, concentrating hard to find the right words in Kikuyu, 'is James always so cruel to you and the other women?'

'Oh no, Mem, James very good as head man, very kind to all.' It was obviously untrue and she hung her head as though in shame.

'There is no need to be frightened,' I said, smiling to reassure her, 'just tell me the truth.'

'I speak the truth, Mem. James very good man.'

I knew I would get nothing else from her, the fear was too great. 'Very well,' I said, suddenly feeling worn out.

'You may rest here for as long as you like, but I trust you to go back to your work when you feel able.'

Dan was inclined to be sceptical when told my story that evening. 'Darling, are you sure she is so old? You know as well as I do that many women here look positively ancient when they're only in their early forties.'

'I'm *quite* sure, and I tell you he shouted at her, making her try to run when she was almost collapsing.'

'But, Mäuschen, she's one of his own people and they all work so well under him. Perhaps you misunderstood?'

'How can anyone misunderstand a kick?' I demanded angrily. 'And I think they work so well because they're frightened to death!'

'I'd hate to think that,' Dan said thoughtfully. 'We certainly can't have him using violence.' He took a few steps about the kitchen before adding decisively: 'Yes, I'd better have a word or two with Master James in the morning, to make absolutely sure he knows how we feel. And don't worry, darling, I'll not let him work anywhere near you in future. Now, let's talk about getting the kerosene fridge and the water heater – '

In the excitement of having these two longed-for appliances, I soon forgot about James and instead began to think that in the following year it might be possible to fence the front of our property, to put a five-barred gate across the opening and to flank it on each side with a Kaffir-boom; and to make a proper lawn in front of our rondavels with flower beds all around. Then, I thought euphorically, we could hold a modest sundowner party on the lawn . . .

We had lived without radio or newspapers for so long that it came as a shock to hear through our new socializing of the widespread disturbances which had been occurring over the past months; these ranged from mysterious grass fires to strikes, and the firing of certain Kikuyu huts whose occupants were known to be loyal to the

Government; the words 'Mau-Mau' were heard more often, although few people knew anything about this outlawed secret society whose name made no sense. There was universal anger that no action had been taken by the out-going Governor, Sir Philip Mitchell, whose departure had left Kenya without a Governor for three months, and many considered that they would have to take matters into their own hands if the new Governor, Sir Evelyn Baring, did nothing. 'But he won't be here until the end of September,' I heard more than one settler say, 'and meanwhile the situation everywhere is deteriorating.'

From these sources, too, I learned that safaris were proving to be a great tourist attraction, for although Europe generally was still bankrupt, there were those who had made fortunes out of the war and they, like the jaded rich of America, found safaris the perfect antidote to boredom. This gave me an idea and, bolstered up by my local success, I wrote to the manager of the New Stanley Hotel asking if he would be interested in selling my paintings in the gift shop. When he replied asking to see a portfolio of my work, I was galvanized into action and did not even have to leave the farm to find subjects, but of course I had my favourites: the family of hyraxes, enticed from their tree home by my large rounds of orange peel, their little furry bodies crouching in tender new grass and wild gladioli; green parrot fledglings and minute bee-eaters, like emerald and ruby puff-balls; exquisite humming birds hovering before gold Peruvian lilies, and butterflies of turquoise and orange clinging to the jasmine-like flowers of Limuria bushes.

Then, growing ever more confident, I turned to the *shambas* of our labour force, finding there only the very old who, nevertheless proved to be wonderful subjects. In their faces – shrunken-cheeked, often toothless and always deeply wrinkled – lay, I thought, all the age, mystery, strength, cruelty and kindness of Africa itself.

To each I gave a handful of cents, hoping that these and my interest would buy them a few more weeks of life. I knew that, no longer able to work, they were waiting for death, when their sons would take them into the forest, to be left for the hyenas. I saw the resignation in their rheumy eyes for I believed that sometimes there was still a flicker of life left when they were put out, and I longed to help.

'But you must not,' Patrick said forcefully, 'truly, Minette, you must *not*!' He turned to Dan in mute appeal, but Dan merely said: 'It's no use looking at me, old boy, she won't take any notice of what I say! I don't mind telling you, she's a most wilful little thing when she get's a bee in her bonnet!'

Of course I knew that Dan was joking, but Patrick did not even smile as he faced me once more. 'You must understand, Minette, that this has been going on since the beginning of time. I have even heard that the old ones often drag themselves off into the forest, if they are able to move that far. I know it makes our flesh creep but there is nothing we can do.'

'Yet how can we stand by without doing *something*?' I protested in distress.

'Because it is their custom; just as we burn or bury our dead, so the Kikuyu leave theirs to be devoured. And, of course, another custom is that if an old person dies in the family hut, that has to be burned, together with all hoarded seed, and everyone has to move to a new *shamba*.' Patrick paused and the merest flicker of a smile touched his eyes. 'Try to look at it from their point of view, Minette: the deliberate destruction of precious seed so essential for their own survival; all the time and effort required to gather materials for building a new hut; in a new location, and none of it really necessary when all they have to do is to take the old one some distance away and leave well alone.' My feelings must have been all too

303

plain. Patrick looked at me very seriously: 'Remember, Minette, what happened to Hilda Stumpf, the missionary who protested about female circumcision! *That* was in the days when the Kikuyu were very much easier to manage. Now, with all the younger ones in such a surly, unpredictable mood, God only knows what they would do.'

'But Dan would never let them harm me!' I exclaimed.

'Dan would probably be flat on his back, grinning from ear to ear with a slashed throat!' I shuddered, but must still have looked unconvinced. Patrick continued: 'They might decide to stake *you* out in the forest, perhaps smeared with honey, and left for the *siafu* – no doubt you remember them, Minette – the unstoppable blind ants that swarm in huge numbers over any prey? They would fill your ears, your eyes, your mouth and throat, and when you were entirely covered, they would give you one vicious, concerted bite . . . you would die of course, and quite agonizingly.'

'Stop it!' I cried, clapping my hands over my ears and cowering back, but Patrick took my wrists and pulled my hands away.

'Not until you promise most faithfully that you will do nothing, say nothing, nor even *look* disapproving of African customs.'

Of course I promised, but when I heard the hyenas howling in the dead of night I wondered if the old people ever hoped against hope that they would be allowed to remain in the warmth of the family hut, sharing the family cooking pot and gourd of *pombe* . . . or if, in the bitter cold of the black forest, they ever grieved or screamed with agony when the pack first tore at them. Or did they wait calmly, knowing that as ancestral spirits they would be revered by all future generations? Unable to bear my own fantasies, I turned in desperation to the very young: the tiny totos, with their huge soft eyes and wonderful skin: satin smooth, and with the bloom of a black grape, which I could never quite capture.

Then there was Wombi whose age I was never able to assess. Although she was child-like in her constant laughter and chatter, her limbs were those of a young woman. She invariably wore a multi-coloured *shuka* wound around under her armpits, loosely gathered and with the end tucked inside, thus leaving her shoulders and arms bare. In my first painting I depicted her standing gloriously upright, with a heavy gourd balanced on her neatly shaved head, her high pointed young breasts thrusting against the material of the *shuka* whose lower fold was open to reveal a long and unusually slim leg. Dan whistled appreciatively when he first saw the painting, but my favourite was the second, a head and shoulders. By then Wombi had overcome her shyness of me and I was able to capture her fleeting, extraordinary animation. I showed her with head thrown back in uninhibited laughter and black eyes narrowed to sparkling slits, thus epitomizing all the carefree, light-heartedness of her people as I had known them in my childhood.

But my greatest favourite was little Karioki. I had come upon him quite by chance, a small boy aged somewhere between four and six, standing quite alone. He was dressed in an ancient knee-length *kanzu* which showed his thin legs and bare, firmly planted feet. His small round head was bent forward and he looked up at me very solemnly from under straight brows. I might never have considered painting him had I not tried to speak a few words in my halting Kikuyu, a most difficult language with double negatives and words that can be interpreted in different ways. I must have said something extremely funny for suddenly a shy and wholly enchanting smile spread across his small face, revealing tiny white milk teeth. It took a great deal of time and patience to win his confidence, but eventually I succeeded, then painted

305

him just as he stood in the dust, with head on chest and the smile – elfin, shy, but with the merest hint of mischief – touching his lips and eyes. Delighted with my effort, I could not resist giving him a quick hug as I handed over the usual few cents. After that, he tended to follow me about, always at a distance, and often rushing away if I gave any indication of having seen him.

'You pay too much attention to that child,' Dan said, 'his parents may not like it.' But he sounded extraordinarily pleased when he came in the evening before we were to leave for Nairobi and said: 'I've been given a present!'

'Oh, by whom?' I asked, intrigued.

'That child who milks Dainty so well – what's her name, Wombi?'

Some child, I thought, keeping my face straight, but when I saw what the gourd contained, I did not feel like smiling. 'You haven't tasted any of it, have you?'

'Definitely not; the smell put me off! It looks like curdled milk, no doubt from Dainty.'

'It *is* curdled milk,' I said, 'and the gourd will have been rinsed out with Dainty's urine and then smoke-dried before the milk was added. Africans love it!'

Dan grimaced. 'Thank God I didn't even dip a finger in – I'd probably be laid low with the runs instead of setting off for the weekend!'

The trip to Nairobi had been talked over and looked forward to for days, and had come about because I had been asked to take my completed portfolio to the New Stanley on Saturday, 18th October. We had thought of driving there and back in the day until Patrick said: 'But the 19th is our wedding anniversary. Why don't we all go together and spend the weekend? We could stay at the Norfolk, perhaps dine at the New Stanley, and go on to dance at the Muthaiga Club. On the Sunday we could show you the sights and maybe go to the Races.'

306

'Can we afford it?' I asked Dan, who said at once, 'No, but let's go!'

So in growing excitement I got out his DJ and Frau Wendel's last effort – a full-skirted white crêpe with an all-over design of raised silk circles. The clothes smelled rather musty, so I hung them outside on a bush and kept my fingers crossed that no birds would fly over them. Luckily, none did, and by Saturday we were like two school children setting off on a longed-for treat. We travelled in the Keneallys' pre-war Buick, with the children and their nurse following behind in the Land Rover.

'I hope you won't mind if we drop them off at Malcolm and Anne's place in Nakuru,' Terry-May said. 'Usually when we go away for the weekend, we leave them at home, but with everything being so – sinister at present, I didn't dare do so.'

'But, Terry-May, what is there that's sinister?'

'I don't know! Faith, isn't that part of the worry? If we knew what we were up against, we might be able to do something, but there's nothing really to put a finger on, except for the labour's odd mood: half of them bordering on the insolent and the other half seemingly dumb with terror. Sure, I don't mind telling you, it gives me the creeps – oh, would you look at those two now. Aren't they the splendid ones?'

The two Masai standing beside the road were the most magnificent of their kind I had ever seen. Both were considerably over six feet with lean, elegant bodies and shoulder-length, intricately plaited hair. They wore only skimpy toga-type garments knotted over the left shoulder, and stood in the typical stance of their tribe: on one leg, with the other bent and the foot tucked behind the knee of its fellow. They held spears only a little shorter than themselves and, with their splendid carriage, appeared arrow-straight yet totally relaxed.

'All these chaps appear remarkably well endowed,' Dan said *sotto voce* to Patrick.

'Well, as small boys they're encouraged to tie a damned great stone on to it – '

'Good God!' Dan's low laugh was incredulous. 'Poor little devils!'

'Yes, but I suppose it's yet another means of inuring them to pain. It's said that in their fighting days they were completely oblivious both to pain and fear, and I certainly would not have liked to face a line of battle-hardened *Morans* in full gear.'

'Aren't these two rather far from home?'

'Well, they graze their cattle down south around Kili, but a lot of farmers are now employing them as herdsmen. Gilbert Colvile, before he married that *femme fatale* Diana Broughton, always had one or two Masai perched up behind him in his Land Rover, and of course Delamere *Père* not only employed them, but in his early days had them sitting around his fire at night, chatting to them in fluent Masai. They rooked him left, right and centre, but he'd never hear a word against them.'

19

'So many police,' Patrick said as we drove into Nairobi, 'and troops, too.'

'Lancashire Fusiliers,' Dan said, recognizing their distinctive yellow hackles.

'Yes, but they're stationed up in the Canal Zone, so what are these fellows doing here? What's going on?'

I barely heard the worried note in his voice for the jacarandas lining the streets were in bloom, the passing crowds full of colour, and there were shops and modern buildings, all indicating to me that I was back in civilization and should not waste a second.

The cottage allocated to Dan and me at the Norfolk was very simply furnished, but it had electric light, taps that gushed forth hot and cold water, and best of all, a loo that flushed – real luxury after our primitive earth closet. But when we were dressed in our evening clothes, we took one look at each other and burst into spontaneous laughter. We had become so used to wearing trousers, shirts and ankle boots that now we seemed unlike real people at all, more like full-sized dressed-up dolls. Also, our shapes had altered: Dan's already broad shoulders had expanded even more, making his jacket too tight across the back and short in the sleeve, while his trousers were so loose around the waist that he had rushed out to buy a pair of braces: 'Because I just can't trust the belt to keep them from falling straight down!' As for me, my once perfectly fitting gown now looked as though it had been made for a woman twice my size. All I could do was pull in the belt, blouse the bodice and try to arrange all the surplus material into gathers around the waist.

Yet when we met up with the Keneallys they compli-
mented us on our appearance, and when I told them that
all my paintings had been accepted for sale, Patrick said:
'A double cause for celebration!'

And Dan added at once: 'Yes, indeed, so dinner is on
us.'

But they would not hear of this. 'Perhaps on our
next anniversary,' they said, 'when you're really firmly
established, but not now.'

'We could make it an annual event,' Terry-May said.
'When is yours, Minette?'

'My what?' I asked stupidly.

'Why, your wedding anniversary, dear.'

My mind immediately became blank with panic, but Dan
said smoothly: 'It's in June, and' – with a laugh – 'to think
that it's husbands who're always accused of forgetting!'

I did not dare look at him but felt my cheeks flame as I
pulled myself together and said: 'I'm afraid I've not given
it a thought lately.'

'Not surprising,' Patrick commented kindly, 'in view
of everything. Now, what are we going to eat? The
filet mignon is usually very good and I can thoroughly
recommend the Mombasa oysters. Do you fancy a dozen
or so, Dan?'

It was a gorgeous meal and afterwards, when we
went to dance at the Muthaiga Club, I looked around,
fascinated.

'It's really quite ordinary, isn't it?' Terry-May said.
'Yet this is where they all used to dine and dance, that
super-glamorous Happy Valley set, and where much of
the action was too.'

'Did you ever meet any of them?'

'Oh Lord, no! I was just a humble Army Nursing Sister,
newly engaged to an equally humble Army Captain, so
they were as far above me as the stars. Nor would I have
wished to mix with them. They'd given the world a very

310

bad and quite erroneous idea of Kenya. Of course the papers were full of the trial – '

'Was Erroll *so* good-looking?'

'From his photographs I'd say he wasn't a patch on your Dan, but of course there was the glamour of his title – one of the oldest in Scotland – plus his reputation of not being able to resist, or be resisted by, any woman. *And* his fabled charm. Ask any of the old hands here and they'll invariably say it was this that made him so fascinating.'

'Did they break up after the trial?'

'Yes, that and all the scandal raked up by the papers, and then the war finally caught up with the younger ones. But, funnily enough, Diana Broughton has come smiling through it all; of course, she had a tough time at first, but then she married Gilbert Colvile, who's just about the richest man in Kenya, and now she's the queen of society. With any luck, you might just see her here tonight, although I think she goes mainly to the Four Hundred. If she does come here, you'll know her at once by her gorgeous clothes and jewels, to say nothing of her dazzling looks! Oh, but here are some of *our* crowd. Come and meet them, Minette.'

Four couples, whose names I cannot remember, then joined us and the talk turned immediately to the present situation:

'It's all due to that bastard, Kenyatta. He could have stopped all the nonsense at once.'

'But he *did* speak to a gathering of Kukes telling them that Mau-Mau was evil and must be given up.'

'Yes, old boy, I *know* he told them that, but I also know that he made secret signs even as he was speaking, which left them in no doubt that his real views were quite different!'

'Oh, come on now! You haven't any proof of that.'

'Maybe I haven't, but it's damned funny that when

Kenyatta told his mob to stop drinking British beer and wearing British hats, they stopped at once.'

'But haven't you *seen* the crowds that gather to hear him? Christ, man, they're there in their bloody thousands, and all hanging on his words!'

'Well, it'll be interesting to see how the new Governor deals with Kenyatta. It's a good sign that he decided to go straight off on that fact-finding tour. Now that he's back, surely he'll do something.'

'It'll have to be a State of Emergency, nothing else for it.'

'But what would *you* do?'

'I'd organize the entire Masai tribe and get them to do themselves up in full gear – lion's mane headdresses, painted faces, monkey fur, and armed with those damned great shields and spears – and then I'd let 'em loose among the Kukes!'

'But the Masai are not what they were.'

'Perhaps not, but they'd still be more than a match for the other mob. Can't you just imagine the reaction of all the city spivs and lay-abouts to a party of senior-grade *morans*? I wouldn't mind betting that the sight of those five-foot spears would be enough to send the wide boys packing!'

'No, I don't think that would be the answer. For a start I'd bulldoze all the brothels and shanties in this city. Not only are they a disgrace, but also perfect breeding grounds for every kind of vice and violence.'

I was glad when Dan quietly asked me to dance. It was obvious that the conversation would continue, with everyone giving a different viewpoint and none able to find a real solution.

As I stood up, I realized that this would be the first time we had danced together since those far-off days in Germany. Dan was smiling down at me. 'No buckles or buttons to bounce off now,' he said lightly.

'Oh, you remember!'

'Well, of course I do!'

'Did you guess the real reason?'

'Yes, and I knew then that I should not see you again.'

'I thought just the same!'

'Yet here we are, all these years later, together in Kenya, of all places!'

'Any regrets, Dan?'

'Yes, I wish I could give you a better life-style.'

'But I only want a loo that flushes!'

'A loo! And here am I, wishing I were an Air Commodore and you my wife, living a comfortable, civilized life moving around the capitals of Europe!'

'But I don't know whether I would have liked that. Living in various capitals, oh, yes, *that* would have been wonderful, but think of all the duty dinner parties and inane cocktail sessions where one could never hear a word because of the noise!'

'Maybe you're right, but I do wish that these last months could have been less of a roller-coaster, especially for you.'

'Oh, but the main thing for me is that we've been together and have come through it all so far.'

'What a good little soul you are, Mäuschen! Too good for me, that's for sure!'

'This is wine talking,' I said, trying to look severe.

'No, it's not, and I'll kiss you to prove it.'

'But you can't – not here! They'll all see!'

Dan's laughter was teasing: 'Well, from what I've heard, no one would even notice.'

'Anyway, darling, you can't because you'd have to bend down too far and might split your jacket.'

'Oh, Christ, yes! I'd forgotten that. Never mind, this party can't last much longer. And think, Mäuschen, just think, we won't have to get up early tomorrow.'

'Tea at six-thirty in the morning?' Patrick asked,

straight-faced, when we were bidding them good-night.

Dan whirled: '*What!*'

Patrick grinned and clapped him on the back. 'It's all right, old boy, just tell them not to bring it until you ring, and we'll see you both in the bar at around twelve-thirty, if that's all right with you?'

Always in our turbulent months together Dan and I had found comfort and strength in our physical closeness, but so often exhaustion had caused us to fall into bed and instant, drugged-like sleep, only to wake and rise to the strident sound of our alarm, even though it was invariably still dark. So that night at the Norfolk was very special and we certainly made the most of it, even lingering the following morning before bathing and having breakfast brought to us.

This must be what a honeymoon is like, I thought dreamily, sitting here in our dressing-gowns, with the sun streaming in and all the time in the world to eat this delicious breakfast: thick pinky-yellow slices of papaya, very slightly chilled, with light-as-air croissants wrapped in hot napkins for me and a full English breakfast for Dan – 'Because it is very necessary that I keep up my strength' – and wonderful coffee. We were smiling at each other over the rim of our cups, remembering the joy we had shared, when Patrick appeared. Dan and I both started up guiltily and began to apologize.

'No, no,' Patrick answered hurriedly, 'you're not at all late, and I'm so sorry to disturb you, but Terry-May and I have just come back from Mass where we were given some very disturbing news.'

'Go on,' Dan said very quietly.

'A very old friend of mine, who is close to the Governor, was there and told me in strictest confidence that a State of Emergency will be declared tomorrow; Baring has only been waiting for the OK from London, and will broadcast the news at noon. This will be followed on Tuesday by the

314

arrest of Jomo Kenyatta. Nobody knows what reaction this will cause among the Kikuyu, but widespread riots are expected. The Lancashire Fusiliers – that must have been their advance party we saw yesterday – are being air lifted in from the Canal Zone.' Patrick paused momentarily, then added: 'I don't know how you feel about this, Dan, but I want to be back on my own *shamba* and in command if the balloon really does go up in a big way.'

Dan nodded instantly. 'Yes,' he said decisively, 'we must be.'

'So how do you feel about going home now?'

Dan answered for us both. 'Fine. When would you like to start?'

'I thought perhaps in an hour? Terry-May is organizing a picnic which we can eat at Naivasha – it'll only be a short detour and quicker than lunching here. We should be home towards late afternoon.'

'It's such a shame that your only break has to be cut short like this,' Terry-May said as we got into the car. She looked tired and, for the first time ever, rather depressed, so I smiled and said: 'Never mind; it's been wonderful and something to remember for a long time to come.'

I could not resist turning for a last look at the Norfolk as we drove away. Would we ever stay there again? I wondered wistfully. And, if we did, what would we have faced in the meantime?

I believe we were all feeling uncertain and sombre but when we came to Naivasha our spirits rose. This lake is one of Kenya's most beautiful. On that day of golden sunlight, with the limpid blue of the sky reflected in the water and the distant ring of mountains hued in lavender, it was also a scene of utter tranquillity and peace. There were no visible signs of habitation and, except for a cormorant perched on a post at the water's edge and a duck paddling past with her tiny brood strung out behind her, we appeared to be the only living creatures in the vicinity.

We sat beneath a huge yellow fever tree to eat the Norfolk's excellent picnic lunch and Dan sighed contentedly, 'What a lovely spot this is.'

Patrick nodded: 'Yes, I've always thought it one of the very best, a kind of fairy-tale wilderness with all the harshness removed and only the hippos in the lake to remind one that it is still in Africa.'

'"Here with a Loaf of Bread beneath the Bough, a Flask of Wine, a Book of Verse – "' I murmured, more to myself than the others, but Dan took it up at once:

'"And Thou Beside me, singing in the Wilderness – "'

'"And the Wilderness is Paradise anew",' I finished, smiling at him.

'Summed up perfectly,' Patrick said. 'You two will have to retire down here after you've made your fortune from farming.'

Dan's laughter held only a hint of harshness. 'That'll be the day!'

'But what a wonderful idea!' I exclaimed. 'We could buy a small plot of land and build a little home, definitely in the rondavel style, but with proper windows and all mod. cons. We could even have a spiral staircase to an upper floor, and it would all be in the shade of a huge tree, with a beautiful garden all around, and, oh, yes, a dovecote!'

'She's off now,' Dan said, jerking his head in my direction. 'I guarantee that by the time we get home, she'll have worked out the colour schemes and decided on the curtains!'

'I think it all sounds quite perfect,' Terry-May said. 'I hope you'll have a guest cottage so that we can come and visit.'

'Oh, yes, of course. Or you might even retire here yourselves.'

'Well, I don't know,' Patrick said. 'I certainly wouldn't want to run such a large farm forever, but we're very fond of the house. All our married life has been spent in it and it holds very special memories, doesn't it, darlint?'

'Very,' Terry-May confirmed quietly, 'although I suppose it all depends on whether Sean wants to take over the farm. If he doesn't, the house will be far too large once he and Bridie have grown up and married.'

'But then you'll have grandchildren to stay.'

'Please God,' Terry-May answered. 'Anyway, it's all a long time ahead, and meanwhile we've got to cope with the present.'

'Remember, friends, we know nothing of the Emergency,' Patrick said as we drove up to the Wilsons' farm to collect the children. 'We've only come back early because of the tense atmosphere in Nairobi and all the strange rumours circulating. And don't stay chatting forever, Terry-May, there's a good girl.'

'I don't even want to go in,' she answered with unusual tartness, 'and I'm certainly not in the mood to chat.'

Malcolm Wilson came out to meet us. 'Hello there! Coming in – no? Well, you're wise to get back at once, now that the balloon has finally gone up.'

There was the tiniest pause, then Patrick said: '*Has* gone up?'

'Yes – oh, perhaps you didn't hear the twelve o'clock news? A woman has been stabbed on her own verandah, just seventeen miles outside Nairobi. Name of Wright, I believe.'

'Jesus,' Patrick said in a hissing whisper, 'do they know who – ?'

'No, only that it was a gang, not a servant or ex-servant with a grudge.'

As the children appeared, Terry-May and I got out to meet them, but I just heard Malcolm Wilson say quietly: 'If it can happen only seventeen miles from the capital, what's in store for us poor sods out here? Time to get

317

out the guns, Bwanas, and don't let your womenfolk go anywhere unarmed.'

The children were the only ones in high spirits as we drove away. Under cover of their excited chatter, Dan and Patrick talked very quietly, leaning towards each other. When we came to our drive, Patrick waited only until Dan and I got out before driving off at speed, the children kneeling on the back seat, waving to us with both little arms flapping energetically.

'It all seems very quiet,' Dan said, looking keenly around.

'Well, it *is* Sunday afternoon, darling. While I light the stove, could you get some water in for tea? I'm longing for a drink.'

He seemed to take longer than usual fetching the water and was frowning when he did eventually appear. 'There's something not right here,' he said at once. 'The girls are still in their *boma* – in an absolutely filthy state – and I don't think they've been let out at all. While the hens, on the other hand, are all out but don't appear to have been fed. You know how they charge about in all directions whenever anyone goes near – '

'Do I!'

'Well, not now! The moment I got up to the run they all rushed to the wire, poking their heads through and squawking loudly!'

'Damn! That means I'll have to get their mash ready,' I said crossly, not having really taken in the full meaning of his words.

'But that's not all! I went up towards the labour lines and I couldn't see any smoke rising from their huts. Surely that's most unusual?'

'Yes,' I said slowly, trying to puzzle it out. 'Oh, I know! I bet some old witch-doctor has foretold the Emergency and they've all gone off to some meeting or other.'

Dan's brow cleared. 'Ah, yes, perhaps that's it! But I

318

wonder where it's being held? Wilson would surely have known if there was a meeting of any size in the Nakuru area.'

'Perhaps over the other side of the mountains?' I suggested. 'Don't forget their God, Ngai, lives on Mount Kenya, so they may have gone to invoke his help.'

'One hell of a walk,' Dan said. 'I wonder how long it'll take them to get back?' He had moved to stand in the doorway, but suddenly turned, white-faced. 'Mäuschen, there are two Land Rovers full of police *askaris* coming up the drive.'

'Oh, Lord, what now?' I asked. My head was beginning to ache and I longed for my tea.

'I-I'm afraid they may be coming for me,' Dan said hoarsely.

'Coming for you?' I echoed stupidly. 'But whatever for?'

'When I was up in the Sudan, I had to give all my Service details; the Squadrons in which I'd served – or commanded – and what I'd done after the war. Suppose they checked and found that I have an undisclosed prison record?'

'But . . . but surely they wouldn't send two vehicles full of police, just to interview you?'

'Perhaps not, but if they intended to deport me, they might.'

'But that's absurd! Why on earth would they want to do that?'

'If they consider me an undesirable resident. I'd better go out to meet them.'

I ran after him. 'We'll fight it!' I cried wildly. 'You haven't done anything wrong here, and if we make a clean breast of everything – '

Dan put his arm around my shoulders and held me close. 'Darling Mäuschen,' he said with a catch in his voice, 'I'm so sorry, so terribly sorry.'

The European Inspector in the leading vehicle stepped nimbly out and came towards us, looking affable enough. 'Good afternoon to you both,' he said, 'I can see you don't remember me – John Gregory – we met at the Wintertons' party about six weeks ago and before that you, Mrs Cleary, had done a charming little painting of my baby daughter, Caroline.'

My mind was still focused upon deportation and I could remember nothing, but I tried to smile and nod while Dan said quickly: 'Of course I remember now! But what brings you to our neck of the woods on a Sunday afternoon?'

'I understand you've been away for the weekend with the Keneallys and probably have not yet heard that they returned to find most of their cattle killed or terribly mutilated, and almost the entire work force gone.'

'Good . . . God,' Dan said slowly. 'How appalling, how utterly appalling – I'd better get over there to see if they need any help.'

'Oh, they need all the help they can get, that's for sure. We've spent as long as we could finishing off the animals not already dead, but now I have to check the rest of my area, and that's why I'm here: have *you* had any trouble?'

'No, but the fifty or so families we had living and working here have disappeared.'

'Ah, that's interesting. I'd very much like to look round their *shambas*.'

'Of course, I'll show you the way.'

John Gregory turned and spoke in crisp Swahili: instantly two of the *askaris* leapt out to stand rigidly behind him. They had all been sitting in their vehicles, immaculate in their khaki drill, with rifles pointing skywards, but each face beneath its red fez was entirely without expression. They might have been robots, and I could not suppress a slight involuntary shiver. Dan took my hand and, as my fingers laced with his, gave them a reassuring squeeze.

There was something definitely eerie about the deserted *shambas*. Usually, even when all the adults and older children were at work, there were some signs of life, if only the activity of hens and pi-dogs. Now there was nothing, and all the granaries had been emptied of their maize.

'But,' said John Gregory, as we stood inside the first hut, 'although the cooking fire is out, the three cooking stones are still here.'

'I'm afraid the significance is lost on me,' Dan said.

'Well, the fire is lit on a couple's marriage and is never allowed to go out while they remain in habitation. These ashes,' John Gregory said, stirring them with one stoutly booted toe, 'indicate that the people have no intention of returning; yet the three stones, which are sacred, are *never* voluntarily left behind. So I deduce that these people left under duress and at great speed, possibly at the coercion of the same gang who spirited away the Keneallys' labour.'

Dan stood with hands in pockets, looking around. Like John Gregory, he had had to stoop to enter the hut, and I sensed his surprise at the primitive dwelling with its smoke-blackened walls and overpowering smell of grease, babies, goats and bodies living in close contact; the ammonia content actually stung the eyes, and I was glad to get back into the open air.

'Are these people really ready to govern themselves,' Dan asked, 'if they can live happily in such conditions?'

'Of course they're not ready,' was the crisp answer, 'and even the most Westernized of their emerging politicians would be too busy feathering their own nests and disposing of their opponents to govern effectively. But these up-country people are still riddled with superstition and therefore extremely gullible which makes them easy prey for the new breed of bully boys, the ones with a bit of education who've become street-wise in the slums of Nairobi. We're beginning to think that these smooth-talking types have been quietly going about the farms,

321

coercing the labour into joining this secret society – this Mau-Mau – and there's even one report that head men have been promised ownership of their Bwana's farm once *he* has been driven out of the country. That reminds me. I believe your head man was James, the younger brother of Patrick Keneally's Joseph, who had also worked for you?' When Dan nodded, John Gregory continued: 'Both have vanished and although Keneally will not hear a word against either, they're just the type I've been describing. How did you find them?'

'Both very efficient and seemingly able to get the very best out of their fellow workers.'

'Exactly!'

'I never liked either,' I said, entering the conversation for the first time. 'There was something about them: sullenness certainly, but something more which I was never able to put a finger on. D'you know, the only time I ever saw Joseph smile was when I once admired his bicycle. And I *know* James was capable of cruelty.'

'Ah, yes. The Keneallys have both said how proud Joseph was of the machine, and they also insist that he must have been forced to leave with the rest, but an hour ago we found the bicycle buried under the floor of Joseph's hut, which certainly indicates to me that he left voluntarily.' John Gregory halted a little ahead of his vehicles and spoke quickly to the two *askaris* who had accompanied us; they saluted with parade ground smartness before climbing back into their Land Rover. 'I think one of our main problems is going to be the trust our people have in their labour – understandable in cases where they have worked side by side and known each other most of their lives. But now,' John Gregory looked from one to the other of us, 'I must recommend you not to trust anyone and to expect the unexpected: the African is cunning by nature and I fear the Mau-Mau will rely on this cunning and stealth for their success. I would suggest you secure all your windows and doors before nightfall and think very carefully indeed before opening them during the hours of darkness.'

As he climbed into his vehicle, he added: 'I hope you've got plenty of firearms, because there's not a gun of any description to be bought anywhere now. I suggest you wear revolvers at all times and keep them beside you, out of their holsters, when you are indoors, ready for instant use.'

'Well,' Dan said as the two vehicles swept away, 'there's certainly never a dull moment in this country! I'll just get our revolvers and then, darling, I think I'd better see what help I can give Patrick.'

When Dan had left everything seemed unnaturally quiet and the forest, which I had always loved, now looked darkly sinister. Get hold of yourself, I told myself sternly, and don't let your imagination run away with you! So to fight off the sense of foreboding, I fed the hens, cleaned out the girls' *boma*, and lastly scrubbed them both down. But all the time I was listening for the sound of the old van – and for what else? I did not know, but twice when there was a slight noise behind me I whirled, hand on revolver. There was nothing, but for the first time I felt totally vulnerable and alone, without any means of communication, and with the nearest homestead five miles away. Before the light had finally faded, the shutters were up, with extra stones to hold them even more firmly in place, the lamp was lit and the door barred, but when at last I heard the van, I rushed out.

'Oh, I'm so glad you're back!' I cried. 'So glad!'

'I'm sorry, darling, I meant to leave long before this but everything was in such a ghastly state that I hadn't the heart to do so before anyone else, and then Patrick offered us drinks – which we desperately needed – no, no, it's all right, this is only animal blood.' Back in the light I had uttered a short scream at the sight of his clothes: from ankle to chest level they were covered in dark dried blood.

'I have never seen a sight of such utter bestiality,' Dan said, when he had bathed and changed. 'Those fiends had driven the cattle from their *bomas* until they were spread all around the house and drive; then they must have set about mutilating them – and, God, what mutilation! There were some with legs hacked off, others with eyes gouged out, and many with stomachs ripped open, standing on their own entrails, those in calf with the foetus hanging out. Very few were actually dead, so the noise was pitiful in the extreme. We just went round as quickly as we could putting them out of their misery, but then of course the carcasses had to be moved, otherwise the house would have been surrounded by every wild animal for miles around. Fortunately, the valley farmers still have most of their labour, so they lorried them up and we managed to get the carcasses away. One of the most awful things was that the children had to see all the maimed creatures as they drove in. I'm afraid they're both in such a state of shock that neither has spoken a word since. Then, when Wilson arrived with their nurse, she promptly had some sort of fit: flat on her back, frothing at the mouth and eyes rolled up to the top of her head!'

'Oh, I should have been there to help,' I cried remorsefully.

'No, they all said they were glad you were not, and some of the other wives drove up with their husbands, so Terry-May was not without very competent help.' Dan paused and looked at me keenly, as though assessing my strength. 'Of course, this means a very big financial loss for the Keneallys and I'm afraid everyone is of the opinion that we're all in for a very bad time, so you must promise me, Mäuschen, that you will have your revolver ready wherever you are and that you will stay *alert*, with none of your usual going off into some delicious little day-dream.'

But I was not even awake when Dan began shaking me. I came up slowly from the depths of sleep, hearing first the knocking and then Dan's urgent whisper: 'Wake up, Mäuschen. *Wake up!*'

'What – ?' I began, only to have him put his hand over my mouth.

'Be very quiet, but get up and put some clothes on,' he whispered, close to my ear. 'There's someone outside and I think it's a trap.'

The knocking began again and a voice, whining and curiously hoarse, called out: 'Please hurry, Bwana! Please!'

'Just coming!' Dan shouted as he lit the lamp. 'Come on,' he whispered to me, and I padded after him through the passage. At the outside door he called out: 'Who are you and what is it you want?'

'Please, Bwana, open the door, it's very cold here!'

'Yes, too cold for me. Now, what do you mean by waking me up in the middle of the night like this?'

'My son, the toto Karioki who the Memsahib loves, is very ill and his mother asks that the Memsahib comes up to our *shamba*.'

Startled, I swung round to Dan, but he shook his head. 'Impossible,' he said authoritatively, 'the Memsahib is asleep and cannot walk all the way to your *shamba* at this hour. She will perhaps come in the morning.'

'No, no, Bwana, by then my son will be dead.'

'How is it that he is suddenly so ill, and why weren't you on your *shamba* all day?'

'Bad men came, Bwana, and told us we must all go as a *thaku* had been put on your *shamba*.'

Dan smiled as though in triumph and nodded silently. 'Well, I'm sorry, but there's nothing I can do. I'm going back to bed now, so don't bother me any more!' He turned the lamp down very low and placed it on the floor inside the passage so that we were not left in total darkness. Then, taking my hand, he led me into the kitchen to stand against the far wall, facing the door. 'The bastard thinks we're so ignorant we'd believe an African would return before a *thaku* had been properly lifted by a witch-doctor,' he whispered into my ear.

'Do you think he's gone?' I mouthed.

Dan shook his head. 'But we'll know very soon.'

I shivered, partly from cold, mainly from fear, and Dan put his arm around my shoulders. I rested my cheek against his heart and marvelled that its beat was so steady. But then he drew in his breath sharply and I raised my head to look at the door: there was a faint noise, like the scratching of a mouse, followed by the slightly louder sound of wood giving under pressure. In terrified fascination I watched as a point of metal appeared between the door and its frame, just beneath the wooden bar that held the door fast. As this slowly began to rise, Dan whispered: 'It's too narrow for them all to pour through at once. I'll take the leaders if you'll try for ones behind on your side, but don't fire until I say.'

I nodded, terror encasing me in ice as I took out my revolver and held it in both hands at arms' length, with legs braced and wide apart.

Then it all happened simultaneously: the bar shot up, the door crashed open, and wild figures filled the opening. Just for an instant they checked at the sight of us, and Dan fired twice, sending the two foremost sprawling across the threshold; two others trampled them as they surged forward, closely followed by a third, all brandishing their broad-bladed pangas and howling like wild animals.

'NOW!' Dan yelled, and I fired at the third, aiming at his chest, but as I did so the falling body of Dan's last victim crashed into him, spinning him sideways, and my bullet hit him in the right arm. He squealed, dropped his panga and, as I fired again, vanished into the darkness.

Obviously we could not tell how many others were outside, but the glint of an eye here and there, and the faintest outline of heads against the night sky, suggested at least four or five more. And Dan, my darling, gentle Dan, did not hesitate: snatching my weapon and uttering something very like a battle cry, he leapt for the doorway where he blazed away into the darkness with both revolvers. A series of cries, yelps, even groans was followed by total silence, and after a few seconds Dan came back to me. 'Reload for me, please, Mäuschen,' he said, holding out his revolver but never taking his eyes off the doorway. In normal circumstances I would have found the heavy Webley hard to break. Now with every ounce of strength rapidly draining out of me, it was extremely difficult.

'Are you all right?'

'Yes, thank you,' I said, absurdly polite.

'Then hurry, darling. At any minute we can expect another attack and I'll only have the rifles.'

At last the gun gave and, with trembling fingers, I began filling the cylinder as Dan said: 'I wish I could get those four bodies clear of the entrance so that we could close and bar the door again. That might just deter them. They'd know we'd be waiting for them this time. I'll hold on for a bit and then try.'

'Oh no, no, you can't!' I cried wildly. 'That's probably just what they're waiting for, and if they charge in while you're busy dragging a body away, I won't be able to cope alone.'

'OK, darling, don't panic now, after you've done so well.' He actually started to hum under his breath and I looked at him in amazement.

'I do believe you're actually quite enjoying this.'

'Well, I wouldn't call it enjoyment exactly,' he said seriously, 'but you must understand, Mäuschen, that after

327

so many months of trial and mainly error, it does feel quite good to be doing something reasonably well, or even just to *know* what I'm doing. Now, what the hell's keeping them. Come on, you bastards, COME ON!' But nothing disturbed the silence except for the usual sounds made by night birds and hunting animals.

'They've gone, they must have done,' Dan said at last. Still I clung to him. 'Wait just a little longer – remember how patient they can be, how for centuries they've been used to waiting, completely motionless, while hunting animals.'

'All right, five minutes, just to please you.'

'Make it twenty,' I begged.

'Ten,' he answered lightly, 'and that's my final offer!' But long before the ten minutes were up he was showing signs of impatience, with foot tapping and fingers drumming on the table. This must have been what he was like in the war, I thought sadly, just like a tightly coiled spring, hardly able to wait before going into danger, even death, because anything was better than just hanging about. 'Right,' he said at last, 'you wait here while I just nip out and do a recce.'

I cringed inwardly at having to leave the comparative safety of the hut, but said firmly: 'There's no way I'm going to stand by and let you face alone whatever danger is outside.'

Dan laughed. 'Darling, look, dawn is breaking! Which means that by now those thugs will be back in their forest hideouts.' I did not even bother to reply but followed him, grimacing with distaste as I stepped over the four bodies. Already a terrible stench was rising from them and it was so good to breathe in the crisp cold air of very early morning that I almost forgot my fear.

Dan was looking keenly around. 'Just as I thought,' he said. 'Nothing here except a trail of blood going towards the *shambas* and forest. I wonder how many we finally got? And why they did not press home their attack?' As I remained silent, he turned to look at me, then came to put an arm around me. 'My poor love,' he said gently, 'it's been a terrible ordeal for you and now you look all in. Come back into the warm while I get rid of these – these objects then we'll light the fire and get some water on for tea. Why not go and rest on the bed until I call you?' But what I wanted most was to have the bodies removed, and obviously if I helped the job would be completed more quickly. So I insisted on taking the feet of each as Dan took the arms, and together we half carried, half dragged them to the drive. 'I'll have to inform the police,' Dan said, 'then presumably they'll come and collect this lot.'

But first there was the floor to be scrubbed and a large pot of tea to be drunk, by which time I no longer felt tired, but slightly light-headed, even giggly. So that when Dan said: 'Well, I'd better be off,' I interrupted at once: 'But what about me? Don't I deserve a cuddle or at least a kiss after being such a Brave Little Woman?'

Dan looked at me in astonishment, then leapt to his feet: 'You're on!'

I rushed outside, saying over my shoulder: 'You'll have to catch me first!' I heard his laughter behind me and of course he soon caught me, bringing me down in a rugger-type tackle, but letting me fall against him rather than the hard earth. He turned me over gently and propped himself up on an elbow beside me. 'You know, you're becoming a real little sexpot,' he said, trying to sound severe, 'with only one thing ever on your mind.'

I twined my arms around his neck. 'Well, if I am, it's all your fault for always making it so lovely,' I retorted. And so on that sparkling, brilliant morning, we made love on a bed of fallen, sweet-scented Limuria blossoms because it was so wonderful to have survived the terrors of the night, because the air was vibrant with sounds of life, and we were so joyful to be part of it all.

When at last Dan pulled me to my feet, he said: 'The next thing I must teach you is the way to run properly. Not like this.' He went up on to his toes and began to run on the spot, knees high and arms outstretched at his sides with hands flapping in such a ridiculous stance that I was soon helpless with laughter.

We were walking with arms around each other, still laughing, as we came to the front of our home just as the two police Land Rovers were drawing up. It was a haggard John Gregory who gave us the news in short, staccato, sentences: The Keneallys had been massacred during the night, together with Wanjiri and the few old people still on their *shambas*. Even the dogs and Sheba, with her six newly born kittens, had been hacked to pieces.

20

There are some things in this life that one never really gets over and even now, writing so many years later, I still grieve for the Keneallys. Not only had they been such wonderful friends to us, they were a warm, loving family, asking little of life except to remain on their land and live at peace with the world. At the time my mood veered from total disbelief to a continuous silent screaming within me at the horror, the obscene bestiality of their murder; I could not sleep or weep, and lived in a strange twilight world of waking nightmare. Yet at the same time, I seemed always to be listening for the distinctive sound of Patrick's Land Rover. And so, when I did hear it, some four weeks after the funeral, I did not stop to think but jumped up, exclaiming joyously: 'Oh, here they are at last!' and rushed out.

It was certainly Patrick's vehicle, but only Janni Verhoeff was in it. 'Good morning, Mevrou,' he said briskly, but I just stared at him, unable to move or speak at the sight of that Land Rover without any of the family in it. It suddenly made me realize as nothing else had done, that they were really gone, that I would never see them again.

'Good morning, Verhoeff,' came Dan's calm voice behind me, and Janni Verhoeff said: 'Your wife, is she ill?'

I felt Dan's arm, warm and strong, around my shoulders. 'No, but she was expecting someone else. So, what can I do for you?'

'I have a proposition for you.'

'Well, you'd better come in then.' Inside the kitchen, Dan righted the chair which I'd overturned in my

331

eagerness, and pressed me gently into it. He offered the only other chair to Verhoeff and went to lean against the stove, arms crossed. 'I'm waiting,' he said curtly.

'You know there was no sign of forced entry into the Keneallys' homestead on the night of the murder,' Janni Verhoeff began without preamble, 'and so – '

'One moment,' Dan said and turned to me. 'Darling, d'you want to be in on this or not?'

But he was my lifeline, my one remaining link with happiness, perhaps even sanity, and I could not bear to be away from him. 'I'll stay,' I whispered.

'Make this brief,' Dan ordered the Afrikaner, who might have been discussing the price of wheat as he said: 'So obviously Patrick let in the killers whom he knew, and my guess is that they were led by that Kaffir bastard, Joseph. And I tell you, man, I am going to get him!' In a sudden burst of fury, Verhoeff clenched his huge fist and smashed it down on the table. '*Ja, ja*, I will get him, and when I have finished with him, there won't be much left for the hyenas – not much, but just enough to make him long for death!'

'What makes you think you will be able to find him and his gang?' Dan queried coldly. 'When the Kikuyu people are said to know the forest like no other tribe, except perhaps the Athi.'

Verhoeff's smile was sinister in its triumph: 'Because I, too, know this part of the forest very well; the farm on the far side of Sweetwater used to be owned by South Africans and I was often sent there to stay with their son, Piet. We spent all our time exploring the forest and found several caves which I doubt are known to any other white men around here. I guess we'll find our gang holed up there.'

'And so?' Dan prompted.

'And so, Mynheer, I am getting together a commando made up entirely of Patrick's friends and we are going to smoke out these filthy animals. I think you would like to join us, *ja*?'

I instinctively thought: Oh no, and for once even Dan seemed lost for words. Then he said: 'But what good would I be? I don't know anything about the forest!'

'You can shoot, can't you?' Verhoeff demanded, the harshness in his voice becoming even more pronounced.

'Yes, of course, but I don't know how to track or how to move silently through dense forest and bamboo thickets. Surely I'd be more of a liability – '

'We shall have trackers, and you should know from your war experience, Mynheer, that when a man's life is at stake, he learns very quickly how to save it.'

'Rubbish!' Dan retorted with something like a snort. 'Highly skilled, specialized training is needed to do that. And even if I had it, how could I possibly leave Minette?'

'All the other wives will be left.'

'But surely they've all lived here for years? We're still new to this country and therefore Minette would be far more at risk – '

'Then get her a dog!'

'Oh, don't be so bloody stupid, Verhoeff! A dog needs to go out at night and that would mean Minette having to unlock the door after nightfall – the one thing we've all been advised not to do!'

Verhoeff shrugged. 'A dog can be let out before dark and left out all night. So! Am I to believe that you will not help to avenge your friends' deaths? The friends who did everything for you? Who were hacked to death, with their heads taken for use in some filthy oathing ceremony? You will not stir from your paltry little *shamba* for them?'

'Of course I would come without any hesitation if it were not for Minette – '

'*Ja*? But I know you, *Group Captain Cleary*. You had enough courage to sit in your little plane and drop bombs on innocent civilians, and perhaps even to throw an

333

unwanted wife down a staircase, but not enough to face a group of savages in the forest!'

As Dan stood, turned to stone, I rose up like the wrath of God and slapped Janni Verhoeff twice across the face. 'How dare you?' I shouted, almost choking in my rush to get the words out. 'You're only a great, stupid ox of a man. You know nothing, nothing! So don't you *dare* sit here in judgement on Dan!'

To my utter astonishment, he smiled at me. 'I admire your spirit, Mevrou,' he said, sounding as though he meant it, and I was reduced to trembling silence.

Dan said with the utmost calmness, 'How long have you known?'

'From the beginning,' Verhoeff answered without hesitation. 'I was in England at the time of your trial and I recognized you from all the newspaper photographs. The Keneallys made me promise not to say anything.'

I knew then that Dan would have to go. If he did not, Verhoeff would undoubtedly blab about the past and Dan would also be labelled a coward. I looked at him, and he nodded very slightly. 'When does this commando of yours set off?' he asked in the same calm voice.

'At dawn, a week today, from Sweetwater.'

'Right, I'll be there. But for now, I'd be grateful if you'd get off our land.'

The Afrikaner heaved his great bulk out of our small canvas chair and, looking at Dan from beneath shaggy brows, said: 'You realize I shall lead the commando?'

'Yes,' Dan said curtly, and went to hold open the door.

'*Ja, ja*, I am going,' Verhoeff rumbled, 'but I will be back.'

And he was, two days later, greeting us as though he had never humiliated Dan or questioned his courage. 'I have brought you a Sten, Mevrou,' he said, 'so you will be quite safe now.'

'On the contrary,' Dan answered with great coldness,

'the Sten gun is a cheap and often very unreliable weapon. It is as easy inadvertently to shoot oneself in the foot as it is to shoot an enemy.'

Verhoeff looked at me in unhurried assessment, just as he would a cow, I thought, glaring back at him. 'No,' he said at last, 'your wife will not shoot her own foot; she has much spirit and will kill any murdering Kaffirs who try to chop her!' I could not repress a shudder and he added as an afterthought: 'Also, a night watchman will be provided, as on all the most isolated farms where women are alone.'

'Just how long is this commando of yours going to be in operation?' Dan asked.

Verhoeff shrugged. 'For as long as it takes. But if the gang is in one of the many caves I know of, it should not take any longer than a fortnight.' He pointed a thick finger at Dan. 'I am placing you in Johnny Brandon's half of the commando. You know him, no? Very pukka English Lieutenant Colonel, ex-Gurkha Brigade, who knows all about jungle warfare. Farms at Njoro. I think you have met his wife, Mevrou.'

'I don't remember.'

'Scrawny old hen of a woman.' He turned to Dan. 'No breasts,' he said conversationally.

Dan blinked rapidly before saying coldly: 'Indeed? But no doubt the lady has other less obvious charms.'

'Ach, but it is not good always to bed with a woman whose body is like a flat iron. It should be like a cushion filled with the finest down – you agree, *ja*?'

'A matter of personal preference, surely?' Dan answered, sounding bored, but for the first time in weeks I felt a giggle rise in my throat and that night I said: 'Mind my downy softness now!'

'Oh, I will, I will!' Dan laughed. 'But who would have thought old Verhoeff could suddenly become poetical like that?'

335

'Yes, and the odd thing is that Aletta doesn't look very downy, does she?'

'I suppose that's it: the poor devil's tied to a flat iron when all he really wants is a nice *boule de suif*!'

We needed to laugh. They were difficult days for us both: Dan was frequently assailed by terrible doubts over leaving me alone; and while I, as frequently, reminded him of all the other women who would be similarly left, I never forgot for a moment that he was going into terrible danger.

'I wish to God we'd never met bloody Verhoeff!' Dan exclaimed as we waited in the pre-dawn for Malcolm Wilson to pick him up. 'And I should certainly never have submitted to his emotional blackmail!'

But by then I had learned that in so many of life's crises, it is the female partner who must be the strong one, so I said firmly: 'But we *did* meet him, and all the other couples are in the same boat, so you mustn't worry, darling, you really must not. Just take great care of yourself and come back quickly and safely.'

As he heard the Land Rover's approach, Dan folded me in his arms and we clung silently together. Then there was a discreet hoot from outside, and Dan held me away from him: 'Don't forget now, you *promised* always to wear your revolver and have the Sten slung over your shoulder during the day, and both beside you at night. And you *promised* never to open the door at night, no matter what.'

I forced down the great lump in my throat. 'I promise to remember the promise,' I said, attempting lightness, 'and you remember you promised to take care of yourself.'

Dan nodded, picked up the automatic Verhoeff had provided and the shoulder pack which contained a blanket, plastic raincoat, a small first aid kit, and a flask of whisky. He wore old Army waterproof trousers over his corduroys, tops tucked into high mosquito boots, and his pockets bulged with ammunition. A thick sweater with the webbing revolver belt buckled over it and a small bush hat, also ex-Army issue, completed the outfit. 'Don't come out,' he said, emotion making him brusque, and so I just stood there, gazing at the closed door and listening to the vehicle's fading sound.

21

The days were not too bad. I was up at dawn, ready to take the eggs and vegetables down to the hospital, and afterwards there was the usual non-stop work. But it was the solitude that was hardest to bear. Not only did I miss the work of our labour force, but their actual presence. I found myself listening in vain for the distant shouts of 'Har-am-bee' as men and oxen strained to uproot trees; for the chatter of women and totos; even for the mid-day whistle, always the signal to stop work and for the women to sit beneath the nearest trees, legs outstretched, while babies were fed, then cleaned with a leaf and re-slung on to backs. Without their work our land very soon began to look neglected for the weeds, unless constantly hoed, quickly formed a stranglehold around the precious vegetables and even more precious pyrethrum. I had to leave them, and also to tell the hotel that temporarily we could not keep up supplies. Instead, I concentrated on picking the pyrethrum, filling huge gunnies with the flower-heads and taking them to the processing plant in Nakuru.

Once I had made these daily deliveries, I did not speak to another soul until the police vehicle arrived with the night watchman, and I could not talk to him because he appeared unable to understand my Swahili. He was a pathetic old man, wizened, and with stick-like legs just visible below an ancient Army greatcoat at least two sizes too large for him. He was armed only with a spear. Dear God, I thought, remembering the broad, razor-sharp pangas and double-edged simis, what earthly good could he do with a *spear*? I almost felt that I should be looking after him, and would have been happy to let him sleep on the kitchen floor, but of course I did not dare, lest he should be coerced into opening the door. So all I could do was to make him a flask of hot cocoa and dig out a Balaclava from my tin trunk. It had been the first I had knitted for the Forces during the war and had turned out such an odd shape, that I had kept it. I showed the old man how to put it on and tried to indicate that it would keep some of the bitter cold from his grey woolly head and ears. I had no idea where he spent each night, for there was never a sound from him, but he was always waiting outside the door each morning for a mug of hot tea before being collected.

It is said that one can become used to anything and, looking back now, I am amazed at how quickly I adjusted to the situation during those two weeks. Yet the hours of darkness seemed endless and I missed Dan most terribly. In the deep silence every small sound brought me to an immediate standstill, holding my breath, but invariably all I could hear was the loud thudding of my own heart. At other moments I was driven almost crazy by picturing Dan in the icy wetness of the forest, without shelter or protection from wild beasts – or the men who had become more savage than they.

Dan had spent a lot of time fixing iron bars to the windows and bolts to the shutters and door, and every morning when I opened up, my thoughts swung between his survival of the night and my own. I would then cross off the previous day on the calendar and listen to the news bulletin, which frequently gave details of yet another horrific murder. I would imagine all the other lone wives listening like me, and no doubt wondering how it was all going to end.

On the twelfth morning there was even a mention of the Verhoeff 'Safari' – some safari, I thought, and almost missed the smooth voice saying that it was proving to be 'Very successful, with plenty of game available.' So perhaps he'll be home tomorrow or the next day, I thought happily, and rushed around with a surge of renewed energy.

By the late afternoon, when I was securing the tarpaulin over the van load of produce ready for the next morning's delivery, I found I was even humming. Then I shut up the hens and shepherded the girls into their *boma*, where I spent a few minutes tickling them behind the ears and talking to them. They seemed to dislike being away from me and looked particularly forlorn. 'I'd love to have you both sleeping in the kitchen,' I told them solemnly, but supposing Bwana Daddy were to come back and find you there? He'd not be best pleased. And, once there, I don't think you'd want to leave, so how could I get you both out?' The two animals looked back at me with their huge, rather sad eyes, their breath already misting in the sudden chill of approaching night. I knew if I stayed longer I'd weaken, so with a quick, 'I'll see you in the morning, girls,' I rushed out, carefully securing the door. Then I walked down to the beginning of the drive to light the hurricane lamp which hung from a tree. The police had requested that every farm should have such a light, the idea being that if this was still burning when the night patrols passed, they would know that all was well; if the light went out, they would investigate. The lamp was meant to be hung on some attachment to the house, but I was too afraid to hang mine on one of the posts supporting our roof lest a gang, unable to get in, decided to hurl the lamp on to the thatch. So I hung it on the nearest tree. Though if I'm still alive after they've chopped off my arms and legs, I can't quite see myself being able to blow out the light, I thought sardonically. But perhaps this will be the last night before Dan returns.

Time seemed to pass even more slowly that evening, although my routine was the same: bath, supper, listen

340

to the latest news bulletin, then bed. Only now it was not into bed but on it, fully dressed, even to wearing boots, propped up by pillows with a blanket covering me, the Sten and revolver by my side and the lamp turned low. It was not possible to sleep for long, since I invariably awoke when my head fell forward, but that night my cheek was snuggled comfortably against a pillow when I awoke and I knew that something else had roused me.

I sat up, holding my breath, but could hear only the tiny pings of insect bodies hurling themselves against the light. I swung my stiff legs to the floor, feeling cold and very much afraid, then clutching the Sten, I tip-toed to the door and put my ear against it. I was sure I would be able to hear any untoward breathing or whispering on the other side, but it was the unmistakable 'huh-huh-huh' breath of a big cat that I heard. Normally this would have reduced me to instant terror, but now it seemed almost like a friend, for surely no gang would be near if a hungry animal were around. I just hope the old man is all right, I thought as I went back to bed, making a mental note to tell Dan that we must contact a Game Warden.

It was obvious that the forest animals, with their usual cunning, had sensed the absence of humans and were invading our land. Only a few days before I had come face to face with a buffalo in one of the fields. We had glared at each other for a few seconds, both motionless, before he had ambled off; on another day I had been on my knees picking peas when I had looked up to see an absurdly thin tail pointing skywards and moving at a leisurely pace through the runner beans. I had held my breath in great apprehension. The tail possessed the unique squiggle of a wart-hog, an animal as ferocious as it is ugly. As she had emerged on to open ground, I saw that she had a tiny replica of herself trotting alongside, and I thanked my lucky stars that I had been downwind of the pair.

341

It was with these thoughts that I went back to bed. I must have slept heavily then because when I next awoke I was huddled on my side with knees drawn up. I seemed to come up through layers and layers of sleep, my head very muzzy. But this time there was no mistaking what had awakened me: Dainty and Tiffany were screaming loudly and in the utmost agony. One of those great cats has got to them, I thought, stumbling out of bed, with spinning head. I thrust my revolver into its holster, grabbed the Sten and a torch and could not lift the heavy bar or pull back the bolt fast enough before opening the door and rushing out. I was only conscious of my toe stubbing against something as I ran.

The bitter night air cleared my brain almost immediately, making me realize how easily I had fallen into a trap, but I checked only momentarily, for in the bright moonlight I saw that Tiffany had been impaled on the huge spiked tops of the *boma* fence, while Dainty stood with udders ripped off and one hind leg almost severed. A great slash in her side pumped out blood with every scream.

Dan had teased me about not running properly, but that night desperation seemed to add wings to my feet. The animals' agony had become my own, and my one thought was to give them release before I, too, was cut down. As I got to them, Dainty's glazed eyes looked at me imploringly and, without hesitation, I flicked the Sten to 'manual', put the gun to her ear and shot her. Then I reached up and shot Tiffany too.

I don't know how long I stood there, gasping for breath, my heart seemingly about to burst out of my chest, but when I heard a slight noise behind me, I whirled instantly, flicking the Sten back to 'automatic' and bringing it up to waist level. But there was nothing there, and the familiar ground all around was open, the only hiding place being the *boma* itself. I turned again, stood in its doorway and fired into the dark interior, sweeping the gun in a wide arc once, twice, as Dan had taught me. The fire-power gave me sudden confidence and when no sound or movement came from within, I thought if I could reach my home, I might yet be safe. So once more I ran, more slowly now as I was still short of breath, and expecting any minute to hear the pad-pad of bare feet behind me.

When I reached the doorway I rushed in, head down, slamming the Sten against the wall while I pulled down the heavy bar and thrust home the bolt. Then I turned, leaning against the door, still gasping for breath . . . and brain, heart, and sight, seemed to explode with terror. They were there, locked in with me and seen only dimly from the bedroom light, three of the wildest-looking creatures I had ever set eyes on, with long matted hair and beards, dressed in a weird assortment of European clothes, all grinning at me with lips drawn back in utterly savage triumph . . . I lurched sideways for the gun, missed it, and as it began to fall I half turned and grabbed it, but before I could straighten or bring the Sten up, my hair was seized from behind with such ferocity that I felt my neck must break. My knees did buckle, and my feet all but slid from under me as an inner voice screamed: He's going to cut off your head! In a purely reflex action, I swivelled on the ball of one foot, poked the gun into him and fired, slicing him neatly in two. The falling panga all but knocked the Sten from my hands and the upper part of the body fell against me, drenching me in its blood and causing a half-strangulated, gurgling sound to come from my throat.

The remaining two then darted forward from the far side of the kitchen, one slightly in advance, with his panga sweeping wildly through the air, while from the throats of both came the most ferocious, blood-curdling sounds I had ever heard. In a last superhuman effort, I thrust the body off me, brought the gun round and riddled the first man as he leapt at me. The force of the bullets sent him crashing back against the wall, arms upflung, and then, as the other was almost upon me, I pumped bullets into him so that he danced and spun, and the walls ran with his blood.

I suppose deep shock can affect people in different ways, and while it is impossible for me to describe my immediate reaction to such terror and carnage, I remember clearly the total detachment and the almost complete paralysis of brain-power, except for the voice inside my head which said quite distinctly 'magazine'. I immediately stepped carefully over the bodies, tip-toed through the blood, and walked into the bedroom. Then I very calmly unhooked the key from my belt, unlocked the tin trunk and took out a fresh magazine of ammunition which I clipped on to the Sten; when the voice said 'lamp', I unhesitatingly opened the door and stepped out into the night. Once again the cold air must have brought me partially to my senses. I remember looking carefully around, but by then I think I had complete confidence in the Sten and my use of it. I walked quite slowly down the drive, took the lamp and blew out the light, and as slowly walked back. Only at the door was there great reluctance to step inside. It seemed perfectly logical to take a chair and sit outside. And that is just what I did, cradling the gun, and oblivious of the cold. I do not believe the danger of attack by any prowling animal occurred to me, or if it did I must have immediately dismissed it as negligible. Nor have I any idea how long I waited there for the patrol, but I do remember that when they came I had difficulty in standing, so numb had my legs become.

It was an Army patrol led by a sergeant who was obviously astonished to see me when the light of his torch focused on me. I cut short his questions, and in a hoarse voice merely said: 'In there.'

When I heard him exclaim: 'Jesus H. Christ!' I thought with mild curiosity, That's an American blasphemy. I wonder where he picked that up? Oh, of course, he must have been posted here from Korea . . . I must try and see his ribbons when he comes out . . . but then, I don't know if a GS has been issued yet for Korea and, anyway, I wouldn't recognize it . . .

Although I was not conscious of it at the time, I believe I was trying to blot out all remembrance of the terrible present by filling my mind with totally unimportant thoughts. When the sergeant came out and asked in an awe-stricken voice: 'Ma'am, did you – ?'

'Yes,' I said curtly, 'but I don't know where the night watchman is. Will you try to find him?'

As the patrol fanned out and began to move towards the back of the farm, the sky behind the forest was suffused with a delicate lemon light, heralding the dawn of a new day. I knew I should be giving thanks for my survival, but instead I was inwardly cringing away from the new trials and terrors it would undoubtedly bring.

Only half aware of what I was doing, I began to walk down our drive, then across the track and over to the edge of the escarpment. The valley was entirely filled with cloud – cloud so soft and thick that I felt if I leapt into it I would not fall straight through, but be enveloped in its billowing layers. How long before I have to say good-bye again to all this? I thought suddenly. Although they will not drive us all into the ground as they have vowed, it will still be the end, and perhaps we have brought it on ourselves . . . we took their land, saying they had agreed, but how could they possibly know what was really happening? A Stone Age people to whom the very sight of a white man had been a profound shock, even a terror. And since then there had been much exploitation. We had taken away the life they had lived since the dawn of time, but had replaced it with – what? Religion? The curing of disease? Yes, and the stopping of their tribal wars, which had all resulted in the survival of so many

345

more, for whom there was nowhere to go, nothing to do . . .

All around me were the sounds of waking birds – not the sleepy twittering of English birds but the cacophany which is so much a part of Africa. Yet on that morning the air was almost immediately filled with an even louder sound as thousands and thousands of huge birds rose up from the mist on the far shores of the lake. Silhouetted against the deepening lemon of the sky, they appeared darkly menacing, but then when they wheeled were shown in all their beauty. Seen at close quarters on the ground, the lesser flamingo is not perfect: it has an almost bulbous head with an outsize, inwardly curving bill curiously marked in pink and black, and its yellow eye, with the pin-head black pupil, is definitely ugly. Nor does it take to flight with the natural ease of other birds, but once airborne, with long neck outstretched and flying in close formation, the invariably huge numbers are a rare and most wonderful sight. For it is then that the splashes of scarlet and deep black borders on their wings – barely visible when these are folded – are seen to great dramatic effect against the soft pink of their bodies and the darker shade of their legs. That morning, as I stood awe-struck with the air of their passage fanning my skin, they suddenly planed down in a steep dive and within seconds had disappeared through the clouds. But the sun, as though not to be outdone in splendour, was rising rapidly, changing the sky to apricot, then orange, and through all the most brilliant pinks to red, and the clouds, which had looked so substantial, were transformed into delicately coloured veils wafting upwards to reveal the lake as a vast sheet of molten gold. Later the sun would drain many of the colours from trees and shrubs, but in the freshness of early morning, all were pristine and sharp. I longed to paint the scene, but knew I did not have sufficient skill to capture the vastness or even the colours.

So instead I walked reluctantly away and when I came to the door of my home I saw what my toe had touched as I rushed out into the night: it was the head of the old night watchman. The thick lips were drawn back in agony, and the eyes still bulged from their sockets. The Balaclava helmet had been removed. The hideous sight might have caused me to vomit or faint, but instead a fury such as I had never known seemed to consume me, and instead of conceding defeat as I had been ready to do, I now felt a fierce determination never to give up the land to a mindless people – a people without a spark of creativity, compassion or feeling for their own kind; a people who would cut down all the magnificent trees for firewood and never learn about soil erosion, so that all the rich earth of the wheatlands, pastures, tea and coffee plantations would be swept away even to the sea. I thought of all our toil; of my parents and of all the others whose lives had been sacrificed to this country, and when the patrol returned I said to the sergeant: 'Get that filth out of my home and off my land!' As he looked at me in amazement, I realized that I had spat out the words.

They called up a lorry on their radio and when all the bodies, including the pathetic carcasses of the two animals, had been removed, I might have come to a full stop, except that there was so much to do: the hens were clamouring to be let out, the produce should have been delivered to the hospital hours before, and of course the kitchen looked like a charnel house. I took three baths, yet still felt the dried blood on my limbs, just as I still saw the great stains on walls and floor, even after repeated scrubbing. I knew it was all in my imagination and finally sat down to hear the midday news bulletin. The atmospherics were particularly bad that day and I might have missed the announcement entirely had I not been concentrating: 'Last night *crackle . . . crackle . . .*attacked Moonrise Farm at . . . *crackle* . . . where Mrs Minette

Cleary, aged thirty, was alone, but . . . *crackle* . . . *crackle* . . . she was unharmed. The Home Guard night watchman was murdered. One of the gang *crackle*. . . now identified as Joseph Kamau . . . *crackle* . . .widely believed to have led the gang that murdered the Keneally family at the nearby Sweetwater Farm last month. Another body, at present difficult to identify, is believed to be that of James Kamau . . . *crackle* . . . that is the end of this news bulletin.'

I turned off the set and sat staring at it, unable to believe my ears. Joseph . . . I had killed Joseph Kamau, the man Janni Verhoeff had promised to leave for the hyenas . . . Joseph Kamau, murderer of the Keneallys, and the reason why my poor Dan was enduring danger, cold and discomfort hunting him in the forest . . . and all the time he was coming for me, and I had got him, together with James, for there was no doubt in my mind that one of the others would eventually be identified as his brother. Surely that was why he and the third member had hung back slightly . . . to give Joseph the elder brother, the leader, the sole honour of taking my head, but instead I had got them all. Suddenly, it was all excruciatingly funny, and I was doubled up in a paroxysm of silent, non-stop laughter which somehow changed to an uncontrollable weeping that made my head spin and the muscles of my chest and stomach ache with the emotion that racked me. Eventually only exhaustion remained, and I was already half asleep when I slumped forward on to the table.

When I next awoke the shadows were already lengthening, and standing in the doorway was a figure, bearded and obviously filthy but quite unmistakable. I got up with difficulty, tried to speak but could not. I took a few tottering steps, but then Dan's arms were around me and he was holding me as though he would never let me go.

22

Dan would never speak of those two weeks in the forest, merely saying curtly that the gang's acts were beyond anything a human being should be capable of practising. But for several weeks after his return, he would fall into exhausted sleep only to have terrible nightmares in which he muttered unintelligibly while his sweat-soaked body writhed, until eventually leaping up with a blood-curdling yell. For me it was different; I could not sleep because the moment I closed my eyes, the three men would be there behind my lids, smiling at me in evil triumph, and I would relive the whole scene until I, too, dripped with sweat and shook uncontrollably.

The Emergency lasted almost five years, and at first it appeared that Mau-Mau was unstoppable, even though a pattern of the gangs' behaviour soon emerged: they would attack in the early evening when their targets were just starting or finishing dinner. A houseboy, who was already a member or under coercion, admitted the gang who would then burst into the room; unless the victims had guns immediately to hand, they did not stand a chance, each terrorist taking his turn at hacking the bodies so that guilt would be collective. With some gangs numbering thirty, there was very little to recognize when they had finished and even children asleep in their bedrooms were similarly butchered. As the gangs became more sophisticated, they ransacked houses for warm clothing and broke into gun cases; police posts were also raided in efforts to obtain arms.

Kikuyu loyal to their white employers suffered just as horribly and in very great numbers. Many of the simple, up-country ones who had initially been lured into joining Mau-Mau with false promises might soon have given up had they not been held in superstitious terror of the oaths they had taken, and these increased in obscenity as time went on.

'Why don't they let us deal with these Mickey Mice?' was the settlers' constant cry, but that was just what the British Government would not do. Instead, large numbers of troops were drafted into the country and, although these were a mixture of fresh-faced National Service boys and war veterans, none was a match for the hard-core terrorists and their women who knew the forests intimately, were prepared to endure extraordinary privation, and even to walk miles on the sides or heels of their feet to avoid detection.

All European men between the ages of eighteen and forty were compelled to join the police reserve, leaving their families at night while they were on patrol. Then an order was made that no white woman was to be left alone during the hours of darkness and no casual labour was to be employed on farms; those already with *shambas* were to be locked into these at nightfall for their own protection.

With so many troops to be fed, all farm produce commanded high prices but the uncertain labour situation, plus two years of drought, meant that few if any farmers made money. Instead, most farms quickly began to look run-down, with much of the land reverting to bush.

For some of us there were other hazards too: when it was announced that a squadron of bombers was to arrive, Dan said: 'I wonder what they hope to achieve?' We did not have long to wait. First a spotter plane came over the forest, quickly followed by the bombers. Dan and I, who happened to be working together at that moment, both looked up in astonishment, and he said at once: 'Lincolns, but what – ?' His voice was lost in the noise of the planes flying very low – so low that we could see the bomb doors open and the bombs begin to drop, fins first, then slowly turning, until they pointed downwards. They were not near enough to harm us, but the awful whining sound instantly brought back painful memories and I quickly covered my ears, shuddering at each 'crump'. The planes flew along the whole length of forest, their bombs spewing up trees and earth and then, as suddenly as they had come, they were gone.

'Well,' Dan began, 'what a bloody waste of bombs and fuel that was! How could – oh, what the hell's that?'

It was an unearthly high-pitched screaming and, whatever it was, we knew it was coming towards us by the haze of red dust it was sending up from the normally moist floor of the forest. Our few workers, who were just reappearing after the bombing, now scattered in all directions, eyes rolling in terror, and even I shuddered, for it was as though the bombs had opened up hell itself and all the tormented souls within were shrieking. Dan was the first to guess and, snatching hold of my arm, he pulled me down into the ditch of a fire-break. 'Keep well down,' he shouted, 'but have the Sten ready in case we have to try and frighten them away!'

Then out of the forest they came, the most enormous herd of elephants I had ever seen, led by a giant tusker with huge ears laid back and plate-like feet moving at speed over the ground. He started to trumpet, a cry taken up by the rest, and this was even more unnerving than their screaming, for they were obviously terrified and quite unstoppable. Dan pushed my head down into the ditch and we both cowered there until the earth no longer shook with their passing. When we eventually looked up it was to see that the herd had cut a huge swathe through our wheat. 'Oh, dear God,' I said, 'is there no end to the hardships out here?'

Dan shrugged. 'I doubt it. Let's just be thankful that we still have the other crops. But, God, we'll have to watch out in case they start returning. As it is, I wonder where they've gone? After all, they're forest elephants. It stands to reason that sooner or later they'll start moving back.'

Thankfully, that herd returned to their habitat through the Keneallys' deserted land but many other animals lived in the forest and all, of course, could be dangerous when frightened. So by day we worked with all senses alert and guns slung over our shoulders and by night we barricaded ourselves indoors; it became normal practice for people to lock doors between rooms as they moved through their houses, and as we could not do that, we were always extremely conscious of how vulnerable we were to being burned out.

'And let's just hope the RAF boys know their stuff and don't drop the odd bomb on us,' Dan said grimly, after yet another sortie by the Lincolns. Later we were advised to spell out our name in large stones painted white and set them down on ground nearest the forest, so that pilots were left in no doubt.

Somehow we got through those dangerous years until in April 1954 a massive operation code-named 'Anvil' swept through the bazaars, brothels and bars of the Nairobi slums. Thirty thousand Africans were arrested and, although it is a tragic fact that very many innocent people were treated as guilty, much valuable information was obtained. When Dedan Kimathi, the most notorious terrorist of them all, was arrested two years later and subsequently hanged, Mau-Mau was virtually beaten.

We had just over two years of normal life then, even modest prosperity, with crops doing well and labour once more living in their own *shambas*. I even returned to painting. The departing troops wanted souvenirs to take home and my water-colours were in demand. Soon I began making all sorts of plans for the future, but Dan was more cautious: 'Let's not go over the moon just yet,' he said. 'Multi-racial government must come, and be followed, I'm sure, by complete independence. I *hope* all will be well, but I cannot help having some misgivings.' Yet it seemed he would be proved wrong when the Conservative Party won a landslide victory in England and Ian MacLeod was appointed Colonial Secretary. 'Couldn't be a finer choice,' jubilant settlers said everywhere. 'He has a brother out here, so now we're bound to get a square deal. Let's drink to him. Boy! Same again all round!'

Disillusionment was swift and unbelievable, beginning with the setting up of a Constitutional Conference on Independence which was promised for the earliest possible date. Then came the bombshell announcement: all land in Kenya was to revert to Africans, with each man being given his own plot. Nor was that all. When a delegation of settlers sought assurance that adequate compensation would be made for the loss of their farms, they were bluntly told that no such payment would be forthcoming from the British Government.

'We've been sold down the river!' was the bitter cry, and even the level-headed and charming Johnny Brandon said: 'It's the end of life as we have known it in Kenya, and time to move on, I think.'

But Dan said to me: 'Perhaps it won't be so bad for us. We've never been *gentlemen* farmers and have never known their very comfortable life-style, so it may just be possible to salvage something. Anyway, there's not much else you and I can do.'

When Independence in the Congo was followed by an incredibly savage campaign of murder, many of Kenya's Europeans began to dispose of their farms, even though at great financial loss, and to leave the country. And with Kenyatta's appointment as President of the Kenya African National Union, those settlers who had said they would never take orders from a black, knew it was the end. These included the Afrikaners. Surprisingly, Janni Verhoeff came to say good-bye. I was busy kneading dough for bread when his enormous shadow appeared in the open doorway. As always, my heart sank. 'Good morning, Mr Verhoeff,' I said curtly. 'What brings you here?'

'Just to say good-bye, Mevrou,' he replied, sinking uninvited into one of our two chairs and mopping his streaming face.

'Oh?' I queried. 'Where are you off to?'

'Back to South Africa,' he answered, in a choked voice.

'You have sold your farm?'

'No, we are having to abandon it and hope that before too long a buyer will come. You, too, Mevrou, should go. The bloodshed is not yet over.'

I shrugged as I continued the kneading. 'We're prepared to take our chance here, but of course I do understand that it is different for you – you will really be going home, won't you?'

I had meant to console him, but instead he erupted into one of his sudden rages. 'Home?' he queried, voice rising. '*This* is my home, Mevrou, *this* is where I was born, *this* is where I have lived all my life, and my parents before me! Do you know, that when my *Oupa* and *Ouma* trekked up here from the Transvaal, they came in wagons drawn by oxen – a long, hard journey – and to get over the wall of the Rift, they had to take the wagons apart and carry them piece by piece because the oxen kept sinking into the mud. Then when they reached the high veld, there was nothing except animals, and even Eldoret did not have a name: it was known as Sixty-Four, because that was its number on the only map available. My people had to quarry stone for their homesteads themselves; our women had to make candles from eland fat and scoop out termite hills for ovens; our ploughs and harrows were

354

made of acacia wood and tied with strips of dried animal skin; the first shoes I ever wore were made by my father from dried kongoni skin. Ach, Gott, what we could teach you people about living off the land! Believe me, Mevrou, we wasted nothing.'

Verhoeff paused to wipe his face again and pointed a finger at the dough: 'My mother made yeast from bananas and bread from potato flour, and in very lean times we roasted locusts and put them between toasted bread. *Ja*, out of an empty wilderness we created wonderful ranches with sleek cattle and horses and fields of wheat as far as the eye could see – and now . . . now we have to leave it all.'

It was impossible not to be impressed by such achievement and I burst out: 'But why go now? None of us knows precisely what Independence will bring. It may be quite a lot better than we expect.'

'No!' he said, making it final and unequivocal. 'Better to leave everything than be ruled by some Kaffir with less brains than a baboon!' He hauled himself out of the chair and, surprisingly, held out his hand. 'I know you do not like me, Mevrou, but you will shake my hand, yes?'

I hesitated only fleetingly before wiping the flour from my hand. 'Yes, but don't disable me as you almost did last time!'

His deep belly laugh was appreciative and he held my hand with surprising gentleness.

'Good-bye to you, Mr Verhoeff, and good luck.'

'And to you, Mevrou,' he replied, sounding sincere. 'Your husband is – ?'

'Not back from Nakuru, but of course I know he would wish you well too.'

He shambled to the door, hesitated, then turned back to me: 'Your husband is a very brave man,' he said. 'He proved his worth in the forest and I assure you his secret will always be safe with me.'

'Thank you,' I said stiffly, 'but *I* assure *you* that Dan proved himself long before in the war.'

'In his bomber, *ja*? But then the end would have been quick and in the forest very slow, very painful. Being buried alive perhaps – '

I did not want to hear any more, so cut in quickly: 'The end was not always quick, you know. In fact, when Dan was shot down over the Ruhr he managed to pilot the plane away from the built-up area before ordering the crew to bale out and then, when he was about to do so himself, saw that the rear gunner was still in his turret, badly wounded. Dan dragged him forward, even though the plane was then in a steep dive and on fire, and lashed their two bodies together and launched them both into the night, not knowing if he could pull his parachute cord or if it would take their combined weight; he got it open, but they were so near the ground that if they had not landed in a very tall tree, they would have been killed . . . as it was the German police had to protect them from villagers who wanted to lynch them.' I paused to let that sink in, then said very proudly: 'Dan got a Bar to his DFC for that.'

Janni Verhoeff bent his head. 'I salute him,' he said, 'he is indeed a very brave man.'

Despite my optimistic words to Verhoeff, I think it was from then that I really began to worry about Independence. 'What *shall* we do if they don't pay any compensation?' I asked Dan, who shrugged and said: 'I don't know, Mäuschen, although my guess is that at the last minute money will be forthcoming from some source. But it's no use worrying. After all, we're all in the same boat.' This was not strictly true. Farmers who had lived all their lives in Kenya might be expected to have some savings from the good years, whereas we had no assets, only a large bank loan.

'Perhaps we'll end up being shipped home as – what's

the phrase? – Distressed British Subjects,' I said, trying hard to sound flippant. 'Let's hope the Government has the decency not to send us Steerage!'

And then once more everything changed. Aunt Alexa died and left me the string of pearls and that ring of vulgar proportions. I have to confess that my sadness at her passing was tempered by the knowledge that some money would result, and I immediately cabled her solicitor to sell the jewels. In due course a cheque for £1,000 arrived, a very good sum in those pre-inflation days. Although I gave much thought to its use, I really knew at once that I wanted Dan to have it. His confidence had increased rapidly during our first months in Kenya, but the Mau-Mau years and the Government's seeming indifference to the settlers' future, had subtly undermined him. Although it was doubtful that he knew this – and would hotly deny it if he did – *I* realized that the feeling of once more being in command, even of personal worth, was diminishing in him. To be given the management of an unexpected thousand pounds could only be beneficial, but making him agree would be another matter. So I gleefully concocted a little plan: I would play the 'helpless little woman' part, not capable of adding up two and two and quite unable to cope with such a sum. I chose my moment carefully before saying, straight-faced: 'You take it, Dan, and use it as you think fit.'

'But I can't possibly do that,' he protested, sounding quite shocked. 'It's your aunt's gift to you.'

'Yes, I know, and I shall be eternally grateful to her, but you know how hopeless I've always been with money. I wouldn't know what to do with it.' He shot me a keen glance from beneath frowning brows and I said quickly: 'Haven't I had to ask you time and time again to work out percentages for me? And – and what about that time when I was supposed to be multiplying and you found I

357

was somehow doing long division instead!' As he smiled gently at the recollection, I added pleadingly: 'So, please, darling, do take it.'

He was still unconvinced and quite a long battle ensued, but eventually he said slowly: 'All right, but I still think it should be kept intact for the future. Just think what you could do with a thousand pounds at home!'

But by then I was tired. 'The future can take care of itself,' I said, for once being very practical. 'It's for the here and now that we need funds.'

No more was said and, having given Dan *carte blanche*, I carefully refrained from asking any questions whenever he was busy with figures and papers. At other times he was so rapt in thought that I often had to speak twice before he even heard me, and then he would start visibly and say: 'Sorry, darling, I was miles away. What did you say?' He also seemed to spend much longer over the daily journey to Nakuru and once, when I had another portfolio for the New Stanley, he was not only eager to take it, but to go alone, saying persuasively: 'You don't want to come, darling, it'll be so hot, and going there and back in the day awfully tiring.'

I pretended to agree, although I should have loved to go, and apprehension stirred in me. But, I told myself sternly, don't start getting any silly ideas in your head. After all, you're together all the time here. It's perfectly logical that he should want to be alone occasionally.

And, as the weeks turned into months, I not only forgot my doubts, but also about the money for so much was happening and there were frequent meetings and discussions with other settlers about the future. Then Dan suddenly said one day: 'If you needed a special occasion frock, Mäuschen, what would you choose?'

'A – a special occasion?' I echoed stupidly, taken completely by surprise. 'Whatever makes you ask that when

I'm less likely than ever to be going anywhere special?'

'Oh, I don't know,' he replied almost airily, 'how about a Government House Garden Party, for instance?'

I laughed. 'Darling! That's one place where we'll definitely not be going! We've never signed the book!'

'I did just that, the last time I was in Nairobi.'

That reduced me to open-mouthed silence, and it was Dan's turn to laugh, rather nervously, I thought. 'Sweetheart, there's no need to look like that! I just thought it might be – rather fun. And now, let's get on with the frock. What colour would it be?'

'Oh – I don't know, I can't think!'

'Well, how about a blue? What d'you call that blouse you have?'

'Ice blue.'

'Ah, that's easy to remember, ice blue. And what sort of material?'

'Dan, I've no idea what the women out here wear to a GH Garden Party! For all I know it might be cotton – I'd have to ask the Flat Iron,' I said, speaking of Johnny Brandon's wife in the irreverent term we always secretly used, following Verhoeff's description of her.

'No need to do that yet,' Dan replied hurriedly. 'Of course we may not receive an invitation. So – ice blue, probably silk. Now we want the style.'

I was too bewildered even to wonder why he was going into such detail but, being me, it needed no further effort to see the frock in my mind's eye. 'No waist seam,' I said, more to myself than to Dan, 'but with an inverted pleat on each side of the front and one in the centre back, so that while I was standing still the line would be straight, and only flow out as I walked. And, yes, I think a waterfall collar.'

'Waterfall collar, inverted pleats,' Dan repeated very slowly as though completely mystified. 'I can't quite – why not draw it for me, Mäuschen?'

Obediently, I took the back of an envelope and quickly outlined the design.

'You'd need a hat, wouldn't you?'

'Oh, I'd love a big picture hat! But it would probably be better to have something very small and head-hugging – like this, tilted over one eye, with a tiny rolled brim which should rise a little at the back to give it a bit of height, and perhaps an eye veil, all in the same blue, and ending at the back in a sort of swirl like, so.'

'Looks good to me,' Dan said. 'What about shoes and bag?'

'Ideally, dyed to match, but probably impossible out here, so I think a very pale beige.'

'And gloves, of course?'

'Oh, yes, I'm sure gloves, probably quite long ones, would be worn. After all, HE is the Queen's Representative.'

'Quite!'

The absurdity of it all suddenly struck me, and I burst into laughter. 'Dan! Can't you just see us rolling up in the van, which would probably backfire or stall or boil as we reached the door – '

'Oh, we'd have to hire a decent car.'

That sent me off into such uncontrollable laughter that it was some minutes before I could speak. 'We must be out of our minds!' I gasped at last as I wiped my eyes. 'Here we are, on the brink of being shipped out steerage class, and we're talking of hiring cars and going to Garden Parties!'

'Well, I don't know,' Dan replied, merely half-smiling, 'probably all the more reason to have a last fling!'

At that moment Njorro, our new head man, came to speak to Dan and our conversation was not renewed, nor did Dan refer to it in the days that followed. I almost began to think I'd imagined it all, especially as I could not even find the drawing. Then three weeks later Dan came back from Nakuru one morning, humming softly and looking so happy that I had to run and give him a hug.

'And I've got something for you, too!' he said in the tone of a small boy with a lovely but unbearable secret. 'We're going down to the Coast tomorrow for a holiday – a real holiday beside the sea!'

I backed away so that I could look up at him keenly. 'I don't think I understand.'

'Not difficult,' he replied, gently mocking. 'A h-o-l-i-d-a-y; going on a puff-puff, with swimsuits, suntan oil, buckets and spades. Going to the s-e-a!'

'Oh, don't be so infuriating!' I stormed in a sudden burst of exasperation, which caused Dan to assume a woebegone expression.

'I thought you'd be so pleased,' he said in a voice guaranteed to melt a heart of stone. I was no exception.

'Darling, of course I would love a holiday, but how *can* we?'

He appeared to give this earnest thought, then said lightly: 'Let's have it and afford it after!'

I swallowed hard on another angry exclamation and tried to speak calmly. 'It sounds fun, but I'm just wondering about the farm and – and getting the produce down to town?'

'Oh, Njorro can cope with it all quite well.'

'But is he safe with the van? I thought he was still at the tinka-tinka stage with it?'

'No, he's improved recently, and the van *is* clapped out.'

'But, Dan, it's our only transport. What should we do without it?'

He looked at me quizzically, head on one side. 'You know,' he said seriously, 'although I often teased you about being a romantic day-dreamer, I think, I *definitely* think, I prefer *that* you to the down-to-earth practical lady you've suddenly become.' As I remained silent, totally at a loss for words, he continued, 'Come on, darling, don't look so worried! We're going on holiday. I know you'll love the coast, it's said to be very colourful, so you may like to take your painting gear and – yes – I'll teach you to swim. You'd like that, wouldn't you?'

'Dan, I'm not a child to be lured into a false sense of security by the promise of a few treats. And – and, I think it's mean of you to try!'

He came to stand before me and put his hands on my shoulders. 'Now, Mäuschen, you wanted me to take charge of our finances and I'm doing so – trust me, please!'

I had to leave it at that, but could not suppress a feeling of deep disappointment for I realized that Dan must be using Aunt Alexa's money for the trip and I had thought him to have a far greater sense of responsibility.

I had also thought that was the end of shocks and surprises, but the next day was to prove me totally wrong. When we arrived at Nairobi station I was almost hustled into the nearest taxi and taken to the Hilton. 'What – ?' I began.

'All in good time, darling,' Dan said, 'do come on now!'

The foyer was crowded with an in-coming party of Americans, ranging from middle-aged to elderly, the large, beefy men much slung about the neck with de luxe cameras, the women impeccably made-up, coiffeured and tailored; the floor was littered with their elegant luggage, the air filled with a mixture of cigar aroma and perfume, with *Joy* – at that time the most expensive scent in the world – predominating.

I came to an abrupt halt, saying urgently: 'Dan, I don't know why we're here, but do let's leave – we look so shabby.'

'Nonsense, darling!' Dan's tone was bracing. 'Don't you

see, it's not necessary for us to have beautifully tailored safari suits or wide-brimmed hats with bits of pseudo-leopard skin tied around them, because we're the genuine article, we live here!'

I could not argue with him there, but when I started to scuttle forward, head down, Dan took a firm grip of my arm above the elbow and said: 'No need to hurry!' and deliberately slowed his pace so that we sauntered across to the Reception desk. Oh, Lord, I thought, I bet the staff pretend not to see us and leave us to last, but to my intense surprise one of them came forward at once as though recognizing Dan, who said calmly: 'Good morning, you have a reservation for us – Group Captain and Mrs Cleary.'

It was impossible not to jump almost out of my skin at his use of the rank, but his sudden pressure on my arm just prevented me from swivelling to look at him. 'Yes, of course, sir,' the clerk was saying. 'If you will just register?'

In a totally bemused state I watched Dan take up the pen and begin to write, his hand perfectly steady. 'I trust everything is in order?' he said, only looking up briefly.

'Yes, sir, everything has been completed, as you instructed.'

The lift was crowded so I had to remain silent, but I kept looking up at Dan, who pretended not to notice, concentrating on the lift's movement, a half smile on his face.

Our reservation was not just a room but a suite, beautifully furnished and filled with flowers. 'Quite pleasant, isn't it?' Dan said casually, as though it was normal for us to be in such luxurious surroundings. He went to open another door: 'Ah yes, the bedroom, and bathroom beyond, no doubt.'

He's ill, I thought, panic taking over from bewilderment. Oh, but I should have noticed before. He's not been himself for months, with all those mood-changes from not even hearing me at times to the being without-a-care-in-the-world pose. I must get him out of here and home, but how? I've no money to pay for all this – we'll have to leave the cases and just walk out. Oh, if only it were the Norfolk where eccentricities are so famous, or even the New Stanley where I'm known – but *here*? Perhaps I can make an excuse to go down to Reception and ring someone for help – oh, if only dear Patrick were still at Sweetwater! Who else? Johnny Brandon? He and Dan get on so well, they're very alike. Perhaps he would drive up here and help me get Dan home – but the Flat Iron is such a cold woman, no help there. So how about Malcolm and Anne? Oh, but it'll be so humiliating for Dan . . .

'Your forehead's as furrowed as a bloodhound's!' Dan's happy voice burst in on my desperate thoughts. 'I imagined all this would make you happy.'

Pretend to go along with him, my inner voice cautioned, speak very calmly and choose your words. 'Oh – oh, it – it has,' I said aloud, trying hard to smile. 'It's been the most lovely treat, but now – now, perhaps we'd better go home.'

'Why?' Dan queried bluntly. 'We've only just come, and don't forget, we're leaving on the night train for the coast.'

Oh no, I thought in fresh panic, not that! 'Darling,' I began tentatively, 'I really would prefer to – to postpone our holiday and instead go home, if – if you d-don't mind.'

'Oh, but I do mind! And I'm sure you'll be pleased when you get there.'

'Yes – yes,' I agreed hastily, 'I'm sure, too, but we are rather hard up and – '

'No, we're not! In fact, we're rather well off and are likely to become much more so!'

He *is* ill – oh God, don't let it be a brain disorder, don't let it be *anything* serious. 'Why, yes,' I said brightly, 'in experience and all we have shared – '

'Yes, all that, but in hard currency too!'

Challenge him, my inner voice advised, but gently, very gently now. I manufactured a strange little titter. 'That's nice! So – so how much have we got?'

'Oh, about ten thou.'

His mind's quite gone, I thought, feeling as though my own were about to do the same. Yet he looked so normal, perched on the arm of a chair, smiling up at me as if having the time of his life. As I remained speechless, he added: 'You think I'm off my head, don't you?'

'Why, darling, what a thing to say!'

'But it's a shame to tease you like this!' Dan said, springing up and coming to put his arms about me. 'I just couldn't resist seeing how you would react. I'm really quite sane, I assure you!'

'Then how – ?'

'I invested your aunt's money when you first handed it over all those months ago. It's been so successful that we now have the equivalent of ten thousand pounds, although it is actually in mixed currencies – mainly US dollars and Swiss francs – but all are Gilts, so they're as safe as shares ever can be. I knew you'd find it difficult to believe, so I've brought all the papers and I'll show you later. But now – ' he looked quickly at his watch ' – God, there's not much time so come through to the bedroom, darling.'

It was all too much for me to take in and I thought only that Dan was not mentally ill after all. But then in the bedroom was yet another surprise. Laid out on the bed was beautiful silk underwear: a slip and panties, a wispy bra, and the tiniest suspender belt I'd ever seen, all lavishly trimmed with exquisite lace; beside them were packs of Dior stockings and a box containing pale beige court shoes, with matching gloves and handbag, while on the dressing table a hat stand displayed a tiny ice-blue hat, complete with veil, obviously matching the frock which, encased in polythene, hung outside the wardrobe.

'Mäuschen, do say *something*!'

The anxious note in Dan's voice roused me from my trance-like state and I rushed to fling my arms around his waist. 'You darling! You dear, dear darling!' I exclaimed joyously. 'To have arranged all these *lovely* things, just for me! I can't think how you managed it, but it's for the Garden Party, isn't it? I can't believe we're really – '

I stopped abruptly as Dan slowly shook his head. 'Not a Garden Party, darling, a wedding.'

'A wedding?' I echoed, once more completely mystified. 'But we don't know – '

'Can't you guess?'

'No,' I said, 'I can't imagine.'

'Yet it's very simple: I just decided that it was high time you made an honest man of me, and so you are marrying me at twelve noon, which gives us about two and a half hours from now!'

My heart, my brain, the room, all spun wildly, then stopped. Everything seemed to stop: the muted sound of traffic, the distant purr of the lift, the closing of doors, the murmur of passing voices. In the intense silence I was barely able to whisper, 'You're not serious, are you?'

'Never more so,' Dan's voice was firm and decisive. 'Would I have made all these arrangements if I were not?'

But I was incapable of thinking clearly and could only say truthfully: 'I don't know.'

'Well, I do!' Dan took both my hands in his and looked down at me very earnestly.

'I love you, Mäuschen,' he said, his voice suddenly very quiet. 'Will you marry me?'

All I could do was to smile mistily up at him and nod; he uttered what sounded very like a whoop of joy, lifted me completely off my feet and spun us both round, before kissing me deeply. Then he set me down and said: 'I've made an appointment for you to have a hair-do, facial and manicure, so you must go at once, Angel, or you'll be late.' He pulled out a large wad of notes from his pocket, peeled off some, and added: 'I've no idea how much it'll cost, but if this is not enough, get them to ring through here – 105 – and I'll bring down some more!'

It's a dream, I thought, even as I made my way to the beauty salon, just a wonderful, wonderful dream: the money, the clothes, Dan's wanting to marry me, I'll wake up in a minute ... .

The beauticians must have thought me very stand-offish. Having tut-tutted over the state of my hair, skin and hands, they attempted to make conversation but I was barely able to answer. As time went on, doubts began to creep into my euphoria, and I rushed back to the suite, bursting in to say urgently: 'Dan, we *must* talk before we go any further!'

He looked at me gravely over the top of the *East African Standard*, then put it down and rose to come and stand before me. 'Mäuschen, the vicar of St Andrew's has arranged a private ceremony for us at considerable personal inconvenience, so I think the least we can do is to be punctual.'

'That's just it,' I said quickly, 'I-I don't think we should go ahead with the wedding.'

'For God's sake, why not?'

'Because – because our whole situation appears to have changed. Now that we have money, we shall no doubt be meeting many more people and – and the time may come when you won't want t-to be with me any more . . . then, if we're not really married, everything will be far less c-complicated – '

'What stupid, bloody nonsense! I know perfectly well what I want and with whom I want to spend the rest of my life! *And* I've told you, but you choose not to believe me!'

'Dan – Dan, it's not that!'

'Well, what *is* it then?'

'It's just that I-I – '

'Good God, what are we doing arguing like this on our wedding morning? I can tell you one thing for sure, Mäuschen – I did not have this fuss first time around! Ros couldn't get me to the altar fast enough!'

'But don't you see? That's just it: Ros was so beautiful, so obviously desirable, that any man would have been beside himself with joy and pride to marry her! And the world is full of wonderful-looking women!'

'Yes, I know. Now, Mäuschen, you have three choices: you can go and dress yourself, or I will dress you, or I will take you, just as you are now, to the church – and I don't care if you kick and scream the whole way. Just make your choice!' So I went to put on all the lovely lingerie, the gossamer stockings, the silk frock and little hat, arranging the veil so that it just covered the deepening lines around my eyes. Then, walking a little uncertainly on the unfamiliar high heels, I went to stand in the doorway. Dan was looking out of the window, but swung round at once. I noticed for the first time that he was wearing a new mohair and silk suit, with a tight cream rosebud in his buttonhole. As his eyes ranged silently over me, I felt hot colour suffuse my face. 'I feel a little shy,' I said hesitantly.

'Darling!' Dan's laugh was loud in the quiet room. 'Is that possible after so long?'

'Yes,' I whispered, 'because I've never been a bride before.'

'So you haven't, angel, but you make an enchantingly pretty one and I *love* the outfit, especially the veil! And there's something else I want you to wear: I know how fond you are of your mother's ring, but now will you wear mine instead?' He took a velvet ring case from his pocket and opened it. 'I chose a plain one, but it has a personal inscription on the inside.'

It was the sight of the ring that made me finally realize that I was not dreaming, not fantasizing, but living in reality. For so many years I had longed for Dan to show me such a ring and ask me to wear it – longed for, but never believed it could ever be. 'It's the most beautiful ring,' I whispered, 'and once you put it on my finger I'll never take it off, no matter what happens to me.' Then I slipped off my mother's wedding ring, held it briefly against my lips, and put it in my new handbag.

There was no reluctance to walk through the foyer that second time and I believe quite a few eyes watched our progress. Outside a splendid new Mercedes was drawn up, complete with liveried chauffeur.

'It had to be a Merc, didn't it?' Dan said, smiling as he helped me in. On the back seat lay a small but exquisite bouquet of peach roses and white stephanotis.

'You thought of everything,' I whispered admiringly.

'Yes, well, darling, planning was my job and this was the very nicest one I've ever had.'

Beautiful cars, especially Mercedes, were not so plentiful in Nairobi at that time, and I was conscious of people staring at us from the crowded pavements and buses. I hope they realize we're a bridal couple, I thought, I hope they're wishing us well! Ever since, whenever I see a wedding car, I think of that journey and say a prayer for the couple's happiness.

But when we arrived at the church, doubts and fears assailed me once more. 'Dan – '

'Yes?'

'You don't have to – it's not too late.'

He swung round to look at me. 'You're not starting that again surely!' he said, sounding, I thought, very like a husband.

'Yes – no. Oh, it's just that I'm so afraid.'

As always, his arm swept around me, drawing me close. 'But I assure you, little Mäuschen, that there is nothing, absolutely nothing to be afraid of, not today or any day in the future.' There was no doubting his sincerity and, as he drew my hand through his arm, he said very gently: 'Ready now, darling?'

'Oh, yes,' I whispered tremulously, 'quite ready.'

'Then right foot forward, and stand up straight, Mrs Cleary!'

And Afterwards . . .

Of course, that is not the end of my story, merely the end of the beginning. Indeed, the next few years were highly dramatic, starting on 12th December, 1963, when, at one minute to midnight, all the lights in the Nairobi Stadium were extinguished. When they were switched on again the Union Jack had been lowered, and the new flag of black, red and green was hoisted in its place. The police band played the new National Anthem and independent Kenya was born, with Jomo Kenyatta as its leader. The huge African audience roared its approval, but I suspect that for many of the Europeans it was one of the saddest moments of their lives for a wonderful, and in some ways unique, life-style had gone forever, and many faced an uncertain future.

Dan had been right when he believed that money for the take-over of European farms would be forthcoming at the last minute, and sufficient to buy one million acres was made available with the promise of further grants to follow. But the very low purchase price was fixed by European valuers appointed by the Government and offered on a 'take it or leave it' basis, which many European farmers felt bound to accept. What none of us could know at that time was that some years after Independence this same land was to change hands amongst Africans at ten or even twenty times the prices paid to the previous European owners.

Sweetwater went some time before ours, to be broken up, like most European farms, into small, often uneconomic plots, in order that each African voter should have his own land.

Since the Keneallys' murder I had refused to go near their homestead, but on the morning of our final departure, I took the new Land Rover and drove slowly along those five miles, my heart sinking at every new sight. The few survivors of Patrick's pedigree herd had long since been dispersed, and the once luscious, clover-starred pastures were gone; so were his carefully planted windbreaks – chopped down, I suspected, for firewood – like most of the fencing. But the house and garden were the saddest. The whole front was a large dustbowl with not a flower or shrub remaining, and the house itself bore unmistakable signs of neglect. There were several panes of glass either cracked or missing, and no curtains were left. Instead, the sills appeared to be piled high with a jumble of boxes. Yet just for a second I saw it all as it had been, and they were all there: the children waving, the dogs rushing to greet me, Terry-May with her medical bag, Patrick beside his favourite horse . . . My vision blurred with tears and by the time it had cleared, they were gone.

'*Kwaheri*, my dearest friends,' I whispered, 'until we meet again.'

As I drove away a crowd of young boys rushed out of the house to kick a ball around, their laughter and happy voices filling the air.

Our own departure was no less poignant and we were both silent, remembering all that we had given to the land, all we had experienced in our little mud huts. But we were the lucky ones for thanks to Aunt Alexa's jewellery and Dan's brilliant handling of the proceeds, we were able to buy a plot of land by the lakeside at Naivasha just large enough for our rondavels and a beautiful garden. Later we were able to lease adjoining land from its new African owner where Dan still grows vegetables and I carnations and gladioli, all of which we pack and despatch to Covent Garden within twenty-four hours.

In a few short years we were to see Nairobi grow into one of the most modern cities in Africa, with a large, constantly changing international population and many sophisticated Africans: the girls, pert and pretty with make-up and straightened hair; their male counterparts in sharp Italian suits, invariably carrying slim executive-style briefcases, and often sweeping through city and countryside in splendid limousines. Sadly, though, behind all the new high-rise buildings and luxury hotels, the slums and shanty towns still exist and there is high unemployment.

The Mau-Mau terrorists have long since become folk heroes, known as 'The Men of the Forest' or, more often 'Freedom Fighters', with streets named after them and their barbarous acts of cruelty against hundreds of their own people conveniently forgotten.

One further great joy came to us in 1966 when Emma visited us with her fiancé, Senator James Menzies Black III. She had never believed in the story of Dan's death and had been trying for years to find him. She came to Kenya to ask him to give her away in marriage, but we all had a hard job persuading him. He was afraid the old scandal would be revived to the young couple's detriment. Eventually he gave in, and when I stood with the cream of Bostonian society and watched Dan lead his daughter to the altar, I thought with humble gratitude: My cup runneth over.

Since then we have spent almost every Christmas with them and their two sons and one daughter, whom it has been our great delight to watch grow into the most charming of young people.

Often, when Dan and I are sitting together, perhaps listening to the BBC World Service, with ice clinking in our glasses and a log fire blazing, I think over our lives. I believe that our story might be of interest to others because we have lived through extraordinary times with so many of the values and codes of conduct held sacrosanct by our families now swept away.

Our own life-style, too, has changed completely over recent years. We still work hard, but at the end of the day there are hot baths to take, comfortable chairs to sink into, and excellent servants to cook and clean. We have many friends from among other lakeside dwellers and our home is considered very attractive with all its books and flowers. Uncle Julian's soft English landscapes adorn the walls together with some of my own, and there are pretty chintzes at all the windows. Outside, in the centre of our garden, there is a huge acacia tree with a bird table suspended from one of its lower branches. Every morning when I put crumbs on it for our many birds, I look up into the heart of the tree and remember the day of the lion. But the bitter heartbreak has long since subsided into a deep yet quiet regret, and as I turn away the dogs invariably come to prance excitedly around me, barking as though to say, 'Don't be sad; life is still wonderful.' And there is nothing to fear now except hippos emerging from the lake for their nocturnal wanderings.

And so we have come to our years of contentment; my love is now seventy-four, still amazingly handsome and trim of figure, with thick white hair which adds great distinction to his looks. Together we have survived scandal, privation and terror and through it all our love has remained constant – always and forever.